LAND OF THE FAR HORIZON

Voyage of the Exiles
Angel of the Outback

VOYAGE OF THE EXILES

PATRICIA HICKMAN

BETHANY HOUSE PUBLISHERS
MINNEAPOLIS, MINNESOTA 55438

Cover illustration by Patricia Keay.

Published by Bethany House Publishers
A Ministry of Bethany Fellowship, Inc.
11300 Hampshire Avenue South
Minneapolis, Minnesota 55438

Printed in the United States of America.

Library of Congress Cataloging-in-Publication Data

Hickman, Patricia.
    Voyage of the exiles / Patricia Hickman.
        p. cm. — (Land of the far horizons ; bk. 1)

    1. Australia—History—1788–1851—Fiction. 2. Botany Bay (N.S.W.)—History—Fiction. I. Title. II. Series: Hickman, Patricia. Land of the far horizons ; bk. 1.
PS3558.I2296V69 1994
813'.54—dc20   94–24234
ISBN 1–55661–541–8   CIP

To my husband, Randy,

faithful warrior,

courageous defender of the faith,

passionate love of my live,

my best friend.

The best is yet to come, comrade.

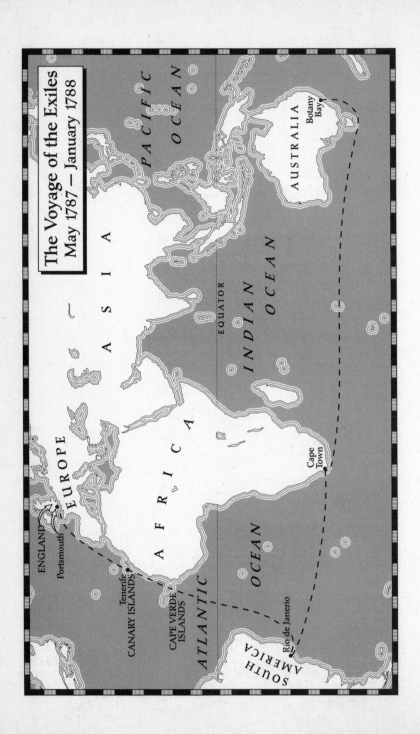

The Voyage of the Exiles
May 1787 — January 1788

PACIFIC OCEAN

ASIA

EUROPE

ENGLAND
Portsmouth

AFRICA

Tenerife
CANARY ISLANDS

CAPE VERDE
ISLANDS

ATLANTIC OCEAN

SOUTH AMERICA

Rio de Janerio

EQUATOR

INDIAN OCEAN

Cape Town

AUSTRALIA

Botany Bay

TABLE OF CONTENTS

PART ONE
The Exiles

PART TWO
The Voyage

PART ONE

THE EXILES

OCTOBER 12, 1786–MAY 13, 1787

1
ENCOUNTER AT TYBURN

It had been a good morning for Otis Skinner. He had dispatched three Londoners with his customary skill and was enjoying the fine fall weather. The autumn sun had melted away the early fog and shone with diamondlike clarity over Tyburn, impeded only occasionally by a gray cloud that sent a brisk breeze and a chill through the spectators.

Acknowledging his own keen flair for detail, Skinner was congratulating himself in jovial, indistinct tones when a wave of complaint began to sweep through the mob below. Still applying the final touches to his last job, Skinner chose to ignore the massive crowd's jeers as the next wagon delivered a new customer. Instead, he turned his thoughts toward more pleasant matters.

He was looking forward to a relaxing afternoon of fishing in the Thames with his ten-year-old son, James. Skinner always gave him a careful account of the day's work on the gallows, and he was gratified to see the boy take a keen interest in his father's profession. He was delighted to teach the boy the finer points of his art. "After all, Meg," he'd often said to his wife, "a man's got a duty to do 'is best for 'is own now, ain't he?"

Still thinking with pleasure of the afternoon's outing, Skinner returned to the elevated platform and turned his attention to the next victim—a pale-faced young woman of no more than seventeen. The sight of her caused the executioner to blink and frown with displeasure, for the frail woman weighed, he estimated expertly, less than a hundred pounds. "The wench don't weigh enough to break her neck," he muttered. He grabbed the rough hemp rope, and when the girl drew back in terror, her eyes haunted like a captured animal, Skinner reached out and grasped her slender neck with his huge hand. "None of that!" he growled, slipping the noose over her head and drawing it tight. The rope biting deeply into her pale skin, the girl moaned and closed her eyes.

"Poor child!" cried a ragpicker with a missing front tooth. "Some say she's innocent as a lamb."

"Who knows but God Almighty?" a blowzy street-woman retorted. "Where's the other one they're 'angin' today? 'E's the one I'm 'ere wastin' me mornin' to see."

The ragpicker blew her nose loudly. "Don't be so impatient! One hour's only worth a sixpence to ya anyway."

The young felon's shoulders stiffened tensely while her slender white fingers clenched and unclenched at her sides.

"Behave yerself, now," Skinner grunted morosely. Seeing she was about to faint, he whirled and grabbed the handle that released the trap. "It won't 'urt a bit," he called out, pulling the lever. The girl dropped, and just as Skinner had feared, her weight was not enough to break her neck. Her frail body twisted and turned frantically; her feet kicked out with a desperate force.

The crowd cheered in sadistic pleasure as Skinner stood staring out at them. "Ignorant apes, that's wot they is! Got no appreciation for a real job of work!"

Finally the rope grew still. "Take 'er down, Oliver," Skinner called to his assistant. The body was carried behind the gallows and laid on a shroud next to the first victims. Oliver blinked when he thought he saw the girl's hand flinch. "Ahh, it's nothin'. They all does that after they dies," he rationalized.

Skinner stared out at the crowd of ragpickers, street-women, drunkards, and cripples. He could see a sprinkling of merchants and even some aristocrats in carriages at the back of the crowd. He felt a lingering embarrassment for the sorry job the young woman had forced on him, but he was soon taken by the sight of a new arrival approaching the gallows in a wagon. "Well, now, this is something like!" he muttered, his good humor restored.

The wagon, an elegant affair decked out with ribbons, carried only one passenger—a handsome man of about twenty-eight dressed as a bridegroom in lavish white, holding a single red rose in his white-gloved hand. He had glossy black hair, a deep tan, and white teeth that flashed in the sun as he waved his hand to the crowd. As he passed by, some of the bawdy women pretended to faint.

"If it ain't Tom Clinch!" Skinner beamed in anticipation, for he had long wanted the pleasure of sending London's most colorful and daring highwayman to meet his maker. He reached down into a black bag and pulled out a coarse brown rope, his best, and rubbed it lovingly with a thick hand. "This un'll do the trick," he grinned. "Take the bad taste of that wench out o' me mouth, it will!" He studied the crowd as an actor studies his audience, and determined to give the affair his best attention.

The crowd broke into cheers when Clinch, jolly as a man going to a party, stood to his feet in the wagon. The mob moved about restlessly, trying to catch a glimpse of the famous outlaw. Through the horde pressed a milling group of street hawkers trying to sell the condemned's hot-off-the-press "Last Dying Speech and Confession." No tear coursed down Clinch's cheek as he bowed deeply to the crowd applauding his final minutes as though he were a hero.

The bells that had clanged his way through the busy thoroughfares of London, from Newgate to Tyburn, suddenly ceased, still as candles in a crypt.

Settling the horses beneath the gallows, which was constructed of three posts linked by crossbars, the driver nodded to the condemned man. Clinch stopped to take one last look at the crowd before dismounting the wagon.

A clergyman waited at the bottom of the ladder holding a Psalter between his hands. He was a reticent man wearing a plain black cloak. His pale gray eyes followed Clinch with a rueful gaze. "Mr. Clinch," the minister whispered. "Did you want to make your peace with the Almighty?"

Clinch acknowledged the minister with a smile. Taking the book from the clergyman's hands, he opened it to the fifty-first Psalm—the "Hanging Psalm"—his final *noblesse oblige*.

Scanning the crowd dramatically, Clinch cleared his throat and took a deep breath, his blue eyes catching the admiring gazes of the women who pressed close to the wagon. "Behold!" Clinch shouted while the onlookers gasped. "Behold, I was brought forth in iniquity, and in sin did my mother conceive me!"

"It ain't true, Lila," the ragpicker whispered to another. "I knew 'is mum and she was a saint, she was!"

Tom Clinch continued, "Behold, thou desirest truth in the inward being; therefore teach me wisdom in my secret heart. Purge me with hyssop, and I shall be clean; wash me, and I shall be whiter than snow."

"Yes, Lord!" shouted a street gospeler who had spent the morning passing out Bibles to the poor.

"Fill me with joy and gladness; let the bones which thou has broken rejoice. Hide thy face from my sins . . ."

"He's a 'andsome one, that 'e is," the street-woman sighed. She gazed into the dashing face of Tom Clinch while the wind blew through the scarlet ribbons on the wagon and caused them to dance about his sinewy frame.

But there was one present who gave no heed at all to the notorious Tom Clinch, but rather gave his full attention to the milling crowd. He was a small man dressed in ragged, colorless clothing—a man not easily remembered. He was able to slip unnoticed through a crowd—a necessary trait for a man of his profession. For George Prentice was a pickpocket, not by choice but by necessity. He had an honest face, with blue eyes and a firm mouth. True, his features were pinched with hunger, but there was nothing vicious or savage in them.

Prentice rubbed his hands on his tattered trousers and be-

gan making his way from behind the carriages of the aristoc-
racy into the crowd, which was caught up in the excitement.
Spotting the scarlet coat of a man enthralled with the hanging, he cautiously reached, and then, deciding an English officer was too big a risk, he chose a gray waistcoat hanging
within easy grasp.

Steadying his fingers, Prentice reached into the pocket
and grasped a smooth, round object. He slid it out cautiously
and found he had fingered a gold watch. While the crowd
cheered Clinch's final theatrical climb up the ladder, Prentice
crept from one easy mark to another, stuffing the plunder into
the lining of his thin coat.

Nearing the edge of the crowd, he heard the familiar
sound of the hinged door falling open, followed closely by the
jeers and screams of the spectators. Looking toward the platform, Prentice saw the highwayman's body hanging suspended, a motionless specter against the blue sky.

Having dallied too long, he turned to make his getaway
but bumped instead against a cushioned barrier.

"Interesting business, pickpocketing!" A constable stood
barricading the man's path. His voice was harsh. "It ought to
pay enough for some new dance lessons, eh? Jolly fun dancin'
on air like ol' Tom Clinch up there, I trust?" Prentice felt his
mouth go dry. He looked around for a quick escape route, but
another officer jumped behind him and blocked the way.

"I've never done this before, sir . . . I can assure you o'
that. . . ." Prentice lied, his stomach starting to churn. A bead
of sweat trickled beside his ear.

The constable's forehead furrowed, pushing his bristly
brows out like quills. "Sure, sure, and I'm King George 'isself.
See me crown?" The constable pointed to his hat while his
other arm, paralyzed from an accident, swung around his ob-
tuse frame like a thick sausage. "Now stand over 'ere next to
this lot," he ordered, jabbing the air and pointing to two other
thieves caught in the act. The men glared wide-eyed at the
blue-uniformed officer holding them at bay.

Prentice, eyeing the other pickpockets, jerked away and
flung the stolen timepiece into the air shouting, "Gold watch!"
The two thieves and Prentice bolted into the scrambling

throng. They serpentined through the mob like a band of cockroaches let loose at a fair.

Raising a stout hand high in the air, the constable began shaking a wooden rattle—London's alarm system—and from three different directions came the "Charlies," the parish watchmen who had been waiting for the constable's signal. Wooden staffs in hand, the officers moved in for the capture, converging upon the crowd enclosing George Prentice. Suddenly an officer yelled over the heads of the confused onlookers, " 'Ay, blokes! I caught the bum! 'E's over this way!"

Responding quickly, the Charlies maneuvered their way through the crowd, prodding the throng like a herd of sheep. As the captor held fast to a big lock of Prentice's brown hair, the others jumped in and began to whack him with their sticks and curse him for giving chase. While the other two thieves disappeared into the mob, the Charlies turned their attention to Prentice. Seeing his luck had run out, Prentice heaved a despairing wail and surrendered. The pain-filled cries of George Prentice were lost in the din.

Captain Arthur Phillip stood on the hillside surveying his modest farm. Behind him was his house, a gable-ended structure with droopy little windows that made the house look as though it were nodding to sleep. Planting his boots upon the crest overlooking his fields, he surveyed his land against the hazy light of an English sunrise. As he pinched off a grain of wheat and held it in his palm, his weary gray eyes narrowed.

After choosing a semi-retirement with half-pay from His Majesty's Royal Navy, Phillip had lived out the last two years alone in a sedentary fashion. He could think of nothing else these days but his life as a captain.

A man of moderate means, he had lived mildly content with his practical and reasonable memories. He had captained a Portuguese ship and delivered four hundred convicts across the Atlantic to Brazil without losing a single man—a task unheard of in most naval circles. Resting his hand on a bony hip, Phillip reminisced about his years on the sea, wistfully recalling the beauty of deep blue water cloven by the plow of a well-manned frigate. He remembered with amusement the mates lolling around a dice game, making up tales with which to frighten women and children when they made landfall. But for Captain Phillip, with no fondness for old wives' tales, the abyss held a more pragmatic meaning. The sea had created a purpose for him in this world, especially since the day his wife left him. *Complicated beings—females.* But that was years ago and time had eroded many of those memories. Now it was the sea and only the sea that put his mind at ease.

As sporadic drops of rain began to fall, a breeze caught his navy cap, and without so much as a blink, he snapped it back into place. For a moment he thought he could smell the tang of salt water wafting across the land. But being a full day's journey from the ocean, he decided the aroma of salt must be permanently embedded in his head. A sigh escaping his lips, Phillip gazed beyond the horizon, scarcely noticing the dark clouds that had gathered. For his mind was captured by a torrent of memories: the unified movement of a well-trained crew in a feisty storm, undaunted by the green wall of water churning over the ship's bow; the fearsome power of a raging sea; a ship being racked in the black of night by a tempest so violent it threatened to squeeze the hull like an accordion.

Phillip's face tightened and his mouth formed a thin smile. The sea had cast its spell over Phillip, forging a bond from which he had never been freed. Thus a perpetual struggle raged within the captain: the pragmatist trivialized his need for exploits, while the idealist yearned for the unseen world beyond the next horizon. It had been with high hopes he had purchased the farm, believing he could settle down and become "respectable" . . . but in whose eyes he wasn't certain.

A faint rumble rose in the distance, awakening the captain from his daydream. The rumbling sound grew more distinct as the clip-clipping canter of horse's hooves upon the clay-packed road drew nearer.

Phillip squinted, causing his thick, graying brows to furrow below his slightly receding hairline. He could make out the King's scarlet on the rider's coat and the brass gorget decorating his throat. The sight of the messenger stirred a faint excitement within him. Reaching to brush away the soil from his gray breeches, the captain stood motionless as the rider approached him.

"What, ho!" the rider hailed, reining the stallion to a halt. "Are you Captain Arthur Phillip, sir?"

Phillip gazed up at the rider's long bland face and rosy cherubic mouth. "One and the same. What be your business today, sir?"

"A letter from King George, sir. He desires your services at once!" The officer handed an envelope to Phillip.

"Services?" The captain turned over the envelope and broke the wax seal. Sliding his thumb across the flap, he opened it, curious, and held a hand over its contents to protect it from the drops of soft rain that had steadily increased. The letter read,

> To Captain Arthur Phillip of His Majesty's Navy:
> It is hereby requested that you appear at once before Lords Sydney and Nepean for further orders to prepare and supply a fleet for the purposes of transporting prisoners to New South Wales. The sea transports will serve both to provide laborers for the new colony in the name of England and to relieve our institutions of the overcrowded swarm of convicts that plague our motherland . . .

The letter continued by naming the persons who would assist the captain in supplying the fleet, including a supply contractor by the name of Duncan Campbell. The document ended with,

> . . . and it is furthermore acknowledged that you are to be appointed Governor of our territory called New South Wales effective upon the day you reach this territory's shores.

"Governor?" Phillip stood gazing solemnly down at the letter while the rider waited impatiently in the drizzle. The responsibility of the farm pierced through him like a jealous wife as the tempting challenge of a new frontier loomed before him. "How soon would I need to depart? There's the harvest, you know." Captain Phillip's mouth was tight and turned up at the ends as he clenched his teeth. He assured himself that he was neither a gambler nor an opportunist. It was to the Crown he must be loyal.

"As soon as arrangements can be made, Captain. Sir Nepean would like an immediate response."

"I see." Phillip studied the field, his lips slightly parting.

"I should like to take leave now, sir, if you've a message for His Highness," the officer stated, taking a firm grip on the reins.

The captain nodded resolutely. "You may say I most humbly accept the invitation and appointment of His Highness. I shall be in London within a fortnight to begin the supply preparations."

"As you wish, sir!" The rider, relieved at Phillip's decisiveness, snapped his arm in a firm salute and turned the stallion down the hill.

"Good day, then," Phillip nodded, peering down at the letter again. Stuffing the dispatch into his pocket, he turned to gaze again over the wheat field. A faint smile dimpled his bristly cheek.

Phillip began immediately to assess the problems that lay ahead. This journey would be the longest route ever ventured by a colonial fleet. His men would be transporting hardened criminals. However much he reasoned, the voyage was more than enough motivation to leave the farm behind.

A thunderclap overhead sent rain pelting down in a sudden torrent. Captain Phillip pulled his coat over his head and turned to see the rider taking shelter in his barn. Digging his heel into the earth, he sprinted down the hill and made fast for the gabled house.

The undertaker stood beside the table with his arms crossed, a frown clouding his grim face. On the table a form stirred slightly beneath the sheet while emitting a faint moan. "The wench ain't dead, Skinner!" he snapped.

"Now it ain't me own fault, is it, Drake? I'm the best they

is an' I'm not the one who'll take the blame."

"You can finish the job so I can be about me business."

"You're mad, Drake! If 'er life was spared, then it was by God's own hand. I can't finish 'er off. It'd be like . . . like murder!"

"Don't be ridiculous, Skinner! She's a condemned felon. She's expected to die and you're expected to execute the girl."

"No, I tell ye! I won't do it!"

Drake looked squarely at Skinner. "What am I supposed to do with her now?"

"How should I know? This 'as never happened before. Just . . . I don't know . . . give 'er back to the courts. They'll know what to do with 'er. She's an absolute embarrassment to 'er family." Skinner pulled a cloak about himself as he marched toward the door. "I wash me 'ands of the whole affair!"

The rusted bell rang dully as Skinner slammed out the door. Drake regarded the girl with an annoyed gaze. "Such a bother," he muttered. He fingered the sharp tool he held firmly in his gloved hand. He could solve the problem with one quick incision across the jugular. "She'll die anyhow, I vow," he argued. "Her sufferin'll end and I'll still collect me fee." The decision was justifiable.

A soft moan was heard again as the girl's face moved beneath the shroud. Drake looked at the name on her tag. Written beside her name were the words "Political offender."

"Blast it all!" Drake flung the blade into a dish and trudged toward the door. "If Skinner ever fouls up like this again I'll hang *him*!" Tossing on his black hat and coat, Drake marched toward the magistrate's building, cursing as he went.

The room was silent except for the ticking of a large clock that stood against the cold wall. The young girl began to struggle again beneath the shroud, and a faint whisper rose against the hollow silence—"Jesus . . . Jesus." As the clock chimed the hour of twelve, the shroud slipped onto the wooden floor of Drake's morgue.

2

PRAYER OF THE DESOLATE

A bright yellow moth looped and skittered like a kite outside the window that was framed and lined with thick iron bars. George Prentice had spent the last half hour gripping and ungripping the cold bars with his tired fingers. His eyes were pinched with worry as he gazed stonily upon the moth that circled continuously, mocking the fifty inhabitants stuffed into the holding cell of Chesterfield Jail. Prentice watched as the winged insect glided through the rear gate and landed on the ground beside a child's ball. Suddenly the area became a flurry of stubby feet kicking wildly as a group of children attacked the ball with hysterical glee. Moving over the dirt like a group of ants protecting a crumb, the youngsters maneuvered the ball away from the gate, down to an open area where the ball could speed about freely. As the lads and lasses departed in a brown swirling cloud of dust, Prentice squinted at the small, flat yellow patch lying motionless against the dusty loam. Oblivious to the tiny creature, the children had crushed the moth under their feet and continued on their way.

"You got any brats o' yer own?" A raspy voice spoke from behind Prentice.

He turned and saw it was the new inmate, Crabbes, a churlish and vulgar man who reeked of gin.

"Yes, I have a little girl." Prentice tried to be polite in spite of the man's rough demeanor.

"I got me six kids in all, scattered around wif a couple o' different women somewhere. I ain't sure where they is." Crabbes wiped his face on his sleeve. "I married one but she ran away with me younguns and I ain't seen 'ide nor 'air of 'em since."

"What about the other one?" Prentice pretended interest in Crabbes' ramblings.

"I beat the wench for crossin' me, and she took up wif a madam sayin' 'ow she'd rather be paid for 'er favors 'stead of 'avin' 'em beat from 'er. Any'ow, I ain't never seen a wench worth 'er snuff, less'n she'd been clubbed a time or two."

Prentice turned stiffly away from Crabbes and shambled to another part of the crowded cell.

The chamber was a dreary structure with walls so thick that breaking out was impossible. Each cubicle, packed with nearly fifty men or women, held a damp, pungent odor that came from the rarely emptied buckets of human waste. The stony floors were covered with a slick puddle of sewage. During the night, rats the size of lap dogs ran along the moss-coated walls, squeaking shrilly before scurrying into their holes. A trembling inmate lay curled up, complaining of his infected hand, which one of the hungry rodents had chewed upon.

A clattering noise caught Prentice's ear. Clanking loudly at the jail door was the stodgy jailer with a heavy set of keys hanging from his waist on a large metal loop. In one hand he carried a walking stick and in the other a whip.

"Listen up, you scum! The magistrate'll be needin' to see some o' you 'ere today." He pushed back his dark cap with the whip handle while the door squeaked open. His assistant stood with a musket pointed at the restless men, who began to shift in their places like rats in a cage. The jailer stuffed the whip into his belt and pulled a piece of paper from his pocket. Full of self-importance, he cleared his throat loudly and stood straightening the wrinkled document while the inmates waited in silence. Peering over his spectacles suspiciously, his thick bottom lip curled out as he read the names and finished with, "An' the last one is George Prentice. Now all o' you file out slowly and follow Jennings 'ere."

Shackled in irons about his ankles and wrists, George Prentice rose silently and shuffled into line behind the others. He thought of his wife, Amelia, and their twelve-year-old, Katy. He tried to send word to them of his incarceration and the likelihood that he would be hanged at Tyburn Gallows, but he had heard no word from them and feared that Amelia had abandoned him.

Amelia had been a jolly wife in the days when he had been respectfully employed as a carpenter. He smiled at the memory of her. He longed to stroke her auburn hair, which hung to her waist when let down. Her fair complexion glowed like a youth's, hiding her age of nearly thirty-eight. With her gold-flecked green eyes, she could have passed for Irish even though she was English through and through. Amelia was a trim, attractive woman with a girlish laugh and a liking for a good joke. George recalled many happy evenings sitting with her and Katy around the kettle, laughing at the political humor circulating about His Mad Majesty, King George, and his mystery ailments. But when Prentice lost his job, a cloud settled over their family. Laughter was a luxury they could no longer afford.

"Move along now!" the jailer commanded gruffly.

Prentice plodded behind the men, his nerves fraught with tension. He had notched up his belt again this morning, his body showing the results of hunger after spending a month in jail. As the men tramped down the long corridors, a labyrinth of no escape, their chains grated against the floor. As soon as they stumbled out into the sunlight, Prentice breathed the air deeply and coughed, cupping his mouth and holding his chest, which rattled from the early onset of an infection.

"I want all you inmates to listen good." The jailer smacked his stick on the ground. "You're to load up in these 'ere wagons and you'll be taken for your trials," he explained in a patronizing manner while pointing his whip at the wagons. "If there's trouble out o' any of ya's, you'll be in for a floggin'."

Prentice hid his face to avoid the stares of the curiosity seekers who were gawking at the front gate. Suddenly a chiding murmur arose in the crowd as a child pushed her way to the front.

"No! Let me through!" the child's voice firmly persisted.

Prentice felt moved by the voice, which sounded familiar to his dulled mind.

With blond ringlets shining in the sun, the girl emerged from the crowd, and Prentice could see straightaway that it was indeed his own precious Katy. The twelve-year-old stepped forward cautiously, her willowy frame thinly clad in ragged garments that billowed in the wind. Her angular face was much like Amelia's—striking and noble in appearance, with a small nose that turned up slightly.

Feeling the weight of the chains that bound his limbs, Prentice gazed in shame at Katy. He considered turning away, but the child's longing eyes impelled him to speak.

"Katy!" His voice broke with emotion.

"Papa!" Her eyes lit with glad surprise. "I found you!" Katy looked up at the gatekeeper with a pleading face. "Oh, please, sir. It's my papa!"

The jailer shrugged, then nodded to the gatekeeper, who motioned her in. She ran and threw herself against her father's shackled arms and wrapped her own around him rapturously. Tears flooded her face as she studied his blue eyes. She had always been able to read Papa's thoughts, and he was too weary to color his mood for her innocent, searching gaze.

Prentice stared into the child's eyes, a deeper blue than his own, fearing this might be his last chance to be near her. "Where's your mother?" he asked feebly.

Katy bit her lip. Mum, who stood within feet of her, had been dragged reluctantly to the jail by the overly persistent girl. Katy was having trouble understanding Mum and her resistance to seeing Papa right now. She refused to believe the unspoken fear that haunted her—that Mum no longer loved Papa. She assured herself that they only needed to get Papa out of jail and he would make things right again, like always.

As Katy struggled for the words, Amelia's low voice muttered, "I'm 'ere." Stepping from behind those who had gathered in front of the gate, she had watched the reunion in silence. How could she hammer George now about the money they owed the tenement owner or about the meager supply of bread and meal that remained in their depleted pantry? Amelia approached George, trying to hide any signs of resentment or disappointment, although both feelings were beginning to consume her. She gazed up and her weary eyes met George's. She decided to tell him nothing. How could he help them now?

Prentice swallowed hard and waited for any show of emotion from his wife. The tear that trickled slowly from her eye as she beheld his ragged shell only served to further disquiet him. Not wanting her pity, he cringed.

Remembering her once loving gaze, now marred by pain and disappointment, caused his soul to ache. He wanted to lift her small frame high into the air as he had done in their innocent days, and once again hear Amelia laugh at his boyish show of strength, and see her eyes full of love and admiration for him. He gazed down at those same arms, which were now bound at his waist, feeble and constrained. Had his weak, ineffectual decisions destroyed everything?

"I've missed you, love," was all Amelia could think to say, but it was just the encouragement George needed.

"I love you, Amelia . . ." his voice quivered, ". . . more than life itself!"

"God, 'elp us!" Amelia's voice broke, her emotions completely shattered.

"Yes," Katy added tearfully, "God, please 'elp us!"

With his arms crossed, Sir Evan Nepean stood gazing out the large window draped with green Harrateen curtains. Serving as undersecretary to Lord Sydney, he had been

handed the laborious task of maintaining the calm as preparations were made to supply the prison fleet. Sir Nepean was
a man of medium build who carried out the king's affairs in
a manner most fitting an English dignitary. Framing his face
was a powdered wig with a double queue tied at the nape of
the neck with a black ribbon. His shirt was of finest cambric,
edged in Mechlin lace that fluttered as he gestured with his
hands.

"Have you met with the contractor fellow yet? What's his
name?" he questioned Captain Phillip, who stood impeccably
outfitted in his military attire.

"Duncan Campbell. Yes . . ." Phillip moved his finger over
the charts spread across Nepean's wide desk. "Seems to be a
difficult fellow to work with. Something about him I don't
trust, I daresay."

"Well, do your best to wheedle the man. He has an enormous task before him. Let me know if he gives you any bother
and I'll see to it quickly." Sir Nepean squared his gray eyes on
Captain Phillip, who stood stiffly, straightening his waistcoat.

"Now, Sir Nepean, about the clothing for the prisoners. It's
an insufficient supply and won't go around to all." Phillip's
tone was controlled but aggressive. "We must have more.
How're they to keep warm?"

Sir Nepean sighed. He was bothered by all this concern
over prisoners, for his mind was heavy with thoughts of the
ailing monarch and the continuing revolt in the American col-
onies. "If it weren't for the rebellious colonists, England
would still be shipping those vermin convicts to America. Oh,
hang it all, Phillip! Give them each a blanket and be done with
it!" he snapped.

"Aye, aye, sir," Phillip answered out of formality, making
mental note to pursue the issue further . . . in writing.

In an effort to change the subject, Sir Nepean cleared his
throat and whirled back around with a smile lighting his face.
"I trust you received your invitation to Baron Thurlow's ball
for this evening. It'll be a merry time for all, with many eli-
gible ladies eager to meet our bachelor captain." His eyebrow
arched as he gazed down his aquiline nose at the man.

Captain Phillip maintained his usual obstinate bearing.

"I'll be unable to attend, I'm afraid. The business of outfitting this fleet has grown so large, I've four bundles of documents to sort through. It's likely I'll still be organizing the whole lot until sunrise."

"Oh, come now, Phillip!" Nepean was persistent. "There will be important dignitaries for you to meet. It's a business affair as well. I insist!"

Phillip tapped nervously at the desk top, annoyed. "Hmm . . ." He paused, reflecting upon how long it had been since he had attended a social event. "I'll submit to your persistent request, I suppose. . . ."

"Splendid!"

"But if I fall behind in my work?"

"You had better not!"

"I see."

"I knew you'd see it my way." Sir Evan Nepean smiled.

The magistrate perused the documents before him, outlining George Prentice's history. His dark wide brows slanted upward pointing to the center of his forehead; his face was carefully expressionless. Bewigged in a powdered and curled toupee, his head nodded as he read of Prentice's recent arrest. "You know the punishment for pickpocketing, Mr. Prentice?"

"Yes, Your Honor, but . . ."

"It is therefore the decision of this court to order that the defendant, George Prentice, be hanged until dead at Tyburn Gallows."

Prentice felt his knees begin to buckle.

"What's this?" The magistrate paused, his demeanor still void of emotion. He studied the documents with veiled interest. "You've some carpentry experience?"

Prentice was taken aback by the magistrate's question. "Yes, sir. I was one of the best until I was put out of work. No money for buildin' right now."

"This court shall then commute the sentence from hanging to that of seven years transportation to New South Wales. You shall be held in one of the hulks at Woolwich as you await departure." He pounded the bench with his gavel.

Transportation sounded better than hanging to Prentice, but what of his family? "Your Honor?"

"Yes, Prentice, what is it?"

"What about my family? Could they travel along with us? Me wife knows something of dressmaking and . . ."

"No, it isn't allowed . . . to my knowledge anyway."

"What? And never see Amelia again? O-or Katy?"

"What do you think this is?" The magistrate was gruff. "A holiday?"

"No, sir, I just hoped . . ."

"Nonsense, Prentice!" the judged snapped. "You're without hope!"

Prentice felt himself being shoved away from the magistrate's bench by two surly guards. How could he explain a seven-year separation to Amelia? She would never wait for him, for he had sensed a change in her when he saw her at the jailhouse gate. *Per'aps if I withhold some of this news . . .* George began to scheme. *Amelia would never understand the whole of it,* he reasoned. "I've got to see Amelia," he muttered, his mind in a quandary. "There is still hope of seeing her again . . . isn't there, sir?" he lamented while the sentries dragged him from the courtroom. When no response was given, George felt panic grip his mind. "I need to see Ame-lia!" His voice echoed down the hard walls of the cold and empty corridor as the courtroom doors slammed shut.

"Next," the judge called indifferently.

The hulks were old troop transports and men-o'-war that were sprinkled throughout the southern naval ports of England and along the Thames. The Woolwich hulks, notorious for their decaying uselessness, were the largest final ships available for convict constraint. As the convict wagon jostled down along the borough's harbor, sea gulls squawked overhead, gliding over the port in search of an easy meal. The smell of dead fish was strong, calling mangy cats from everywhere to feast on the piles of oyster shells and rotting fish heads. Pulling alongside the dock, the wagon drew to a halt. The armed guards were on their feet at once, prodding the hungry and weakened convicts with their muskets.

George Prentice hesitated before standing up in the wagon with the other designated transportees. "How long until we pull out to sea?" he asked a guard worriedly.

"How would I know, scum? Now out with ye!" He jabbed Prentice hard with his gunstock.

Prentice grunted and thrust himself upward. His arms and legs remained locked in the irons, requiring the guards to assist him and the others as they disembarked. An old man beside him, his skin stretched taut across his cheeks, hobbled back and forth until two of the guards impatiently dragged him from the heavy wagon. Two gangly women attempted to entice the guards with promises of a jolly night on the town if they'd set them free for a while. They were shoved into line with the others. Prentice steadied himself and followed the guards and other inmates up the gangway to the lower deck. A hatchway was opened and the convicts were ordered below. As they crept into the dark passageway, the last ray of light pointed the way to their dismal quarters.

"There'll be no candles or lanterns! It's against the rules. Anyone caught with 'em'll be flogged!" the guard coldly established. "As soon as we know which transport you'll be departin' on, you'll be moved at that time."

Prentice retched at the stifling odor that hung in the air. "Smells like a stinkin' corpse," he muttered under his breath nervously. His fingers trembled as he felt his way along the walls. Without hesitation, he found himself praying aloud, "Dear God, I beg you . . . deliver me from this hell!"

"Shut up, convict," one of the guards threatened, "or I'll beat your 'ide to a bloody pulp!"

The hatch squeaked open and the guards filed out. Their abrupt departure filled the hold with a sickening silence for one brief, dreadful moment. George stood quietly in the bowels of the hulk, with only the sound of dripping water permeating the void. But instead of madness consuming him as he had feared, a restless stirring plucked at his heart. Condemning thoughts swirled through his mind. *I've gambled and lost everything*. Prentice leaned forward on one knee and braced a shaky hand against the wall. Swallowing hard, he bent the other knee as well. His faithless journey had left his mind hollow and void of words worthy of heaven. As the hatchway was battened down overhead, the hold became dark as a crypt. Some of the prisoners moaned in despair, while others cursed, but George Prentice fell to the floor and softly wept.

3

TRAPPED ON TURNMILL

"You're already be'ind two months and I've another family that'll pay me for the room . . . in advance!" Making her rounds in the tenement was a woman well known by the renters as old Shea Groggins. She had a long, drawn face, severe brown eyes, and pendulous ears. With a stonyhearted glare, she stood at the door of the Prentice flat with her hand outstretched in Amelia's face.

"But, Mrs. Groggins," Amelia pleaded, "I'm sure I'll find some work soon. If you could just give us a little more time . . ." She pushed the loose strands of auburn hair back up into the beige butterfly cap. Small ringlets of soft hair curled around the nape of her neck.

"Who'd 'ire the wife of a pickpocket?" Mrs. Groggins' words stung Amelia, who wished Katy had stayed out in the hallway.

"Don't call 'im that!" Amelia held her composure. "We just fell on 'ard times is all." Her green eyes rimmed with red, Amelia wiped the tears and perspiration from her face.

"Well 'e is what 'e is, ain't 'e? An' then leavin' you with an extry mouth to feed and no way to do it! It's a fine kettle o' fish 'e's left you in! Now, I'm sorry, Mrs. Prentice, but I'll 'ave to ask fer me room back. The key, please!" The old woman extended her hand again as the door across the way squeaked open a hairsbreadth, and then slammed shut when the occupant beheld the less-than-popular presence of the landowner. Old Groggins' stern gaze never left Amelia's face until she finally pulled a brass key from her moth-eaten pocketbook and laid it in Mrs. Groggins' hand.

"Here's your key, then. No use arguin'. It's obvious you've made up your mind to toss us out." Amelia's face tightened. "I'll send for our beds tomorrow if that'll be satisfactory, ma'am."

"All the furniture is mine!" Mrs. Groggins' voice was firm. "It'll help to pay off what you already owe me."

This time it was Katy who protested. "Our beds! But what'll we sleep on?"

"I can't be worrying about that, now, can I?"

"You're nothing but"—Katy was livid—"a horrible old crow!" Her countenance fiery, the girl stood toe to toe with the woman, ignoring the difference in stature.

Amelia pulled Katy's arm. "That's enough, Katy!"

The old landlady was well acquainted with the testy personality of the twelve-year-old, who was often found tangled in the clutches of bullies bigger than Shea Groggins herself. Mrs. Groggins' eyes grew large as she crossed her arms in a huff. "It's about what I'd expect from the likes o' you. Typical offspring o' George Prentice, if you ask me!"

Katy stood with her mouth open in stunned silence. If Mrs. Groggins had stabbed her with a knife, it wouldn't have hurt any worse. She fought back the tears, refusing to cry in front of the old woman.

"Mrs. Groggins, we'll be takin' our clothes now and leavin'." Amelia's eyes were threatening. "Unless you plan to sell our rags as well!"

"No, go on. Just be quick about it and leave the room tidy."

Amelia and Katy gathered their belongings—a dress and a nightgown each—into a cloth bag, and walked out of the room not knowing where they'd be spending the night. In a sack was the last bit of bread they had saved for their breakfast.

"Let's find Papa again." Katy ran to keep up with Amelia. Her mouth was drawn up as the tears began to spill onto her fair cheeks. "He can tell us what to do, Mum? Can't he?"

"Stop it, Katy!" Amelia sniffed as she gripped Katy's hand. "We're on our own now. No amount o' hopin' can change our situation."

Katy had been expecting Mum to say something of this sort all along. "Don't say it, Mum—that you've given up! You do care about 'im, don't you, Mum?"

"It ain't whether or not I care, Katy. Papa broke the law, not me. I have to think about us now. We have to look at it as though . . ."

Katy stopped and looked into Mum's eyes brimming with tears. "What, Mum?"

" . . , as though he were dead."

"No!" Katy's emotions ignited. "How can you say such things, Mum?" Her hands trembled as she glared into Amelia's eyes. "You *wanted* Papa to be arrested!"

Amelia knew she should chasten the girl for her impertinence, but the words never came. It was true that she had tired of George's mistakes long ago. But she wasn't certain anymore about her feelings for him. She was numb.

"You *don't* love Papa anymore . . . do you, Mum?" Katy's fears had finally surfaced along with her anger.

Amelia gazed into Katy's eyes, which seemed to hold great contempt for her. "Don't say such things." Her tone was soft. She shouldn't expect the girl to understand. Amelia turned abruptly and continued down the busy street, fighting to stifle the sobs that shook within her. "You're no longer a child, Katy. You have to face the truth . . . we both do. It's time you grow up. We have to go a different way than Papa's gone."

"But why, Mum? Papa needs us now more than ever!"

"We can't help 'im now. We can't even help ourselves, love."

Amelia strode firmly and directly as she marched alongside the thoroughfares. She appeared to know exactly where she was going, even though she didn't. "I'm scared, Katy," she confessed. Her voice sounding strained and breathless, she pondered aloud, "I don't know which way to turn. Everyone we know is worse off than us."

With Katy trudging behind, Amelia plodded up the street, past the butcher's shop, and around the corner. Straightening her brown skirt, she stepped into the tailor's shop where she had sought employment before. The small room was painted a lively green with yellow trim, and smelled of cotton and silk.

"Hello?" she called timidly. "Mr. Devonshire? Are you about?" She quickly wiped her face. No need to alarm the tailor. He had been a nervous sort since his wife had passed away.

The tailor walked into the storefront carrying a large pair of shears in his hand. His stout frame was covered with a dark-bibbed apron, and a pair of spectacles was planted on his balding forehead. "Oh, 'ello, Mrs. Prentice. Sorry to 'ear about George."

Amelia cringed. Word of George's arrest had traveled quickly. "I'm ashamed to talk about it, Mr. Devonshire. I can't do nothin' about it anyhow."

"Oh, of course not." He was fast to agree. "I know it's been difficult, Mrs. Prentice. I'm glad for George he has you. I'll vow his transportation is a welcome relief when you consider the alternative."

Amelia stared at the tailor in alarm. "You know somethin' I don't know, Mr. Devonshire?"

Devonshire bit his lip fearing he had betrayed a confidence. But it was the talk all up and down the street this morning. Surely . . . she knew. He cleared his throat uncomfortably. "You *do* know that George's sentence was commuted from hanging?"

Amelia shook her head, retying her bonnet at the neck. "No, sir, I suppose I don't know anything. My George is getting transported?" Amelia recalled the brief letter she had received from George only yesterday. He simply mentioned that he would contact her with further news about his sentencing. Amelia felt panic welling up inside of her. *Has George lied to me again?*

"Now, where they're sendin' the poor bloke, I don't know,

ma'am. But last I heard he was bein' moved to one o' those Godforsaken hulks."

"The hulks?" Amelia dabbed at her eyes once again. Everyone had heard the horror stories of disease and riots aboard the hulks. "Dear God, help 'im!"

"I'm sorry to be the one to tell you, Mrs. Prentice. I feel bad about all this business." Devonshire stared at the floor.

"No need to apologize, sir. I'd rather know the truth." Taking a deep breath, Amelia stuffed the handkerchief back into her pocket and regained her composure. "All that aside, Mr. Devonshire"—she swallowed hard—"I came by for a good reason today. I wanted to see if you'd be needin' a seamstress to replace the one you lost this week?"

Mr. Devonshire shook his head. "No, sorry, Mrs. Prentice. I 'ired someone yesterday late and she's a good worker."

Amelia forced a smile and curtsied politely. "Well, if you should change your mind, I'm sure you'd let me know."

"That I'll do!" He tried to sound encouraging as Amelia turned away to hide her disappointment. "But, say," he remembered, "there's a lady that came in inquirin' of a seamstress just this mornin'. Said 'er name was Marcella . . . yes, that's it . . . Marcella Briggs. Wanted a girl to do 'er chores and 'er sewin' for 'er."

"Where?" Amelia could no longer hide her anxiety. "I'll go see 'er now, Mr. Devonshire!"

"Now let me think a bit. She said she 'ad a place down around Turnmill Street. Oh, but I'd be careful down around those parts, Mrs. Prentice. A lot o' riffraff crawlin' around lookin' for an easy mark, and you with the child and all. I'd be careful, fer sure!"

Amelia bit her lip and stretched a smile across her face. "I wouldn't do anything to bring 'arm to us. But it would pay us to inquire . . . don't you think, Mr. Devonshire?"

Katy crossed her arms in front of her and said, "Yes, and if we can speak up to ol' Mrs. Groggins, we shan't be afraid of anyone, right, Mum?"

"Oh?" Mr. Devonshire tapped his finger beside his face. "Is Mrs. Groggins givin' you a fit?"

"It's nothing, really!" Amelia motioned Katy toward the front door.

"She's an old crow, and we told her so, didn't we, Mum?" Katy swung her fist into an invisible object and smacked it into her other hand.

Mr. Devonshire chuckled as Amelia nudged Katy through the doorway. "But mind my words, Mrs. Prentice. If you have to go, be careful!"

"We'll do it, sir," Amelia called back to him, grasping the cloth bag in one hand and Katy's slender arm in the other.

"Can't we go to Papa . . . now that we know 'e's alive?"

"First we better find us some work, love. Let's take comfort in knowin' 'e's still alive for now." Amelia quickened her pace, leading the girl briskly down the street. She'd not be steered by a twelve-year-old again.

Turnmill Street was an hour's walk from the lower-class neighborhood where the Prentice family had lived. This Marcella lady might be the answer to their problem. Amelia divided the bread and handed the largest portion to Katy, who gobbled it hungrily. Amelia chewed her own morsel slowly to make it last the whole way.

Leaving behind the aroma of fresh-smoked meats and cheeses, they soon found themselves wandering the sooty streets of London's crowded rookeries. Amelia stopped beside a decaying tenement and glanced up and down the street. The indigents of Turnmill Street seemed to take life at a more melancholy pace. Straggling down the road came a heavily ladened man and his wife, both dressed in tatters and surrounded by a string of raggedy, dirty-faced waifs. Bleary-eyed men sat on doorstoops, passing around bottles of white spirits flavored with crushed juniper berries. Two derelicts "tonicked up" with gin lay sleeping on the ground, curled up in stained newspaper. A young boy, his cheeks smudged with black, peddled shoeshines.

"Let's ask the bootblack if 'e knows anything, Mum." Katy tugged her mother's arm.

Amelia hesitated, then deciding the boy was harmless, approached his side. "You, there, boy?"

"You talkin' to me, lady?" He snapped the air with a grimy rag and hit a fly midair.

"Yes, I was wonderin' if you know of a woman by the name of Marcella Briggs. I understand she's needin' a girl to do work for 'er."

"Who? Marcella? She's always needin' girls. She 'ires 'em all the time."

"Good." Amelia was relieved. "Now, how do I find this Miss Briggs?"

"You're almost there now, lady. Go up this street 'ere. See that woman sellin' oysters on the corner?" He pointed directly as Amelia and Katy looked on.

"Yes, I see," Amelia nodded.

"Make a left and you'll see an old two-story 'ouse on the right with pink curtains. There's a big lamp in the window and you might see 'er in there rockin' and knittin' to 'er 'eart's content, you will!" The boy thumped his chest over his heart.

"Why, thank you so much, lad!" Amelia almost hugged the child. Her feet were aching and she hoped the woman would be hospitable enough to offer her and Katy a place to sit, if only for a few minutes.

Up Turnmill Street the twosome trudged, past the oyster lady, and then left. There they saw the old gray house with pink curtains, just where the bootblack had told them. Amelia stepped up on the porch that wrapped around the front of the house and ended on each side under large turreted windows. Inside, an old woman could be seen sipping a cup of tea. At her side was a small black girl holding up her hands with knitting yarn wound around them. Amelia knocked quickly.

The woman peered over her spectacles through the soot-covered glass. Adjusting her frowzy lace cap, she handed her teacup to the child and pushed herself out of the rocker. Amelia could see the lady mouth something to the child.

The big wooden door opened and the old woman stood staring with a sour frown at Amelia and Katy. She was a broad woman with sharp features. Ashen-faced, the woman had gray hair that hung in long tendrils around her shoulders, giving her a witchlike appearance. Amelia couldn't help but notice the woman's thick hands fidgeting inside the large pockets on her apron—pockets bulging with what sounded like dozens of keys jiggling incessantly.

"What do you want?" The woman eyed Amelia first and then Katy, who stood shifting from one foot to the other.

"I'm Amelia . . . Amelia Prentice, and this is my daughter, Katy. We're looking for Marcella Briggs." Amelia forced out the words, trying to hide her anxiety. "Are you Miss Briggs?"

The woman hesitated. "As I said, what do you want?" she asked flatly.

"We were sent by Mr. Devonshire, the tailor. He told us that you were looking for a lady to do your sewing and chores."

"Oh!" Marcella's round cheeks tightened like plums as a wide grin spread across her face. "You're out of work?"

"Yes, and—"

Amelia was interrupted by dauntless Katy. "She's a good seamstress, she is, ma'am. Knows a couple o' fancy stitches and even sewed up a pair o' pants for a baron once!" Katy nodded and smiled, finishing up with, "And no girl works 'arder than me. I can polish silver and clean your rugs—"

"Katy!" Amelia snapped. "Don't boast! It ain't becomin' for a young lady to carry on so!"

Marcella opened the door wide. "Are you 'ungry, lass?" She seemed to eye Katy in a calculating manner, her eyes studying the girl from her head to her feet.

"Oh yes, ma'am. Famished!" Katy held her growling stomach.

Amelia blushed. "I'm sorry about the girl, Miss Briggs. She seems to have forgotten 'er manners along the way today."

"Come on in an' 'ave a sit down. We'll talk about work while you eat."

As Amelia entered, she noticed an aroma of tea and dried roses permeating the room. But the room also held a dankness, and most of the walls had cottony webs stuck along the corners. *Needs a good airin' out*, Amelia thought.

"Sit yerselfs 'ere." Marcella pointed to a red tufted sofa that was beginning to lose its stuffing. As mother and daughter seated themselves, Marcella pushed her big hips back down into the rocker. "I keep a business 'ere. Lots of rooms in this 'ouse for . . ." She hesitated. ". . . boarders." The old woman reached a stout hand toward the servant girl, who was still standing with yarn wound about her hands. The child couldn't be older than six or seven, Amelia estimated. Her bony frame seemed to wilt at Marcella's presence, and at the sight of the old woman's hand, the girl flinched and batted her eyes. "Pour these two ladies a cup o' tea, Esther," Marcella snapped.

Esther dropped the yarn into a basket and ran to a mahogany table that held a tray of cups and saucers. Setting two of them on the tray, she loaded hot sliced bread into a basket and carried it over to the table in front of Amelia and Katy. As she poured the cups full of steaming hot tea and added cream, she watched for any sign of disapproval from her mistress.

Marcella continued speaking in a loud manner. "I don't give no 'andouts. Everyone around 'ere 'as to earn their own way."

Being able to stand the hunger no longer, Amelia handed Katy a large slice of bread with jam and began stuffing another piece into her own mouth. Katy slurped hungrily on the teacup and emptied it, scarcely noticing the tiny pink rosebud painted in the bottom of the cup. "More, please, Mum." She held out her cup, her voice low.

"Now your daughter, Katy, 'ere will be treated same as a grown woman. She 'as to do as I say or you're both out in the streets again." Marcella sat forward, her icy gaze directed at Katy. "Is that understood, young lady?"

Katy gulped down the soft bread and jam and felt an odd fear inside of her. "Yes, ma'am." She nodded, then caught Amelia's eye with a worried glance of her own.

"Katy's a good girl." Amelia almost sounded defensive.

"Now me customers likes things a certain way and I better not 'ave any complaints from 'em."

"Well, no, I should 'ope not," Amelia tried to assure the woman as she picked up two more slices of bread and poured herself another cup of tea.

"All me customers are men, and they likes ya to be nice to 'em . . . if you know what I mean." Marcella's eyes met directly with Katy's.

Amelia felt her frame go rigid. "No, Miss Briggs, I'm beginning to think I *don't* know what you mean! Per'aps you should explain."

"Oh, I think you're beginnin' to understand. 'As the girl ever 'ad any men?"

Katy stared at the woman, confused. Her stomach churned, feeling close to nausea.

"I should say not!" Amelia was furious. "We're respectable people!"

"So are me customers. But they likes 'em young and this' un 'ere is just about the right age to get broke in. Actually, a little younger'd be better, but she'll do." Katy stayed close to her mother, who began to rise from the couch. "I don't think we can work for you, Miss Briggs!" Amelia snapped.

A smug grin curved Marcella's face. "Seein's how you already ate up all me food 'ere, I figure you already owe me a day's wages."

"Well, I can earn that with sewin' or 'ousework, but I'll warn ya to leave your 'ands off me daughter!"

Marcella frowned again. "Now, I 'ave a mind to call in ol' Dring. He don't like it when Miss Briggs is un'appy."

Esther ran and hid behind Miss Briggs' chair. Her thin ankles wobbled behind the rocking chair legs as she squatted to conceal herself. A bull of a man with a rough beard and dark eyes overshadowed by a thick cranium peered into the room. He had been standing in the kitchen, out of sight of the visitors. His mouth was full of onion, and he stood slicing another piece with a sharp blade. "What's wrong, Miss Briggs?" His eyes narrowed suspiciously. The sleeves of his coarse shirt were ripped, whether from a brawl or from the weight of his heavy flesh Amelia couldn't tell.

"These two came in 'ere askin' for work, but after they ate up me grub, they decided they didn't want to work for it." Marcella's bottom lip protruded as she crossed her arms.

"Miss Briggs don't give no 'andouts. All the girls 'as to work for their meals. You want me to take care of 'em, Miss Briggs?" He tossed the onion into the kitchen and ran his broad thumb down the knife blade. With his other hand, he smoothed his greasy hair that hung to his shoulders.

Katy began to panic. "Please don't let them 'urt me, Mum!"

Amelia tried to remain calm. "I told ya I'd do some work to pay fer me food, Miss Briggs. There's no need to threaten me."

"Dring, show these ladies to their quarters. Then show Amelia 'er cleanin' tools. She's got a full day ahead."

The burly man lumbered over to Amelia and Katy and nudged them toward the hallway. They reluctantly complied and entered a hallway lit by a dusty lantern. Old portraits encased in grimy frames lined the walls. "Your room is in 'ere with the other girls." Dring pointed to a splintered green door, aged with neglect. "The rooms upstairs is where ye takes the customers." He ogled Katy. "Those rooms 'as to be cleaned before tonight."

Amelia groaned at the thought of treading up that stairwell. "Katy, you stay with me," she whispered.

Dring stood with his arms folded across his chest. "Take your belongin's on in and pick a bed. I'll be out 'ere in the 'allway waitin' fer you."

As the two entered the room and closed the door behind them, they saw Marcella's "girls" sitting on thin cots. Some looked to be mere children, while others appeared as old as eighteen. They were clothed in worn, faded gowns that were cinched at the waist. The girls stared vacantly at Amelia and Katy.

"Well, don't just stand there. Come in!" The girl on the farthest cot, a titian-haired beauty, turned to draw up her stockings. She had a well-endowed figure with a tiny waist and struck a pose with the flair of an actress. But Amelia thought she detected a glimmer of vulnerability in the young girl's blue eyes.

Amelia cleared her throat. "Mind if we take these two beds over 'ere?" She pointed to two uninhabited iron frames each covered with a scanty mattress.

"Not at all. You can 'ave them," the titian-haired one smiled, her full lips slightly smudged with red cosmetic. "I'm Rachel . . . Rachel Langley. What're your names?" she asked.

Amelia drew a deep breath. "I'm Mrs. Prentice and this is

me daughter, Katy. But we're 'ere by mistake. We won't be stayin'."

"That's what we all said," a thirteen-year-old piped up. Her eyes were pale blue and bloodshot, and her freckled face was in need of a fresh bath. "But we 'ad nowhere else to go and Miss Marcella keeps us fed and gives us a place to sleep."

"But you're all just children." Amelia's maternal instincts prevailed. "How old are you, Rachel?"

"Fifteen." Rachel threw back her shoulders. She had played this game before with nervous customers, eventually becoming a pro at convincing others that she had attained the adulthood that was forced upon her. As she stood beholding the frightened newcomers, she asked cautiously, "Are you . . . scared?"

"Scared out o' me wits is more like." Amelia glanced nervously at the door.

"Don't be, lady." Rachel shook her head. "They'll just chew you up and spit you out. Act like you don't care and no one'll bother you much."

"Goodness, child, who taught you such things?" Amelia's brow furrowed.

"Life itself, lady."

"Life is both good an' bad, Rachel. Don't we learn lessons from both?"

"Some people's born with good lives an' others gets the bad. We're the bad ones. There's no way out fer me . . . fer any of us. We're trapped on Turnmill, we are."

"What about your mothers and fathers?" Amelia persisted.

"Mine are dead," said a young girl with a blond braid trailing down her back. "Me papa was 'anged and me mum died o' the consumption."

"Are all of your folks . . . dead?" Amelia questioned.

"No," Rachel answered matter-of-factly. "But me mother 'ad too many mouths to feed and she turned 'er oldest ones out—me and two sisters. I don't know where they are now. I just 'ope they got it better'n me. They're both smarter than I am, I vow."

Amelia could feel the despair closing in on them. Surely

life offered alternatives for little ones like these. "There's no other place for you to go?"

"Beats the work'ouses. After we've done our mornin' chores, we 'ave the afternoon to ourselves." The thirteen-year-old tried to sound convincing. Her voice quieted as her eyes glanced sideways toward the door. "Miss Marcella's customers don't get 'ere 'til after sundown."

Amelia crept to Rachel's side. "We 'ave to get out o' 'ere," she whispered. "I'll die before I'll let 'em take my little girl and use 'er for their shameful purposes."

"If I knew 'ow to break free from 'ere, don't you think I'd be gone meself?" Rachel pulled her red tresses back into a comb. "You'll starve"—her eyes pointed to the window—"out there."

Amelia refused to accept defeat, if only for Katy's sake. But if they were to escape they would need Rachel's help. She had to shake the blinders from her eyes. *But how?* "Don't you ever dream of leavin' this place?"

The girls glanced at one another, their faces perplexed at the idea.

"I once did." Rachel twirled and seated herself with legs crossed on the rickety bed. "I dreamed of living in a 'ouse with a 'usband who would love me more than life itself . . . with eight children . . . an' they would've all been so smart. Smarter than I've been."

Amelia froze upon hearing her statement. Hadn't George said he loved her more than life itself? She stepped toward Rachel, stopped at her bedside, and placed her hand on the girl's shoulder. "You can 'ave those things, Rachel."

"Surely," Katy chimed in. "Why not?"

"Impossible!" Rachel retorted bitterly. "I'm ruined . . . nobody would 'ave me now. It's all over fer me."

"It's never too late." Amelia couldn't believe her own words. She had been the one tempted to give up on life just this morning. She sighed and pushed George out of her thoughts.

Rachel lifted a cracked mirror to her face. "I'm used up. I feel so old. Like me mum . . . she was always old." She gazed into Amelia's face, which appeared so caring. Without inten-

43

tion, Amelia was unearthing a graveyard full of emotions inside of Rachel. Perhaps it would have been better if this woman and her daughter had never appeared. "Never mind . . . I'm makin' no sense at all."

"You make an awful lot o' sense, Rachel. Hard times makes all of us feel old beyond our years, it does."

Rachel felt herself drawn to this woman. *What would you dream, Rachel?* The question nagged at her. "I suppose if I could wish for a thing to happen . . ."

"Go on." Amelia detected a spark of life in the young prostitute's eyes.

"If I could feel young again, that would be a good thing, now wouldn't it?"

Amelia nodded. "It would be a good thing, Rachel."

Shrugging, Rachel asked, "What makes you so good, Amelia?"

"What?" Amelia chuckled. "I'm no example. What with me bad temper an' all. Only God is good."

Frowning, Rachel looked down at the floor. She knew about God. He was that far-off entity that sat hoarding gold as all kings did. Rachel found no comfort in something she couldn't taste or feel. But if the thought of God gave Amelia comfort, far be it from her to criticize the woman.

"I'm glad you're 'ere, Amelia." Somehow Amelia's presence gave her solace. She saw in Amelia the strength that she had always lacked.

"I'm not stayin'!" Amelia persisted, though Rachel cautioned her to be quiet.

"What's takin' so long?" Dring stuck his head through the doorway. "Miss Briggs wants this upstairs cleaned right away!"

"They 'ave to make their beds, Dringy. Will you give 'em a few minutes, love?" Rachel smiled sweetly and fluttered her long, black lashes at Dring, whose face lit up at the sight.

"I'll wait if *you* ask." He grinned and shut the door.

Rachel waited for a moment and then flung her pillow to the floor. "I rue the day 'e ever lays a finger on me!" she cringed.

"You know 'e's sweet on you, Rachel. It won't be long until

'e'll be askin' Miss Marcella to make you 'is own." The thirteen-year-old shook her finger at Rachel. "Dring'd be a fine
'usband now, wouldn't 'e?"

"The onion-eatin' dolt!" Rachel's thin nose pointed upward
as she placed her hands on her hips. Then, leaning toward
Amelia, she whispered, "You go clean the upstairs for Miss
Marcella. I'll think o' somethin'."

"I'll be ever indebted to you, Rachel." Amelia and Katy
straightened the blankets on the bed frames but left their belongings in the bag. Opening the door, they found Dring holding a straw broom in one hand, a pail of rags and soapy water
in the other.

"Take all this and follow me upstairs," he ordered, handing
the cleaning supplies to Amelia. Katy reached for the broom.

After ascending the stairs, Amelia stepped cautiously onto
the tapestried rug. It was deteriorated and frayed, especially
in front of the six doorways. Dring took a large set of keys and
unlocked each door. The last, a large oak door with a glass
doorknob, was already unlocked. As he pushed it open, the
bed sheets flew back and a stodgy man with thick legs jumped
to his feet.

"Beggin' your pardon, Your Honor, sir. I didn't know you
was still about this mornin'!" Dring bowed low as the gentleman pulled his waistcoat around himself.

Her eyes meeting the judge's, Amelia stepped back, but
Katy peered around Dring's stomach. She eyed the under-
wear-clad fellow, who fumbled for his powdered wig.

"Is it daylight already?" The magistrate seemed frustrated.

"It is, sir. You 'ad a merry time last night if you don't remember."

"Oh!" he moaned. "My head! Too much ale."

"If I'da known you was 'ere, I'da woke you fer sure!" Dring
scratched at his bristly jowl.

"Can't sleep at home . . . sleep too long here!" the judge
muttered to himself.

Katy continued to stare while the judge pulled back the
heavy drapes, letting in the sunlight. Turning around he
looked at her with an impish grin creasing his cheeks.

"And who might you be, child?" His voice reflected the previous night's lack of sleep.

As their eyes met, Katy suddenly felt a shamefulness even though she had done nothing wrong. She backed away and fell over the broom handle. Amelia caught her shoulders and lifted the girl back onto her feet while the magistrate chuckled.

"We'll be about our business now, sir. You need yer breakfast?" Dring motioned behind his back for the women to leave.

Amelia and Katy gathered the supplies and scurried into the room across the hallway, closing the door behind them while the two men chatted.

"We've got to leave this place, Mum!" Katy's hands were trembling as she began to sweep the wooden floor.

"I promise you, love, before sunset . . . we'll be out of 'ere or we'll die tryin'!"

4
RACHEL'S FIRE

The glass bottle was carelessly tipped, filling the base of the lantern with kerosene. Nervous fingers fidgeted with the cap, dropping it once, then quickly screwing the lid into place. While excess oil seeped over onto the dusty glass, two dark eyes darted down the hallway keeping vigil over the green door. Dring was waiting for Rachel. He had swept the hallway around her door numerous times, and straightened the old carpet runner again and again in an effort to maintain a surveillance of the girl. Finally, the hinges squeaked shrilly, sounding the alert to the lumbering loner that his prey was emerging.

"What do *you* want?" Rachel snapped sharply, seeing the dark figure who stood blocking the doorway. Masking her alarm, she stood defensively with her chin up and shoulders straight.

Dring leaned toward Rachel without hesitation. With only a few minutes remaining before the first customers would start arriving, he knew his time was brief. Taking in the sight of her, Dring's eyes grew wide with anticipation. Rachel's blue dress hung off her shoulders, and the faded satin bodice clung to her waist. Her fiery hair glistened like gold under the hallway lantern. Dring moved toward her, his gaze menacing. "What do you think I want, Red?"

"I don't care, and besides, I'm in a hurry . . . and don't call me Red! If you don't move I'll call Marcella." Still refusing to show her fear, Rachel glared defiantly at him, narrowing her green eyes as she planted her hands on her waist.

"You were nice to me today, Red. You want me, too . . . don't you?" Dring reached for her pale shoulders, which were wrapped in a thin shawl of dingy lace.

"No! I wanted you to leave that lady and her daughter alone, and that's all! Now get out of me way or I'll—"

Dring grinned lecherously and pulled Rachel closer. "Since when do *you* care about someone else?"

"Leave me alone!"

"One kiss," he laughed. His dark eyes widened like two black pits. Thoughts of Rachel had occupied his mind all morning—the memory of her face, her feisty walk, and her perfume had blossomed into a full-blown fantasy. He would force her to love him, even if it meant a flogging from Miss Marcella.

Panic choked Rachel as she struggled to free herself from Dring's tight grip. She had spent a great deal of time avoiding him, but now he had finally succeeded in cornering her. His thick fingers were immoveable, reaching completely around each slender arm.

"No, Dring!" Rachel begged, shuddering. "Leave me be or I'll scream!" Twisting her head, she opened her mouth to cry out for help, but the enormous man swiftly clamped his hand around her mouth.

Angry tears spilled from Rachel's eyes. She had often had to please men she didn't like, but Dring was worse than them all. He was loathsome, despicable. How she hated him . . . and Marcella . . . and all the users who bought and sold misery like a priceless commodity. Her brow pinched in anger, she slashed her fingers through the air, clawing his face with her long nails and cutting into his skin. Instinctively, he jerked her away and held her at arm's length, out of reach from her clawing fingers.

Suddenly the door behind them flew open. "What's goin' on out 'ere?" Amelia stepped through the doorway with Katy. In shock and horror, they both watched Dring tossing Rachel around like a rag doll.

Startled, Dring's head snapped around to see the intruders. "Go away, wenches! We're busy!"

Gasping for breath, Rachel screamed, "Help! Let me go!"

Her face full of fear, Katy shrieked, "Mum!" as the doorway behind them quickly filled with the other girls, who began to scream angry curses at Dring. "Leave 'er be, ya big ape!" shouted one.

With a hollow sigh, Dring loosened his grasp, and dropping his arms, he backed away from Rachel. He glared at the girl, who fell sobbing to the cot, covering her face with her hands. "I'll see you again, Red." Blowing her a kiss, Dring proclaimed, "You're mine!"

"No you won't, you beast!" Rachel sat upright and shook her fist at him, the torn shawl flapping around her arm as she threatened him. "I'll wait for you to fall asleep one night, I will . . . and you'll never see the sunrise again!"

Dring laughed aloud, his heavy stomach shaking and protruding through his torn shirt. He wiped at his blood-streaked face. *She won't refuse me again or I'll make her pay!* He turned to gaze at her once again. "If we die . . . we die together, my sweet!"

"You!" Rachel shrieked. "Get out o' here!" She threw her shoe at his retreating back.

Amelia grabbed Katy, and they stepped aside as Dring angrily pushed his way through the girls and stomped down the hallway.

"Where's Marcella?" Rachel yelled as the girls gathered around her. She adjusted her dress, pulling the sleeves back up on her shoulders and jerking the hem of the skirt down around her ankles. Her face was stained with tears; her eyes were full of rage.

"Marcella's waitin' at the front door, she is, wavin' at the men and grinnin'," one of the girls answered.

The thirteen-year-old tried to offer comfort. Patting Rachel's shoulder, she spoke softly. "He's gone now, Rachel. Calm down."

"Don't touch me! Everyone just leave me alone!" Rachel drew up her knees and hid her face in the folds of her skirt.

Amelia noticed that the haughty facade had drained away, and the fifteen-year-old child had emerged from within Rachel. "There, there, love. Nasty ol' Dring is gone. Let Amelia wipe your face." She took a cloth that was quickly handed to her by one of the girls.

Slowly Rachel's face turned up in response to Amelia's soothing, steady voice. Amelia sounded much like her own mother, although this lady seemed more protective of her offspring than Mama had. Perhaps Mama had given up too soon, throwing away Rachel and her sister in order to save herself.

Amelia dabbed under Rachel's eyes. "You're such a lovely child."

Rachel felt some new tears surface. She hadn't been called a child in many years. It sounded sweet and innocent, and she was neither. What was innocence? She had been bought and sold so many times that she had often wished for death as she lay motionless on the bed at night, listening as the last customer tramped down the stairs and out the door. Some were filthy like Dring, but many wore fancy clothes and spoke in an educated manner. Sometimes Rachel imagined them traveling back to their cozy homes, finding a warm stove full of embers and a wife and children sleeping soundly in their beds. Perhaps the meaning of innocence had been lost with this age—trampled underfoot by a society's self-indulgence.

"Rachel?" Amelia whispered in a kind tone.

Rachel lifted her eyes to Amelia, who was a blurred image. "Yes?" she sniffed.

"Anywhere is better than 'ere, right, love?"

Rachel hesitated only for a moment, then nodded.

"Ain't no place better'n Miss Marcella's!" A voice cut through the silence. Marcella stood with arms crossed. She glared at Amelia and Rachel as the girls scattered back to their cots. "You all 'ave five minutes to be out front and ready to greet the customers or you'll go without your vittles!" she ordered.

"Yes, Marcella!" Rachel jumped up from the bed.

Katy looked at Amelia worriedly. "What now, Mum?"

"Time to work fer yer grub an' no nonsense out o' either one o' you!" Marcella barked, then turned to go answer a knock at the front door.

The room was silent. The girls stared down at the floor, despairing in their hopelessness.

Finally, it was Katy who spoke. "Well, I'm gettin' out o' here! I'll climb out that window, I will!"

"It'll do you no good." One girl shook her head. "There's a big fence round the back and then where'll you go? To the workhouses?"

"We'll worry about that later, me an' Katy," Amelia answered the girl boldly. "Rachel, you said you'd help?"

Rachel bit her lip, then nodded. "But I'll 'ave to leave for good, meself, or stay and deal with Dring."

Men's voices and laughter could be heard coming from the front room. Rachel motioned to the other girls. "You all go up front and greet the men. Tell Marcella that Amelia's 'elpin' me put on a fresh dress. This one's torn . . . see?"

The girls filed out and Rachel shut the door behind them. Running to stuff her belongings into a bag, she tossed it down for a moment and pulled a frayed cloak out of a trunk. "The window's nailed shut. If we break out the glass, we'll 'ave Dring and Miss Marcella in 'ere right away." She slipped into the cloak.

"So what else can we do?" Amelia's voice quivered with anxiety.

"Oh, burn it all down!" Katy sounded the most desperate.

"What?" Amelia was incredulous.

"Wait a minute! Katy might have something there," Rachel interrupted. "I'll go lift one of the lanterns off the nail and smash it right in the 'allway. While they run around getting water buckets to douse it, we'll break out the glass and climb out the window."

Katy almost cheered.

Amelia grabbed their belongings as well as Rachel's bag

and ran to toss them under the windowsill. Lifting a heavy chair, she prepared to heave it through the glass upon hearing Rachel's signal.

Katy threw on her thin coat. The temperature outside had dropped to a frosty chill and she and Mum might be on foot for hours, but she didn't care. The streets were sounding better to her now than they had this morning.

Rachel slipped out into the hallway. She could hear loud conversations as the customers guzzled down Marcella's homemade wine. The girls were talking louder than usual; they surely knew something was in the works. Rachel slipped the lantern off the peg and twisted the cap from the base to spill the kerosene onto the wooden floor. The past year raced through her mind, haunting her with the dire memories she had unknowingly collected. The laughter drifting down from the parlor only served to rekindle the fury that raged within. Her hands trembled. *Can you do it, Rachel?* She cursed herself and her own shallow weakness. Lifting the lantern high above her head, she froze as Esther's soft voice spoke behind her.

"What're you doin', Miss Rachel?"

Rachel had forgotten about the child. Esther was innocent and helpless in this wretched place. Rachel would never do anything to harm her . . . not even to save her own life.

"Esther, go out the back way. Miss Marcella needs more liquor. Go to Gin Henry's up the street and tell him Miss Marcella's runnin' outa gin."

"But I'll need some money, Miss . . ."

"Hush yourself now, girl. You want Miss Marcella to beat you again like she did last week? Ol' Henry's a customer. You won't need any money."

Esther nodded, her face fearful. She dreaded a beating worse than anything. "I'll go right now, Miss Rachel." The little girl ran for the rear exit at the end of the hallway.

"That's a good girl. Oh, Esther?"

"Yes, ma'am?"

"Take care o' yourself . . . I want you to know . . . just take care o' yourself, that's all."

Esther stopped with her hands on her hips. "Are you all right, Miss Rachel? Nothin's wrong?"

"No! Go, hurry!"

After waiting momentarily for Esther to disappear out the doorway, Rachel lifted the lantern once again. A new courage, laced with hatred, raced like lightning through her blood. With a groan, she smashed the lamp violently to the floor and leaped backward toward the doorway. The floor ignited quickly, the flames licking up the spilled kerosene. As the fire climbed the walls, the dusty hallway acted as a vacuum, sucking the flames down toward the attic opening. Rachel stepped back into the room and slammed her door shut as the fire swept past. Suddenly a crash exploded behind her. Jerking her head around, she saw that Amelia had thrown a wooden chair through the window.

Katy was frantic and ran to grab Rachel's hand and pull her toward the window. "Let's go, Rachel. We're free now!"

"No, no! You go first, Katy!" Rachel insisted. She struggled with her own will, hesitating once again at the thought of fleeing. *Where will I sleep or eat tonight?*

Amelia threw a sheet across the broken glass and quickly helped her daughter out the window. Katy landed safely in a patch of grass. "Hurry, Mum!" she called up to Amelia.

Rachel saw smoke beginning to seep in around the doorframe. Her mind raced with fear and indecision. *I could throw a blanket on the fire and help to put it out—blame the Prentice woman for the entire incident!* Looking out the window, Rachel could see nothing but the blackness of night. An urgency within seemed to speak to her, imploring her to run. She gazed at the anxious stranger who had somehow given her reason to hope again.

"Comin', Rachel?" Amelia wrapped her thin scarf around her throat. She pretended not to notice Rachel's hesitation.

"I'm comin', Amelia!" A vague smile lit her face. "I'm truly comin'!"

Within moments the ceiling was turning black and flames were inching into the room. The attic had caught fire.

"It's your turn, Amelia. Let me 'elp you!" Rachel steadied the older woman's arm while Amelia tossed out the bags and then scrambled out herself, landing beside Katy.

Turning to look back one last time, Rachel gasped in terror

when she saw the door kicked open and torn from its hinges. Dring stood like a demon in the doorway, flames all around him as he stepped into the room. Rachel ran to leap for the window, but her cloak caught a nail on the wall. She could hear screaming from the front room as the men tossed the girls aside and scrambled for the front doorway, racing to escape the fire, now raging out of control.

Dring plodded toward Rachel, his arms outstretched, his eyes piercing. "Thought you'd gotten away from ol' Dringy, eh, Red?" he leered, watching Rachel tug helplessly at the cloak.

With one final yank, Rachel ripped the cloak from the nail as Dring lunged toward her. Above him, the ceiling began to give way as the fire rapidly consumed the decaying wood structure. In a blazing crash, a beam tore through the thin ceiling, catching Dring across the back as he grabbed for Rachel. Rachel whirled around to jump through the window, but Dring snatched at the girl, seizing her slender ankle. Around them crashed the fiery ceiling, turning the room into a scorching inferno. Watching helplessly from the ground as they listened to Rachel's shrieks, Amelia and Katy screamed for her to jump.

His clothing afire, Dring groaned painfully and grasped onto Rachel's ankle even more tightly. "I said we'd die together, Red!"

"No, dear God, no!" With a sudden burst of strength, Rachel kicked forcefully away, freeing herself from Dring's burning hands. Her side pierced by the jagged glass, she fell onto the ground below as the ceiling caved in on Miss Marcella's place.

Captain Phillip stopped his carriage at the entrance to Baron Thurlow's country estate. He could see the lavish home just beyond the front gate, the tall windows illuminated by candlelight. Merry music drifted through the night, soothing away the worries and drowning out the cares of the day. Inside would be ladies expecting his company and dignitaries expecting his adoration. He sighed at the thought of both.

Although an emptiness pervaded his lonely life, Phillip found the choice of bachelorhood to be less complicated and less painful than married life.

The sound of a horse neighing behind him was followed with, "Excuse me, but may we pass?"

He turned to see a coachman sitting atop a fine carriage, no doubt occupied by a wealthy lord. The driver's droll expression suggested his boredom with the whole affair. Phillip's farmhouse staff included a coachman as well, but Phillip decided the drive alone would offer more relaxation.

"So sorry, sir," Phillip apologized, whipping his team and entering through the great gate, which stood open and guarded by the gatekeeper. As Phillip's team cantered down the long drive flanked by stately elm and spreading oak, he sighted ahead the mansion's entrance, and a woman being assisted from her carriage by several servants. Her head was top-heavy, with an extravagant hairstyle accented by large colorful plumes. He chuckled at the sight as she struggled to maintain grace and balance while unfolding the paniers of her skirt. As he reined his carriage up behind hers, Phillip was met by a servant who offered to take his carriage for him. Acknowledging the lavishly dressed groom, he alighted and proceeded up the steps to the front doors.

Upon entering the magnificent residence, Phillip noticed a group of women standing in one corner, fanning flirtatiously at the men passing by, their painted eyes flashing above their colorful silk fans. He groaned inwardly. A servant in black formal coat and long tails stepped forward and whispered to Phillip, "Your name, sir?"

"Captain Arthur Phillip," he replied quietly.

The servant then shouted to announce the captain's arrival, causing all to stop and gaze. "Captain Arthur Phillip of His Majesty's Royal Navy!"

The women stared with mild interest at the amiable-looking captain, who blushed at the unwanted attention. A pink-gowned woman with roses braided into her wig turned to whisper to the others. "He isn't married, you know."

"What happened to his wife?" queried a woman with heavy bags under her eyes. She poked at a loose curl that had fallen onto her forehead. Her royal blue satin dress gleamed under the chandeliers while the violins swelled to the lively strains of Vivaldi.

"They divorced some time ago. Left him a miserable bachelor." The lady in pink seemed to know a lot.

"He has some land I hear, but I'd never make it as a sea captain's wife. I want someone home at night to stoke the fire," said an older woman with a cane.

"I don't mind that as much as living out on a farm. Why, I'd lose my mind chasing around with pigs and chickens!"

"Well, he's looking this way. What should we do?" the woman in blue satin asked anxiously.

"Oh . . . act interested!" the one in pink chided. "None of us are getting any younger!"

Their chins tilted, the ladies smiled with exaggerated expressions and curtsied in Phillip's direction. Their fans flapped like a flock of pigeons.

Phillip fingered his sword nervously as he eyed the ladies, who, with their white towering hairstyles and twitching smiles, had the appearance of a huddle of anxious white rabbits.

Phillip groaned. *It's faces like those that keeps me married to the sea*. He was chilled by the thought.

"I see you *did* come, Phillip." Sir Nepean had stepped up to rescue the captain. "Splendid!" The dignitary was dressed smartly in black velvet knee breeches and an ornately embroidered waistcoat. From each side of his waist hung a bejeweled watchfob—one a clever fake.

Phillip cleared his throat uncomfortably and raised his voice slightly to speak over the violins, which had switched to Handel. "Yes . . . as you ordered, Sir Nepean."

"Confound it, Phillip! Enjoy yourself!" Nepean was frustrated with the man.

"Yes, sir."

"Ah, what have we here?" Nepean glanced up at the lady who had just entered.

Captain Phillip, following Nepean's gaze, recognized the woman as the one who had arrived ahead of him. She had evidently taken a few moments to straighten out her dress and hair after the carriage ride. She smiled sweetly; her round cheeks glowed a merry rose in the candlelight. Her headdress sparkled from the small circles of diamonds adorning it. As she stepped into the ballroom, her black gown rustled to her movements, and her pudgy fingers clutched a gold-topped walking stick.

"Now there's a lady you'll need to meet, Captain Phillip. She's the widow of Admiral Bennington and quite a catch for a bachelor like yourself."

Phillip sighed. It wasn't that he didn't like women. They just didn't seem to like him much. Or perhaps it was his frequent absences they detested. This one, however, had been the wife of an admiral, which meant she understood the life of a seaman. He smiled at the thought.

"Excuse me, Sir Nepean. What is her name?"

"Martha. Martha Bennington. Quite a bedwarmer, eh?" he winked. "Phillip, why not ask her to dance?"

"I don't care much for dancing."

"Oh, go on! Here . . . I'll introduce you." Nepean grasped Phillip's sleeve and pulled the reluctant officer along beside him.

As Martha Bennington pointed her toe and stepped down onto the ballroom floor, Nepean planted himself in front of her, flashing his white teeth and bowing graciously. "Madam Bennington," he said in a chivalrous tone, "please allow me to introduce to you Captain Arthur Phillip, soon to be Governor Phillip of New South Wales."

Martha smiled, her chin tilted slightly as she curtsied. The heavyset woman stood an inch taller than the captain. Her rounded nose was cushioned by a portly face, but her eyes sparkled as she spoke, adding interest to an otherwise homely countenance.

"It's a privilege to meet you . . . Governor Phillip." Her voice had a deep rumbling quality to it, with all the overtones of a well-bred woman.

Phillip felt awkward. "Well, actually, Madam Bennington, I'm not governor just yet." He hadn't courted in years. He wasn't sure he remembered how to dance. Hadn't the minuet gone out now? He did manage to bow politely, adjusting the sword at his side. "But it is I who should be privileged, Madam Bennington," he said quietly.

"I've heard of your expedition—to Botany Bay, is it?" The refined lady was obviously knowledgeable in naval matters.

"Yes . . ." Phillip grew more interested upon hearing his favorite subject. "I'm beginning to wonder if we'll ever depart Portsmouth. Things are moving a bit slow to my liking, anyway."

"Tut, tut, Phillip!" Nepean bustled. "Let's not weary Madam Bennington with naval politics."

"I don't find it wearisome at all," the lady smiled. "I love politics, as a matter of fact. Who or what is holding up the voyage, Governor Phillip?"

Phillip cleared his throat knowing Nepean's piercing eyes were directed at him. "For one thing, I need more clothing for the prisoners. I can't help but suspect someone is skimming a profit from the backs of these poor wretches. To observe them all wasting away in the freezing cold is nothing less than pathetic."

"Poor creatures!" Madam Bennington shook her head.

Nepean was growing impatient. "Poor nothing!" he retorted. "With all due respect, Madam Bennington, they deserve their lot in life. They're a scourge on society!"

The widow's eyes narrowed. "Sir Nepean, might I remind you they're all human beings."

"My sentiments as well, madam," Phillip smiled.

"Please, Sir Nepean, can't you find it in your heart to help these poor souls with clothing?"

Nepean stood with his arms crossed, agitation darkening his countenance. "The problem lies not with me but with the supply contractor, Duncan Campbell. He has eleven ships to stock with supplies. Remember, madam, the colony has to survive after it arrives."

"I know all about survival, Sir Nepean." Her brow furrowed. "The admiral and I lost two children before he died."

"I'm sorry." Discomfiture marked Nepean's gaze. Carefully calculating his answer, the dignitary smiled. "Not to worry, Madam Bennington. The prisoners will receive their clothing or Campbell will answer to the Crown!" Nepean bowed politely. "If you'll both excuse me, I've more guests to greet." Anger tinged his words.

"Good evening, sir." Phillip bowed in kind, which helped conceal his tight-lipped smile. His gaze remained upon the floor until Nepean had walked away.

"I hope I didn't get you into any sort of trouble." Madam Bennington's smile was burnished with triumph.

"I'm not worried, madam, so you needn't be either."

"How does your wife feel about your going away?" Her brows raised slightly while her eyes scanned the ballroom to belie her interest in the captain.

"Oh, my dear madam, there's no problem with that sort of thing. You see, I'm not married."

Madam Bennington smiled broadly, her extra fold of chin resting upon an ornate strand of semiprecious stones. "I see!" Her face exuded a warmth that endeared itself to Phillip. "As a matter of fact, I believe I wish to dance."

Phillip gallantly held out his arm to the woman. Madam Bennington beamed as she took the captain's sinewy arm. He was somewhat handsome, and she admired a man who would dare challenge the Crown on behalf of society's castoffs.

Phillip could hear bits and pieces of polite conversation as he steered Madam Bennington past the dancing couples, trying to find an area large enough to accommodate both her and her wide paniers. Taking her plump fingers in his stout hands, Phillip bent to kiss her hand while glancing up roguishly. She smiled serenely, stirred by the captain's charm. Counting off the music mentally, Phillip led Madam Bennington around the shining floor as the music swelled. Perhaps he understood women after all.

5
GAUNTLET OF TERROR

The heavy wooden door groaned and swung open, slamming against the wall. Yellow light flooded the hole where George Prentice lay in shackles. Prentice could hear his fellow prisoners stir and swear when the sudden light hit their sensitive eyes. They had been on board the hulk at Woolwich for a month without seeing the light of day. Pushing himself upward, Prentice winced in pain at the stiffness in his joints; his hands trembled from the weight of the shackles binding his wrists. Infection had set in around the dried blood encircling each limb, preventing the open wounds from healing. Near starvation caused his stomach to ache constantly, but he had seen many men punished for complaining about the maggot-infested food, and he had no intention of inviting that punishment upon himself. Leaning against the wall, Prentice stood with silent hatred seething from his eyes. When the guard stared down at him, he turned his face quickly toward the floor, for he had come to understand the posture of a slave. Humiliation was now a way of life for him.

"Listen good, you vermin!" the husky voice snapped from the oily stairwell. Deville, the wide-faced guard, had a week's growth of beard framing his snarling mouth. His cruel temperament was well known among the inmates, who cursed him angrily behind his back.

"The commander's comin' aboard fer inspection an' we needs you all to file out fer a head count. So on yer feet, dogs!" Frigid bursts of white air blew from the mariner's thick lips as he spoke. December had descended on London with a polar grip, bringing with it winter's first ice storm.

McGuire, an Irish inmate, growled angrily. He had been flogged several times for brawling. He spat at the floor contemptuously while attempting to rouse the convict next to him.

The ship's mate standing next to Deville held a rag to his nose to mask the odor coming from the hole. Turning to retch, the young man stumbled back up the stairs, cursing and gasping as he went. Prentice sniffed at his clothes, then shrugged slovenly. He had grown so accustomed to the stench he hardly noticed it.

Standing to his feet, Prentice observed the two motionless men on either side of him. He prodded one with his foot. "You there, Bobbitt, we're goin' up fer a look-see. Come, let's take a stroll, shall we, mate?" Prentice mocked feebly. Cruelty had so become a way of life that Prentice found himself growing as soulless and sarcastic as his wicked keepers. "Hurry it up, Bobbitt, or they'll kill us just for sport." In the pale light, he could see Bobbitt's face, covered with festering sores. His dark, graying hair hung past his ears.

Coughing weakly, Bobbitt raised his head and squinted. His beard, a blackish frizz with silver intertwined, was matted and unkempt. Grasping at Prentice's trousers, Bobbitt struggled to pull himself up. "What day is it, Prentice?"

"Blamed if I know, Bobbitt! Let's call it Friday. I always liked Fridays in London, when all the ladies paraded around in their finery." Prentice sneered with his eyes toward London. He remembered Katy and Amelia standing in front of the jailhouse in their tattered dresses.

"Friday it is, then." Bobbitt coughed again and pulled the

thin blanket around his shoulders. "It's so cold, Prentice." He shivered, rubbing his palms and pinching his numb fingertips.

"Must be December, then. Merry Christmas, Bobbitt!"

"To you too, Prentice. Better wake ol' Finster. He could use some fresh air. Smells like the devil 'isself, 'e does!"

Prentice prodded Finster's shoulder with the toe of his worn shoe. "Wake up, Finster. It's Friday. Time to 'it the pubs, mate. Rise and shine!"

Prentice and Bobbitt stared down at their friend, who didn't move. "Come on, Fin-boy! Time to chase a few skirts," Prentice bantered, turning his face to cough hoarsely.

Reaching his trembling hand toward Finster, Bobbitt checked the man's pulse. Glancing at Prentice, he shook his head, his voice grim. " 'E's dead, mate. Dead as a doornail, 'e is."

Prentice heaved a heavy sigh. "Another one. Poor bloke." Finster had been a nice enough fellow. Like Prentice, he had been without work for a while and had the misfortune to get caught with some stolen silver. "His missus'll be upset, she will. He talked about her a lot. They 'ad five children . . . or was it six?" His gaze lingered over the lifeless body, which within hours would be hauled out and tossed into one of the "poor holes" in London. "If I die, Bobbitt, don't let 'em bury me."

"What?" Bobbitt fumbled with a worn-out book that protruded from his pocket.

"Put me body on a pile o' sticks an' set it afire. I don't want to be buried like a dog."

"Stop it, Prentice!" Bobbitt coughed. "I'm in no mood for your jokes today. Have a little respect for the dead, will you?"

Prentice smiled sardonically. "It ain't a joke."

"Let's move those feet, prisoners! Hurry it up or you're all in fer a floggin'," Deville yelled from the top of the stairs.

Prentice trudged up the creaky steps, followed by Bobbitt, who stared after Finster with a melancholy look in his eyes. He could hear Bobbitt muttering a prayer for Finster. But it wasn't for his soul; the prayer was for Finster's wife.

Devising a scheme, Prentice whispered to Bobbitt, "Don't

say nothin' about Finster bein' dead down there, mate."

"Are you insane?" Bobbitt's brow furrowed. "We can't just leave Finster's dead body down there! It ain't Christian."

"Quiet! They'll hear us." Prentice clamped his hand over Bobbitt's mouth. "When they bring his rations down, I'll give you half."

"God help you, Prentice! I believe y'are insane!"

"Move along!" Deville snapped. His eyes focused on Bobbitt. "Here now! What's that you're stuffin' down yer trousers?" The guard grabbed Bobbitt tightly by his collar.

Bobbitt jolted, grappling for the old book he had shoved inside his pants. He pulled it out and waved it at his accuser, who was fast pulling out a musket. "Only a Bible, mate. Nothin' to fret about . . . really!"

Eyeing the small, frayed Bible, Deville chuckled in a mocking manner. "A lot o' good this'll do ya!" he sneered.

Bobbitt held his tongue, hoping Deville would tire of his cruel game. Finally the mariner thrust the Bible at him and pushed him back into line.

"Move along, scum!"

As the men shuffled into line around the stern, Bobbitt hobbled up beside Prentice, taking his place again between him and another inmate. "I *won't* eat the food of a dead man, Prentice." Wrapping his hands with cloth ripped from his shirt, he shivered from the biting wind that whistled through the men, taunting them with the distant sounds and aromas of London. "I'll starve to death first."

Heaving a sigh, Prentice capitulated to Bobbitt's badgering. "Blast it all, Bobbitt, I didn't mean it! I'll tell Deville that Finster died if it'll shut you up!" He cupped his hands to his mouth. "Hey, Deville!"

Deville snapped around to glare at Prentice. "This better be good, convict!"

"There's a bloomin' corpse down there! Ol' Finster's died."

"Shut up, Prentice, or you're next!"

Prentice sighed and stepped back into line, muttering under his breath.

Bobbitt turned to look straight ahead as a sentry passed. "Thanks, Prentice. I knew you wouldn't do it," he said quietly.

He stationed himself next to Prentice, who looked at him curiously.

Prentice couldn't help but wonder about Bobbitt's strong sense of right and wrong. "You carry a Bible, Bobbitt?"

He nodded. "It belonged to me sister."

"I've never understood the thing meself."

"Well, all the more reason to study it then, eh, bloke? We've nothin' but time now."

"I suppose. But they won't let us have a candle or lantern down in the hole, so how you gonna read it?"

"I memorized some of it, I did." A subtle smile curved Bobbitt's face. "Even in the dark, it's still up 'ere"—he pointed to his head—"and in 'ere too." He tapped over his heart.

Prentice shrugged. He had no patience with those who were overly religious. Believing in God was one thing, he had often told Amelia, but devotion was a waste of time . . . and fanatacism? Too dangerous. Moreover, life was too short to fill it with religious baggage.

"It eases me misery when I reads it, it does," Bobbitt quietly explained.

"Go on." Prentice shook his head. He was too weary to argue. "Quote me somethin' to ease me misery, then."

"All right." Bobbitt tapped the side of his face with a grimy finger. His brown eyes seemed to study the air in front of him as his lips parted. "Every valley shall be exalted, and every mountain and hill shall be made low: and the crooked shall be made straight, and the rough places plain: And the glory of the Lord shall be revealed, and all flesh shall see it together: for the mouth of the Lord hath spoken it."

Prentice blinked and then stared at Bobbitt from the corner of his eye. Even though the words stirred something within him, he wouldn't admit it. "Makes no sense."

A sanguine gaze lit Bobbitt's face. "One day, Prentice, all the wrongs in life'll be righted. Beyond what I see in all me misery, I can still hope."

"Hope fer what? Gettin' out o' this place?"

"Hope for eternity . . ."

"Did the priest tell you all that?"

"Didn't 'ave to. God'll reveal it if you ask."

"Aah!" Prentice waved his hand. "I'll leave it to the priests to figger out."

"Quiet!" A naval officer walked down the line, eyeing each prisoner with an intimidating glare. Simmons was a large man with a cruel bent, who was hated by all the prisoners. It was suspected that he sold the good rations for profit and tossed the rotting rations to the prisoners. He had been known to spend time on the docks, conspiring with the fleet contractor, Duncan Campbell.

With a disparaging frown, Simmons crossed his arms. The convict assemblage gathered under his watchful gaze was a pathetic sight to behold. Most of the men were stoop-shouldered with long, filthy hair and nails. Some had lost teeth while others had gangrenous limbs. Their clothing was literally rotting off them and their body odor was unbearable. The officers standing behind Simmons backed away from the prisoners, wincing at the smell.

Suddenly a prestigious-looking gentleman appeared on the gangplank. He was outfitted in the King's red and carried with him an air of authority and a quiet sense of dignity. As he rounded the stern, every officer snapped to attention. "Welcome, Commander Phillip," said the chief officer.

"As you were." Phillip saluted in return. He studied the faces of the prisoners, appearing shocked at their wretched appearance. "They look dreadful . . . like beasts, Simmons."

"Makes sense, Cap'n. They're just a bunch o' animals," Simmons replied indifferently, wrapping another scarf around his neck while the other officers seemed to gloat.

"They look starved," Phillip assessed with a concerned gaze. "Did you get their rations to them we sent last week?" His face grew stern, his eyes latent with suspicion.

Simmons shifted uncomfortably. " 'Course we did, sir. Aye, aye, Commander."

Phillip scribbled a few notes. "Well, we're going to send more aboard. I trust you'll see that the prisoners are fed this time?"

Simmons stood stiffly at attention. "Aye, aye, sir!" he snapped.

"Take me to the kitchen, Simmons," Phillip ordered.

Turning on his heels, the officer complied, riveting his eyes threateningly on the convicts.

Deville and the other mariners stood guarding the prisoners, but not close enough to observe McGuire speak in a whisper to another. McGuire, the largest and most formidable of the inmates, held a venomous hatred for his British captors. He turned to Vinson, the prisoner beside him. "When the commander leaves the ship, I'll give the signal," he muttered with an insidious sneer. "Pass it on."

Vinson turned to the convict next to him, and the message was passed down the line, causing a restless shifting among the prisoners. The mariners sensed a mood change in the prison ranks.

"Quieten down, you bunch of rats!" Deville pulled up his musket and aimed it at the prisoners, halting the passing of the message to Prentice and Bobbitt. The prisoners came to attention, paralyzed by the sight of the weapon.

McGuire muttered to Vinson, "I'll take *him* out first thing. It'll be my pleasure." His yellow-green eyes narrowed as he smiled in cold-blooded anticipation.

Prentice gazed around at the prisoners, sensing something beyond their somber expressions. *Somethin's amiss!* he thought to himself. But not having received the message, he sighed and looked wistfully out over the port, turning his thoughts to Amelia.

Captain Phillip reappeared with a muttering Simmons following close behind.

"I'll be looking for an improvement in the condition of the prisoners." Phillip shot a warning glance at Simmons, who saluted dutifully.

"Yes, sir. I'll see to it, Commander Phillip, sir!"

As quickly as he had arrived, Phillip departed from the hulk and was assisted into a carriage that quickly pulled away.

McGuire yanked the brim of his cap over his forehead, casting a shadow across his brow. He strained to watch as the captain's carriage made a right turn and disappeared into the fish market. Pulling out the knife he had concealed for a month while down in the neglected ship's hold, McGuire slid his foot sideways, inching toward Deville. He had deliberated about the knife, debating whether to take a sentry captive or to wait for another chance. Choosing to wait, he fantasized about the pleasure of power he would experience the day he seized the ship. But the waiting had fostered a bitter hatred for the guards, and he knew that the time for revolt was now or never. In spite of the chill, beads of sweat appeared on the Irishman's forehead. His jaw dropped like a cobra's as he prepared to strike out at the unsuspecting officer. Suddenly he found himself within inches of Deville, who turned in surprise to meet McGuire's deadly stare.

Deville's brow furrowed deeply as he scowled at McGuire, his mouth opening to protest the Irishman's close position. But in place of a protest, his eyes grew large as the icy tip of McGuire's blade lashed into his abdomen. Deville attempted to cry out, but no sound emerged save that of a low guttural noise made by a man trapped in a nightmare. Tearing out the blade, McGuire lunged at Deville's throat while the mariners around him scrambled for the swords and muskets they had left out of reach . . . an omission they would never forget.

"Die, you treacherous beast!" Wild-eyed, McGuire grinned savagely at the mariner.

His fingers extending stiffly, Deville dropped his weapon onto the deck as his body, drowning in its own fluids, slumped forward onto McGuire.

Instinctively, the prisoners erupted, seizing and overpowering the mariners before they could reach their muskets or draw their knives. Lashing their captives down with rope, the inmates began to drag the mariners around the deck, beating them with any weapon they could find—brooms, whips, shackles—and stripping their uniforms from them.

"Keelhaul the vermin!" yelled a grisly thief.

"Look at these! See what I found!" shouted another, waving the keys that would free them from the dreaded shackles.

Escaping down the gangplank, Simmons and two of his officers ran for reinforcements. Behind them erupted the sound of musket fire and the heightened pitch of revengeful men.

"Harkins, you run for more men that way!" Simmons ordered. "Fowler, you come with me!"

68

A pain-filled cry rose from the bow as another mariner was stripped and flogged ruthlessly.

"Prentice!" Bobbitt yelled to George, who was standing in a shocked stupor, gazing upon the rioting rabble that had waylaid the old hulk. "Quickly! Let's go below . . . where it's safe!" Bobbitt tugged at his friend's sleeve.

"No, wait!" Prentice grabbed the prisoner who was running by with the keys to the shackles. "Unloose me, man!" His voice sounded desperate. "I want to be free, Bobbitt! Don't you, mate?"

"I want to be alive, Prentice! Don't you know they'll hang whoever goes along with this lot? Go below, man! Keep your shackles!" Bobbitt tried to shout over the mob's furor.

Ignoring Bobbitt's pleas, Prentice trembled as his hands and feet were freed from the iron bonds. He groaned, first from pain, then from relief, when the weight was lifted from his limbs. He rubbed his sore wrists. "You next, Bobbitt?"

"Not me! I'm payin' me debt, then startin' over, Prentice. No shortcuts for ol' Bobbitt anymore."

Prentice shook his head in disbelief. "I'm leavin' while the leavin's good, mate!" He turned to make his way from the ship. "Goodbye, my friend. Good to know you. Good luck!"

As Prentice neared the gangplank, he stopped dead. His eyes widened in fear at the sight of Simmons bearing a sword and musket, followed by what appeared to be a hundred men.

Suddenly Simmons stopped short; his eyes narrowed upon seeing the bloody body of Deville hanging limply over the ship's bow.

Prentice groaned and backed away. "Bobbitt, ol' mate, looks like you were right," he muttered, surrendering to defeat.

Simmons raised his weapon in the air shouting, "Ready! Aim! . . ."

Prentice leaped for the deck, his bruised body rolling under the feet of stampeding prisoners running for cover.

"Fire!" Simmons' voice resonated above the heads of the inmates scrambling over one another in a frenzied panic. The guns rang out with musket fire blasting through the air over the rioters. As a second blast echoed across the bay, Bobbitt appeared from the stern and ran toward Prentice, his face tightened in a confused gaze. Falling forward, he slumped next to Prentice, who grabbed him and pulled him close.

"Are you crazy, mate? Lay low 'til the firin' stops!"

His eyes half-closed, Bobbitt regarded Prentice with a weary gaze. "Some bloke stuck me wif a knife, 'e did! I'm dyin', Prentice!"

"Don't talk such stuff, Bobbitt!" Prentice worriedly studied the knife wound in Bobbitt's chest. "Remember? You're the one what's gonna do it up right! Pay your debt . . . start over! Don't give up now, mate!"

Bobbitt's face suddenly assumed an expression of serenity. He smiled as his eyes opened, gazing upward. "Aw, now that's a nice light, it is. Bright and warm to take the chill out o' ol' Bobbitt, it will."

Prentice looked all around in confusion. "What light, Bobbitt? I don't feel nothin' warm on me."

"Goin' home, Prentice . . ." he softly uttered. Bobbitt's body grew still and lifeless as his eyes continued to stare up at the gray, cloudy sky and a chilly breath—his last—escaped his lips.

Prentice looked down at the still form of the man he knew so little about. He felt his lip tremble, whether from anger or sadness he wasn't sure, as he reached to close Jack Bobbitt's eyelids for the last time. "Why'd you 'ave to go back there, Bobbitt? You can't take care o' yerself, you know! You should've listened to ol' Prentice . . . stayed with me. I'd 'ave looked after you, I would!" His voice quivered almost silently as he picked up a rag and spread it reverently over Bobbitt's face.

The shouting of officers and sailors could be heard while they rounded the deck, flogging the prisoners and rechaining their shackles. "You blasted rabble! You'll 'ang for this one, you will!" one growled, his fist pounding on a prisoner's head.

Fingers trembling while his eyes shifted nervously, Prentice slowly reached for a set of shackles within his grasp and clamped his ankles tightly. Then with a groan, he latched first one wrist and then the other and planted himself head down against the wall. Prentice could hear the pounding of the sailors' boots as they neared him, yet he remained motionless.

Flinging obscenities at him, they kicked Prentice fiercely. "To your mutinous feet, convict!"

Raising his head slowly, Prentice swallowed hard and pulled himself upward. He could see three sailors dragging McGuire to the flogging post. A mariner stepped forward, his face bleeding from a cut over his eye. "Where were you during the riot?" the mariner demanded to know.

"My friend and I weren't a part of the riot, sir." Prentice pointed to Bobbitt's body. "They killed him, but I got away," he lied, his voice low, not wanting McGuire to hear.

"How do I know you're tellin' the truth?" the mariner frowned.

Prentice held out his bound wrists. "I'm still in shackles, ain't I, now?"

The mariner studied Prentice's hands suspiciously. "All right . . . fer now." The sailor turned to Simmons. "I don't recognize him as bein' one o' the ones who beat me, anyhow, sir."

"Be seated, scum!" Simmons ordered Prentice.

As the sailors continued around the deck, interrogating and flogging as they went, Prentice felt his head bump the wall when the old ship listed in the bay. He was safe for now. He remembered what Bobbitt had tucked inside his pants and began to feel around the waistband of his dead friend's trousers. "Here it is," he muttered to himself sadly. Pulling out Bobbitt's cherished Bible, he flipped through the pages. Blowing out another wintry breath, he sighed, closed the book, and tucked it inside his prison shirt.

"Here's a bit more wood for you ladies." A thin man in a tattered coat smiled down at Amelia and Katy, who nodded warily. Setting up a primitive camp along the banks of the Thames was not the most desirable living arrangement for the female fugitives. But it was a welcome refuge from the brothel that had surely burned to the ground. The survivors of the blaze were still unknown to both of them. After hiding in a passing hay wagon headed out of town, they were consumed with one thought only—survival.

Katy dabbed at the wound on her mother's arm. It was a painful gash that bled easily, so after cleaning it, she wrapped the arm with a clean strip of fabric torn from the nightgown in her cloth bag. Amelia smiled faintly at her daughter. "You're 'avin' to grow up too fast, you are. You'll be a grown woman before you know."

"Here now, Mum! You still 'ave a bit of a weed in yer 'air, you do." Katy pulled the weed from Amelia's tousled curls. The midnight ride in the straw wagon that followed their flight from Miss Marcella's had left them both exhausted. They had spent the last two and a half weeks in an abandoned lean-to near the Thames. "Will you find a job, Mum?" Katy's brow was pinched with an uncharacteristic look of worry.

"Don't you fret, Katy, me love. Yer mum ain't givin' up yet."

"Wonder if Rachel made it to West London, Mum?"

Amelia sighed, gazing at the sunrise that peered over the Thames as it broke through the wintry morning sky. "We may never know, love. I ain't so sure she even has relations there, like she said she did. Girl like that gets a funny thought in her head and she's gone . . ." Amelia snapped her fingers. "Gone like the wind, she is!"

The silence of daybreak cast a melancholy over the mother and daughter as they gazed out at the river, which was frozen solid around the banks, thinning out to a slow-moving current midstream. Ghostlike wisps of mist rolled across the ice and up through the holes that had once been cut by red-cheeked boys determined to ice fish. The biting freeze of winter had left the holes abandoned, to freeze over again, giving the ice a pocklike appearance.

"I'm glad I 'ave you, Mum," Katy mused, rubbing her hands next to the fire.

"Me too, love. I don't know what I'd do without you."

Katy leaned and kissed her mother's cheek, feeling the numbing cold against her lips.

"We'll 'ave to put out the fire and get on our way soon, Katy. There's some fine 'ouses up the road and we can see about a position at one o' them. Right now I'd work a week for a bowl of gruel."

"Me too, Mum. Or . . ." Katy was thoughtful, ". . . I'd trade a week's wages to find Papa."

"You lost your papa?" The thin vagrant had continued to stand over the women, eavesdropping on their conversation.

Amelia felt alarm. She didn't think the man should be so inquisitive about their circumstances. "Sir, we thank you for the fire. It saved our lives when the frost hit so harshly last night. But we can't be tellin' our business to a stranger."

The man wiped at his raw nose and pulled his coat tighter. "I can't say as I ever met a stranger. But whatever your business, you can't stay another night out here alone, I vow. If you don't die of the cold, you'll 'ave worse things to contend wif than the likes o' me. I ain't one to be bringin' no 'arm to you."

"Nothin' personal to *you*, sir," Amelia sounded apologetic, "but we 'ave every reason to trust no one, if you know what I mean."

"Likely I do, ma'am. But maybe I could help you with findin' your husband. I been around all these parts an' I know London like the back o' me 'and."

Amelia's brow furrowed as she caught Katy's hopeful gaze. She shook her head at the girl, trying to discourage any further business with the simpleminded vagrant.

"Please, Mum." Katy seated herself closer to the fire. "Per'aps the gentleman can 'elp us."

Amelia sighed. "Oh, all right, then. His name is George . . . George Prentice. He's been transported to one o' the hulks, but where, I don't rightly know."

The tramp scratched at his bristly chin. His blue eyes held a faint glimmer of intelligence. "I can't say as I know a George Prentice, but"—he had a sudden thought—"I'll venture to say I know who *would* know."

"Go on, then." Amelia felt herself growing weary of the man.

"It's a man who's takin' the fleet to Botany Bay. Man by the name o' Captain Arthur Phillip."

"And where might I find this Captain Phillip?" Her interest stirred. Amelia decided to exercise patience with the man.

"Well, 'pears to me he ought to be found somewhere

around Portsmouth, right around the harbor he should be." The man grinned.

Katy's face lit at a sudden thought. "Oh, Mum! We're goin' to find 'im, ain't we?"

Amelia stroked Katy's hair with fingers stiff from sleeping in the lean-to. She hated to quell the girl's enthusiasm for her father, so she answered simply, "We might at that, Katy. We just might at that."

Amelia sighed with anxiety as her mind once again filled with troubled thoughts of George Prentice.

6

CASTLE IN THE SNOW

"It's a black eye on His Majesty's Navy, Lord Nepean . . . that's what it is!" Commander Phillip paced in front of the large window in Nepean's office. Absently, he noticed that snowflakes had given way to sleet, which was pelting the window in a steady beat. Repeated onslaughts of snow and freezing rain had encased the bare trees in a hard shell of glassy ice, giving the sooty square around the government buildings the appearance of an arctic fairyland.

"We're not speaking of John and Mary good-neighbor down the lane, Phillip!" Nepean gazed over his spectacles arrogantly. Commander Phillip, with all his worthwhile ability, was a trying man. "We're speaking of the vile lowlife of our society. . ." He tapped his fingers impatiently, seeking the full attention of the officer gazing out of the window. ". . . the swinish multitude that burdens Mother England with beggars, thieves, and murderers, and offers no worthwhile contribution, mind you, only never-ending needs . . . needs that can't be met! Are you listening, Phillip?"

75

"But, sir, you should see the women aboard the hulks. They are, well, for all practical purposes . . . naked! And in this ungodly weather as well! Clothing prisoners is not uncommon, is it, sir? It's rather expected, I would think."

Nepean heaved a heavy sigh, drumming his fingers on the mahogany desk. "And what of the riot? Your hands are obviously too full of dealing with prisoner woes to attend to their discipline. Is this not true?"

"Not at all!" An indignant frown marked the commander's face. "Officer Simmons quickly brought in reinforcements from the other hulks. They overpowered the mutinous convicts and rapidly regained control of the ship. All the culprits were duly flogged and threatened with hanging." When Nepean gave no response, Phillip went on. "But riot aside, sir, could we have some more cloth for the women? Should they be expected to do without?"

Nepean's face grew tense. "No, blast it, they shouldn't do without! I'll see you get your bolts of cloth!" The dignitary hurriedly grabbed a quill and jabbed it into the ink bottle. "I'll inform Lord Sydney once again of the situation."

Phillip paused, holding his words. *Then it'll never be done*, he thought wearily. Lord Sydney lived too far above those isolated in the lowest caste of English society to place any urgency on this request.

"Will that be all today, Phillip?" Nepean's voice carried a tone of finality. He tightened his mouth and lifted his chin expectantly, waiting for the answer he wished to hear.

Phillip walked away from the window and retrieved his cape from the plush sofa, still warm from the fireplace. "Yes, that's all today. I'll be turning in a new supply list once we transport the prisoners in a few weeks to Portsmouth."

Nepean was relieved at the new direction in their conversation. "Going down there soon yourself?"

Phillip nodded slowly, lost in thought. "In a few days. The *Scarborough* will be mustered at anchor soon on the Motherbank. Likely the others will follow quickly thereafter."

"Good show, Commander! I trust you'll keep things running well." Nepean stood to see Phillip politely to the door and to hurry the captain along so he could get to more important affairs than the hulks' miserable rabble. Surely the fleet would depart soon and all of England's problems would be solved. "Have a merry Christmas, Phillip." He feigned joviality. "And try to forget about those prisoners for a while."

Phillip saluted respectfully. "Aye, aye, sir. And you have a good holiday as well."

As Phillip left the warmth of the building, he pulled on his gloves and drew his cape tightly together to block out the cold. Glancing up at Nepean's office window, he could see the glow of the fireplace that had warmed the hands of many powerful and prestigious men. But the yellow gleam kindled no warmth for the dark city that surrounded its impertinent glow. Rather, it instilled an even deeper despair in those who looked upon its faraway light . . . a distant point that shared its hoarded essentials with no one.

The wagon rolled along, bumping up and down over the rutted mounds of iced-over road. Amelia braced herself against the side of the wagonbed while Katy sat up front with the farmer who had kindly offered them a ride. After satisfying her hunger with the farmer's bread and milk, the twelve-year-old chatted endlessly with him about Christmas and bowls of pudding and skating on the icy Thames with her papa . . . all things she dearly missed. The farmer listened with animated interest, his brown eyes reflecting sympathy for the girl. His stout frame, contrasting with Katy's small form, presented a sweet, almost humorous portraiture against the backdrop of the country snowscape. People passing by could easily take them to be grandfather and granddaughter out for a brisk ride in the early evening. How Amelia longed for this sort of normalcy again for Katy.

Amelia rode silently, viewing with sadness the winter white countryside that seemed to stretch limitlessly before them. This time of year had once brought a spirit of merriment and joy to the Prentice home. She remembered laughing with George as the first flakes of November snow began to fall. How they loved to watch the wonder in Katy's young eyes as they bundled her warmly for a quick outing to engineer the first snowman of the year. But with George now locked away on one of the hulks, leaving Amelia and Katy to fend for themselves, the winter now brought with it nothing but impending hardship and the cruel threat of death.

"You might start lookin' fer work along this stretch of road, ma'am," the farmer spoke, rousing Amelia from her pensive reflections. He pointed to a narrow side road down which the only building visible was a small white church, crowned with a tall spire and stained-glass windows. "It's gettin' late, though, Mrs. Prentice. You'd best hurry. There's several rich folks that lives down this road, although I can't say as I knows any of 'em, save the Bennings family that buys a Christmas goose from me each year."

He pulled the two horses to a halt. The animals stomped at the road and snorted, their skin flinching at the cold. "I wish I could 'ire you both, but me wife 'as all the 'elp we can afford." He pulled a snuff box from his pocket and pinched some powdered tobacco between his fingers.

"I understand, sir." Amelia stood, pulling her skirts about and retying the shawl around her shoulders. "We could never repay you for the kindness you've shown us, offerin' us the ride an' bread an' milk an' all."

"It did taste good, sir." Katy smiled, feeling as though she might be able to trust someone again.

"I wish I could do more, ma'am, I do. Can you think o' anythin' else I might do for you?"

"Well," Amelia hesitated.

"Go on! It don't hurt nothin' to ask, Mum." Katy was insistent.

"All right, then," Amelia went on. "I was wonderin' if you knew how I might get a message to Portsmouth?"

The farmer grinned and nodded. "Why, certainly! I'll be takin' the wife down this week to sell some of 'er prized geese for Christmas. With Christmas bein' in only two weeks, she'll be makin' a bit o' lolly to buy our youngsters some shoes. Who is the message for, ma'am?"

"It's for Captain Phillip of His Majesty's Navy."

"I heard o' him, I 'ave." The farmer nodded as he scratched

his bristly sideburns. "Right famous, 'e is! The Botany Bay captain I read about in the *Times* . . . is that 'im?"

"One an' the same, sir. If you could find 'im and tell 'im that I would be glad to exchange work for passage for meself and Katy to follow me husband, George, I'd be appreciative, I would at that."

"Oh, Mum!" Katy was elated to hear her mother suggest such a plan.

"Will they let a man's family go along with him these days . . . one that's bein' transported?"

"I hope so, sir. Just tell the captain I can do a lot o' jobs. I can cook and clean like no one can and me fancy sewin' stitches can outdo anyone's. I'm the best they is, I am!" Amelia decided it was time to brag a bit of her abilities.

"You don't say! Well, I'll tell him, then! And the captain'd be a fool to turn you down, now wouldn't he?" The farmer laughed in a convivial manner. "So try an' meet me at this same spot in the afternoon on Christmas Eve. Can you do that?"

"I'll do it, or I'll send Katy." Amelia smiled at the confidence the farmer seemed to show in her. She had seen little sign of encouragement in many months. For some reason, she believed the man would somehow get a message to Captain Phillip. Maybe Christmas would bring a glimmer of hope.

Amelia and Katy waved farewell to the farmer, their insides partly satisfied by the goat's milk and bread.

"Do you think he'll do it, Mum?" Katy whispered as the wagon pulled away."

"Let's hope so, love." She pointed, a new interest catching her gaze. "Look at the pretty church. We'd do ourselves a world of good to stop and pray, we would at that."

A faint, thin smile graced the girl's face. "We 'aven't been to church in a while, 'ave we, Mum?"

Melancholy washed over Amelia. "No, love."

The two of them stopped in front of the church and Amelia stood silent for a moment. Feeling somewhat awkward, she sighed and bowed her head. "Dear Lord, it's me, Amelia," she began. "I'm sorry I waited so long to talk to you. I need your help to find some work and a place to stay fer me and Katy.

Keep us safe and watch over George. Let 'im know you're there with 'im, dear God. I thank you much fer listenin'."

Katy glanced up at her mother. She could see small pools of tears in the corners of Mum's eyes. Reaching around Amelia's frail waist, she hugged her gently.

"Please, God . . . only you can help. Please. Amen," Amelia concluded. Her eyes remained shut for another moment.

"Me too, Lord. Amen," Katy said politely. She wanted to pray like Mum, but somehow the words didn't come. Papa told her once that God was for old women and little children. But to be on the safe side for Papa's sake, she breathed the "amen" part for luck.

Amelia sighed as she started down the road with Katy. "It's been too long since I did that. God forgive me fer puttin' it off."

As they walked the long road, stopping at one expansive house after another, they were mesmerized by the sight of candlelit hallways bedecked with holly and the smell of cinnamon, cloves, and orange peel. Rosy-cheeked children bounded down carpeted staircases, squealing delightedly while their mothers made preparations for Christmas.

But no one was interested in hiring the weatherworn pair clad in smudged and tattered attire. Amelia stopped by a fountain that held a basin of ice. She took a stone and broke the surface of the ice, then shuddered as she wiped the grime from her face with the frigid water, using her bandages as a washcloth. Smoothing her hair, she took Katy's hand once again and headed for the next manor. The maid at the last home had informed them that Stoney Manor, owned by widow Emily Breach, might be seeking a new housekeeper. Amelia and Katy soon came upon a high stone arch, flanked with tall cedars. They couldn't see a house, but since the gate was wide open and no gatekeeper was in sight, they decided to go through the entrance. After walking a great distance and leaving the gate far behind with no sign yet of the main house, Amelia felt herself growing weary and discouraged.

"Look, Mum!" Katy sounded excited. "I see a puff o' smoke ahead, I do!"

Amelia looked up to see the smoke, a puff of charcoal gray

smudged against the blue twilight sky, which had faded to pale yellow along the horizon. As they rounded the bend in the icy road, they saw the chimney tops—seven of them—and the turreted roof. Continuing past the thick grove of trees that blocked further view, Katy and Amelia turned the final curve and stopped dead still. Before them, the grand estate stood in regal splendor, punctuating the end of the road with an impressive display of magnificent architecture. The property was aptly named, for the manor was built entirely of large gray stones that gave it a castlelike appearance. The front property was elegantly landscaped with tall, thin shrubs that stood in shadowy formal rows and bordered an elaborate circular garden.

"Look, Mum! Could be a duchess might live here—or King George 'imself!" Katy pointed at the house without inhibition as Amelia trudged toward the entrance.

Tiptoeing slowly up the stone steps, Amelia approached the front door cautiously. It was a massive oak door with a bell on the side. After ringing the bell, which seemed to harshly pierce the solitude of the English countryside, Amelia thought perhaps she should grab Katy and run away. But Katy stood watching the door, her jaw set with such courage and determination that Amelia couldn't let her down. Finally the door creaked open and a scowling dim face with ice blue eyes peered around it and studied the two lost-looking souls standing on the doorstep.

"What do you want?" the old woman snapped, pulling a black scarf so tightly around her neck Amelia thought she would surely choke.

Amelia pulled herself up as straight as she could. "I understand you needs a new 'ousekeeper and I'm the best there is!" Amelia shuddered at her own sudden show of false confidence. Perhaps she was being too quick to sell herself. Too forceful . . . too cocksure.

"That remains to be seen." The old woman eyed Amelia warily, her jaw rigid. "Well, let me see if Mrs. Breach can see you tonight. It's almost Christmas, you know. Lots o' things goin' on." The old woman drew in her head and slammed the door shut, startling Amelia. Several minutes passed and the door reopened . . . this time much wider.

"Well, come on in and 'urry it up. Don't want no wind blusterin' through an' makin' Missus Emily sick." The woman paused, taking the scarf from her gray head as she held out a tallow candle. "I'm Portia Thorn. I does all the cookin' round 'ere. But take heed! I don't make no chitchat with the 'ired 'elp. That's 'ow I been able to stay so long with Missus Emily. She don't take to no socializin' amongst the workers, and she'll dismiss you in a snap!"

Amelia and Katy followed Portia obediently, their shoes making rhythmic echoes down a long corridor. Katy stared wide-eyed at the large paintings that lined the walls of the corridor. Most were of people dressed in the finest clothes she had ever seen. But one picture that drew her eye in particular was of a large sailing vessel. The ship sat squarely in the center of the canvas with white clouds framing it in. The ocean depicted was a placid sea swarming with gulls. At the bottom of the frame was a small brass plate engraved simply—*The Europe*.

"You, girl!" Portia's tone was both demanding and hostile. "Don't be gawkin' at all Missus Emily's things. We've no time for sightseein'!"

Katy felt her face blush red. She quickened her steps and fell into place behind her mother. "Beggin' your pardon, ma'am," she apologized. "But that's a right fine-lookin' ship, ain't it now?"

"Sure and it ought to be! That was her nephew's vessel. He's an important man now in . . ."

"Portia!" A woman in a black dress stood pounding the floor with her cane. Her back was severely bowed, but her threatening scowl indicated she was anything but helpless.

At the sound of the raspy voice, Portia stopped dead, her face reflecting alarm. She curtsied to her glaring employer, who stood at the end of the long hallway. The glowing candles along the corridor gave the old woman a jaundiced appearance.

"I'm sorry, Missus Emily! I didn't hear you come in," Portia apologized.

"It's a good thing I did or you'd be sharing my life history with these complete strangers!" She rested on the black cane topped with a brass bird's head.

"Oh no, ma'am. Not at all! I swear I was just tellin' the youngster 'ere about the ship, that's all. Really, ma'am."

Mrs. Breach stood with her arms folded, teetering back and forth impatiently.

Amelia hesitated for a moment, then a slight smile lit her face. She curtsied politely and directed her conversation to Mrs. Breach. "It's nice to meet you, ma'am. I'm Amelia Prentice and this is me daughter, Katy. You've a lovely home 'ere. I don't blame you for keepin' it so private what with so many thieves runnin' about this city." She hesitated, remembering her husband's own sentence for pickpocketing. She would be certain not to share that bit of news with Mrs. Breach. "But I can assure you that me and Katy 'ere don't 'ave any interest in your private affairs." Amelia continued explaining as though it were her last opportunity to squeeze out all she wanted to say. "I understands you have need of a 'ousekeeper. We'll work hard keepin' your place clean and when you has your special guests over, we'll jump in and help out all we can!" Amelia beamed, her face full of sincerity.

"Well, of course you would!" Mrs. Breach's tone was no less terse. "*If* you were hired. Do you have any references?"

Amelia hesitated, for all of her references related to sewing and assisting tailors. She certainly couldn't offer Marcella Briggs' endorsement. "Well, Mrs. Breach, I can give you three references, but I must tell you that all of 'em was with folks that I sewed fer. I always cleaned up spotless when I finished me work, though, and I think me work record'll speak fer itself."

"So you're not an experienced housekeeper?" Mrs. Breach asked dryly.

"Not an' bein' paid fer it, no, ma'am."

"But you say you can sew?" Her face reflecting her pleasure at a new opportunity, Mrs. Breach arched her brow approvingly.

"Yes, ma'am!" Amelia was quick. "Is there some sewin' I could do fer you after I finish all the cleanin'?"

For a moment, Mrs. Breach said nothing. Leaning on her

cane, she stood there observing the pair. *A seamstress*, she thought. Smiling to herself, she realized this woman was obviously willing to do anything that was asked of her just to be employed. And what with it being Christmas, it wasn't likely one could locate a maid to serve at her parties on this short notice. She could always dismiss the woman later if she didn't work out. *The ballroom windows could use some brightening up*, she reasoned, calculating the uses of a seamstress. "Well, yes," she decided. "How quickly could you sew up some new drapes for this window over here?" She pointed to a room off to the side.

Amelia glanced over Mrs. Breach's shoulder. "May I step inside, ma'am?"

"You may."

Amelia tried to mask her astonishment at the bare elegance of the room, never having seen anything like it before. Hanging from the white ceiling, a crystal chandelier caught the light in small teardrop-shaped prisms and sent flecks of red, gold, and violet dancing around the stark white room. In the corner, an ornately carved pianoforte was adorned with a single item—an empty crystal vase that captured the light as elegantly as did the chandelier overhead. Save for two Duncan Phyffe chairs that faced the fireplace, the rest of the room was void of furniture.

"Indeed, those are right tall windows, ma'am, they is!" Amelia gazed at the six windows stationed around the room in pairs. They reached from floor to ceiling and overlooked a wooden porch that appeared to encircle the rear of the home.

"Well, these are the windows that need draperies. We use those windows as a passage to the rear porch, so I want the drapes to remain open at all times. I want them made long enough for the fabric to gather in a heap on the floor . . . about six inches too long should do it."

"You want them too long, ma'am?"

"Yes!" Mrs. Breach snapped. "It's a sign of good taste for a lady's curtains to have extra fabric. It's a measure of one's wealth. Don't you know anything?"

"Don't I learn somethin' new every day!" Amelia decided to humor the lady and acted thoroughly astounded. "How soon would you be needin' 'em, ma'am?"

"It would have to be after the holidays. It's much too late to get them all up now. We must prepare for our party tomorrow night."

"That soon, ma'am?" Amelia smiled. "Well, I guess I better get busy spiffyin' up this place. Where do we put our things?"

"Well!" Indignant, Mrs. Breach blinked, thinking the woman impertinent. "I haven't checked out your references yet, Miss . . ."

"I'm Mrs. Prentice. But why don't you let me 'elp with your party? Then if you ain't 'appy when me references come back, I'll pack me things and leave and you won't 'ave to pay me for the work this week."

Mrs. Breach was astonished. "So you're willing to risk working for nothing just to get this job?"

"I think when you get me references back you'll be glad you 'ired me, that's what!" Amelia swallowed hard, refusing to show worry, although Katy's mouth fell open upon hearing her mother's proposal.

"Well, the pay is only three shillings a week plus your room and board."

Amelia nodded her grateful approval. "I'll take it and thank you fer givin' me the chance, ma'am!"

Mrs. Breach shook her head. But she had to admit the woman's tenacity was admirable. "Portia, show these two to the servants' quarters behind the house. Explain everything to them. You know the rules better than I do."

Amelia and Katy followed Portia down another hallway, through an enormous kitchen, out the servants' exit and through the snow to a long building full of doorways. The structure was beginning to look run-down, but to Amelia it looked like the answer to her prayers. Stepping inside, Amelia saw the housekeepers' quarters held three small cots and a rickety bureau for storing their meager belongings.

"If you keep this job, you'll be sharin' the room with whoever else Missus Emily 'ires. She goes through a lot o' housekeepers, she does." Portia spoke matter-of-factly.

"Well, I works harder than most, Miss Portia. I can't see meself throwin' away what God just handed me." Amelia began pulling their things from the bag.

"Oh, it don't take much to rile the missus," Portia said. "The last one just chitchatted with a fellow at one o' her big parties and she was fired for fraternizin' with the guests. Another one was fired when she was caught inquirin' about another position up the road. Missus Emily fired her first, then sent word to the neighbor and gave the girl a horrible reference. She was out in the cold that night!"

Amelia remembered the message she gave to the farmer. If Mrs. Breach caught her trying to find employment aboard the prison fleet, she'd dismiss her immediately. She had to be careful.

As the two women and the girl busied themselves with lighting lanterns and filling a small stove with kindling, they were too occupied to notice the watchful gaze of one who stood surveying them from the window of the woodshed.

Bending to spit out his wad of tobacco, the man made mental note of the newcomers. *Two pigeons for a new game*, he thought to himself. Taking the side path around the manor, he disappeared as the shadows of evening cast their shroud around the old quarters of Stoney Manor.

❖

"Let me go, please!" the young female convict screamed, kicking the mariners who tried to subdue her. "Dear God, please help me! Let me go! I'll die on this hulk!" The desperate look in her eyes spoke of a past filled with hopelessness and hunger. The other female prisoners stared apathetically. Most who were sent to the Portsmouth hulks arrived starved and willing to do anything for a bit of food and a place to lay their head. For an hour or so of meaningless love, a hungry woman could have an extra portion of rations and, if she was lucky, a bottle of gin.

"What's her problem, mate?" one of the mariners chided another.

"She says she's not a criminal."

"What's she doin' 'ere, then?"

"She fenced some stolen goods—a lace handkerchief and

some silk stockings. Not worth six shillin's, I vow."

The mariner shook his head smugly. "Once a thief always a thief, I say."

That she was risking severe punishment didn't seem to deter the girl from struggling with her captors. As the men tossed her flailing body once more onto the slick deck, she fell in a heap.

"Let me go!" she wailed, tears streaming down her face. "I'm not a convict!"

One of the mariners made a suggestive remark while the others laughed cruelly. Then, as quickly as they had begun their mockery of the girl, they were stopped by a voice of authority breaking through their laughter.

"What goes on here?"

They looked up to find Commander Phillip had arrived for a surprise inspection. After a brief stop-in at *The George* on High Street, the local haunt where the officers frequently gathered, Phillip had determined to monitor the hulks before retiring for the evening.

He approached the girl, who lay sobbing on the deck. She looked up and pulled her long red locks from her face, her eyes filled with fear and bitterness.

"Please, don't touch me!" she begged, her eyes pleading.

"I won't hurt you, miss. I'm Commander Phillip of the Botany Bay Fleet."

"Commander?" The girl fell at the captain's feet. "I can't go aboard this hulk. As surely as I go, I'll die . . . somethin' tells me so! You 'ave to 'elp me, sir!"

As the mariners chuckled, Phillip sighed and ordered them all away. The girl watched in guarded amazement as the men quickly obeyed the command of the benevolent-looking officer.

Staring down at the deck, she asked suspiciously, "Are you really the commander of the fleet?" She straightened her worn skirt, trying to cover the burn mark on her calf. Pulling a tattered cape around herself, she fidgeted with its ripped hem.

"I am at that. And who might you be, child?" Phillip bent slowly, studying the inflamed open wound on her leg.

The girl licked at her bottom lip, chapped and sore from exposure to the elements and from spending too many nights in the streets. "Rachel," she answered cautiously. "Rachel Langley."

7

CHRISTMAS AT STONEY MANOR

"Oh, Mum, you look like an elegant lady!" Katy cupped her hands to her mouth as Amelia danced around the small room in a pale blue dress, her lithe form making long shadows on the wall in the dark, chilly morning.

"They give me two o' these blue dresses to wear, Katy. Mrs. Breach wants 'er people to look right smart, she does." Amelia tucked her hair inside a white bonnet trimmed with lace and blue ribbon. Reaching for the other dresses hanging on a nail on the wall, she smoothed them with her chapped fingers. The third dress was solid black with a train and white apron. "Portia told me to wear this'n tonight at the Christmas party. It's right elegant, ain't it, love?"

The blue dresses were of plain design and simply cut; the long skirt hung just above the floor. Six small blue buttons ran down the bodice front and a small bustle adorned the seat. The last housekeeper must have been larger than Amelia for the seams hung off her shoulders. "No matter!" she said cheerily. "I knows how to fix that!"

Katy watched her mother with admiration. "With your hair all done up in a fine bonnet like that, you look so proper, Mum."

Portia had even promised Katy some fabric for a uniform if Amelia would sew it for her, but for now, Amelia and Katy had quickly washed out Katy's better-looking dress, as well as her underthings, and hung them near the stove to dry. The dress was stiff, so Katy hurriedly worked the fabric with her fingers, smoothing away the wrinkles before putting it on.

"Let me run a comb through your pretty hair, love," Amelia said.

Katy braided one side as Amelia combed the other, then pinned it up in a circle around the crown of her head.

After a quick check in the cracked mirror that hung over the bureau, Amelia handed Katy her thin coat and tossed a shawl around her own shoulders. She sneezed loudly, then shuddered. "This place is right drafty, it is. Let's get to the big 'ouse where it's nice and toasty."

Amelia grabbed the lantern to light their way up the snow-covered path, for sunrise wouldn't appear for another hour. The workday started early for the servants of Stoney Manor. Other domestics were filing out their doors, their faces looking weary in the light of the swaying oil lamps.

"It'll be so nice, Mum, won't it?" Katy followed Amelia out the door. "Get to meet some new folks, we will." Katy turned to two men dressed in heavy coats and thick boots. In their hands they each carried an ax and one also toted a musket. "Good mornin', sir!" Katy said cheerily to one.

The man nodded, half noticing the girl while the other one, a surly-looking man in brown leather boots, smiled. Behind him came several women wearing bonnets, and under their cloaks, blue dresses similar to that of Amelia's. They walked silently, their faces tense.

One whispered, "Think we'll make it through the day, Mary?"

The maid shook her head, her thin face pulled into a scowl. "Who knows, Elnora? Last Christmas party she had, she fired half the servants!"

Behind them tramped the male servants, looking somewhat distinguished, and two boys who joked quietly with each other.

"And who might you be?" A gravelly voice startled Amelia.

Amelia turned to see the man had an ill-shaven face and shabby, unkempt clothes, looking nothing like the neat liverymen who served Mrs. Breach. "I'm Mrs. Prentice and this is me daughter, Katy." Amelia suddenly assumed a new coolness in her voice, trying to ward off further conversation with the man. It wasn't his appearance that made her uncomfortable, but rather the way he leered at her as though she were an available woman.

"Leave the women alone, Jiggs! They've enough to do today without worryin' about *your* foolishness!" a liveryman remarked disdainfully.

"I'm only bein' friendly to the new one!" he snapped, his resentment toward the higher-class servant evident. "I'll be remindin' ye to mind yer own business!" Jiggs fell into line behind the other men, muttering under his breath, expletives exploding in an Irish brogue.

Amelia rubbed her hands, which were beginning to sting from the cold. "First thing we'll do, Katy, is buy us each a pair o' proper gloves, that's what. An' a scarf, too!"

"Fer Christmas, Mum?" Katy glanced over in a trusting manner.

Amelia hesitated. "We'll see, love."

The kitchen was cozy, the warm air laden with the aroma of mincemeat pie, baked apples, and smoked meats, all as Amelia had imagined. Portia and her kitchen maids had, as was the custom, entered the dark and chilly kitchen an hour before the others to stoke up the fire, light the lamps, and begin mixing the biscuit dough. Portia had made a batch of hot bread, which the servants gobbled hungrily.

"Mrs. Breach says fer ya all to eat in a hurry and get about yer chores. This party's got to be near perfect . . . a lot o' important people comin' tonight, they is."

Katy and Amelia took their serving of biscuits and jam and quickly swallowed them down with milk. Glancing around the large kitchen, Katy noticed it was as large as the entire flat they had rented from Shea Groggins. The kitchen was surrounded by windows on two sides and had two big ovens. A large wooden block in the center of the room overflowed with onions and potatoes. A stone fireplace, larger than any Katy had ever seen, had an iron kettle in it filled with beans and salt pork, which bubbled over the fire and dripped hot sizzling streams over the sides. Portia and three other women passed around fruit and gave each servant a slice of cold meat pie. It tasted heavenly to Katy, who hadn't eaten meat pie in years.

"Does we get this every mornin'?" she asked Portia hopefully.

"Sometimes we just gets a bowl o' gruel, but at Christmas there's extras around the kitchen, like fruit an' such, an' Missus Emily has a mad fit if anythin' goes to waste, she does," Portia explained quietly. "So enjoy it while you can." Portia directed her next statement to Amelia. "I'll be wantin' your girl to 'elp me an' the other cooks in the kitchen. We'll be needin' someone extra to run fer things as we need 'em, we will."

"Katy'll be 'appy to help, won't you, love?" Amelia smiled and tucked a strand of hair back under her bonnet.

Katy nodded at Portia. "Where will Mum be, Miss Portia?"

Portia studied the young girl with skepticism. "Don't you be worryin' about your mum. She'll be runnin' around polishin' silver and 'elpin' Missus Emily with the ballroom . . . a chore I'd never undertake!"

"Why is that?" Amelia asked cautiously, her brow furrowing from a sudden dull pain that started to throb in her head.

" 'Cause nothin' ever pleases Missus Emily when she starts her decoratin'. And I know nothin' of such things, anyhow."

From another room in the house came the sound of a bell ringing. Portia jumped to her feet, followed immediately by the other servants, who grabbed the fruit and stuffed it into their aprons and pockets greedily.

Portia placed her hand on Katy's shoulder. "You, girl, go over to that basin and start washin' that heap of vegetables. It'll take half the mornin' to peel 'em and chop 'em, I figures. Hurry it up, now!" Portia's voice sounded even more strained than it had the day before. "Elnora'll help you, she will."

As her mother nodded to her, Katy jumped from her chair and did as Portia bade her.

Speaking to Amelia, Portia barked, "Hurry now and get to the ballroom! Missus Emily'll not wait long fer you until she'll be yellin' and fussin' at me. And I don't 'ave time to be chasin' around after a new housekeeper."

Amelia practically ran the length of the hallway, backtracking her steps mentally from yesterday's brief time in the manor. As she came to the end of the long hall, she could hear Emily Breach's familiar voice screeching, "Portia!" which made Amelia's head hurt all the worse.

"Portia's in the kitchen, ma'am." Amelia entered the ballroom quickly and curtsied to Emily Breach. "May I be of service?"

"How we'll ever get this all finished and train a new staff at the same time is beyond me!" Mrs. Breach blustered. "Now, Amelia"—her gaze was direct—"a new woman is coming by today for the ladies' maid position. She's experienced in cleaning large homes and you should work under her direction. Is that understood?"

Amelia nodded.

"Good! Now I want you to drape this hollyberry all around the fireplace mantel. Don't be slow about it! Then arrange these candles in the center so they'll reflect in the large mirror over the mantelpiece. Is that clear, Amelia?" Mrs. Breach studied Amelia's face with a critical eye. Her piercing gaze and stooped posture gave the woman a vulturelike appearance.

"Oh yes, ma'am!" Amelia curtsied again, feeling nervous. "And was there some silver you wanted polished?"

Emily Breach walked to the end of the ballroom and opened a wooden door. "It's all in here." She directed Amelia, waving her hand inside the small room. "Quickly now! Come see!"

Amelia hastened across the white wooden floor and stopped to stand next to her mistress. Peering into the room, she saw a long table jammed inside. From one end to the other the table was filled with silver bowls, platters, candlesticks, goblets, and other serving utensils, none of which was familiar to Amelia. Her countenance fell as she realized the huge task before her. *I'll be lucky to finish polishing it all by Christmas day, let alone tonight!* Exasperation added further pressure to her mind—she and the new housekeeper still had to decorate the ballroom and clean the entire house in preparation for showing it to all the guests arriving for the party. Taking a deep breath, Amelia affirmed, *I'll get it all done and just to the lady's likin', I will.*

Mrs. Breach studied the worry on Amelia's face. "You could quit like the others, you know." She half smiled, remembering the desperation in Amelia's voice the previous day.

"Oh no, ma'am! I'll get the work finished or me name ain't Amelia Prentice!"

The bell outside the front door rang loudly. Mrs. Breach sighed as she heard Portia bounding down the hallway. "Portia, you stay in the kitchen! I'll tend to the door until the new butler arrives," she snapped.

Portia peered fearfully around the doorway. "Are you sure, Missus Emily?"

"Yes, you'll never be finished in time for tonight if I don't. At any rate, perhaps the ladies' maid is here for her interview." She turned to Amelia.

"You know what to do now, Amelia?"

"Yes, ma'am." Amelia nodded and curtsied as she stepped toward the fireplace, but then remembering the silver, she looked back toward the room in confusion. Her head felt light and she had great difficulty remembering all that her employer had just said to her. She gripped the mantel in bewilderment.

"What's wrong now? Can't remember?" Now it was Emily Breach who was exasperated, but the woman's words sounded distorted. *What is wrong with me?* Amelia thought worriedly.

"Finish the mantel first . . . then polish the silver . . . then clean the house! Can you remember all that?" Emily asked coldly, her gaze patronizing as Portia rolled her eyes and shook her head in kind.

"I understands, ma'am." Amelia blushed, feeling humiliated as the elderly matron seemed to regard her as she would a hardheaded child. She had worked for difficult men before, but none were as intimidating or as demeaning as Emily Breach. And Portia, after serving the woman for so many years, had learned to agree with all her mistress said, which further added to Amelia's humiliation. She shook her head. She couldn't let Mrs. Breach defeat her. *I'm a better person than she knows, that's what!* "I'm feelin' a little lightheaded, ma'am, that's all. No need to worry. I swear it."

"Good. I've much to do today." Mrs. Breach hastened from the room, and Amelia reached for the bag that held the holly-berry branches.

Amelia began arranging the branches along the mantel's edge, feeling awkward and unsure of herself. Decorating for Christmas had always been a lighthearted affair for their family when Amelia was a girl. She recalled her mum didn't seem to bother with where everything was set, but instead, significance was placed upon the fact that all family members joined in and worked together, from the oldest child to the youngest. The joy was found in one another. Misplaced strands of strung berry only added to the quaintness of the occasion. Their family was one that ascribed more importance to the child in the manger than to the decorations. Although she had prayed earlier, Amelia felt so very far from Him today. It had been many months since she had gone to church, perhaps longer. George had never been one to attend services regularly and she had somehow fallen into the same pattern. Her faith seemed as dry as dust now, her spirit weary and hollow. *I'll find out about that church up the road*, she decided.

Peering around the ballroom, Amelia noticed how quiet it was. *Strange to decorate without children about,* she decided. She felt that Katy had missed a special joy in life by not having any brothers or sisters, such as she herself had enjoyed as a child. But try as they did, with Amelia suffering two miscarriages in the process, she and George had never been able to conceive successfully again. Masking his disappointment, George boasted often of his joy in fathering Katy, but Amelia couldn't help feeling inadequate. Their disappointment in each other was mutual and became one of their few common bonds.

Feeling anxious and troubled about George once again, Amelia sighed and refocused her thinking so she could again concentrate on Mrs. Breach and her dreadful party.

As she worked her way around the long mantel, her eyes fell upon three miniature portraits encased in silver frames. Not having noticed the pictures until now, Amelia picked up one of them and dusted around it with a cloth from her apron. The miniature was of a man in full naval dress—an officer with a receding hairline and smallish eyes. She knew by his uniform that he was a high-ranking officer.

"That's Missus Emily's nephew," a voice spoke from across the room. "Captain Arthur Phillip."

Amelia flinched, startled by the sudden interruption. She glanced around to find Jiggs standing in the doorway, gawking at her. Pretending only mild interest, she asked, "Did you say this man is Captain Arthur Phillip . . . *the* Captain Phillip?"

"Was and is the one and only Captain Phillip. Why? Do you know him?"

Amelia hesitated, remembering the caution she should exercise. "Shouldn't you be about yer chores, Mister. . . ?"

"Jiggs is all anyone calls me, Missus Amelia." His eyes narrowed as he peered at her sideways. That same repulsive voice chafed at Amelia as he drew out her name. "I *am* doin' me chores! Portia asked me to look in on you before I rearrange the tables in the ballroom."

"Well, you needn't bother lookin' in on me. I'm about to finish with this mantel o' Mrs. Breach's, then I'll be polishin' her silver. So get your tables ready and leave me to me work!" Amelia turned her back toward Jiggs.

"Well! Aren't you the one to be givin' orders!" He answered in a thick Irish brogue. "You must be used to orderin' around a man. Did yer 'usband leave ya?" he smiled, his thick brown eyebrows arched.

"Me 'usband is none o' yer business, Mr. Jiggs! Now, if you'll excuse me . . ."

"Oh, so y'are married." Jiggs pushed the conversation further. "So poor ol' Jiggs doesn't have a chance to win the affections of a lady as lovely as yerself?"

Amelia sighed, feeling weary and exasperated with the man. "And if I were not married—which I am—if it were any o' yer business—which it ain't—I wouldn't be interested in the likes o' you!"

"Oh, lass! A low blow to ol' Jiggs . . . a downright punch in the ol' stomach! Now why'd you have to go an' hurt ol' Jiggs' feelin's . . . eh? How's about a little kiss to ease the pain?"

Amelia glared at him, her patience spent. She felt her temper rising and her voice grew more intense. Her knees grew weak, and she was certain now she was strangely ill. "Would you please leave . . . me . . . alone!" she shouted, confusion rising in her tone. Those words were all she remembered saying before the room began to churn, spiraling downward into a blurry void as the white floor flew up to meet her face.

Jiggs watched in a shocked stupor as Amelia fainted dead away, falling to the floor in a limp heap at his feet. He leaped to catch her but was too late. Her head had struck the floor, and she lay still and lifeless in front of the fireplace.

"Mrs. Breach!" Jiggs panicked. "Portia! Quick! Someone . . . help! Amelia's fallen dead on the floor!" Jiggs jumped away, his face flushed.

Portia came rushing into the room, followed by the cooks, Mrs. Breach, and the new ladies' maid.

Behind them ran Katy, gasping, "Mum! Dear God, help 'er!"

The women gathered around Amelia's still form while Portia checked her pulse. "It's all right, Katy," she tried to assure the girl.

"It's an omen!" Jiggs held his cap to his chest.

Turning to Jiggs, Portia snapped, "She ain't dead, Jiggs!" She shook her head at the shaken Irishman. "Maybe a little worn out's all. Here now, help me get her into the study and lay her on the couch."

Jiggs lifted Amelia cautiously in his arms. As he looked at her ashen face, he wondered if she would accuse him of causing her to faint. Would she get him dismissed? *She'd best keep 'er mouth shut if she knows what's good fer 'er.*

Portia patted Amelia's face with a cold, wet towel. "Look, now! She's beginnin' to come to." Portia tried to sound encouraging.

"Oh, Mum, you're all right!" Katy buried her face in Amelia's skirt. Her thin fingers gripped her mother's cold, clammy hands. Amelia moaned softly and her eyes half opened. She squinted at the faces that hovered all around her.

"Give her room, now," Mrs. Breach ordered. "She needs air!" The old woman began waving back the servants.

"I . . . I'm sorry, Mrs. Breach," Amelia whispered. "I'll 'ave that silver polished soon, I will." She tried to make her voice sound reassuring and reached to stroke Katy's head, which remained on her stomach.

Mrs. Breach groaned, muttering to herself, "I *would* have to hire a sick one, now wouldn't I."

"I'll be fine, really." Amelia wearily tried to brace herself up, propping on the backs of her wobbly arms. Her head hurting where she had fallen, she reached and rubbed the tender bruise.

"You hit yer head when you fell, Amelia," Jiggs apprised with a nervous laugh. "You'll probably have a bump back there the size of a goose egg!"

Amelia sat up straight. Her head was beginning to clear and her memory was returning. It was Jiggs with whom she had been arguing, she remembered. Her eyes narrowed as she studied his face. *He's a troublemaker, that one! But what in the world caused me to faint?* She and George had been known to go a round or two quibbling over their circumstances, but she never collapsed from it.

"Amelia?" Mrs. Breach touched her hand to Amelia's shoulder. "How do you feel now?" Her face was close to Amelia's as she stretched a smile across her wrinkled jaw.

"Much better." Amelia attempted to return the smile and forced a cheery sound into her tone.

"I think me mum ought to be in bed, I do!" Katy was adamant, her eyes looking determined.

"Posh!" Amelia steadied herself as Portia helped her to her feet. "I feel as fit as a fiddle, I does! And I've some silver to polish and a great grand house to clean!"

Portia shook her head, expressing worry. "I don't know, Amelia. Perhaps Katy's right."

"Well, if the woman says she feels fine, then let her work!" Mrs. Breach interjected, taking Amelia by the arm. "I'll fix you a spot of rum to warm your insides. I can see you're a lot like me, Amelia—a woman of determination."

"That I am!" Amelia beamed as she felt a sudden comradery with Mrs. Breach. *Perhaps the lady isn't such a bad lot after all.*

Portia sighed and shook her head. She had seen Mrs. Breach manipulate scrub girls who were dead on their feet, just to get another hour's work out of them. "Mrs. Breach, I . . ."

"That'll be all, Portia," Mrs. Breach quickly interrupted. "Thank you for reacting so quickly and helping Amelia."

Amelia nodded. "Oh yes, Portia, thank you for helpin' me." She smiled at the others. "Thanks to you all."

"Everyone back to your chores." Mrs. Breach clapped her hands, her tone carrying an uncharacteristic lilt. The women dispersed slowly, watching Amelia with worried faces as they left the room. Jiggs followed them out, but stopped and turned to study Amelia suspiciously.

"Jiggs, haven't you work to do?" Mrs. Breach inquired impatiently.

"I do at that, Missus Emily. I'm on me way." Jiggs whirled on his feet and was gone.

Accepting Mrs. Breach's offer of rum, Amelia did find that the liquor warmed her insides. Mrs. Breach had given her a cushioned chair on which to sit and she soon found herself humming and polishing away.

"Hello?" A woman stood in the doorway, feather duster in hand. "I'm Cozette Frye," she introduced herself. "You gave us quite a fright, Amelia."

"For that I apologize." Amelia shook her head and continued rubbing the teapot in her hand.

Cozette was an older woman, a widow who had lost her husband to the plague. She had a stout build and the stern appearance of a schoolteacher as her blue eyes peered over her wire spectacles. "I'm the new ladies' maid," she explained.

"I'm glad to meet you, Mrs. Frye," Amelia answered respectfully.

"You may call me Cozette. Shall we get busy?"

Amelia smiled at the woman's pleasant demeanor. She was grateful for the help.

After several hours of rubbing and polishing, the table was loaded end to end with sparkling silver. Cozette was quick to point out tips to help Amelia do the job more speedily and soon the women were chuckling and beginning to enjoy the afternoon. They strolled back into the ballroom and began covering the tables at the entrance with antique-lace tablecloths. Jiggs had brought in the tables at Mrs. Breach's request and seemed to take his time setting them in place. Amelia stood with her hands behind her back and her eyes cast down at the floor until he departed.

"I just don't trust the man!" she whispered to Cozette, who shook out the tablecloth before handing two corners to Amelia.

"And why not?" Cozette asked curiously.

"He's a rounder, that one, Cozette," Amelia warned. "He was harassin' me this mornin' when I fainted. Askin' things he ought not be askin' of a married woman."

"You don't say?" Cozette watched Jiggs, who seemed to pass by the window outside more than was necessary. "He likes the ladies, does he?"

"More than 'e should, I'm afraid. Makes me nervous."

"Oh, posh! I wouldn't pay him any mind, Amelia. He's probably as harmless as a kitten, he is."

Amelia shrugged her shoulders. Shaking out the last tablecloth, the women placed the finishing touches on the ballroom, and filled the large crystal vase on the pianoforte with Christmas greenery and berry-ladened vines.

The afternoon slipped away quickly. New servants seemed to keep appearing as quickly as Mrs. Breach could hire them. Even a butler appeared and took care of setting the silver place settings in the dining hall and took charge of answering the door.

As the sun sank into the horizon, Stoney Manor was beginning to take on a festive appearance. The aroma of cin-

namon permeated throughout the hallway and into the ballroom, where Mrs. Breach paced with her cane. She had called
the servants to assemble in the ballroom, and they all stood
stiffly at attention, their shoulders erect like soldiers for inspection.

Her mouth twisted in a scowl as she fidgeted with a long
strand of pearls that hung from her neck. Mrs. Breach examined each domestic with cold arrogance, sighing as though
frustrated with a litter of dumb pups.

Amelia realized that the sympathy offered to her earlier by
Mrs. Breach had now disappeared, and was replaced by the
same calculating demeanor she had detected from the beginning.

Mrs. Breach picked at the hollyberry on the mantel. "It
could be better!" She eyed Amelia who swallowed the lump
she felt in her throat. "But we're out of time, and I need you
all to prepare yourselves for tonight. After you've changed
your uniforms, I'll expect each of you to report back in an
hour. I want you all to clean the downstairs once again before
the guests arrive. Cozette, is my bath drawn?"

"Yes, ma'am." Cozette curtsied. "I've laid out the burgundy
dress of yours, ma'am, just like you said, along with your
fancy shoes. Will you be needin' me to dress you, ma'am?"

"I will at that, and you can assist with my hair as well."

"Yes, ma'am."

Emily Breach jerked her head around and fixed her eyes
on the other servants. "Well? Get to your quarters, then!"

The servants bowed, almost in unison. "Yes, Mrs. Breach,"
they answered.

Katy flinched and turned to follow her mother down the
hallway and out the kitchen door. She stiffened her lip, her
eyes wide when she heard the servants around them muttering under their breath and quietly swearing at their employer.

"I'm a liveryman. What's this woman think I am . . . a
bloomin' scullery maid?" one groomsman spewed under his
breath.

"And why does the butler get to stay in the big house, I
wants to know? Ain't I paid my dues to this family? Well, ain't
I?" Portia complained.

Amelia remained silent and turned to enter her room. When she opened the door and went inside, Katy hesitated at the door, watching the servants scurrying to their rooms.

After the men and women disappeared behind their doors, Katy closed the door and breathed a sigh of relief. "You still 'ave a job, Mum. Now if we can only make it through Mrs. Breach's party."

"Oh, dear girl! I think it will be a miracle!" Amelia lamented as her blue dress dropped to the floor. "Well, let's hurry, shall we, and be the first to return. I'll warm this morning's water on the stove. Everything will be fine, Katy. You'll see." Amelia seemed to have returned to her cheerful self, the fright from this morning behind her.

Resting the pail on the stove, Amelia bent to stoke the wood. Her lips thinned as she pondered the picture she had seen on the mantel. Would she meet Captain Phillip sooner than she had expected?

The black domestic dress was hanging on the nail as she had left it. Grasping it from the peg, she pulled it over her head and smoothed it around her waist. Stroking her stomach, a troubling thought struck her mind . . . one she dared not share with Katy. *No*, she reasoned. She was fatigued; that was the only reason she had fainted. With all she and Katy had been through, she had every reason to faint from exhaustion.

Amelia peered from the tiny window, staring pensively at the snow that hid the earth from view. She sighed and whispered quietly, "What does our future hold, dear Lord?"

8

WINTER'S EMPTY HAND

The coachman stopped the black carriage along the snowy road and disembarked from the driver's seat. "Sorry, Captain Phillip. One of the horses is actin' lame on me. I'll check it out right quick, I will."

Phillip pulled his head back inside the coach. The sun had just set, taking with it the last ray of warmth for the day. He pulled his coat together more tightly and wrapped another scarf around his neck. The trip to Aunt Emily's was always a lovely ride in the countryside, but much too lengthy for Phillip, who lived in Lyndhurst on the other side of London. "How's it coming, Mr. Sebastian?" he asked hoarsely, beginning to feel an achiness in his joints.

The coachman moved carefully, assuring each step by thrusting an old tool handle into the snow as he walked around the carriage, his boots waffling through the icy crust. "Right fine, Captain Phillip. Me mare just had a stone in her hoof. We can leave now. Should be at your aunt's estate in a few minutes."

103

"Thank you, Mr. Sebastian."

"Might as well light these lanterns while I'm stopped." Sebastian opened the glass lanterns on the carriage and lit their oily wicks. Then taking his seat again, he flicked the reins, commencing the horses on their way.

Phillip took another glance out the window. Hues of pink and violet streaked across the sky for a brief moment, before dissolving into evening shades of blue. In the east, a solitary star sparkled, shedding its ancient light on land and sea. Phillip recalled navigating many a ship by that same star. It was a celestial oddity to him; it hung in the air on nothing, yet remained a constant guidepost for navigators of captains and ships . . . and kings and camels.

"We're pullin' into Mrs. Breach's place now, sir."

"Thank you, again, Mr. Sebastian," Phillip answered, his throat scratchy and sore. He dreaded this party more than them all. Aunt Emily Breach was his mother's sister. Since his mother's death, Phillip had tried to maintain occasional contact for his family's sake. But, also, he had always felt a certain sympathy for the lonely old woman who seemed to place her own value on how many "things" she could accumulate. Within all the luxury, he had decided long ago, must be hidden a good measure of insecurity.

Emily had few real friends but many social connections, and she loved to brag to them about her officer nephew. She had even paid a high price for an original painting of a ship, *The Europe*, he once commandeered. Phillip knew he would spend the evening being dragged about from room to room by Aunt Em to meet her guests. But her cuisine was always the finest, with platters upon platters of smoked meats, fish, vegetables, fruits, breads, and desserts of every description. He loved to tease her head cook, Portia, about needing a long winter's rest after Aunt Em's Christmas party. Portia usually said little as did most of Emily's servants, staying as hidden as possible except to keep the ale flowing and the platters replenished.

The carriage door opened and Phillip looked out to see a footman dressed in a brimstone-colored waistcoat, covered by a pigeon-tailed sky blue overcoat, and wearing white stockings. The man squinted as sleetlike ice blew from the rooftop, pelting his cocked hat.

"Welcome to Mrs. Breach's," the footman winced, not at all enjoying his lot. "I trust you're ready for a jolly evening, sir?"

"Quite. Are you new?" Phillip asked as he stepped from the carriage.

"Quite."

"Aunt Em must be at it again," Phillip jested, "hiring and dismissing."

"I wouldn't know about that, sir." The footman's face was bland, although he shuddered from the biting wind.

"Good answer, footman!" Phillip laughed, patting the servant's back.

"Have a jolly time, sir. When you're ready to leave, allow me to send for your carriage. My name is Bones, sir. Danson Bones."

Phillip laughed again. "You can't be serious! Your name is actually Bones? Danson Bones?"

"It is at that, sir." The man heaved a sigh, obviously growing weary of the comments.

"Well! Before the night is out, I hope your bones'll be dancing!" Phillip laughed all the way up the steps, securing his footing on the ice and grabbing the stair rail for balance.

Mr. Bones groaned and motioned for Mr. Sebastian to move the horses around to the rear, where he could find warmth inside the servants' parlor. "Watch your step, sir," Bones cautioned Phillip.

Peering through the window, Phillip could see his aunt teetering about the floor, her skirts swishing to the violins' swell as she hobbled around with her cane.

Emily had been in the kitchen three times already to threaten Portia's kitchen maids for not keeping the drinks properly filled for her guests. With a full complement of newly hired servants, she would have to watch closely to see they served the party well. In the corner of the room stood the new butler awaiting Portia's signal to call the guests to dinner in the great dining hall.

Emily moved through the crowded ballroom, grasping

each hand firmly, making eye contact, and smiling—she worked a party like a politician, making each guest feel important.

Suddenly Emily heard the familiar bell and the sound of the front door opening once again. She crept into the hallway to see who was arriving fashionably late. As the new groom ushered in the man, Emily's pale green eyes lit with joy. It was the first sincere emotion the old woman had shown all evening. How she loved it when her sister's son came to her parties! "Nephew!" she cried, extending her arms to Phillip. "You're finally here!"

Phillip rushed to meet his aunt and embraced her warmly. "Aunt Emily! What a joy it is to come to your grand party!" Phillip lied. "And you're looking so elegant in your wine-colored dress. Those aren't . . ." He pointed to the shiny baubles adorning the beaded epaulets on her shoulder seams.

"Yes they are, Arthur!" Her nose wrinkled as she winked. "Rhinestones!"

"Oh, Auntie, you'll have every man in London chasing after your money if you don't stop advertising it like that!"

"They do and I'll set the dogs on them!" she snapped coldly before her face broke into a warm smile again. She peered down the hallway, hearing the clattering sounds that issued from the kitchen. Emily shook her head. "What's taking them so long with the drinks?"

Behind the kitchen door, the servants scurried around like scared mice, mixing hot wassail with floating orange slices as they prepared to serve the sweet mixture to those who had just arrived. "This'll help to save the better wine for the last leg of the party," Portia instructed. "Pour in a little rum to give it a kick, Mary."

"Portia," Amelia whispered while keeping her eye on Katy, who was decorating a platter of fish with greenery.

"Yes, what is it?" Portia stirred in the rum while the kitchen maid poured.

"Could I 'ave one o' those tarts for Katy . . . if there's enough of them, I mean. Today's her birthday. I bought her a few things from that peddler but I thought . . ."

"Birthday? Well, why didn't you say somethin' sooner? I'd

have fixed her somethin' meself. You help yourself, Amelia. Why not take two or three? Fer sure we'll be throwin' some o' this food away, we will. Most of it's for show, anyhow. Most o' that lot'll be too busy impressin' one another to eat much."

Amelia couldn't help but smile at Portia. She was more caring than she allowed others to know. Amelia wrapped some of the cakes in brown paper. She would surprise Katy with them later tonight.

Turning around, Amelia tiptoed to the doorway when she detected the sound of Mrs. Breach's voice above the others. She cracked the door just enough to see her employer standing in the hallway talking animatedly to a man in military attire. He had aged a bit, but with the thinning hairline and eyes just like the man in the picture on the mantel, she knew in an instant that he must be Captain Arthur Phillip. *Oh, drat! If I could just have a moment to talk to him!* But first she'd have to wait for Emily Breach to leave his side. Mrs. Breach would never stand for one of her housekeepers to be "fraternizing" with her precious nephew.

"Amelia!" Portia was headed for the door with a serving tray. "Open the door for me quick like," she ordered, although her tone had somewhat softened since Amelia's fainting spell. "Elnora, you grab the other platter."

"Oh, Portia, look there!" Amelia pointed to a red spill on Portia's apron. "Mrs. Breach won't want you runnin' around with a soiled apron on like that! Let me take the tray out and serve the guests while you go change your apron." Amelia decided to act quickly. "Katy, love, why don't you help Portia with her apron?"

Portia looked to see that Amelia was correct. "Thank you, Amelia! Missus Emily would surely be fussin' at me fer that now, wouldn't she?"

Amelia checked the initials sewn into the apron that lay on the countertop. "This one's mine, but you take it, Portia."

"Thank you kindly, Amelia." Portia grasped the apron while Amelia left with the drinks.

Amelia balanced the tray carefully in her hands, the china cups clanking against one another as she walked down the hallway. Ahead she could see Mrs. Breach leading Arthur

Phillip into the ballroom. Amelia counted the thirty or more cups of wassail she had to serve. She would simply take her time and wait for the right moment.

A friendly smile gracing her face, Amelia offered each person a drink as she moved slowly among the lavishly dressed visitors who filled the ballroom to capacity. The room was lit with hundreds of candles that added an elegance to the evening and glowed amidst boughs of holly and arrangements of fruit. Suddenly the room grew quiet momentarily as the pianist began the first few measures of a Mozart sonata. Amelia stopped to listen and a feeling of melancholy swept through her. She remembered the night she and George had stood outside a little bistro arm in arm, their bodies swaying to that same melody. It had been a warm evening, and the street cafes were so crowded that she and George had found a place under a cluster of trees where they could be alone. It was the night of their first kiss. *When was our last?* she tried to remember.

"Miss? Miss?" A guest had grown weary of trying to flag Amelia's attention.

Amelia, startled, flinched when she realized the man was impatiently waiting for a hot cup of wassail. "Oh, I'm so sorry, sir. Take one . . . or take two if you like!" she overcompensated.

Suddenly a clattering racket and a great crash came from the kitchen. The guests reacted with loud gasps, turning to look first toward the kitchen and then back at Mrs. Breach, whose forced smile could not shroud her irritation. She glanced apologetically at her visitors. "I'll go and see what could possibly be wrong!" The agitation rose in her voice as she hobbled out of the ballroom, followed by a worried-looking butler.

The guests turned back to resume their conversations—all except Arthur Phillip, who opened one of the floor-to-ceiling windows, just as he had many times as a boy, and allowed himself out onto the back porch, closing the window behind him.

Amelia glanced down the hallway again. She could hear Mrs. Breach snarling at the clumsy servant. *At least it wasn't me own Katy!* She breathed a sigh of relief and stepped casually toward the window, passing out the remaining cups of punch as she went—all but one.

Lifting the window handle with one hand while balancing the tray with the other, she cautiously stepped out onto the porch and closed the window behind her. The wind snapped at her apron and sent a shiver down her spine, raising chill bumps on her arms and legs.

"Here, Captain Phillip, sir. I brought you some hot punch to warm yourself." Her voice was shaky. "You *are* Captain Phillip, aren't you, sir?"

Phillip turned to see the pretty maid who stood in the cold bringing him hot refreshment. "Why, thank you, miss! I am indeed Captain Phillip. But you shouldn't have come out here in the cold like this for me."

Amelia noticed the kindness in his eyes. But still, he was related to Emily Breach, which caused Amelia to hesitate and choose her words carefully. "I don't mind at all, sir. I suppose you're accustomed to standin' out in the cold like this, bein' a captain an' all that."

Phillip nodded. "I suppose. Well, thank you for the punch, miss." Phillip turned and leaned on the porch railing, his ear inclined toward the paddocks where the horses could be heard stamping and neighing. "I'll extend my appreciation of your service to my Aunt Emily. Good evening to you."

"Oh, no need to do that, sir. It's just me job. I'd do it for anyone, really." Amelia hesitated, beginning to feel awkward. "Captain Phillip?"

"Yes?"

"Is it true that you'll be takin' a fleet of ships to Botany Bay in New South Wales . . . a prison transport fleet?"

"Why, yes," Phillip grew curious. "You're familiar with such matters?"

"Not a lot, really, but I might have a relative goin' on board one o' them ships, I'm sorry to say. But I ain't fer certain. Is there a way to find out if he's on one or not?"

Phillip hesitated, noticing the desperation in the young woman's eyes. She stood before him looking as helpless as an insecure child. Realizing the woman's plight, as well as the risk she was taking by inquiring of such matters at Aunt

Emily's party, he sighed. "Well, if you could give me the name, it's possible I could get a message to the man, if indeed he is one of our prisoners. No promises, though—understand? Can you write him a note?"

Amelia looked back inside and saw Mrs. Breach hobbling into the ballroom. Watching the old woman craning her neck all around, Amelia knew she must surely be searching for her nephew. "I can write, but look see there!" She pointed. "Your aunt's come back. I better get inside or she'll dismiss me fer talkin' to you!"

"Here, miss!" Phillip pointed to a gateway on the porch. "As a boy, I became an expert in disappearing from my doting aunt when it was convenient. You can take this path down around back and into the servants' entrance to the kitchen. She'll never know!" Phillip grinned conspiratorially.

Amelia smiled back at the captain. "I'll bet you were a handful as a tyke, you were!"

"I can't say as I remember." Phillip scratched his slightly graying head. "But before I leave, I'll be sending for my driver, Mr. Sebastian. You'll find him nosing around the kitchen, I'll vow, nibbling on Portia's Christmas ham and swilling down her wine. Take a quill from the study and write a note with your relative's name on it. Tell Sebastian it's for me. Understand?"

Amelia nodded. "I can't believe you're such a nice man, sir. Not and bein' kin to—" Amelia stopped and clamped her hand over her mouth. Her eyes, clouded with discomfiture, were cast sheepishly up at Phillip.

Phillip laughed. "Not to worry . . . I know Aunt Em well, miss. Now hurry along before she sees you!"

Amelia tucked the tray under her arm and stepped toward the gate. Stopping, she suddenly remembered her second request. "Captain Phillip?" She looked at him, feeling a bit fearful about asking. She could be dismissed for asking this question for certain.

"Yes, miss?"

Amelia sighed. Captain Phillip would never hire her. She couldn't embarrass the man by asking. "Never mind."

Amelia turned sadly to leave. Biting her lip as she held

back tears of disappointment in herself, she walked through the gate. "Good evenin', Captain Phillip, sir."

Captain Phillip watched her go, feeling pity for her. It appeared this frail woman carried an enormous weight on her shoulders—one too large for her to bear. "Miss?" He decided to ask the question he was thinking.

"Yes, sir?"

"Would that relative be your husband?"

Amelia sighed and continued down the icy steps. "Not likely, sir. It don't really matter now, anyway," she replied in a monotone voice.

Captain Phillip shook his head. "I'm truly sorry."

Amelia nodded but turned her face away from the man. What more could she say or do? She felt as though she had met the end of her road where George was concerned.

As she tramped around the rear of the house, the dogs started barking from their kennel. "Oh hush, you mangy animals! If I only 'ad *your* life," Amelia snapped bitterly. Nearing the door, she pulled back her shoulders and took a deep breath. "Chin up, Amelia, ol' girl! Can't have Katy seein' you so down, can you?" she chided herself. At least now she had the opportunity to get a letter off to George—a luxury she hadn't anticipated.

Amelia felt snow melting into her black fabric slippers as she plodded through the deep mounds behind the house. She would hurry in and warm her stockinged feet by the fire, but not until she had written the letter. After checking in with Portia, who quickly filled her hands with a platter of cherry tarts and cream, she headed for the study. She and Cozette had polished the furniture in the study that day, and she well remembered the quill pen on Mrs. Breach's desk.

Amelia paused in several of the rooms, serving the dainty desserts to the guests who were wandering through the manor—some were admiring the large rooms while others were escaping the stuffy ballroom that was packed with ladies and gents engaged in the waltz. Amelia walked through the large dining hall where many were seated, sipping Jardiniere soup from silver spoons. She hurried through the door that led to Mrs. Breach's private study. If the old woman found her wandering around, she could feign ignorance, pretending to be looking for lost guests.

Observing that no one had noticed her, Amelia closed the big oak door behind her. Her eyes studied the room's interior as she searched for the quill. The study's high walls were covered with bookshelves. Because Mr. Breach had been a lawyer, the shelves were filled with old law books that gave the air a quaint library smell—a musty, educated smell, Amelia decided. "There they are!" She spotted the quill and stationery on the large desk that had also belonged to Mr. Breach.

Setting the dessert tray on a Chippendale table, Amelia crossed the room to the desk and picked up the quill pen. A piece of stationery was lying atop the desk with some notes scribbled on it. Amelia pulled open the desk drawer and found a clean sheath of paper. As she drew it out, she heard the door squeak open behind her.

"What are you doin' in here?"

Amelia turned with a start and found Katy staring at her wide-eyed. "Oh, Katy! Come on in! You nearly frightened the wits out o' me!"

"But what're you doin', Mum?" Katy came in and closed the door behind her.

"I had the good fortune to meet up with Captain Phillip himself, love! Mrs. Breach's nephew, if you can believe that!"

"Oh, Mum! Will he let us go with Papa on the ship?"

Amelia paused, deciding whether she should delay giving Katy the news. Then making up her mind, she answered, "I'm sorry, love. I was too afraid to ask. It's no use anyway, Katy. But he said he'd be happy to give yer father a note from me, he did. I gots to be quick about it, though, or Mrs. Breach'll be in here chewin' me ears down!"

"I'll write it, Mum," Katy sadly replied. "Give me the quill." Katy sighed and reached for the feathered pen and began to write as Amelia dictated.

> *To Mr. George Prentice:*
>
> *I lament your loss my der husbund since I herd of your Tryal. If you be on one of the transport ships write me a letter and tell me of it. I will then expect to see you if it will not break my Heart that I may take my last farewell of you as I*

*never shall think of seeing you again after you leave. Katy
sends her heartfelt love and her sadness at the loss of her
Papa. I ham very well and want you to no I has a good job
with a place to stay. I shall wate to hear from you soon and
send my deepest love for you, my der George. You may send
your letter to the home of Mrs. Emily Breach—good aunt of
Captan Athur Philip.*

*Your love,
Amelia*

Katy looked up at Amelia with tears clouding her blue
eyes. "Never see Papa again, Mum?"

"We mustn't fret, Katy. I've done all I can do now. I has to
worry about keepin' you safe. If God wills us to be with Papa,
then He'll have to make a better way, for I've none to speak of,
child." Amelia stuffed the letter into an envelope. On the outside she scrawled, "For Captan Philip to deliver to Mr. George
Prentice." She shoved the envelope into her apron pocket and
grabbed the tray of pastries.

Katy cautiously opened the door and watched to be certain Mrs. Breach was nowhere to be seen. The dining hall had
filled with guests who were finishing up the main course of
lamb cutlets and roast duckling.

Amelia handed Katy the cakes. "Here, love, you finish
passing these out 'ere in the dining hall and then return the
tray to Portia. I'll get this letter to Captain Phillip's driver."

Katy nodded and took the tray, although she felt resentment rising toward her mother. *I'll ask Captain Phillip meself.
I ain't afraid o' no one!* she firmly decided.

After slipping back through the dining hall and into the
kitchen, Amelia found Mr. Sebastian in the servants' dining
parlor, just as Captain Phillip said she would. With her heart
full of sadness, she explained the letter's purpose to
Sebastian, who took her letter and placed it in the pocket of
his waistcoat. A bit tipsy from the wine, Sebastian headed
outdoors for some fresh air.

"Thank ye for the good food, Portia. If you weren't so old
and cranky I'd marry you meself!" He tipped his tricorn hat
to Portia, who shot him an angry glance as she stood chopping cabbage.

"And I'd be a fool to marry up with a gamblin', drinkin' scoundrel like you, now wouldn't I?" Portia drove the cleaver forcefully through the large head of cabbage. The drivers still seated around the table roared with laughter as Sebastian stumbled out into the chilly night air.

He breathed deeply, then groaned and squinted at the bleary horizon. The moon, half-hidden by snow clouds, cast a violet haze on the blanketed slopes. Sleet was beginning to fall again, and from the side of the manor Sebastian could hear the steady crunch of boots in the snow. He peered around the corner to see Danson Bones on his way to find him.

"Hello, Mr. Bones!" Sebastian staggered.

"Captain Phillip is wanting to leave now, Mr. Sebastian. He's sent for you."

"Always the first to leave, as usual!" Sebastian muttered to himself.

Sniffing, Sebastian felt a great sneeze building in his head, so he pulled out the handkerchief from his waistcoat just in time to cover his face. Taking a deep breath, he stuffed the cloth back into his pocket and followed Mr. Bones around the great house. In the hazy moonlight he failed to see the envelope that fluttered down to the snow near the rear exit. It was Amelia's letter to George. It had fallen from Sebastian's pocket when he pulled out the handkerchief.

"Coming, Mr. Sebastian?"

"I'm on me way, Bones, ol' boy!"

Katy rushed to the ballroom, leaving the pastries on a hallway table. Upon entering the room, she found Captain Phillip saying his final farewell to his aunt and her guests. She swallowed hard. Approaching him now could cause her and Mum to be dismissed for certain. *Why didn't Mum ask him when she had the chance?* With a heavy sigh, Katy turned and trudged back to the hallway.

Amelia had stationed herself at the front window, which was draped with holly and ivy and lit with tapered candles. She could see the first few carriages pulling away. Upon hearing of Captain Phillip's departure, she ran to the window in hopes of seeing him handed her letter. But the windblown sleet mixed with snow blinded her view, and all she could see were the vague silhouettes of horses and carriages trotting under the winter moon's waxen glow.

She smiled, thinking how happy George would be to hear from her. This year, winter had dealt their family a poor hand, an empty one from which they could never recover. But perhaps it was possible that one of those black carriages carried the potential of a proper farewell to Katy's father—one last embrace, one final tender kiss—if she could only find him. *I must find you, George, and tell you the one thing I failed to say at the jail gate*—"I love you so deeply, George," her voice whispered.

She watched the carriages disappear into the raven black woods, shrouding the lanterns' yellow light—a memory that would remain a faded glimmer of hope in Amelia's mind.

9
ARRESTED!

"Leave the barrels on the dock and load the flour sacks first!" Simmons stood beside Captain Phillip, his arms crossed and his face drawn up in a scowl as he yelled at the ship's hands. Under Commander Phillip's watchful gaze, he had spent the morning ordering supplies loaded onto the *Scarborough* and the *Alexander*, both anchored in Portsmouth since dawn that morning.

"Did you get my orders regarding the transportees?" Phillip questioned without taking his eyes from the supply loaders.

Simmons shook his head. "Which ones was that, sir?"

"I wanted the male prisoners loaded onto the *Scarborough*, Simmons, with the women constrained on the *Alexander* . . . for now, anyway," Phillip instructed, watching a group of grungy jack-tars carelessly overloading their makeshift conveyors with barrels of salt meat. He rubbed his face, frustrated as he observed the load of barrels tumble down into the street. "Blasted mariners are useless." Phillip shook his head.

"Well, they've done nothing but nursemaid a bunch of worthless lowlifes, Captain, sir!" Simmons was defensive. "They're ready to see some sea action again. They get rusty as nails standin' guard duty to this lot, sir. I'm sure you can understand."

"Poorest excuse for nursemaids I've seen in a bit, Simmons. I want you to exercise the same discipline with the mariners that you administer to the convicts. Any trouble out of them and they're to receive the same lashes the prisoners are dealt."

"But, sir, these are just ordinary men . . . just human . . ."

"Aren't the convicts simply that, Simmons—humans?"

With arms crossed, Simmons stood glaring out over the port. "Not the ones I've met, Commander."

"I'll return tomorrow to follow up our conversation. I trust my orders will be followed."

Simmons evaded his directive. "Any idea of our departure date yet, Captain?"

"Soon, I hope. We've nine more ships to bring in and we have to supply all eleven of them. It can't be done overnight. With the sort of help they're sending us, it could be a millennium." Phillip turned to signal for his carriage. Pondering the supply dilemmas, he spotted Duncan Campbell speaking with another officer. His initial judgment of the supply contractor had been accurate, and the man's stinginess with supplies was placing more stress on Phillip's plans than he had bargained for.

Simmons sighed. "Well, I followed your orders about the transportees, Captain Phillip. We stopped at Woolwich this mornin' and transported them onto the *Scarborough*. The men are loaded up now as we speak. The *Alexander* is being loaded with the females right now, sir, bein's how all of 'em were sent here to Portsmouth, anyway." Simmons pointed with a gloved hand.

Phillip looked in the direction Simmons was gesturing. He could see the wretched women being herded up the gangway like sheep. Their clothing looked just as ragged as it had his last visit. He watched as one tripped on her skimpy shoes. He recalled having seen the young woman once before. Remembering that she was considered a troublemaker by the sailors, he felt pity for the girl. She looked like a child tramping up the plank, as did all the others milling around her. He shook his head as the girl turned to help an older woman step onto the ship.

Pulling her toes back inside her right shoe, Rachel Langley grumbled as the sole flapped loose again. She had tacked in the nails so many times they could no longer hold the shoe together. "Ragged things!" she muttered. "How am I to stay alive without proper clothes to wear?" she complained a little too loudly.

"Oh, why don't we just run down to London and have this lady a fine dress made!" a mariner mocked sarcastically in a falsetto voice. "And then to the hatmaker's for a proper hat!" He pulled his hat down around his ears and flailed his hands in an effeminate manner.

"How about a red one to match her lovely hair . . . and her temper!" The mariners laughed and one swatted Rachel's backside, which only ignited the girl's temper further.

"Don't you touch me, you animal!" She shook her fists in his face, her chains swinging dangerously close to the man's head.

"I'm gonna pound this girl good if she gives me any more grief!" The mariner's face turned beet red as he dodged Rachel's fists. "She's not worth the trouble she causes, I can tell you that!"

"Go on, Langley!" Another mariner shoved Rachel back into line. "Or I'll let ol' Clyde here give you the licks that's been comin' to you, I will!"

Rachel glared at the mariner menacingly. She no longer felt afraid. What could they do to her that hadn't been done already? Tossing her hair in the man's face, she jerked herself around and trudged into line behind the other female prisoners.

A lanky woman with hard eyes and rigid posture turned toward Rachel and spoke between her gritted yellow teeth. "It would make things easier on you if you'd just be nice to 'em.

I got an extra day's rations just by cooperatin', if you knows what I mean."

Rachel leaned close to the woman's face and looked straight into her eyes. Her tone was direct. "I don't 'cooperate' anymore! I does fer meself and fer no one else! That's the law o' Rachel!" Rachel's face was full of defiance as a thought smoldered in her mind. *And as soon as I break free from this place, that's the way it'll be, too!*

"Look, Mum! It's so pretty inside, and if you twist the handle the lady and her man dance in a circle."

Amelia looked up from her dusting to see Katy had picked up a music box from the mahogany tabletop. She was studying the object with one eye while closing the other. Amelia smiled at the sight of the girl as she stood in front of a tall window draped with gold velvet fabric. Katy was wearing a green dress Amelia had helped her make—sort of a belated Christmas gift. With a floral pattern that ran vertically up and down the length of the dress, Katy looked refined, as though she "belonged" in the room. Amelia had been given a remnant of the material after she had sewn Mrs. Breach's drapes for the ballroom. The sight of the girl poised with the box was picturesque as she stood by the window with her hair draping down over her shoulders and cascading past her waist. Her figure was becoming slimmer at the waist and fuller at the hips. Katy was becoming a woman, however hard she fought it.

"Katherine Mercy Prentice! If you don't look like a grown-up lady standin' there, I don't know what you are!"

"It's the prettiest thing I've ever seen, Mum! Take a look!" Katy pointed at the music box.

"I've no time, love. Mrs. Breach woke up in a bad way this mornin' and wantin' this room made ready for a guest that's comin' in."

"Who is it, Mum?"

"I'm not one to be askin', Katy . . . and don't you neither. Mrs. Breach don't like no one inquirin' about her personal affairs, she don't. Besides, she's just startin' to act as though she might be trustin' me." Amelia muttered under her breath, "Although I doubt she ever fully trusts anyone." Amelia tugged at her bodice, feeling the tightness against her waist. She had adjusted the dress to make it smaller, but now she wished she hadn't done so.

"Maybe it's Captain Phillip again, Mum."

"It wouldn't matter. The man offered us no hope o' bein' with your papa, anyhow."

Amelia thought of the farmer who had returned on Christmas Eve with the news that Captain Phillip had left for the holidays and that Amelia's message had never reached him.

Suddenly the bedroom door flew open and Portia came blustering in, motioning with her hands. Her face flushed and mouth stretched in a tight frown, she panted, "Everyone's to meet downstairs immediately! Mrs. Breach has ordered the entire staff to report in the ballroom at once!"

"What's wrong, Portia?" Amelia touched the woman's shoulder, sensing the alarm in her voice. "Blamed if I know! All's I know is that she's fit to be tied and she'll not be satisfied until she's found fault with someone!"

Amelia stuffed her cleaning supplies inside a pail and followed Portia out the door. Katy quickly returned the music box to the tabletop and ran behind Amelia. As the women filed into the ballroom, they found the servants assembling in the usual line, grumbling to one another and muttering to themselves about the interruption of their work. Mrs. Breach paced slowly back and forth in front of them, the brass tip of her cane making an annoying tapping noise on the wooden floor. Her face bore a hard scowl that made her look even older than her eighty-two years.

Amelia stood in line between Portia and Mary. From the corner of her eye she could see Jiggs glaring at her. He had scarcely uttered two words to her since the day she had fainted, but took every opportunity to give her a cold stare that made her feel uncomfortable. She felt as though he were watching her every move.

"I want you all to listen carefully, for there's a reward involved!" Mrs. Breach stopped her pacing and stood staring at her hirelings, making certain she looked each in the eye. "I've a large amount of silver missing from my collection."

Startled gasps could be heard from all around.

"But what sickens my heart is to know that someone would stoop low enough to be off with my crystal vase, the one my dear late husband gave me on our last anniversary."

Portia shook her head. "I'm so sorry, Mrs. Breach."

Amelia glanced toward the piano to the bare spot where the vase once stood.

"The vase was old and a rare find, but its value to me could never be measured in terms of money. More than anything else, I want this piece returned to me. I discovered it missing at dawn this morning, and after a careful search I realized some of the silver is missing as well."

Jiggs spoke up. "Mrs. Breach, did you find any of the doors broken into?"

"No, Mr. Jiggs. But I did find a window left unlocked on the back porch to the ballroom. Had I realized it was un-locked I, of course, would have secured it. My question is this—who left it unlocked? Have any of you recently departed through this opening for any reason?"

Katy suddenly remembered and opened her mouth to speak, but being too fearful she took a deep breath and said nothing.

Mrs. Breach turned and studied the girl's face suspi-ciously. "You, girl . . . what is it you have to say?"

Katy swallowed hard. The cold, intimidating glare of Mrs. Breach was enough to shut the mouth of the bravest soul.

"Speak up, girl! Tell me what you know!" Mrs. Breach in-sisted.

"Go ahead, Katy," Amelia nudged her gently.

"Well, ma'am, I usually go through that window to beat your rugs off the back porch. I didn't mean any harm by it, though. It's much quicker than goin' all the way through the servants' exit in the kitchen." She took another breath. "Last I remember doin' it was yesterday, late, I did, ma'am. I'm so sorry if I've caused this to happen." Katy's lip began to quiver as she saw a glimmer of anger in Mrs. Breach's countenance.

Cozette cleared her throat. "Beggin' your pardon, Mrs.

Breach, but I know about Katy goin' that way to clean the rugs. She did do it yesterday, which is why I went right behind her and locked the window up tight. As a matter of fact, I check them windows every day before I retire to me quarters. I promise you, ma'am, they was locked up tighter than Newgate, Mrs. Breach, ma'am!"

"Then how did I get robbed?" Mrs. Breach pounded her cane against the floor.

Jiggs stood pinching his bottom lip as the room went uncomfortably quiet. Nodding his head, he snapped his fingers and spoke up. "I saw somethin' kind of odd this mornin', I believe."

"What is it, Mr. Jiggs?" Mrs. Breach asked.

"Must have been around three in the mornin'. I was sittin' up takin' a smoke . . . couldn't sleep. I heard a squeakin' noise in the distance. Sounded like someone drawin' water early from the well. I thought perhaps Cozette or Amelia had gone for water, for when I looked out me front door I could see fresh footprints leadin' from their door. Did one o' you ladies see anythin' when you were out this mornin'?"

Cozette and Amelia looked at each other and shook their heads.

"No, Jiggs!" Cozette sounded annoyed. "We drew our water last night before bed. I didn't get up until our usual time. I had to wake Amelia. It wasn't us out late, I vow."

Jiggs continued matter-of-factly, his eyes fixed on the ceiling as he stroked his bristly chin. "Well, then, as time went by, I didn't hear anyone returnin', so I went and looked out me window and I saw up on the hillside, just beyond the barn, two figures standin' in the snow. One had a lantern and the other carried a large bundle thrown over her back."

"And you just sat there, Jiggs?" Mrs. Breach was growing even more annoyed.

"Sorry, Mrs. Breach, but I was beginnin' to feel sleepy an' when I see's what I thinks to be a housemaid outdoors, I thinks their business is none o' mine, that's what!"

Mary and Portia looked at each other while the other maids, including Amelia, began to shift restlessly.

"Are you lyin', Jiggs?" Mary was defensive.

"I swear, I'm tellin' the truth, Mary! As sure as my name is Jedediah Meriweather Jiggs!"

"Why do you think you saw one of our housemaids, Jiggs?" Mrs. Breach interrogated coldly as she slowly approached the laborer.

"Well, I guess it was because . . ." He scratched his head. "I remember now! It was dark, granted, and I thought at first glance I was lookin' at two men. But one of 'em turned and in the lantern light, I could've swore I saw one o' those white aprons, I did . . . a-an' a bonnet! Sure as the world, I did!"

The females in the group glared at Jiggs, shaking their heads in outrage.

"It wasn't me!" one yelled.

"Nor me, either!" another chimed in.

"Well, we can search their quarters—and their aprons! But I'll vow that all my things have already been sold to a fence! Watson, you and Mr. Finney come with me! The rest of you stay right here until we send for you—is that understood?"

The line of anxious-looking domestics nodded.

"Portia and Mary, we'll search your quarters first. Watson, just to be thorough, you go check the well and have Jiggs show you where those two hoodlums were meeting."

The hired hand nodded and left the ballroom. Close behind him tottered Mrs. Breach, who led the other three servants.

Amelia shook her head and whispered to Elnora. "As long as she's known Portia, I can't believe she'd even think to search her quarters!"

Elnora whispered, "She don't trust nobody. It don't matter how long she's known 'em, Amelia. I'll just be glad when this is all over. This happened a few months ago and two of the maids were caught with some of Mrs. Breach's good butter and bacon. They swore they didn't steal it, but there it was . . . in their room! They were also blamed for some gold coins that were missin' from Mr. Breach's study on the very same day. We never found the coins, but the girls were arrested and hanged."

Amelia shuddered. "How awful! Did *you* think they were guilty?"

Elnora shrugged her shoulders. "I don't know anything. I just keeps meself clear o' any o' that business."

Finney returned to the ballroom, followed by Portia and Mary, who entered looking relieved. Finney waved his hand at Amelia and Cozette. "We need you two next . . . your daughter might as well come too."

Amelia sighed and, together with Cozette and Katy, followed the man out through the kitchen. Mrs. Breach was unlocking their door when they arrived. Finney began pulling the sheets and blankets from their beds, shaking them in the air while Mrs. Breach began going through their extra aprons and dresses that hung from the pegs on the wall. Cozette shook her head at Amelia and sighed.

"I only see one apron here with this dress. Where's the second one?" Mrs. Breach questioned, her feeble hands grasping the everyday dress belonging to Amelia.

Amelia's brow furrowed. "I'm sorry, Mrs. Breach, but I soiled that one yesterday. I left it in the kitchen so's I could give it a good scrubbin' this afternoon."

"So what you're saying is that it should be in the kitchen, Amelia?"

Amelia nodded. "Oh yes, ma'am. I swear it!"

"We'll see! Finney, assist me back to the kitchen."

The weary band followed the old woman back to the kitchen. Mrs. Breach looked all around the room, checking through a pile of towels. In a corner, she found two white aprons. "Is one of these yours, Amelia?" She held one dangling from the tip of her cane, holding it in front of Amelia's face.

Amelia took the apron and studied it carefully. "Not this one, ma'am. I stitched me initials inside mine like the other women did, so's we can tell 'em apart. Let me look at the other one." Amelia picked up the other apron and found the initials in it—M.T., for Mary Thaxton. She shook her head, confused. "Mine's been tossed somewhere else. I'll ask Portia if she put it somewhere for me, Mrs. Breach. But I ain't worried."

Leather boots squeaked through the doorway. "Perhaps you should be, Amelia." Watson stood in the doorway with Jiggs. He held in his hands a soaking wet white apron, bundled in a small heap. He unfolded the saturated cloth to reveal a heavy object. Holding up the object, he handed it to Mrs. Breach.

"My crystal vase!" Mrs. Breach gasped. "Watson! It's cracked!" she wailed.

"I fished it out of the well, Mrs. Breach," Jiggs frowned. "The vase was all tied up in that apron. But there's no sign of your silver anywhere."

"Give me that apron!" She snatched it from Watson's grip while cradling the vase in her other arm. Searching the apron carefully, Mrs. Breach stopped upon finding two initials stitched in the hem in blue thread. She looked up slowly, animosity etching her face. "The initials are A.P., Amelia! This is your apron!" The old woman held the wet apron out for Amelia to see.

"She must have dropped the vase, ma'am, then tried to hide it in the well when it wasn't no use to her anymore," Watson analyzed.

Amelia studied the initials, alarmed at what she found. "But, Mrs. Breach, I would never do such a thing! I swear it!"

"Watson, have her arrested! And get her out of my sight at once!"

"But don't you see, Mrs. Breach? Someone stole my apron to make it look like I was the thief!"

"Who do you suggest would do such a thing?" Emily Breach frowned.

Amelia glared at Jiggs, who stood next to Finney with his arms crossed. "It was you, wasn't it, Jiggs? You've hated me all along and now you do this!"

Jiggs' eyes grew large, his countenance surly. "Don't you be blamin' me fer your thievin' ways. I hardly know you, woman!"

Cozette gripped Katy's arm as the girl began to cry. "Me mother wouldn't do it! She's not a thief!" Katy ran to Amelia, who wrapped her arms around her.

"Mrs. Breach, you must listen to reason! I've every reason to stay out o' trouble, don't you see? First of all is me responsibility to Katy."

"Perhaps your devotion to the girl was all the more reason

to want more for her. But you've been caught and there's nothing more to say. I'm sorry, Mrs. Prentice. Perhaps this'll be a lesson to the other servants! Watson, you hold her at bay while Finney goes for the law." Mrs. Breach turned to walk wearily from the kitchen, an angry scowl marking her countenance.

"But you can't arrest me, Mrs. Breach! There's something you must know!"

"And what is that?" she snapped.

Amelia's face paled as she pleaded with the woman. "I think I might be with child, ma'am!"

"A thief and a harlot! I might have known. May God have mercy on your soul, then!" Emily Breach turned coldly and walked out of the kitchen as Watson and Finney took up their muskets and escorted Amelia Prentice all the way back to her room.

Heartbroken, Katy fell into Cozette's arms and sobbed uncontrollably.

10

THIEF IN THE CELLAR

Katy lifted the corners of her apron to carry the potatoes from the cellar. She hated going into the cellar. It was cold and dark and she was fearful of finding a rat or a slimy reptile curled around her foot. Lifting both corners, she pinned each side to the strap of her apron top and secured the potatoes. Peering through the darkness of the cellar, Katy stepped toward the shafts of light illuminating the stone steps. The loose wooden clogs she wore scraped the dirt floor with each burdened step.

"You ought not to come down 'ere by yerself, lass." The low voice seemed to come from the darkest corner of the cellar. "Somethin' might grab you."

Katy jumped, her left foot stumbling out of the clog. "Who's there?" She backed away. "Jiggs?" Her eyes searched the darkness.

"The bogeyman, lass."

Katy's throat tightened. "What do you want?" She stumbled toward the steps, sensing the man drawing near. "Keep away!" she threatened. "I'll call for . . ."

"Who?" the voice laughed. "Your mum? She'll be hanged soon. You've no one left." Leather boots squeaked as the man stepped toward her.

"Portia!" Katy cried out weakly toward the cellar doorway.

"She can't hear you. She's busy with Mrs. Breach's tea." Another step closer he drew.

"H-How do you know that?" Katy strained to see, but there was only blackness.

"I know everything," he hissed. The figure drew near enough to touch her. "And I know all about you. That's why I 'ave a little proposition to offer you. If you're smart, you'll do as I say."

"What do you mean?" She eyed the light that fell across the man's feet. He was now within inches of her.

"We could work together . . . you and me. Make a lot o' money for some pretty dresses. No one would suspect *you* o' bein' a thief."

"Thief?" Sudden realization flooded the adolescent's mind. Drawing back her one clogged foot, Katy kicked toward the sound of the voice. "It's you!" she yelled. "You're the thief! Not me mum!" She missed her mark and swung around, which sent her stumbling toward the wall.

"Settle yourself, girl!" The intruder sounded impatient.

Katy felt his presence near her. She could hear his steady breathing and the boots shuffling as he placed himself in front of her.

Katy's hand fell against a wooden object. Sliding her fingers down the smooth surface, she realized she was grasping a shovel. Drawing it up slowly, she lifted it parallel to her shoulders then drove it downward in front of her.

"You . . ." the man roared painfully, pulling up his injured foot while steadying himself with the other.

Katy turned and ran up the steps in her stocking feet. She coughed, her chest feeling tight, as she stumbled out into the yard. Streaking past the rose garden, she made haste for the rear of the manor. "God, please help me!" she cried. Running blindly, she slipped on a mound of muddy snow. Her hands slid through the cold slush as she dove headlong into a brown-

tinged furrow that had been shoveled up by the liverymen.
The potatoes, still pinned inside her apron, slammed against
her stomach, bruising her. "Mum, please come back to me!"
she sobbed while pulling herself upright. Katy's eyes narrowed as she wiped at her face. "What's this?" She spotted a
piece of paper stuck in the shoveled mound. She tore the paper from its snowy grave and struggled to get to her feet again.
Running for the servants' quarters, she stumbled up onto the
small porch and closed the door behind her.

The enclosed area, where the men often sat sharpening
knives, provided a good lookout point, and just beyond it was
the kitchen entrance. She felt safe. Katy took a deep breath
and leaned against the wall, her eyes staring cautiously
through the thin opening between the curtains. She saw no
sign of the man in the cellar. "Who was it?" she tried to think.
The man had never spoken above a whisper. Katy's eyes fell
on the paper she still held firmly in her grasp. She saw at once
that it was a white envelope, soaked through to the contents.
The blurred writing across the front was scrawled in blue ink
and was smeared beyond legibility, although the lines were
vaguely familiar. Suddenly a thought struck her mind. Her
face filled with anxiety and then disappointment. Was it the
envelope that Mum had written to Captain Phillip the night
of the Christmas party? "Captain Phillip never got it, 'e
didn't." Angry tears stung her eyes as she stuffed the envelope
into her pocket and ran out into the rear yard. Looking back,
she checked to see that the man in the cellar wasn't following
her. She must hurry straightway and tell Portia so the thief
could be captured. "Then they'll have to free Mum from
prison!"

As she ran through the backyard, Katy held her arms
tightly for warmth. The sky overhead was gray and the air was
chilly, unlike the previous week, which was sunny and warm
enough to start the snow melting. Glancing down at the letter
again, Katy burned with anger. She had watched the road's
end so many evenings, wondering if Papa would be sending
a letter to her, telling her she could come be with him. She
had gotten only one letter from Mum, telling her to pray for
her release and asking Katy to always remember that she was

innocent. She had said nothing more of the baby she carried, causing Katy to worry through many sleepless nights.

Katy rushed past the rear porch in despair, the letter still in her grasp as she carted the potatoes to the kitchen. She didn't notice the two faces that watched her from the window of the study.

"Have you informed the child yet, Aunt Emily?" Captain Phillip watched the girl disappear around the corner.

"No. I'll inform her tonight. Watson will take her to Lambert mill tomorrow. I'm just getting too old to deal with the girl's foolishness. It's bad enough she's the child of a thief, but with her mother gone, she's been difficult to deal with. She's gone completely mute . . . won't even speak to me when I address her! Of all the nerve!"

"Perhaps it's you she blames for her mother's confinement."

"I don't care what the waif thinks about me. I just want her gone. She's trouble, I tell you!"

Phillip turned to his aunt, remembering something about a maid he had met at the party. "Aunt Em, I met one of your servants the night of your Christmas party. You remember . . . the evening I left early and feeling poorly."

"Which servant?" Emily held up her cup while Cozette served hot tea from a blue and white china teapot.

"She was a maid who brought me something to drink when I was out on the porch—a good-natured woman with a quiet spirit. Her hair was brown and she was attractive. Was this woman the girl's mother?"

"I don't know, Arthur," Emily shook her head. "She sounds more like Mary, Portia's kitchenmaid. She's gone today to the market."

"Does Mary have a relative on one of the hulks?"

Emily contemplated for a moment. "Seems like she does have a nephew that got into some trouble. I don't let it reflect on her, though. She seems honest enough. Not like that Amelia Prentice . . . building my trust, then robbing me blind!" She turned and motioned to the maid. "More wine, Arthur?"

"A little." He held out his glass while Cozette poured.

"That will be all, Cozette." Emily nodded at the maid.

Phillip sighed as Cozette walked from the room with the tray. "I suppose I haven't met the woman, then." He fingered the glass as Emily seated herself in a cushioned chair.

"No. You know I don't allow my employees to fraternize with the guests."

Phillip sipped at the wine while walking away from the window. "Aunt Em, I hate to see this girl sent to the cotton mill. It's a dreadful place. Anything could happen to her there. Where's the girl's father? Wasn't this woman married?"

"I don't know! I don't know, Arthur! She was only here a few weeks. I always assumed the woman to be a widow."

Phillip sighed. "Aunt Em," he resigned himself. "Let me take the girl with me. If she's an orphan, then she might as well come with me to the farm and help my cook. Gertie's always complaining of being overworked. Maybe the girl would do her some good."

"No, Arthur! I don't want you to involve yourself with this rabble. You've enough to worry about with your supply problems and all. Forget the girl. She'll at least learn the meaning of work. Maybe she won't turn out as badly as her mother."

A voice spoke from the doorway. "Captain Phillip, sir. Your mount is ready if you wish to take a ride." The groom was standing with a riding whip in his hand.

Phillip waved his hand at the groom. "In a moment." The captain placed his hands on Aunt Emily's shoulders. She was a tough old woman with a hard will, but he knew she had a soft place in her heart for him. "Aunt Em," his tone was direct, "I've made up my mind! The girl is going with me. If she gives me any bother, I'll take her to the mill myself. I promise!"

"Don't do it, Arthur," Emily pleaded. "You're too softhearted about these matters. Let me deal with the girl in my own way."

"You're wasting your time, Aunt Em," Arthur smiled. "The decision is made. You know how obstinate I can be when my mind is set."

"Oh, Arthur! You're as stubborn as I am. But if this girl robs you like her mother did me, don't come back complaining that I didn't warn you!"

"I swear I won't. Why don't you call her in here? Her name is Katy, is it?"

"Yes. Katy Prentice. Finish your wine first, Arthur," she fussed at her nephew.

Katy rushed into the kitchen out of breath and found Portia oiling the large cookstove. Mrs. Breach required the cook to shine the stove like a mirror. Unpinning the apron, Katy laid the potatoes out on a cloth.

"All right, Katy, you can peel all those now after you've rinsed them." Portia shoved the potatoes onto a wooden block and placed a knife next to them. Spotting Katy's mud-stained apron and stocking feet, she fretted. "Sakes, child! What've you done to yourself?"

"Portia! You've got to listen to me!" Katy's eyes were large as she ran back to the kitchen window to guard the cellar with her eyes. "Oh no!" she fretted to herself. The view was blocked by the servants' quarters. She pushed down the muddy stockings with her fingers and peeled them from her feet.

"Why, what's wrong with you?" Portia laid a piece of smoked pork and a slice of bread on a plate for Katy.

"There's someone in the cellar! He frightened me, Portia! Said he wanted me to be his thief. Portia, we've got to catch him!" Katy ran to pull on Portia's arm. "Don't you see, Portia? It's the *real* thief that stole Mrs. Breach's silver, not me mother!"

"Calm yourself, girl. What man in the cellar?"

"I'm not sure. It was dark, and he could've disguised his voice," she hesitated. "But I think it was Jiggs!"

Portia chuckled smugly as she carried the plate toward the servants' parlor beside the kitchen. "Come 'ere, child." She motioned for Katy to look into the parlor.

Katy crept to her side, still catching her breath. Peering into the parlor she saw Jiggs sitting with the kitchenmaids as they ate their noon meal.

Jiggs smiled sarcastically. "So I'm hidin' in the cellar now, am I? And *I'm* the thief, not your mum, am I?"

The maids held their hands to their mouths, stifling their laughter.

"I think you owe Mr. Jiggs an apology, Katy. He's been in 'ere with us since you been gone."

Portia turned to the manservant. "As a matter of fact, Jiggs, you've been in 'ere too long. You'll be workin' late tonight if you don't finish up this second plate o' grub and get to choppin' the wood!"

"Aye, aye, Captain!" Jiggs saluted while the women laughed.

Katy blushed and then grew worried. "I'm sorry, Mr. Jiggs! Please accept me apologies, but someone needs to listen to me! There *is* a thief in that cellar. We've got to catch him before he runs away!"

Jiggs wiped his mouth with a napkin after gulping down his pork with a swig of warm beer. "Ah, me!" he sighed. "Guess I'll have to go and have a look-see and catch this 'ere thief in the cellar."

Portia shook her head. "Don't do it, Jiggs. You've enough to do without chasin' around after imaginary crooks."

"He's not imaginary, Portia!" Katy retorted angrily. "I'll take you there meself!" She ran for the door.

"You'll do no such thing, Katy Prentice!" Portia snapped. "You get to peelin' those potatoes immediately!"

Katy crossed her arms in a huff. Then resigning herself, she turned around and pulled the muddy apron over her head, laid it in a pile of soiled rags, and put on a clean one. Wiping her feet with a cloth, she slipped on a clean pair of shoes. Whisking the knife from the board, she began peeling the potatoes, all the while keeping an eye on the back door.

Portia put the maids to work, sending them throughout the house. The kitchen grew quiet as their chattering voices disappeared down the hallway, leaving Portia and Katy alone in the kitchen. Portia pulled a plucked duck off the hook that hung beside the cookstove. She had cleaned it this morning for Mrs. Breach's evening meal. As she fidgeted with the bird, chopping it into smaller pieces, she eyed Katy nervously. "I needs to talk to you, Katy."

Katy looked up at the cook. She had come to know the

woman well enough to realize an anxious look when she saw it. "What's wrong, Portia?" She tossed two potatoes into a bowl.

"I know you're unhappy about your mum and you blame Mrs. Breach for your predicament. That's why you won't answer her when she speaks to you now, isn't it?"

Katy shrugged and continued peeling.

"But . . ." Portia hesitated, then turned her back to Katy and busied herself with salting down the duck. "Mrs. Breach feels that there's somethin' wrong with you now . . . somethin' that she can't deal with and . . . she's come to a decision about you."

Katy swallowed hard, watching Portia's rigid profile.

"She wants to send you to the Lambert mill and—"

Katy's face grew livid. She threw down the knife and potato with such a force that Portia flinched when they ricocheted inside the lead sink.

"Don't be throwin' one o' your fits now, girl! It's bouts like this that's caused Mrs. Breach to turn you out in the first place." Portia shook her finger at Katy.

Katy yanked the apron from her waist. She wasn't about to stand around waiting to be taken to the cotton mill. The stories about children being chained to their work stations and hung from the ceiling to keep them working were no mere rumors. She bolted when she heard Mrs. Breach's voice echoing down the hallway.

"Katy!" Mrs. Breach called. "I need to see you this instant!"

Katy shook her head at Portia. Her face displayed her panic as she ran for the back door.

Portia's mouth fell open. Afraid that Mrs. Breach might be angry with her for telling Katy too soon, she ran after the girl. "Wait! You can't leave, Katy!"

But it was too late. Katy fled from the house. Running down the path to her room, she ran inside and gathered her belongings into her old knapsack. There was no time to grab any food, but she did have six shillings she had saved from her wages. She could take the pig trail through the woods and hike the back way to the main road. If Mrs. Breach truly wanted her gone, she wouldn't spend much time looking for an unwanted chore girl. Katy remembered seeing an old shack along the road when she and Mum had hitched the ride with the farmer that first day. She could sleep there at night until she found permanent work for herself again.

Throwing on the coat and gloves Mum had bought from a peddler for her birthday, she tossed the knapsack over her shoulder, looping its rope through her arm so it could hang down her back. Racing for the exit, her eyes grew wide with fright as the door flew open.

"Why, what's wrong with you, child? You're as pale as a ghost." Cozette, finished with serving Mrs. Breach's afternoon tea, had stopped by to take a brief rest. She saw immediately that Katy was dressed and packed to leave. "What's happened? Where are you goin', Katy?"

Katy bit at her lip. From down the walk she could hear the kitchen door squeak open and slam shut. She stepped toward Cozette, her eyes sorrowful and full of dread. She felt trapped like a rabbit in a snare. Taking a deep breath, Katy lunged for the door, zigzagging around the confused maid. Out the doorway and up the sidewalk she flew.

Mrs. Breach rounded the corner. "Katy Prentice!" Her voice pierced the air. She was hobbling as fast as her cane would allow. For an instant, Katy turned. She saw the anger in the woman's eyes and knew she would beat her for this outrage! *Run, Katy, run!* her mind commanded as her feet obeyed. Running past the servants' quarters, she rounded the corner of the building and made haste for the woods just ahead.

A large bell outside the quarters began clanging loudly. Mrs. Breach, not one to be easily defeated, summoned the liverymen. "Someone stop her!" Her voice cracked as she shouted.

From all over the grounds came the men, and in a moment's time, they had gathered the dogs and were off into the woods chasing the runaway girl.

"Katy!" Jiggs yelled. Behind him ran Finney, followed by a string of liverymen and footboys. Watson came flying up through the rose garden yelling, "What's goin' on?"

Katy fled down the path, too afraid to look back, and too

afraid to stop and hide. "God! Can you hear me?" she cried out. She could see a fork in the road ahead. From the corner of her eye she saw a red coat flash through the trees. "The man in the cellar!" She jerked her head to find a rider on horseback racing down the second path that paralleled her own. Reining his horse to a dead stop in front of her, the man's eyes met Katy's frightened blue ones.

Katy stopped on her heels, breathing heavily and coughing. The man gazed sympathetically at her and slowly dismounted from his horse. Behind her, Katy could hear the voices of her pursuers and the howls of the hounds as they drew near.

"You don't have to run, Katy," the man's voice was calm and reassuring.

Katy turned to run again as he called out to her, "I'm Captain Arthur Phillip. Perhaps—"

Katy froze at the edge of the path, her shoulders rigid. *Captain Phillip?* Turning to look at the man, she nodded. *But of course! Look at the eyes—the mouth.* Her eyes were moist and pleading as she entreated, "Please, sir, you've got to help me!"

Arthur Phillip held his hand out to Katy and nodded. "I know."

11

VISITED IN
THEIR
AFFLICTION

"I feel poorly, Rachel." A voice spoke from the darkness next to Rachel Langley.

Rachel had been aboard the *Alexander* for months and she too was feeling weak and nauseous. She had been incarcerated in one of the small convict quarters—seven feet by six feet—where the women were crammed four to a room. Divided by thick bulkheads, the cubicles were jammed in the between decks of the merchant ship and were so small that the women were forced to stoop when they stood. Rachel tried to stretch but found no room to do so. She blinked and rubbed her dry eyes. "Like livin' in a bloomin' coffin, it is! How'm I supposed to breathe?" she grumbled to herself, loosening her frayed dress at the neck.

"Rachel, did you hear me? I'm sick. I can't hold up my head."

Turning to the side, Rachel recognized the voice next to her as that of Betsy Brady, a young woman of seventeen. On the other side of her was an elderly woman named Wanda. To

Betsy's side was their fourth cellmate, Hilda.

"What's wrong, Betsy? Seasick from last night's storm?" Rachel held her own head.

"I don't know. My head's spinning and it hurts fiercely . . . like it's going to explode."

Rachel felt for the girl's face. It was hot with fever and Betsy flinched at Rachel's touch. Betsy's auburn hair, which usually hung in soft ringlets around her shoulders, was matted against her hollow cheeks. Her eyes, dark brown and deep set, were indistinct in the dark cell.

"Oh—" Her groan was long and weary sounding. "Even my skin hurts. I think I'm dying, Rachel. Please get help!" Betsy strained to hold back the tears.

Rachel doubled over and coughed. Her chest hurt now and she didn't feel like helping anyone but herself. "They're not goin' to help us, Betsy. They're just goin' to leave us down here until we rot, that's what. Bunch o' stinkin' dogs!"

"Can you get me some water?" Betsy pleaded softly. "My throat hurts and my back's in pain."

"I'll try, Betsy." Rachel stared into the darkness, feeling ill at ease. She had seen death more than once on the hulk and had learned to turn her back to pain. It would have been better to have never befriended the seventeen-year-old. Betsy was unlike the other prisoners, and she talked little about her previous life. She spoke with refinement and seemed to be knowledgeable of political matters. She often spoke of God and rarely complained about anything . . . except to reiterate the fact that she was innocent of the charges brought against her.

For Rachel, society had chewed her up and spit her out, and she was ready to return the favor. Eventually she had concluded that growing insensitive to the pain around her might offer protection. In contrast, Betsy's sensitivities seemed to grow more acute the longer she was exposed to the harsh realities of convict life. *I can't be like you, Betsy*, Rachel had decided. No longer the victim, she would be in charge of her world. That was the only right and wrong Rachel understood.

Wanda slumped against her, moaning in unintelligible syllables. "Not too close, lady!" Rachel winced. "I don't want your sickness, I don't."

The woman groaned again and Betsy spoke softly. "Don't you see, Rachel? There's something wrong with all of us. Please beat on the hatchway . . . make someone help us!" Her voice sounded desperate.

Hilda had been sitting silently weaving back and forth. She had listened to this impudent young woman long enough. "I've a fever meself. Do as yer told, girl! Get us some help!"

Rachel cursed and turned toward Betsy. "I'll do it just to shut you all up so you'll leave me be!" Rachel twisted around and stood up. She raised her arms so that her elbows were parallel with her chin. Heaving with all her strength, she beat at the hatchway several times until she had no strength left. She fell back in a heap, swearing under her breath.

In a moment she heard the sound of bolts being unlocked overhead and the thud of the oak stanchions being removed. Fresh air seeped in through the hatch when the barricade was lifted from the cubicles, and Rachel stood upright, stretching and lifting her face toward the hatchway to breathe deeply. The dawn of day broke into the cell, awash with the coolness of morning sea air.

"What's the commotion down below?" a sentry barked.

"There's somethin' wrong with Betsy and these other women." Rachel looked at Betsy still slumped on the floor, and could now see the red rash across her skin. Wanda was muttering in a delirious fashion, her words garbled. Hilda gazed up glassy-eyed, her cheeks inflamed.

The guard stepped down into the cubicle, halting in the doorway. His eyes grew large as he looked at Betsy and the other two women. "Dear God! Looks like typhus again!" He scrambled up the ladder more quickly than he had come down.

"Typhus?" Rachel shook her head. Why hadn't she recognized the symptoms earlier? She had seen it in her family when her youngest brother had died of the illness. Rachel felt a twinge of guilt. "I'm sorry, Betsy. I didn't realize you were so sick. Really I didn't."

Rachel climbed the ladder and took another deep breath.

She saw a cabin boy scurrying by and waved him down. "Here, now! Get the doctor quick like! Bring us some fresh water and towels and a bottle o' gin or somethin' like."

The lad scowled at Rachel, his freckled complexion blistering in the March sun and wind. "Says who, prisoner?" he demanded to know as he stood glaring at Rachel.

"Don't come near here, boy, unless you want typhus," Rachel threatened as she pointed down the hole where the sick women lay.

"What?" The boy backed away.

"Just do as I say and get the doctor!"

Betsy doubled over, moaning and retching as she lost her meager meal of the previous evening.

Rachel turned her head, shuddering at the stench. "Oh, Betsy! You're really sick, aren't you? Help's on the way . . . I promise!"

Rachel climbed back down the ladder and moved Betsy away from the soiled floor. Taking the girl in her arms, she stroked her hair away from her face and cradled her. "You feels hot, you does."

"I feel confused, Rachel. Like nothing's real. Pray for me, Rachel."

Rachel shook her head. "I don't know how to pray, Betsy."

"Well, talk to me, then, Rachel. I want to live. Keep me alive . . . will you?"

"All right, if talkin' will help. What shall we talk about, Betsy, ol' girl?" Rachel watched the hatchway, anxiety filling her mind. *I hope they hurry!*

"Oh," Betsy moaned and gasped for air, "I don't care. Tell me where you came from. You never told me that, did you?"

Rachel thought for a moment. "That's right, Betsy, I haven't told you that about meself. I know all about you and your mum's farm and your sisters. I been livin' on Turnmill Street in London at a—ladies' boardin' house. Yes, that's it. Only it caught fire, sort o', accidentally." Rachel plucked at strands of thread from the scarf Betsy always wore tightly tied around her neck.

"How awful!" Betsy coughed and rubbed her arms.

"But I got out all right. A lady by the name of Prentice

helped me out a window. She and her daughter made it out all right. But I got burned and cut up a bit."

Betsy acknowledged weakly, "I saw your leg."

"It's gettin' better . . . not to worry. But then, the Prentice lady wanted me to come with her. Said we could all live together. I almost did it, I vow. Probably should have done it, but I . . ." Rachel hesitated. Her eyes softened at the memory of Amelia and Katy.

"You what, Rachel?"

"I don't know, Betsy. I felt pity for them. They seemed to have as much bad luck followin' them as followed me. I decided I better set off on me own. I'd just be more bad luck for them."

"Oh, Rachel, you believe in luck?"

Rachel sighed and stared up at the hatchway again. "I don't know, Betsy. I don't know what I believes." The two women sat in silence for a moment.

"Rachel, I know what I believe . . ." Betsy gasped for more air and clung tightly to Rachel's arms.

"I know, I know, Betsy. You believe in the Lord God Almighty . . . Creator of heaven and earth. But if He's so Almighty, then why'd He let a girl innocent as yourself get thrown into a mess like this?"

"I don't know, Rachel. I can't answer all your questions. I simply trust there's some sort of plan."

Trustin' yourself right into a grave, if you ask me, Rachel thought to herself. But she said nothing more to Betsy. *Let her believe what she wants and die believing that some far-off God'll rescue her. But I won't fall for that fairy tale!*

"What's wrong down there?" a voice called from the hatchway opening.

Rachel looked up to see a bearded man staring down at them tiredly as he adjusted a pair of spectacles on his nose.

"Are you the doctor?" she asked.

"I'm the ship's surgeon, Dr. John White. What's the problem?"

Rachel held Betsy's head in her hands. "I'm sorry to say, sir—it looks like typhus."

The doctor shook his head. "I'm afraid this isn't the first

case. We've found four more this morning. You, Fred!" he yelled at the cabin boy. "Get some men. We need to move these women to the upper deck! On the double! Mr. Tench! Tench!" he shouted to the mariners' officer. "Better plan to check all the cells. This could be an epidemic!"

Rachel listened as the sailors rushed around on deck in a frenzy. Perhaps this epidemic was the opportunity she had been waiting for—a chance to escape the transport. There had been talk among the sailors of weighing anchor soon. Perhaps an opportunity would come her way. She had no intention of wasting seven years in isolation at Botany Bay.

"Everything'll be just fine, Betsy. We're goin' to get you out o' here, we are," Rachel whispered to her weak friend.

The cabin boy returned shortly with six sailors, and they carried the female prisoners from their cells.

As Rachel assisted with carrying Betsy and the others to the quarterdeck, she carefully eyed the port just beyond the foremast. She could see wagons of goods being driven in and out of the bay . . . perhaps they would be her mode of escape.

"I . . . need my sister. Where's my sister Grace?" Betsy whispered, confusion in her eyes. Her head fell on Rachel's shoulder as she was carried with the help of a disgruntled mariner. Rachel adjusted Betsy's scarf, shaking her head at her friend's ramblings. She feared the worst . . . that Betsy was gradually becoming delirious. Behind them, three men carried Wanda, who was nearly comatose, followed by Hilda, who stumbled along on her own, holding her feverish brow.

The women were taken to a small cabin inside the fore-castle, the superstructure at the bow of the merchant ship. In this small room they were placed on beds made of iron laths and ticking that had been meagerly stuffed with what appeared to be seaweed.

"Mr. Tench, we must inform Captain Phillip at once," the doctor advised the young First Fleet officer.

"I agree, Dr. White," Tench answered as he scribbled some quick notes.

The young officer whirled around and called out to a stocky sailor in naval dress. "Take a wagon up to the port admiral's office on High Street and see if Captain Phillip is with the admiral. Tell him of the typhus outbreak immediately!" He turned to the other five men. "Get some mops and creosote and swab those holes with quicklime."

"Aye, aye, sir!" The sailors saluted and turned to make haste to go and sanitize the cells, while the first sailor scurried down the gangplank and headed for High Street.

Tench turned his attention to Betsy as Dr. White administered cold towels around her face and limbs.

Rachel eased out from the doorway and watched the sailor disappearing down the street. Taking a deep breath, she stepped slowly and cautiously toward the plank. Not a sailor was in sight as she made her way past the wheel and the mizzenmast. While easing her way across the creaky deck, she heard a girl's voice cry out. It was Betsy, obviously in a great deal of pain.

Rachel remembered her own brother, Tom, before he had died. His head hurt so badly that he cried constantly and began talking irrationally about nonsensical things that frightened her. He had complained of seeing gray cherubs with horrid ugly faces and begged for someone to make them go away. Rachel had wanted to help, but her mother was too listless and weary to decide what needed to be done. Mama sat in her rocker and watched the boy sink into a coma.

"Why don't you do something?" Rachel had demanded. But her mother was unable to cope and had simply stared vacantly with the lost look of one without hope.

Shaking the memory from her mind, Rachel turned and looked back toward the forecastle. "Oh," she sighed in reluctant resignation. Wheeling around, she marched back to the sickroom. Stepping inside, she could see Officer Tench sitting at a desk recording the surgeon's observations. She walked between the beds and slid a chair over beside Betsy's cot.

"Excuse me, Mr. Tench. I'll see to her, I will!" Taking the wine bottle from the tabletop, she began dribbling small drops of the liquid into Betsy's mouth. Betsy's back arched and her eyes seemed to roll back under her eyelids.

"Oh, Mum, help me! They're killing me! I'm falling . . . fall . . ." Betsy moaned.

"There, there, Betsy." Rachel stroked her face with a wet

cloth. In a low voice she whispered soothingly to the sick girl, "Mum is here. I'm goin' to take care of everything."

Mum longs to have your company, my der Katy. I keeps trying to get a message to Captan Philip. So if you see him will you tell him about me and that I did not take the silver from Mrs. Breach. I was not hanged as some suppose but am also being transported as your der father. He nose nothing of my truble but I shall keep trying to get a message to him of my Tryal and sentence to Botany Bay. I love you der more than life itself and will continue to pray fer God to bring us together again. Do not lose hope my der Katy.
Your mother,
Amelia

Glancing up from the torn shard of paper, Amelia regarded the hard-eyed women who slumped against the damp cell walls of Newgate Prison. Without hope, the females merely survived from dawn until dusk, from ration to ration, never viewing life with any expectancy. She folded the paper and wrote *Katy Prentice* across it, along with Mrs. Breach's address. Some mail had arrived that week, but Katy had yet to send her any news or acknowledgement that she knew of her mother's condition or whereabouts. Amelia worried that Mrs. Breach had ordered Katy away or sent her to the workhouses after her own arrest.

The guard took the quill and paper from Amelia and stuffed the letter in a mailbag. He stepped out quickly and slammed the door behind him. Amelia shifted uncomfortably, holding her stomach, which was beginning to show her pregnancy of six months. She worried about the little life growing inside of her. How could she care for a baby on board a prison fleet, and would the authorities even allow her to keep the child? With her history, would she be able to carry the baby to full term? Amelia rubbed her stomach again and sighed as she felt the sturdy kick. "Oh, little one, Mum prays you're a fighter, I does."

Several inmates glanced her way, and one older woman seemed to regard her with pity. But the others turned their backs on her apathetically.

Sympathy was at a low ebb in Newgate. Even less sympathetic had been the magistrate, whom Amelia had recognized as the gentleman customer in the upstairs room at Miss Marcella's. He had stared at her for a long period of time, his eyes shifting as he tried to place her familiar face. Suddenly, her eyes met his and the two at once found recognition. Amelia gasped at the realization. "Why, I know you!" she exclaimed, her eyes wide.

"Tut, tut, madam," he had chided. "I've a face known by many, but can assure you we have never chanced to meet."

Shaking her head, Amelia had answered him forthrightly, "Dear sir, I tell you it's unmistakable that you're the one I saw at . . ."

Amelia had never been allowed to complete her statement. Being threatened with hanging, she had been silenced with the promise of a commuted sentence . . . to Botany Bay. Knowing she was innocent and trusting God for mercy, she lived with the knowledge that she might again see her dear George . . . and prayed to see Katy.

12

Brief Encounter

"See, look at all this, Captain Phillip, sir!" The ship's cook aboard the *Charlotte* sifted the grain through his hands, allowing the rice to scatter onto the floor of the kitchen. The bag was next to several others that were marked identically—"FLOUR."

"Rice? Rice!" Phillip raged. "Duncan Campbell has done it again!" Phillip scooped up a handful of the fraudulent product and eyed it closely. His lips pressed together tightly, he drew back his fist and hurled the rice through the open porthole. "A blight be on his soul! He's shortchanged me again!"

"I'm sorry to be the one to tell you, sir." The moon-faced cook stood with eyes cast to the floor. He turned to grab a broom and began sweeping up the rice.

Phillip gripped the doorway on his way out and shook his head. "What about the citrus, Meeks? Did he send the anti-scorbutics?"

Meeks shook his head. "No, sir, I'm sorry."

Phillip tromped to the quarterdeck and gazed overhead before entering the officers' quarters. A black thunderhead

149

was blowing into port. He would have to hurry if he wanted to complete his inspection aboard the *Alexander* and finalize the clearance to allow more convicts aboard. As soon as the disease had been isolated, he had ordered the *Alexander* to be evacuated. The convicts had been divided up and transferred to the *Lady Penrhyn*, the *Charlotte*, and the *Scarborough*.

Phillip entered the cabin and found it occupied by Mr. Tench and another officer, who were reviewing the maps for the First Fleet's voyage.

"Mr. Tench," Phillip said.

The two men stood to attention. "Aye, aye, Commander," Tench saluted.

"I need to send a message to Lords Sydney and Nepean immediately!"

Tench, seeing the urgency in Phillip's face, seated himself quickly at the small desk and penned while Phillip dictated.

> *April 12, 1787*
> *To Lords Sydney and Nepean:*
> *I send news of an urgent request to inform you, my Lords, that Mr. Duncan Campbell has once again short-changed our supplies by providing us with rice instead of flour, and only a half pound per convict instead of a full pound. In addition, no antiscorbutics have been provided. As you are aware, we must have citrus for scurvy prevention, and I cannot in good conscience set sail until my request has been made good. With the small supply of bread Mr. Campbell has delivered, we will only have enough to allow each convict two slices per day.*
> *As I inspect the number of supplies provided, I regret to say that they will never last an eight-month journey. In fact, my Lord, the fleet is being sent to the extremity of the globe as if it were being sent to America—to survive a six weeks' passage. Having never been consulted about the supply contracts, is it fair that the public should say of me hereafter that I departed in ignorance and would lose half the garrison and convicts undersupplied in such a manner for so long a voyage? I pray you will assist me with the remedy to this situation as our time is growing short while my patience grows thin. Thank you, sirs.*
> *Sincerely,*
> *Commander Arthur Phillip*

"Will Campbell stop at nothing to fill his own pockets?" Tench shook his head. Placing the letter in an envelope, he pressed the commander's seal onto it and hurriedly addressed the message for Phillip. Standing to depart, Tench offered, "Commander Phillip, before I leave may I introduce one of our new marine officers stationed aboard the *Charlotte*?"

Phillip acknowledged politely.

"Commander Phillip, meet Corporal Brock Chaney. Officer Chaney and I attended the same military school. I was most surprised to see him walk through my door this morning." Tench smiled broadly at his friend.

Chaney patted Tench's shoulder and tipped his hat at the commander. "Most honored to meet you, Commander. I must say the news of this First Fleet's voyage has all of London buzzing!" Chaney boasted. He was a handsome young officer, with broad shoulders and a tall stature. His dark eyes glistened as he regarded the commander.

"London is always astir about something. If it isn't one thing, then it'll be quite another!" Phillip returned the smile courteously. "Well, I must be off. I'll be finishing up the inspection of the *Alexander*. Then I've much to do, what with closing up my farm and making final plans to depart Portsmouth. Good day, Tench . . . Corporal Chaney." He turned on his heels and departed.

Tench crossed his arms and gazed contemplatively. "Well, we'll certainly have our hands full aboard the *Charlotte*."

Chaney leaned on the desk corner with his arms crossed. "It's an enormous ship, eh?"

"No, I don't mean the size. It's those women, Chaney. They're a mangy lot, they are. Full o' the devil, if you ask me."

Chaney chuckled. "Well, we'll keep 'em on their side o' the ship and try to stay on ours."

"If you can keep 'em on their side, Chaney. They get to carousin' around at times. We'll have to take to floggin' 'em soon."

"Why don't you show me their quarters, Watkin, ol' boy?"

"You're a brave man, Brock Chaney. But I'll put you to work at the same time. We've opened the hatches to give the females their fresh air. With the storm blowing in, you can help us batten down the hatchways."

Chaney followed Tench out of the cabin. Leaving the quarterdeck, they proceeded midships where two guards stood watch over the female convicts who were sitting lethargically around the hatchways. The officers were surprised to find Commander Phillip conversing with one of the convicts.

"I just wanted to commend you, young woman, for your bravery. You probably helped save a number of these women's lives. Your name is Miss Langley, correct?"

Rachel looked up from braiding Betsy's long hair. Nodding, she answered, "Rachel Langley, sir." She stared at the commander in silence for a moment. "I thank you, Captain Phillip, but I don't feel I did all that much."

"Of course you did, Rachel." Betsy smiled. "I would've died if you hadn't been there for me. She was there night and day, Captain Phillip."

"Most people in your situation would've done nothing at all, Miss Langley. I just wanted to commend you myself."

Rachel laughed quietly and shook her head as the admiral turned and walked away. But something began to stir within her . . . a vague feeling that perhaps she had accomplished something of worth, after all. Sensing a drop of rain splatter across her nose, she looked up to find two officers watching her as she fastened Betsy's hair with burlap string.

"Hello, Rachel." It was Tench who spoke first. He had come to know her well and seemed to be kinder than the other mariners.

"I suppose you'll be lockin' us up tight again, eh?" Rachel studied the clouds, pregnant with rain.

"Sorry, but yes. You'll all have to go below."

Betsy eyed the handsome officer who stood quietly beside Tench. "Excuse me, but I don't remember seeing you before, sir."

Chaney cleared his throat uncomfortably. He wanted nothing to do with these convict women and preferred they didn't call him by name.

"This is Corporal Brock Chaney," Tench broke in. "He's just joined us aboard the *Charlotte*."

Rachel looked up at Brock. He was a head taller than

Tench with a square jaw and dark skin. She set her teeth firmly on her bottom lip and pretended to concentrate on finishing the braid. But wanting another look at the handsome face, she took a quick glance before lowering her eyes to the task of finishing Betsy's hair.

Brock started to look away, but he wasn't expecting to find such a pretty girl on this lifeless transport. Rachel's red hair shone like spun copper and her fair complexion carried a rosy glow after having spent the afternoon on deck. Her upturned nose gave her a mischievous appearance and her blue eyes sparkled like a placid lake. But those eyes seemed to veil a life of pain hidden deep within them. *Still and all*, he reminded himself, *she's a convict*.

"All prisoners, please advance below! All hands on deck to batten the hatches!" Tench called loudly.

As the guards began to shove the females back into their holds and bar down the hatches, Rachel and Betsy were the slowest to comply. Rachel fidgeted with her own hair, straightening its long tresses and running her fingers down the length of it to smooth the flyaway hair. Turning her eyes purposefully away from the two officers, Rachel stooped to retrieve the loose strands of rope she had placed at her feet.

"Come on, Rachel." Betsy noticed the hesitation in Rachel's steps. She glanced toward the officers and then again at Rachel before turning to stroll back to the cell.

Brock turned away to assist in barring the hatches. Suddenly rain began to pelt down upon the deck. Thunder rumbled loudly as lightning streaked across the sky.

In the space of only a few minutes the streets of Portsmouth were muddied, and carriages scurried about to transport those who had been caught in the storm. Down High Street clattered two wagons, fully open to the elements, with more transportees from Newgate. The miserable men and women aboard shivered in the rain and pulled their thin wraps over their heads. One female convict handed her shawl to an older woman.

"Thank you for your kindness, but it'll do no good at this rate. Bloomin' rain would have to start with us out 'ere like this. At least they could've given us a cover of sorts," the old woman muttered. The convict woman smiled at the elderly prisoner, catching her off guard. "What was your name, ma'am?" the old woman asked her.

"I'm Amelia Prentice. But I think we're almost to the port. They'll put us in a dry place when we arrive." Amelia drew her arms about herself. She did dread the thought of being placed in a soaking wet cell overnight. But with all she had seen at Newgate, surely the transport itself would offer a welcome relief from the rat-infested jail. "I think we're supposed to be placed aboard a ship called the *Alexander*," she said aloud as the wagon drew to a halt.

"Hey, blokes! Got more prisoners to deliver from Newgate," the driver hollered at two sailors nearby.

The sailors ran up the plank of the *Alexander* and returned in a moment with an officer.

"Commander Phillip couldn't complete his inspection, so I can't allow them to board here!" the officer instructed as rain dripped from his cap and drenched his face.

Amelia sat forward, her interest piqued upon hearing the name. *Phillip?*

"As a matter o' fact, he's disembarkin' right now and goin' back to the port admiral's until the storm blows over. We'll have to divide 'em up and place 'em aboard the other ships."

Amelia looked up the gangway of the *Alexander*. She could see a group of officers making their way rapidly in the rain. Their faces were covered, but in the gale she thought she saw the red coat of the admiralty.

Being able to contain herself no longer, she called out, "Captain Phillip? Is it you, sir?"

"Quiet down back there, you vermin!" the driver shouted to Amelia.

"Sorry, sir," Amelia apologized as she saw one of the men hesitate.

"Does she know you, sir?" the officer asked Phillip.

"Well, I don't see how." Phillip squinted to make out the woman's features in the rain. She was soaked to the bone and staring at him anxiously. He shook his head. "I don't know her. Get my carriage for me please, one of you."

"I will, Commander." An officer splashed through the mud, calling out for Phillip's driver. "Mr. Sebastian! Commander Phillip is ready to depart!"

"Sebastian? Don't I know him, too?" Amelia jumped to her feet. "Mr. Sebastian, it's me, Amelia!" She began waving her arms wildly. "Did you give the captain me message?" she shouted naively.

"If you don't quiet down, woman, I'll flog you myself!" The officer jumped up on the wagon, reaching to strike Amelia's cheek.

"But I have to speak to 'im, please, sir," she pleaded.

"I said, shut up!" The officer slapped her face violently.

"Better do as they ask, Amelia," the old woman cautioned, spying Amelia's enlarged stomach. "She'll do it, sir. I'll see to it," the woman assured the mariner. "But have mercy on the lady as she's with child, sir."

After seeing the old woman had spoken the truth, the mariner turned away angrily and stepped down from the wagon. He muttered under his breath. "Just do as I ask or I'll not stop the next time!"

Her emotions crushed, Amelia seated herself on the hard wooden seat and watched as Phillip was assisted into his carriage. Her cheek was slightly swollen, and burned almost as deeply as her anger.

The admiral turned and looked toward the convict wagon once again from inside the vehicle. A portly woman already seated inside the coach leaned and gazed toward Amelia while the two conversed. Phillip shrugged his shoulders and seated himself next to the female passenger. The footman latched the door, and the carriage pulled away in the midst of the torrent.

"All prisoners prepare to depart!" A voice ordered in a singsong manner. The officer stepped up, taking the list of convict names from the driver. "All females will be taken aboard the *Lady Penrhyn*. All men will board the *Scarborough*. You'll be reassigned your permanent quarters before we launch." The officer instructed them quickly as he wished to be rid of this nuisance and get to his own dry bunk.

Amelia sat trembling, her hands against her cheeks. Although most of the prisoners had scarcely acknowledged the incident, tears of humiliation streamed down her face. Sorrowfully, she wrapped her arms around her stomach. Her worries increased for the child who was due to be born around the first of June. The First Fleet would probably be at sea by then and she would deliver the child all alone, without George or Katy to witness the small miracle that God in His mysterious way had decided to give to her. But instead of a blessing, it had become a hellish nightmare.

As the female prisoners were marched to the *Lady Penryhn*, Amelia began to weep openly. She felt as though she would die of remorse. What a painful world she was bringing this child into, should the baby live. *It ain't fair*, she decided, *for this child to live and only know pain and sufferin'*. Amelia shuddered at the thought that now haunted her mind. *End the life!* The words taunted her, causing a shudder of horror to rush down her spine. *No! I can't, God! You do it—take back this child!* she inwardly pleaded. "Mercy, dear Lord, show us your mercy!" Standing over the gaping hole that would confine her for the next year, Amelia felt her world spin as she collapsed in a heap.

13

THE CAPTAIN'S GIRL

Katy stood with her back to the door. Her head was cocked as she eavesdropped on the conversation taking place in the breakfast room. Beside her, also listening, stood two grinning housemaids.

Captain Phillip was preoccupied with departure details while he finished his morning meal of biscuits and beef. Gertie, his longtime cook, stood beside him. She was a thin, middle-aged woman with a sad oblong face and droopy blue eyes.

"What did you tell your lady friend, sir?" Gertie glanced toward the kitchen door.

"What lady friend, Gertie?" Phillip's eyes remained on the letter in his hand.

"Oh, I think you know, sir. That widow woman you been visitin' from time to time—Madam Bennington, is it?"

Phillip glanced up from his work, his face reflecting mild annoyance with Gertie. "She's been nothing more than an acquaintance, Gertie. I've no information beyond that for you and those curious maids hiding behind the kitchen door."

A shuffling of feet and nervous giggling erupted from the kitchen.

"Love don't come along often, sir, is all I gots to say about things . . . if you ask me, anyway."

Phillip shook his head, his eyes narrowing skeptically. "I don't remember asking you, Gertie."

Gertie crossed her arms in exasperation and rolled her eyes. "I'll be about me work in the kitchen, sir, gathering me things for the trip, if that's satisfactory with you." The cook stood rubbing her palms nervously. She glanced back toward the kitchen, where Katy peered out between the partially open door and the doorframe. Wide-eyed, Gertie quickly motioned for the girl to back away from the door.

"Certainly, Gertie. Take everything you'll need to set up a kitchen in New South Wales," Phillip muttered as he perused a letter from Nepean's office. "It's a Godforsaken country and there'll be no shops available where you may run and buy your supplies."

"Yes, sir." She hesitated and glanced at the kitchen doorway again, finding Katy still peering through, her eyes wide in an expression of adolescent anxiety. She mouthed silently through the parted doorway, "Ask him, Gertie . . . please!"

Gertie bared her teeth at Katy and shook her head, motioning again for her to shut the door. "Captain Phillip," she paused.

"Is there something else, Gertie?" After a moment of silence, the captain put down the letter and looked up at Gertie curiously.

"Well, I understands how you wants some of your servants to stay behind to tend to the farm and all, but do you think it might be possible to take just one helper for me?"

Phillip shrugged. "It doesn't really matter to me, Gertie. If you really see the need, then you may do so. Ask Bertha to go. She's a hard worker and she isn't married."

Katy had cracked the doorway again and was gesturing wildly. "No! No!" she shook her head.

"No, sir!" Gertie shot back before she had time to think, and then covered her mouth as Phillip scowled.

"Why, what's wrong with asking Bertha?" he wanted to know.

"Well, Bertha gets sick a lot in the winter and she's gettin' on in years, as you well know, sir. Why, she might not make the voyage and wouldn't that be just awful, sir?"

Phillip seemed to be growing impatient. "Well, who then?" He tapped his fingers on the table.

"I think I should be allowed to ask young Katy Prentice, Captain Phillip, sir!" Gertie finally announced boldly, while Katy stood with fingers crossed.

"Katy Prentice?"

"Katy Prentice, sir. She's young and no one works harder. She has few personal belongin's and wouldn't take up near as much space aboard the ship as an adult might do."

Phillip shook his head. "I don't know. She's still a child."

"Why, sir, she's half grown! The girl's thirteen and quite mature for her age, if you ask me."

Sighing as he reached for his teacup, Phillip finally nodded. "I don't care, Gertie. Ask her if you wish . . ."

"Hurrah!" came a shout from the kitchen.

Phillip laughed as Gertie blushed and added, "Well, Captain, I think she just gave us her answer."

"May I read my letter now, Gertie?"

"Go right ahead, sir. And I thank ye kindly." Gertie lifted her skirts and paraded triumphantly into the kitchen. Swinging open the door, she found herself quickly embraced by the excited youth.

Katy's face was filled with elation. "I can't believe it, Gertie. You're wonderful!"

"I ain't so wonderful," she argued. "I just don't wants to be without me help again in that wilderness land. That's all!"

"Oh, Gertie. Thank you for not tellin' him about me papa. Captain Phillip might not understand."

"I still thinks you ought to tell him about your father. He might be more understandin' than you give him credit for."

"Oh no, Gertie!" Katy shook her head. "It's bad enough about me mum, but to come from the home of *two* convicts might be the thing to bring my dismissal for certain."

Gertie sighed and nodded. "I understands, I does, lass.

You've me word I'll not tell the captain about your papa. I'm still surprised you've heard no word from your mum, yet."

"I left a letter with Mrs. Breach to send to Mum once she heard news of her sentencing. And Mrs. Breach knows she can send news to me here at her nephew's farm." Katy looked confused. "I can't understand why Mum hasn't sent me a letter yet of her trial."

Emily Breach sat at the desk in her study. Hammering out the monthly bills and paying the servants' wages was the most unpleasant time of the month for her. When her husband was alive, he had always tended to such matters. But since his death, she had never trusted anyone with her finances, except Arthur, and he was much too involved in naval matters to tend to her personal affairs.

The door opened suddenly and the butler appeared, bearing what looked to be several letters in his grasp. "For you, madam," he said dryly, straightening his waistcoat and jacket.

Emily took the letters without so much as a blink and laid them out before her. "Thank you, James. Would you ask Cozette about my morning bath?"

"As you wish, Mrs. Breach." He turned slowly and departed, closing the door behind him.

Emily opened the letters one by one, finding the usual contents inside: a relative asking for money, a pleasant note from the vicar, a letter from a niece. She adjusted her spectacles to better read the roughly scrawled writing across one of the envelopes. The letter appeared to be stained and swiftly thrown together. "What's this? A letter for Katy Prentice?" She scratched her head.

She laid the worn-looking letter aside, planning to give it to Arthur tomorrow when she bade him farewell on his voyage. Then quickly changing her mind, Emily snatched it from the desk top and turned it over hesitantly. Peering toward the doorway, she made her decision and tore open the flap. "Aha!" she tapped the paper. "It's a letter from the girl's convict mother. Dear me!" she fretted. "It's a good thing I opened it.

That's all Arthur needs—more problems from *those* people." Reading the letter's contents, she shook her head. "Transportation?" She was indignant. "What is England coming to? The woman needs to be hanged as an example!"

Emily took the letter and tore it in two pieces before stuffing it into the wastebasket. Then pulling out Katy's letter to her mother from the stationery drawer, she held it between her fingers and tore it as well, allowing it to drop beside Amelia's letter into the trash. "As it should be," she quickly pointed out to herself.

Katy awakened from her sleep to the sound of the wagons being loaded. The last two days had been filled with packing. As of late, her world seemed to progress in two fashions—rapidly and forward. Their last evening on the farm had been bittersweet. They had bid farewell to the servants who were staying on at the farm until the eventual day of Captain Phillip's return. But Katy had allowed her mind to be filled with a new expectation—that she might soon be reunited with Papa.

Emily Breach had come and gone late yesterday and had simply shaken her head when Katy asked, as politely as she knew how, if she had heard any news from her mum. Torn between staying behind and waiting to hear from Mum, or going with the captain and finding her father, her mind was tormented by anxiety and guilt. Fearing her mother to be hanged, she had mourned in her bed that night, feeling lost and so alone. Remembering her promise to Mum to pray, she had done so, and found a certain amount of peace in the process. If she could just find Papa, he would know what to do.

The sound of sheets snapping overhead roused Katy, and stretching lazily she looked toward the right side of the room.

"You'd best get movin', Katy, if you wants to be ready when they leave this mornin'." It was Daphne, Captain Phillip's maid. She was going along as well, and was busy covering the furniture to be left behind with sheets and cord to protect it from dust. Daphne was the prettiest woman Katy had ever met. Her hair was dark and her blue-violet eyes were set off by lovely long lashes. She had taught Katy how to walk like a lady and how to fix her hair in the newest fashion. Katy had learned a great deal from both Daphne and Gertie.

Katy dragged herself from the bed to the wash basin, where she splashed cool water on her face and washed the sleep from her eyes. Combing her hair, she pulled the sides back with ribbons, allowing the rest of her hair to hang down her back in blond curls. In a matter of minutes, she had dressed herself in an outfit she deemed proper for sea travel, a blue cotton frock adorned with red rosettes. The frock smelled of household soap and of the wax used to polish the iron. She had sewn it herself and found a hat that matched. "Mum, you wouldn't know your little Katy now," she whispered to herself as she pinched color into her cheeks.

Breakfast had to be made and consumed quickly, so Katy assisted with preparing hot rolls with jam before helping Gertie pack the final kitchen box.

"Have one of the men load this one, dear," Gertie instructed her.

As the wagons were loaded with "must-have" furniture such as beds and dressing tables the coach was filled with luggage and bags belonging to Phillip and his immediate servants, Gertie and Daphne. Because of the lightness of her bag, Katy's belongings were also included among the important baggage—a small luxury she enjoyed.

"We're ready to depart if you're ready, sir," Mr. Sebastian informed Captain Phillip.

The captain made a few notations in his diary as he held to the door of the coach. Nodding, he answered, "Ready to go, Mr. Sebastian. After we've settled in and arranged our transportation in New South Wales, you realize you'll be sent for?"

Sebastian nodded. "As you wish, Captain, but as long as I can keep me feet planted on dry ground, I'll do so, sir."

Phillip laughed at the landlubber. "Oh, you'd love the sea, Sebastian!"

Sebastian walked to the front of the team to inspect the horses' bridles before their departure.

"Mr. Sebastian?" Katy spoke quietly.

The startled coachman turned quickly to see the cook's

young maid had addressed him. "Yes, Katy. You scared me, child! What is it?"

"You remember when me mother gave you the letter that you lost?"

Sebastian sighed, his arms dropping to his sides. "Are you goin' to make me feel bad about that again?" he asked sheepishly.

"No, I wouldn't do that, Sebastian," Katy assured the man. "I just wanted to say that perhaps it's turned out better this way. If Captain Phillip knew about Papa, he might feel differently about me goin'. The way things has turned out, maybe I can find Papa meself."

His lips pursed, Sebastian nodded, then spoke. "Maybe so, lass. I hope things turns out for the best. I hopes you can find your papa . . . and your mum."

Katy shook her head sadly. "It hurts to think about Mum . . . o-or the baby. It's just . . . painful, Sebastian."

"Are we ready, Mr. Sebastian?" Phillip called from the coach.

Sebastian glanced back to see the three wagons were loaded down with household belongings, extra food, and servants. "Why don't you just ride up top with me, eh, Miss Katy Prentice? You look like a full-grown woman, lass!"

"Dear me!" Daphne called from the coach as she stepped inside to speak to the captain. "Ladies don't ride on top!"

"It's all right, Daphne." Katy nodded and the coachman assisted her to the driver's seat.

She relaxed against the seat and gazed at the road ahead, enchanted with the view of nature. The roadside was bordered with blooming May flowers. Laburnum trees with their drooping golden chains of flowers were surrounded by the gay red and yellow colors of everlastings and tulips. Blue and white love-in-a-mist danced in the breeze, clothing the ground in brilliant color. English gardens were miniature bright spots, bathed in color in the daylight and looking larger in the evening shadows. Katy wondered if New South Wales would have flowers as pretty as did England. She had heard the servants speak of the new land as though it were a paradise, with strange creatures and giant plants decorating the landscape like an exotic netherland. Having never traveled outside of London, she had no choice but to believe their peculiar stories. She couldn't help but feel a certain apprehension about the entire trip. How she hated making decisions without Papa or Mum to help.

As the rhythm of the coach rocked her to sleep, Katy drifted in and out of reality for most of the day, waking occasionally to find Sebastian rattling on about one thing or another.

The day stretched into late afternoon, and it wasn't long before the caravan was pulling into Portsmouth.

"We're almost to the bay," Sebastian yelled to the captain.

The servants relayed the news cheerily to one another that they had arrived. Katy waved happily to the others and began straightening her dress, which had gotten dusty and crumpled from the day-long trip. As they neared the harbor, she crinkled her nose at the fishy odors that permeated the bay. Along the dock, she counted eleven enormous ships that were mustered at bay. The ships, all of them new, made the old washed-out hulks along the port look like dull, dreary old maids. She had memorized the names of all of them and was anxious for the day she could sneak a look at the ships' rosters, which were carefully tucked away in the captain's personal files.

The coach pulled up alongside the colorful naval flagship *Sirius* and the brig-rigged sloop *Supply*. Bringing the horses to a halt, Sebastian whistled to the sailors, who jumped to their feet and ran in all directions gathering enough men to unload the wagons.

As Daphne and Gertie were handed their bags, Sebastian assisted Katy from the seat. The three of them were directed to the *Sirius*, and they cautiously began the walk up the gangway. As they did so, gawking mariners rolled their eyes at the three females and called out to the demure Daphne, who blushed appropriately.

"I'll carry that for you, miss!" A mariner grabbed Daphne's bags as Gertie looked on disapprovingly.

Katy laughed. "You're just too beautiful, Daphne!"

Captain Phillip was handed his official commission to

launch, which was duly signed by Lord Sydney. He sighed, knowing they were still without proper victuals and supplies. But it would be disastrous for the convicts to know the ship was underequipped in weapons, so the crew was under strict orders to keep quiet regarding the supply shortage.

"Are we prepared to launch, Captain Hunter?" Phillip asked of his second-in-command.

"Aye, aye, Commander." Hunter snapped to attention. "We can weigh anchor at your command, sir."

"Excellent." Phillip gazed up and down the harbor, surveying the fleet.

Meanwhile, the servants were busy seeing that the personal belongings of the captain were stored away from the ship's provisions. Gertie was well in charge of seeing that her cooking supplies were not intermingled with those of the ship's cook. "All o' mine are marked with me name and are to be stored below in the bosun's stores," she firmly instructed the mariners, who regarded her with annoyance.

Katy wandered above deck and watched the crew bustle about, making last-minute preparations as Second Lieutenant William Gidley King barked orders and checked items off his list. Lieutenant King had been commissioned by the Royal Navy to assist Commander Phillip aboard the *Sirius*. He was a thick, burly officer, with full, bristly sideburns and small penetrating eyes. "All hands make ready! Commander Phillip is preparing to board."

As the sailors assembled on deck, Katy stepped toward the cabin where she had taken her bags.

"You there, girl!" a surly mariner called to her. "What are you doin' aboard? You'll have to leave now. We're preparin' to weigh anchor here shortly."

Katy shook her head. "But, sir . . ."

"No buts! Get along now, girl." He tried to shove Katy toward the gangway.

"Here, here, now!" Gertie appeared from below, after having made sure her supplies were all intact. Behind her came Daphne, scowling at the mariner.

"Get your hands off that girl!" Gertie shook her finger at the sailor.

Katy breathed a sigh of relief as she straightened her collar. "I tried to tell you, sir."

"What?" he questioned. "You goin' on this trip, too?"

Katy nodded.

"Why, don't you know anythin', sailor?" Daphne shook her head. "She's with us. She works for Commander Phillip."

"Don't say?" The mariner scratched his head.

"O' course she do," Gertie chimed in. "She's the captain's girl!"

Katy smiled and turned to follow the women to their cabin.

14

AWEIGH ANCHORS

"What do you mean, they aren't moving, Lieutenant King?" Phillip asked his second lieutenant.

King stood shaking his head while Captain Hunter came charging up from the quarterdeck.

"What's going on?" Hunter demanded.

"That's what I'm trying to explain to the commander, Captain Hunter! I gave the order to weigh anchor . . . see there, sir?" King pointed. "The signal flags are waving, but none of the mariners are setting sail from the merchantmen. I'm going now to check into it, sir."

Quickly dismissing himself, King made his way down the dock to the *Scarborough*, which was anchored beside the flagship and the sloop. Once aboard, he found the mariners sitting lazily under the masts, arms folded across their chests.

"Didn't you hear your orders, you men?" the red-faced lieutenant bellowed, pointing to the flagship. "Can't you see the signal as plain as daylight?"

167

The men looked at one another and stared back at the lieutenant blankly.

"Answer me!" His gaze was stern but the mariners refused to reply. "Where's your officer?" he demanded of the contracted group.

A seaman pointed below deck. King wheeled around and stormed toward the companionway, wiping the sweat from his brow and noting the sun sinking below the English horizon. They should have been pulling out to sea by now. Climbing down the staircase to the cabins below, King entered the common quarters where the mariners were bunked. He spotted Corporal Frederick pacing nervously.

"What's happened, man? None o' your men'll set sail and I've given the order twice!"

Corporal Frederick shook his head. "It isn't my fault or yours, Lieutenant King. It's the owners of the commercial vessels of this fleet who're to blame. They've neglected to pay the men their wages and the crews refuse to leave without their pay."

"What?" King was furious. "Well, why wasn't I given this information beforehand? We could've made arrangements. It's time to leave now! You tell those men to weigh anchor or I'll . . ."

Frederick gazed dryly at the second lieutenant. The crews on the merchantmen were not under the Royal Navy's command, but rather were hired by the owners of the chartered vessels. Lieutenant King's hands, in essence, were tied and Frederick knew it.

"They're behind seven months, sir."

"Seven months! This is an outrage!" King tapped his chin worriedly. "I'll have to speak with Commander Phillip, Frederick." King stormed out of the room and up the stairwell to the quarterdeck. Upon stepping out onto the deck he could see Phillip and Hunter bounding up the gangway.

Phillip's brow was arched, his expression inquiring as he sought out the ship's officer.

"Confound it!" Phillip pounded the deck with his heel. "Where's the crew?"

Hunter spotted King. "Look, Commander! Here comes King."

King bustled up to face Phillip and Hunter. His eyes indicated his worry. "It's the contractors, sir. They've neglected to pay the wages to the crew, and the men refuse to weigh anchor, sir, without pay."

Phillip sighed and shook his head. "One snarl-up after another! Why should one more surprise me?"

"Captain Phillip, sir, if I may speak?" A seaman stood before the officers. He was a stoop-shouldered fellow who stood shifting nervously, one hand in his pocket and the other grasping a bag of mail.

"What is it, man?" Captain Hunter sighed.

"I think I might 'ave some information for ye, if ye'll listen, that is."

"Go on," said Phillip, his impatience evident.

"You see, Commander Phillip, sir, if the owners holds out our wages until we're out to sea, then we're forced to buy our provisions only from their stores on the ship . . . an' they charges a lot more'n we wants to pay. We wants to buy our necessaries here in Portsmouth."

Phillip shook his head, his eyes steeled discerningly. "I might have known!" Glancing appreciatively at the mariner, he placed his hand on the seaman's shoulder. "Thank you for apprising me, sir. I'll see what I can do to negotiate for you men." He turned to the captain. "Hunter, you keep things on the ready here. King, you come with me and we'll figure out what's what."

The mariner saluted respectfully. He was relieved that his complaint had found favor with the commander. At least for now it left him with a renewed sense of well-being. Turning on his heels he began to spread the news among his fellow crewmates that Phillip is "on our side."

"We'll see!" a surly jack-tar snapped as he joined an assortment of sailors in passing around some gin. "If Phillip wants these 'ere vessels to make it out o' port, he'll be on our side, all right!" He snatched a letter from the seaman's hand.

His crewmates laughed and mimicked the officers, but the persistent private shook his head at the man. "Give it a chance, will ye? We've got to work with the blasted Royal Navy, now, don't we?"

The mariner cursed and tilted the bottle, swigging down the white tonic, while the private turned to deliver letters to the convicts. Standing over the hatchways, he said, "Help me lift these hatches, mate. I'm goin' to give these convicts a little air since we ain't pullin' out right away."

The convicts stirred restlessly below. Dark as always, the convict pit had become a breeding ground for insanity and hopelessness. George Prentice lay slumped against the wall of his cell. His cellmates had grown quiet, so he worked absently with a piece of rope. Prentice had become quite expert at tying a bowline in the dark, threading the loop through the knot just to keep his wandering thoughts from driving him to insanity.

A voice spoke, piercing through the deadness of the cell. "How much blacker can darkness be when nothin' is all you see?" The voice next to Prentice was raspy and dry.

"Eh?" Prentice's brow furrowed as he turned toward the voice of his cellmate Smitty. Smitty had been a lively, good-looking fellow from the beginning, entertaining the men with tales of his exploits with women. But his conversation had begun to sound pedantic and confused the last few days. Sometimes Smitty would stop in midsentence, forgetting his train of thought. Prentice had tried to help the man when his thoughts seemed to stray, but keeping Smitty focused on reality was becoming a bit of a struggle.

"I didn't know you 'ad the poet in ye, Smitty," Prentice remarked cynically. "A regular Samuel Johnson y'are."

"Is Samuel Johnson a poet, Prentice?" Smitty asked, his breathing labored as he wheezed and coughed.

"Who knows. I ain't no scholar," Prentice lamented. "I wouldn't give a farthing fer one neither."

The overhead sound of the stanchions scraping the latches brought them all to their feet. Small fingers of light seeped through the hatchway, unmasking the dust before breaking forth into full-blown daylight. A sailor peered in, his gaze reflecting curiosity, as though he were observing a scientific experiment.

"All you below, listen, now!" the seaman called to the prisoners. "We're preparin' to weigh anchor. As soon as we're out o' sight o' land, you'll all be allowed out to exercise on deck, so long as the weather 'olds out . . . an' you don't cause no grief fer us!" He paused, turning his head in search of fresh air. "I should warn ye that any attempt at escape will be punished with instant death."

"Did you 'ear that, Smitty? We're goin' to be let out soon!" Prentice tilted his head, looking upward as he inhaled deeply of the fresh air.

"Oh, me legs!" another cellmate moaned. "I don't know if I kin walk or not."

"Well, I'm goin' to kiss the deck when I step out, I will at that!" an Irish convict remarked.

"Hey, blokes!" Prentice yelled up through the open hatchway. "Where are we headed, anyway?"

"First stop—the island of Tenerife!" the seaman replied.

"Hey, Smitty," Prentice elbowed his friend. "It's paradise we're goin' to!" Turning his face back up toward the mariner, Prentice asked, "Did I get a letter yet from me wife?"

The seaman shook his head. "No, Prentice. Got a letter for Higgins, though." Bridges pulled the letter from inside his coat and tossed it below to the other convict. Higgins' face broke with elation. "From Mary? Me dear, sweet . . ." His face was filled with rapture as he held the letter to his breast.

"Matter o' fact, Prentice," the mariner hesitated, weighing the news he was about to convey. "I'm sorry to say, the one you sent to your wife's been returned. She must've moved away or somethin' like."

Bridges held out the weathered-looking envelope and allowed it to drop into Prentice's hands.

Prentice stared down at the letter. Disappointment and despair rose up, choking him. His fingers curled over the envelope as he lifted the crumpled paper and ripped it in two.

"It's all right, Prentice." Higgins tried to offer consolation. "Probably just a mistake."

"No, mates. It ain't no mistake." Prentice held out the part of the correspondence that was scrawled in his own handwriting. "Amelia's left me, she 'as . . . fer good."

Rachel Langley held the blue scarf, still scented with perfume, up to her nose. The floral aroma draped the air of the damp cell with a pungent fragrance. "Mmm, Cally, this smells lovely, it does. Where'd you get it?"

"From a jailer." Cally, a new inmate, leaned casually against the wall and smiled. She had arrived with the last of the female convicts to be boarded on the *Charlotte*. Two older convicts in the cell had sighed in exasperation when Cally arrived. Placing a fifth cellmate in the already tight cubicle had caused the older women much distress, but Rachel welcomed the new face.

Cally tugged at the neck of her prison garb and spoke in a whisper. "I slipped the scarf under this 'ere sack of a dress they gave me to wear."

Betsy reached for a corner of the scarf and sniffed its edges. "Heavenly, Cally. I almost forgot what perfume smelled like, I did."

"You can 'ave it, Rachel," Cally urged. "I'll get more where that one came from." A smile lit the girl's face. She seemed eager to impress Rachel.

"Ahh . . . don't you know where y'are?" The oldest woman laughed and waved her palm at Cally. "You ain't goin' to find no perfume an' such on board the *Charlotte*." She turned and took her place cross-legged on the hard floor beside her gray-haired cellmate. "Welcome to the real world. Whether you're a man or woman, it don't matter. They treats us all like riffraff."

Cally pulled her raven hair through her fingers and glanced at Rachel again. Her brows were pinched with an air of insolence as she formulated a fast reply for the old woman. "I'm not like all the rest." Then, smiling demurely up at the sentry who stood over the hatchway counting prisoners, she skillfully parried their comments. "I picks the right friends."

Rachel bit her lip. She understood rough-hewn women like Cally but knew Betsy would never affirm such a lifestyle.

Cally turned her face toward Rachel, her eyes taunting.

"You know how to gets what you wants, too, don't you, Rachel?"

Rachel gave a slight shrug, her eyes purposefully avoiding Betsy's. "O' course . . . that's why I'm on this transport," she replied tartly. Everyone laughed but Cally.

Cally's voice grew caustic and defensive as the conversation seemed to be slipping from her command. "You tellin' me that none o' you's ever sold yourself? It's a lie yer tellin' me, if that be so. Ain't a woman alive that ain't learned how to get what she wants. Even the married ones knows how to get around their old men."

"Cally Hodges . . ." Betsy was finally stirred up enough to speak out. "My mother and father didn't *use* each other selfishly. Surely you've heard of love?"

"Only one kind, Betsy . . . the kind that's bought and sold." Cally's eyes were resistive as she turned her face toward the darkness of the cell. Yet she continued to seek the approval of Rachel. "So, Rachel . . . do you agree or disagree?"

Sighing, Rachel felt Betsy's eyes on her. She knew Betsy would speak the truth freely. But as for herself, Rachel still felt bound to her haunted past. "I don't know . . ." She was hesitant. "Besides, we've other things to worry about." She decided it was time to change the subject. "Have you heard any news yet about New South Wales?"

Of course Cally knew everything. As she rattled endlessly, Rachel glanced over at Betsy, whose face seemed to reflect a tinge of disappointment. Rachel sighed. If Betsy expected her to live up to her high expectations . . . well, it just wasn't likely to happen. *She may as well get ready for disappointment. Rachel Langley isn't about to change . . . or be changed. Besides, Cally seems to need my friendship.* Cally reminded her of the girls at Miss Marcella's, the ones who liked to live on the edge and take chances. They believed life was less dreary that way.

"I don't think I'll 'ave to stay long in prison, I don't." Cally smiled. "There'll be desperate old men over there lookin' for a quick wife. One fast trip to the altar and Cally Hodges'll be out o' there faster than you can shake a stick, she will!"

"What, an' marry up with some feebleminded ol' fool?" Rachel laughed at the girl.

"Just fer a short time, Rachel. Long enough to be set free, then once I gets me 'ands on the old codger's fortune, it's back to England fer me!"

Rachel waited a moment before commenting. "I don't know if it'd be worth it . . . marryin' the wrong man an' all. I think I wants to marry up with the right one to begin with." Cupping her hands behind her head, Rachel concluded boastfully, "Then he better keep Lady Rachel in the manner to which she's accustomed."

The women laughed again and continued in their noisy chatter as Rachel leaned against the wall reflectively. A faint smile curved her pale lips as she recalled the handsome mariner she had encountered the day they were allowed to sit out on the hatch. It was a pleasant but fleeting remembrance before the brutal realities of confinement came flooding back to mind. Rachel, disheartened, slid slowly to the floor and pressed her back against the lifeless wall.

The red-orange color that stretched brilliantly along the western horizon like eagle's wings was edged with deep blue clouds—dark billows enveloping the sky from north to south. The English flotilla bobbed in the harbor, soaking up the last rays of hot sun. Salt water jostled the hulls in a warm brackish bath as the sloop *Supply* careened through the bay, acting as messenger for Commander Phillip.

Maneuvering the sloop was Captain Riggs of His Majesty's Navy. Judging the speed to have reached its maximum as the ship heeled over the lee gunwale, he barked coarsely, "Ready about!" thus starting the tacking maneuver. With her head plowing into the ever-advancing waves, and spray exploding over her bow, the little ship was brought about. At the critical point in the tack, Captain Riggs screamed through the flying spray, "Helms alee!" as the wheel was put down and the wind spilled through the jib. "Mainsail haul!" he quickly barked, to fill the mainsail and to maintain speed.

The crew held to the tack at the capstan, maneuvering the rope through the wooden blocks. "They're head in the wind but coming through nicely, Captain!" a crewman yelled back methodically.

"Let go and haul!" the captain ordered as the vessel surged ahead and the wake calmed.

"Bring 'er port side to the quay?" A large corporal questioned the captain as they prepared to dock beside the *Sirius*.

Captain Riggs nodded. "Port side to the quay, mates."

As the *Supply* nosed in left side to the dock, the sailors prepared the mooring to tie her up.

"Get a message to Commander Phillip," Riggs ordered his lieutenant. "We've got a meeting between him and the contractors arranged in one hour at the port admiral's office."

The lieutenant turned and marched purposefully aboard the *Sirius*, in search of the commander.

Katy Prentice disappeared down the stairwell and seated herself at the table with the servants to eat the evening meal. It was their first taste of ship's grub and they eyed their rations suspiciously. Each tin plate held a meal of salt pork, peas, a slice of bread with butter, and a slice of cheese. In addition, they were each handed a tin cup of rum. Katy scowled at the taste and asked for water instead.

"It'll take some gettin' used to, won't it, Daphne?" Katy asked the maid.

Daphne winced as she chewed on the salt pork. "Gertie may have to sneak into the kitchen and whip up somethin'."

Gertie chuckled. "I'm not so certain starvin' wouldn't be 'ealthier than eatin' this pig fodder!"

"Can't we eat from our own stores?" Daphne asked.

"We'll 'ave to eat what we're given, ladies," Gertie pointed out. "When we make our home in New South Wales, we'll fix some grand meals then, we will, workin' fer the governor and all." A broad grin creased her cheeks.

"You're right, Gertie." Katy looked thoughtful. "Commander Phillip *will* be the governor. Won't we all be grand?"

The maids laughed and dove into their meal with a renewed sense of anticipation.

The remainder of the evening passed quietly as groups of twelve or more were routed through the mess. As the sky shaded the port with its drowsy blanket, the crew resigned itself to another evening docked at Portsmouth. The dreaded hatchways were locked up and Phillip's staff bid one another good-night as they went in search of their bunks and a welcome night of rest.

But Commander Phillip did not find rest, nor would he allow his newest adversaries, the contractors, to rest. After many hours of deliberation, compromise, and exchange of partial pay, the complaints were sorted out.

Across the harbor, before the dawn could shed its glow over the bottle-shaped bay, the cry rang out, "Aweigh anchors!"

Katy stirred in her sleep, opening her eyes only briefly. She heard the sound of feet running across the deck and voices shouting as they weighed anchor and pointed the First Fleet toward Tenerife in the Canary Islands.

For the first time she felt the premonition that an orphan feels upon realizing she's separated forever from her parents. Katy closed her eyes and tried to recapture the dream she had of her family—Papa, Mum, and a baby whom she would never be able to hold or stroke or smell. She wiped the tears of regret from her eyes.

"If you see me, God," she prayed softly, "please don't let me die. I feel so alone. I've no one but you to keep me from 'arm. If you'll stretch out your hand, I know that . . . somehow . . . you can find me papa. An' please don't let 'em 'ang Mum . . . I beg you for that, sir." She stopped and bit her bottom lip to prevent the sobs from bursting forth. "I wish I could see your face and know you're here, God. Everythin' looks so dark." Katy lay staring upward, her eyes straining to see beyond the overhead bunk as she struggled to discern her future. "Amen," she softly concluded.

Inhaling deeply, Katy felt a peacefulness envelop her. The feeling didn't surprise the thirteen-year-old or strike her as odd, for she was still a child who didn't question, but merely accepted the sense of well-being as a natural occurrence. Turning on her stomach, Katy yawned and closed her eyes as she was rocked to sleep in the bowels of the ship.

PART TWO

THE VOYAGE

May 20, 1787–January 20, 1788

15

DEN OF
THIEVES

Phillip seated himself at his desk in the straight-back chair. Making a notation in his ship's log he wrote: "The First Fleet has been at sea only one week, and the convicts are suffering great seasickness. With such horrendous need to swab the cells, we've resorted to placing convicts on duty to assist with the frequent swabbing of the decks and cells." Completing his notation, Phillip placed the log in a drawer and began to study the fleet's rosters.

Perusing the rosters, the commander paid close attention to the prisoners' offenses. Of the seven hundred thirty-six convicts aboard the First Fleet, most were thieves. No female prisoners were being transported for prostitution, for that crime was not considered a transportable offense. "Yes," he mused in his practical way, "as it's always been." For crimes against property fetched a higher punishment, property being valued more than human life.

"Commander Phillip?" Katy stood timidly in the doorway. The captain had seemed so quiet and unassuming back on the farm, but now having seen him as Commander of the First Fleet, Katy was hesitant to approach him.

"Yes, young Prentice, what is it?"

"Your Lieutenant William Bradley, sir, has spotted some fish off the starboard bow. He thinks you should like to see them, sir."

Phillip chuckled. "He does, now, does he? Well, we'll just have to go and see about these fish. Have they great wings, lass?"

Katy shook her head. "Not that I know of, sir!"

"Well, then, what's all the bother?"

"I think some of the men should like to drop their lines, sir."

Picking up his jacket and cap, Phillip muttered, "King George would surely throw a royal tantrum if he knew his vessel had been made into a fishing boat." Phillip stepped briskly past Katy.

"Per'aps he would honor the lines if we cast them in his name. Would 'e like that, sir?" Upon realizing she had caused the commander to laugh, a smile broke across Katy's face.

"Now, I've never perceived it in such a way, Katy. If we do all in the name of England, does that make all things honorable?"

"I suppose it does, sir!"

"That's a good lass. Keep it up and they'll make you a duchess." Phillip peered back into the cabin. "So are you going to wet your line as well?"

"I like to fish, sir. I used to fish with me . . ." Katy stopped. She had never made mention of her papa and decided it was best she didn't.

Phillip raised his brows. "You fished with your father?"

Biting her lip, Katy nodded.

"No need to feel bad talking about him, Katy. My aunt told me you had lost him. How did he die, anyway?"

Katy swallowed hard. She had never told Mrs. Breach her father had died. Why did the woman tell the commander such a story?

"That's all right, Katy." Phillip noted her discomfort with

the subject. "We don't have to discuss it now. Perhaps later, when you feel up to it."

Katy looked at the floor, her cheeks flushing. Even though she hadn't said a word, Katy felt as though she had just told a great lie.

"Well, join us if you can, dear." Phillip walked away, the sun glinting off his forehead.

Katy smiled weakly. She had thought she was beginning to build trust with the commander. But how could she ever expect him to trust her if she didn't confide in him the truth about Papa? Katy glanced back at the shuffle of papers Phillip had left behind on his desk. She stepped across the room and reached to straighten his desk top. As she did so, her eyes fell across the title of the top document—"Fleet Roster."

"I can't believe I'm seein' this!" Katy exclaimed, swinging quickly around to see if anyone was watching her. The word "trust" rang in her mind again. *What would the commander do if he caught me going through his things? However, one look couldn't hurt, could it?* she reasoned.

The first page listed the *Lady Penrhyn* at the top. After studying the first few names, listed alphabetically, she could see straightway that the ship was occupied solely by female convicts. She dropped the list and went on to the next. The *Alexander* seemed to be full of men. Katy studied the list intently but couldn't find the name George Prentice. The girl sighed, feeling anxious as she read one list after another without finding her papa's name. "What if Papa was never transported? Was it a lie all along?" As Katy pulled up the last list she heard footsteps approaching. She quickly ran her finger the length of the roster, stopping near names like Potter and Preeks. Suddenly her eyes grew large. "Papa!" she exclaimed as her slender finger found the name George Prentice.

"What on earth do you think you're doing?" a stern voice made its demanding inquisition from the doorway.

Katy gasped and tossed the paper back into the stack, reshuffling them in a frenzy. Seeing Lieutenant King standing with his arms crossed and his eyes narrowed suspiciously on her made Katy feel like a criminal. It was the same censure she felt when Mrs. Breach glared at her from the window of her study.

"I'm sorry, sir! But I was . . . only straightening up, I was!" The statement was partly true. "I works for Commander Phillip, you know!" Katy felt the color drain from her face as King walked toward her and yanked the list from her hands.

"You're lying to me, girl!"

Katy looked up at the lieutenant. He was an enormous man, not as big as Dring, nor as frightening, but nevertheless he alarmed her with his pointed accusation.

"I'm sorry, sir. I didn't mean no harm, I didn't!" Katy felt the tears spill from her eyes.

The lieutenant sighed. He wasn't accustomed to dealing with young girls. Perhaps he had been too harsh. "I . . . I'm sorry, Miss Prentice, but I can't allow your going through the commander's things." He hesitated. "If you'll leave now I won't say anything to Commander Phillip."

Katy breathed a sigh of relief. "I promise I'll leave," she vowed. "But I'll tell the commander meself if it'll help, sir."

King waved his hand. "Don't bother. No harm done, I suppose. But you shouldn't be touching important naval documents, if you understand my meaning!"

Katy glanced back down at the papers, trying to recall the name of the ship her father was placed on. Biting her lip, she resolved that just knowing he was on the fleet would have to suffice for now.

"I understands, Lieutenant King, I do. You're right, you are. I'll not touch 'em again." Katy took a deep breath. "I promise I won't." But behind her back her pale fingers were crossed, and Katy made a silent vow to return later.

George Prentice held the mop loosely, pushing it through the waste that had collected just that morning from the sea-sick inmates. He had fought nausea the first two days, but gaining his sea legs, he had been ordered to assist with the care of the ailing convicts. In the process, he had been freed of his heavy shackles.

Prentice turned his eyes away, feeling queasy as the mop swashed up the putrid refuse. He complained loudly, mostly to himself since nearly everyone chose to ignore him. "When're you bunch o' *women* goin' to get your sea legs? It's like nursemaidin' a bunch o' waifs, it is at that!"

He made his way across the deck, resentment filling him as he regarded the wan faces of the shackled men sitting against the outer walls of the cabin house. Most of the men were in shock from the long periods of confinement and illness, but rather than feeling compassion toward them, Prentice was annoyed that they couldn't care for themselves and he had to assist with the dreadful cleanup.

Stopping to rub his mending wrists, Prentice sighed heavily at the thought of reaching the Canary Islands. Once land was spotted, he and the other convicts would be ordered below and the shackles would again commence the process of mangling his limbs.

Placing the large, stringy mop in the foul-smelling bucket, Prentice pushed the pail across the deck so he could toss the putrid water overboard. He picked up the bucket and hurled the contents across the bulwark, losing his grip in the process. He grappled for the pail, but watched in dismay as it tumbled below into the swirling green wake of the stern. Swearing profusely, he turned to see if any guards had witnessed his bungled throw. Losing equipment could bring him lashes at the flogging post, which had gotten much use in the last week. The guards were busy conversing about the rum they planned to buy in Tenerife, so Prentice veered casually around them with the mop and headed toward the companionway. Lifting the hatch, he climbed below in search of another pail from the hulk's stores.

It was dark below, except for the oil lamp that swung lazily to the ship's rhythmic sway. Nearing the storeroom, Prentice detected voices. Cautiously peering around the doorway of the small room, he was startled to find three convicts arguing over a metal gadget, wrestling back and forth with the object in their greasy hands.

"Not like that, you fool! Give it to me, Worley, and let me do it or you'll botch the whole thing!" Barrett attempted to yank the piece from Worley's grasp.

"Do what 'e says, Worley!" the third man snapped.

"I know what I'm doin', I tell ye, Barrett!" Worley fought for the right to hold the object. "I made plenty o' coins in my day, an' good ones too!"

"Ain't no one that kin run a coinery better'n Thomas Barrett!" Jenkins argued.

"Coins?" Prentice whispered, backing quietly away. Not seeing the stack of pails behind him, Prentice stumbled backward into the containers, and with a mighty crash the pails tumbled to the floor.

Taken by surprise, the forgers spun around in a fury to see who had invaded their hideaway.

"It's Prentice!" Jenkins jerked his head back toward Barrett.

"Grab 'im!" Barrett shouted while the two men jumped for Prentice's arms.

Prentice swung one arm free, catching Worley in the jaw with a solid right hook.

"Ahh!" Worley cursed, blood spurting from his bottom lip. "I'll kill ye, I will!" He lunged for Prentice's throat as Jenkins grabbed the intruder by his coarse prison shirt.

Prentice's eyes grew large, his gaze meeting the glint of a dagger's shiny tip. Though he struggled, Barrett held him securely by the throat, and Worley and Jenkins wrestled him to the damp floor. Worley laughed cruelly and watched Prentice gaze helplessly at his steel blade. He held the knife tightly, twisting it back and forth in front of Prentice's face.

"So, who're ye spyin' fer?" Worley's gravelly voice snarled. "Captain Fox?"

"I'm not a spy, I tell ye!" Prentice argued. "I was only lookin' for a pail!"

Jenkins drew back his fist and delivered a stout blow to the abdomen. Prentice drew up his knees, his face etched with pain while Barrett gripped his hair more tightly.

"Let's draw an' quarter the louse!" Jenkins drew back his fist again.

"What, an' hang for murder, you idiot?" Barrett turned Prentice's face up toward his own, his yellow eyes glaring threateningly. "I've a better plan. We're goin' to make you work, Mr. Georgie. You're goin' to 'elp us distribute our merchandise."

Jenkins shook Prentice by the collar. "No, Barrett! 'E ain't gettin' me share, 'e ain't!"

"Shut up, fool!" Barrett eyed Prentice again. "Breathe one word an' you're shark bait!"

Prentice shook his head. "I won't do it, Barrett! I want no part of this counterfeitin', I don't!"

"We're goin' to have to kill 'im, Barrett, like I said!" Worley pointed the blade at Prentice's throat.

"Is that it, Georgie?" Barrett asked banefully. "You want I should let ol' Worley finish ye off . . . feed you to the fish . . . piece by piece?"

"No!" Prentice replied desperately. Struggling to buy more time, he swallowed hard before answering. "I'll help you, I will. Just tell me what to do!"

Barrett laughed, his sinister brow overshadowing his pockmarked face. He grinned at his two vile cronies, who joined in the levity. "That's better, Georgie." Barrett leered. "Now, your job is simple. We make the coins and you pawns 'em off to the sailors to buy supplies from the stores. Bring back lots o' rum, mind ye! Understand?"

Prentice nodded, feeling trapped and cowardly. Life was beginning to count for less with each passing day. Perhaps he should let them kill him and be done with his miserable lot. Suddenly, a picture of Katy flashed into his mind. It was the very last time he had seen her, standing in front of the jailhouse gate with the wind blowing her flaxen hair. She looked like a miniature of her mother. Even in ragged clothing the girl was lovely beyond compare. *No*, he decided. *If for nothing but the comfort of her memory . . . and Amelia's . . . I must stay alive.*

"Let 'im go, mates!" Barrett ordered while the two convicts roughly unhanded him. "Meet us down 'ere in two days . . . alone! It's a long voyage, Georgie, with nowheres to run! If ye spill yer guts to anyone about us, we'll skin ye alive in yer sleep, we will!"

"I understand." His voice strained, Prentice looked away,

trying to mask his fear and hatred for the man.

Prentice turned on his heels, and without looking back he ascended the stairs, defeat pushing him further into a valley of gloom. As he stepped out onto the deck again, Prentice eyed the lieutenant pacing the quarterdeck. Rubbing his bloody knuckles on his trousers, Prentice wrestled a decision to speak with the officer. But with a sigh, he thought better of it. His hand stopped as he felt a small lump in his pocket. He pulled out the worn Bible he had taken from Bobbitt the day of the man's death. He hadn't read it at all, and had reasoned more than once that he owed it to his deceased friend to read a few words in his behalf.

Prentice stumbled over behind the mizzenmast and took a seat in the sunshine. The northeasterly wind blew warm against his face, scarcely parting his hair, which was cropped short.

Prentice, like most of the convicts, could read a little. Pushing himself up against the mast, he opened the leather cover and scanned a few pages, skipping through passages he didn't understand.

Remembering Bobbitt had died with such peace, he sighed. "Per'aps you were just daft, man," he muttered under his breath. He thumbed through the thin paper, squinting to read the tiny writing.

Prentice struggled to concentrate. Barrett's threats kept tumbling through his mind, stirring his emotions and rekindling his anger. He shook himself and tried to focus on a sentence he had read three times already. But it was no use. His thoughts became consumed with the past. He felt his weaknesses closing in on him. *Strength, man, strength!* he berated himself. He considered tossing the Bible overboard. It would have been an easy choice, but feeling strangely drawn to the worn pages, he clutched it tightly to his chest.

Then closing his eyes, Prentice did something he had not expected to do. *Lord,* he prayed silently. He swallowed and struggled for the right words. *I want to have . . . I need . . . the peace that Bobbitt found . . . if it's possible. I'm not strong enough to reach you. You'll have to find me.* Feeling his bottom lip quiver, Prentice fought back a tear. He could almost see himself in his mind . . . standing in tattered garments, a spiritual pauper. *Make me a man of honor and not a thief. Make me a hero and not a coward.*

Prentice sat quietly for a moment, hearing nothing but the sound of wind spilling through the sails. His eyes remained closed. He didn't want to open them, for something seemed to hold his attention. He couldn't describe what he was feeling; he only knew that he was experiencing something spiritual. "It's you. . . ." he whispered in awe. ". . . God!" Peace flooded his being. "I can't believe it!" he marveled. "You're right 'ere with me . . . with ol' George Prentice!" He wiped the tears from his face unashamedly. "I'm sorry for all the misery I've brought on meself and me family. 'Elp me to do better . . . a-an' thank you, God!"

Prentice once again picked up Bobbitt's old Bible, and this time he became engrossed in reading page after page as the *Scarborough* trailed the *Sirius* and the *Lady Penrhyn*. He glanced up occasionally, but didn't really notice the figure who stood motionless at the stern of the *Lady Penrhyn*.

The obviously pregnant woman eyed the eight ships that followed her transport, the trailing ships being faithfully rounded up by the sloop *Supply*. Straining her eyes, she searched for a familiar figure.

"Amelia?" a woman called from midships. "Time for rations. Better get in line if you want yours."

Amelia Prentice turned and fell into line behind the other hungry prisoners. Her mind was consumed with worry about the family from whom she was separated. She glanced again beyond the stern, then faced the bow and struggled to turn her mind from thoughts of despair to those of hope.

16
A Bottle o' Gin

The fleet had passed unnoticed off the coast of Spain, save for a few fishing vessels whose occupants lazily grumbled at the wake's disturbance before returning to their own business of checking lines and nets.

Sailing on past Africa, the *Supply* trailed behind the fleet in its usual watchdog fashion while Commander Phillip's *Sirius* forged ahead, plowing toward the Canary Islands. The *Lady Penrhyn* and the colossal *Alexander* hugged close to the flagship ahead, while the smaller *Charlotte* churned through the Atlantic at a snail's pace, often losing sight of the other ten ships.

The *Charlotte* slowed when the signal was given from the *Supply* to heave to, in warning of the contrary winds ahead. As the sailors scrambled to shorten sail and to goose-wing the topsail, which stretched overhead like a pyramid of canvas, Rachel watched with interest the baring of the masts. The strong wind flattened her hair back, and when she closed her eyes, she felt the hot Atlantic air blow hard against the bow.

The smell of rain was in the air, and Rachel was beginning to recognize the signs of changing weather, which the sailors reacted to instinctively like wooden marionettes beneath the spars and rigging.

Rachel counted off the days in her head, attempting to calculate the time since they had left shore. With no system of keeping track of the calendar dates, she suddenly realized her sixteenth birthday had come and gone uneventfully.

"Watchin' fer the rain, pretty lady?" A grating voice spoke behind her.

The wind whipping her hair around her face as she turned sharply about, Rachel found a swarthy sailor leering at her. "Just takin' a walk." Her answer was short as she turned her face seaward again. She had managed for three weeks to avoid the attentions of the men aboard, an achievement that was simplified by the eagerness of many other female convicts to keep the sailors company.

"You're a right fine-lookin' woman, y'are, missy."

Rachel blinked impassively, ignoring the man whose persistence was becoming annoying.

"Jake Hessler's been needin' a woman to keep 'im warm at night, he has. I'll pay ye a full bottle o' gin for it too."

Rachel sighed and turned slowly, searching the deck unobtrusively to see if anyone had observed her predicament. Her eyes were drawn back to Jake, who stood square in front of her, picking his yellow teeth with a broom straw in one hand, and shaking a gin bottle in the other.

He was a tall, red-faced sailor with long, sinewy arms. His piercing blue eyes were red-rimmed from the salty air and sun. With a broad jaw set to the side, he ground at his teeth, causing his mouth to gap at one side and the veins to stand out on his thick neck. His short-cropped yellow hair and penetrating gaze gave him the chilling appearance of a fierce Viking who had been too long at sea.

"How about it, wench?" Drawing near Rachel, he reached a firm hand about her small waist.

"No! Leave me alone!" Rachel tried to push him away firmly, placing her hand against his hard chest.

Jake glanced down at the girl's slender fingers and reached

to grasp them in his own. "You ain't sayin' no to ol' Jake, now, are ye?" He pressed her fingers against his bristly cheek. "If y'are—well you're the first fool to do so!" Narrowing his eyes he put his face right up to hers.

Rachel drew back, her eyes widening at the smell of his foul breath against her cheek. "You heard me right, sir—I *am* sayin' no! Now, please go find someone else—there are plenty o' others more willin' than meself!"

"I ain't interested in another, wench. It's you that's caught me eye and it's you I'm tellin' to march yerself below. They won't miss us if we're gone for a bit."

"No!" Rachel pushed furiously away from the sailor, fleeing toward the quarterdeck. The gin bottle spun in the air twice before it fell and exploded onto the deck. Swearing profusely, the sailor lunged for the girl and seized her arm, yanking her back toward him.

"I don't think you understands! You're goin' with me!" Jake gripped Rachel's arms cruelly.

Her head pounding thunderously, Rachel's mind flashed back to the horrid night when Dring had trapped her in the fiery brothel. "No! No! No!" she heard herself scream above Jake's laughter. But the gusting ocean winds muffled her screams, and no one seemed to hear her frantic cries for help.

Jake lifted Rachel and threw the fighting red-haired young woman over his shoulder. She pounded him violently with her fists and kicked him with her feet, desperately trying to free herself. They passed a group of mariners checking the spars and rigging, but the crewmen just laughed as Jake winked at them, and turned back to finish their task, their minds callous to the complaints of another worthless convict.

As they approached the companionway, Rachel took a deep breath and with tears streaming down her face shrieked, "Help me, please—someone!"

"Hessler!" A shout rang behind them.

Jake whirled around while Rachel screamed again. His eyes met suddenly with the marine officer Brock Chaney.

"Yes, sir"—he eyed Chaney defensively. "Did you need me fer somethin'?"

191

"I don't think the woman wishes to go with you," Brock confronted Hessler boldly.

"She's a bit feisty, Corporal, but I'll have her submitted in a bit."

Brock shook his head. "No, Hessler. Put her down—now!"

Jake's eyes narrowed as he gripped Rachel's legs more tightly, almost threateningly. "You wants to go with Jake, don't you, lass? Tell Corporal Chaney you does!"

"No!" Rachel shouted. "Put me down!"

Brock folded his arms across his chest, his feet planted squarely. "*Now*, Hessler!" he commanded. Hearing the confrontation, curious mariners and convicts gathered behind him.

Muttering under his breath, Jake bent and slid Rachel off his shoulder, dumping her in a heap on the deck. As he did so, he glared into her face and hissed, "No one gets away with crossin' Hessler! I'll kill you fer this, wench!"

"What's that, Hessler?" Chaney stepped toward Hessler and gently took Rachel's arm, drawing her beside him. Then pointing toward the hatchways he ordered, "Go and swab the cells, Hessler—all of them! And when you're finished—"

Hessler glared at Rachel again and then back at Chaney, "Yes, sir?"

"Do it again!"

Jake Hessler stormed toward the hatchways as a grinning mariner handed him a mop.

Brock turned Rachel toward him and dropped his hands to his sides. "You'd best stay clear of the man. He's as rough as they come and I can't be around every minute of the day."

Rachel looked into the handsome face she had tried so many nights to shake from her thoughts. "I don't know how to thank you Corporal Chaney. I . . ." Rachel hesitated when her eyes met with the corporal's.

"It's only my duty. Nothing more." Chaney was determined to keep his distance with the convicts, and had been successful thus far in doing so. "I must take leave now, Miss Langley."

Rachel smiled. "Miss Langley" sounded so . . . respectable.

Looking into her eyes, Brock shook his head. "Good day. Excuse me, Miss Langley." He turned and walked quickly away as Rachel stood looking after him in bewilderment.

Rachel turned slowly to fall into line while the guards began counting heads and reshackling the women's limbs. She watched Brock disappear around the forecastle. The corporal was so different from the other men. Certainly nothing like the Jake Hesslers of the world who regarded women as chattel, to be taken at will. She felt unworthy even talking to the man, because in her view he was too good for her. *Who is there for me?* she wondered. Her former choices had pushed her too far over the edge. All she could see beyond her horizon was deeper despair.

The clouds looming overhead, Rachel turned to go back to her cell, but stopped abruptly at seeing Hessler eyeing her while grabbing a swab and descending the companionway. Perhaps Jake was the best that life had to offer her.

"Please stay away from him, Rachel. He's a dangerous man, that one." Betsy stood with her arms wrapped about herself.

"You're right about Jake, Betsy," Rachel nodded. "But what can I do? Do I 'ave to be Jake's woman or die if I'm not?"

"Don't say such things, Rachel. That man makes me shudder." Betsy wiped her moist face. "I felt so helpless. I prayed for God to send an angel to save you."

Rachel mused, "Maybe 'e did, Betsy—maybe 'e didn't."

"I choose to believe He did."

Rachel shrugged. "How do you know?"

"You're safe, aren't you?"

Rachel kept her face away from the hatch where Jake stood leering. She couldn't bear to look at him again. "Not for long, I vow." She adjusted her chains and made her way back down the ladder into her cell. "There's no hope left in this place, Betsy. I'd be better off just givin' in."

The older woman squeezed a cold, wet cloth between her fingers. Holding it over Amelia Prentice's hot forehead, she pressed it gently into her brow as Amelia gasped and held her abdomen.

"There now, Amelia, take a deep breath and draw on this other rag." She held another cloth in her hand that had been soaked in wine. "This'll help ye with the pain—not too much now."

Amelia drew the cloth between her lips and sucked gently to squeeze the moisture into her dry mouth. "I'm so thirsty, Ollie!" She turned to the side, her face contorting as she grabbed her stomach.

The old woman moved to the foot of the bed. "I've delivered many babies in my day, Amelia, I have. Just be calm now. Everything'll be just fine. You'll see."

Amelia shook her head, her sweat-soaked hair sticking to her cheeks. "No, Ollie! You don't understand! Somethin' ain't right!" Her body began to shake violently.

"I'll be the judge o' that, now, missy." Ollie Feldman carefully checked Amelia to see how the birth was progressing. After examining her, she stood with a perplexed frown and slowly brought her eyes up to meet Amelia's.

"What? What is it?" Amelia asked between short breaths.

"Baby's breech, I'm afraid. Nothin' I kin do but wait. If it doesn't turn soon . . ." She sighed and sat on a stool at the foot of the cot, staring down at her own two feet.

The ship's surgeon, Arthur Bowes Smythe, stepped into the sickroom to check on Amelia and the three ailing convicts with her. "I've arranged another room for these sick women, Ollie. We'll move them out of here so this woman can have her baby without all this disease around."

"She may not be havin' it anytime soon, Dr. Smythe."

"What's wrong?"

"Breech, sir."

Dr. Smythe examined Amelia and found Ollie to be correct in her assessment. He sighed heavily and shook his head.

"No, dear God, no!" Amelia sobbed. "Did I come this far just to have it die inside of me?" She continued praying, muttering quietly while Ollie and a young convict girl attended her with damp cloths and wine.

"If we could stop the labor, we would, Amelia. It's in God's hands now."

Dr. Smythe motioned for a sailor to enter and instructed him to carry out the sick patients one by one. After the last girl was removed, Smythe stood looking ruefully down at

Amelia. "I'm sorry, ma'am. We'll do whatever we can to ease the pain. These things just happen sometimes." Turning, he followed the sailor out the door.

Ollie crawled over onto the empty cot next to Amelia to rest a bit. She had delivered four babies aboard the *Lady Penryhn* so far, with many more pregnant females awaiting delivery before they reached New South Wales. Some of the infants would die of illness, while others would likely waste away from starvation. Perhaps if this child died in the womb, it would be a blessing from God, for the sake of the poor baby as well as for the mother. She reached to untie the scarf that covered her gray braided hair and held it tightly in her long bony fingers. Ollie sighed and closed her eyes to catch a few moments' sleep to strengthen her for the long night ahead.

17

KISS OF THE ISLAND MOON

"Land ho!" rang the cries of the seamen posted above the topsails, as the seaport of Santa Cruz de Tenerife stretched before the First Fleet like an oasis, a white line of foam marking the reef. The sailors below whooped and shouted like restless spirits upon sighting the volcanic island dead ahead. Rum hungry and sea weary, the men maneuvered the rigging with eyes to the loam as the sloop *Supply* glided past them effortlessly. In the bay, the surface of the brine was as smooth as a freshwater pond.

"All prisoners report to their cells immediately!" the lieutenants barked imperatively, while the marines shoved the reluctant convicts back into their holds and began barring the hatchways. "Any convicts caught out of their cells once landfall is made will be flogged severely!" The orders continued until the cells were filled with the grumbling exiles.

Phillip made quick notations, then handed the charts to Lieutenant Bradley, who promptly began storing the navigational records and equipment. Phillip kept daily observances in a logbook, which was to be delivered to the fleet's chronicler, Corporal Watkin Tench, once they made landfall. Tucking the logbook under his arm, Phillip turned to Captain Hunter. "Good work, Captain!" Phillip shook the officer's hand vigorously as the two of them gazed toward the island.

"I'll be grateful to step foot on dry land again, sir." Hunter smiled at Phillip, who nodded. "Too bad we can't colonize the Canary Islands, eh, Commander?"

Phillip chuckled, seemingly at ease, and replied dryly, "No, Hunter. I believe it's been done already."

Hunter smiled. " 'Twas just a thought, sir." The two glanced at each other silently, chuckling under their breath for a moment before fixing their eyes once again on the shore, where a party of island greeters awaited them. The coconut palms lining the beach appeared to be standing proudly at the water's edge, admiring their reflections in the lapping water. As the crew of the *Sirius* scrambled to dock at the port of Santa Cruz, Phillip gave last-minute instructions to his personal staff. "Gertie, keep an eye on all the women and never travel alone without an escort. Try to stock up on as much fresh meat and vegetables as possible."

Pacing through the commander's cabin, making notations as he spoke, Gertie nodded, "I'll do it, sir. Can't wait to get to market. We'll all be like birds set free from a cage, we will at that, Commander!"

Katy stood obediently behind her mistress. After changing into a simple pink dress and bonnet, she stood eagerly awaiting the opportunity to assist Gertie and Daphne at the Santa Cruz market. She had managed to keep out of trouble since being caught with the rosters by Lieutenant King. Deciding to approach the search for her father more cautiously, she resigned herself to a slower, well-planned strategy. With plenty of free days ahead, she would surely have time to locate Papa. Undaunted in her mission, she quietly schemed while Gertie worked on her needs list. Abiding patiently for the right opportunity would perhaps bring the reward Katy had long awaited.

As the *Sirius* was secured to the dock, Katy stared up at the volcanic peak of Tenerife rising out of the island like a giant cone. Seeing the island surrounded with thick tropical foliage, she felt as though she were being given a glimpse into Eden. Surely she would find the time for exploring this veritable paradise. She was beginning to feel a certain freedom and privilege working under the most important man aboard the First Fleet, and decided she must use it to her advantage.

"Hello, Miss Katy." The rowdy cabin boy, Robert, peered around the door at her. He had passed her many times without so much as tipping his cap to her, but now he spoke with familiarity. He was a tall boy of fourteen with long, reddish brown curls that bounced as he energetically bounded around the deck, running errands for the officers. His complexion had tanned to a golden bronze under the Atlantic sun. Katy had noticed his teeth were white and perfect, usually a sign of privilege and position. But the boy's rough-and-tumble behavior betrayed his common beginnings.

"May I . . . escort Miss Katy, Commander Phillip?"

"I'm goin' with Gertie and Daphne," Katy quickly interjected.

"It's not a bad idea, Sir Robert." Phillip called the boy by the name the sailors had awarded him because of the lad's outlandish ambitions. Phillip studied the boy for a moment. "Keep an eye on these ladies and help them stay out of trouble, will you?"

"Aye, aye, sir!" Robert saluted, his long arms extending several inches beyond his sleeves.

"Commander Phillip?" Lieutenant Bradley appeared quickly.

"Yes, Bradley?" Phillip cleared the top of his desk, locking the papers in a trunk.

"The governor of the Canary Islands has sent a welcoming party to greet us. They're ready to meet you, sir, and they want to give a grand feast for you and all the officers tonight."

"Oh?" Phillip rolled his eyes. "We'll be ready for some island food, now, won't we?"

Robert held out his elbow to Katy, who walked briskly past him, her nose to the clouds.

Amelia ran her hands over her abdomen while Ollie and

Sybil packed some blankets under her shoulders.

"It's a bloomin' miracle is what it is . . . that's what!" Ollie exclaimed as she shook her gray head. "Never saw a baby turn around so fast like that, I ain't."

Amelia laughed shakily and gave in to the urge to push.

"That's it, love!" Ollie encouraged, taking her place on the stool at Amelia's feet. "You can do it with all your might now. Push!" she commanded loudly.

Tears streaming from her eyes, Amelia strained, pushing as hard as she could to free the baby from her body.

"Ye has a fighter, ye has, Mrs. Amelia!" Sybil smiled and dabbed Amelia's forehead again as she had done all night and all morning.

"Lass! I see the head o' the child. . . ."

"Is it a boy or girl, Miss Ollie?" Sybil asked naively as Ollie shook her head at the girl incredulously.

"Give us a few minutes, Sybil!"

Amelia gripped the rails of the bed so tightly Sybil thought the bed would surely bend. Her lips white, Amelia bared her teeth and held her breath as the baby's shoulders appeared, followed by the tiny hands and then the perfect feet. Amelia pushed and cried out so loudly her voice was heard across the deck of the *Lady Penrhyn*.

"God! He's yours!" she cried unrestrainedly.

Ollie looked up at Amelia in surprise. "How could she know that?"

"What?" asked Sybil.

"That it's a . . ."

Sybil stood gazing over Ollie's shoulder, her eyes full of wonder as she beheld the tiny Prentice baby. "Look, Mrs. Amelia. It *is* a he, it is! Look at yer fine baby boy!"

Ollie held up the child, slapping his backside vigorously. With a gasp and a sputter the baby expelled a lusty wail and filled his lungs with his first breath of air.

Amelia laughed as relief flooded her mind with joy. "Oh!" she cried. "Let me hold him! Let me hold little Caleb."

After washing the infant carefully with a soft cloth and wrapping him in a towel, Ollie handed a vigorously kicking, blue-eyed Caleb Prentice to his proud mother.

"Oh, Ollie! He looks like his big sister, Katy! Look at the soft, golden hair." Amelia stroked the top of his head tenderly.

"He's beautiful, Mrs. Amelia." Sybil wiped her eyes and handed a rag to Ollie, who had to do the same.

"Where are we, Ollie? I don't even know where me child's been born."

"We just landed in the Canary Islands, lass, just before sunset. He's an island baby, he is!"

Amelia stroked the small nose and the little ears sticking out on the sides just like George's. "Oh, George Prentice! Where are you?" she lamented, slowly tucking the infant at her breast to feed. "Sybil, see if I can get another message to Commander Phillip."

"I'll try, Mrs. Amelia. But the captain o' this ship thinks you're crazy in the head fer tryin' to speak to the commander."

"Per'aps I am, Sybil. I'm sure George has long forgotten about me." Amelia pulled Caleb close to her side. "Maybe it's time to put the past behind us, dear love," she whispered to the wriggling infant.

Far above the tiki torches, the dark gold moon was fixed in the summer sky like a celestial ornament, hanging over the tall volcano of Tenerife. With the ships snugged down in the small port, the sound of laughter and drumbeats could be heard as the guests of the Sicilian-born governor were lavished with food and entertainment. Above an open pit in which two butchered pigs sizzled over the fire, smoldering wisps of smoke spiraled through the banana trees, draping the air with mouth-watering aromas. In a cleared sandy area five native women danced barefoot to drum music as the governor sat next to Commander Phillip, conversing and laughing.

At a fruit-laden table stretched under the trees, officers of the First Fleet reclined and gazed upon the dancing women, fascinated by their dark skin, exotic eyes, and glistening black hair. The officers' heads nodded hypnotically to the rhythm of the drums and the shaking, rustling grass skirts.

Two large rocks, graced with palms on either side, served as twin backdrops to the festivities, offering a perfect lean-to for an officer who was already ailing from overeating and overdrinking. Steadying himself against one of the rocks, the man turned and staggered back to the feast while a figure hidden in the shadows sat motionless.

Peering out cautiously to see that her presence had not been detected, Katy Prentice sighed with much relief. Earlier, she had tiptoed down the gangway after assuring herself that Gertie and Daphne had fallen soundly asleep. After having spent an afternoon watching the servants haggle with the street merchants over the price of onions and Canary wine, Katy had waited with quiet anticipation. As she had suspected would happen, the ladies had collapsed on their berths, scarcely taking the time to change into their nightgowns. Wearing a pair of small trousers that had been left out on a barrel to dry, Katy tucked her hair inside a sailor cap and slipped away undetected, disguised as a cabin boy. Following after one of the officers who lagged behind, she crept a safe distance from the man as the island birds fussed overhead. After crossing a bridge constructed of palm trees stretched side by side, she had found a hiding place in the cleft of the rocks.

Katy sniffed the delicious aroma of the roasting pork. Watching the stout governor kick back in his chair and gnaw on a leg bone, she wondered how she might snitch a taste of the food for herself. He was a dark-skinned man who slumped in a heavy, ungainly attitude, his great belly thrust forward and his plump legs set widely apart.

Settling back between the two large rocks, Katy had just resigned herself to the fact that observation would be her only amusement, when a hand slipped quickly around her mouth. Yanking her from between the rocks, two strong hands carried the girl several feet away and dropped her beneath a tree.

Katy swung in the dark at the figure, who wouldn't release her until she promised not to scream.

"It's me," said the voice. "Robert!" The boy stood before her clad only in a pair of frayed trousers.

"Are you daft?" Katy whispered in an agitated tone. "I

thought I was bein' kidnapped or somethin' like!"

"You *were* kidnapped, Miss Prentice! Shanghaied by a pirate," Robert answered with mock wickedness. "And I'm Pirate Robert who's demandin' the ransom!"

"What are you doin' out 'ere? You're supposed to be aboard the ship asleep!"

"So are you!" Robert retorted, crossing his arms in a patronizing fashion. "So here we both are, Miss Prentice . . . on a deserted island. What shall we do for sport?"

"It's not deserted and I *was* havin' great sport until you came along to spoil it all!"

"Tut, tut, my dear Lady Katherine. The sport has just begun!"

Katy turned away so as not to reveal the smile she wore as she observed the handsome young boy jumping through the air, waving his invisible sword. "Well, I'm not stayin' out here with the likes o' you, I'm not!" Katy rejoined. "I've better things to do with me time."

"Like what?" Robert dropped his arms to his side and took a place on the ground beside Katy.

"Like sneakin' back to me bed before Gertie finds me missin'. She might beat me . . . or worse!" Katy's eyes grew large at the exaggeration.

"Beat you? Why I'd never hear of it! I'd . . . I'd . . ."

"You'd what?" Katy smiled coyly.

"I'd have to tell you a story. That's what!" Robert stared curiously up at the moon, which seemed to sink behind the black outline of the banana trees, making the sky a dull purple.

"What story?" Katy was suddenly interested.

"A witch doctor told me about it today. It seems the moon over this 'ere island is bewitched by a spell." Robert waved his hand in the air.

"Go on!" Katy shook her head.

"It's true, it is!" Robert's eyes were wide as he spun the tale. "And it can give you good luck if you say the magic words."

"What magic words?" Katy regarded the boy skeptically.

"Oh, they're much too powerful for me just to spill 'em out like that! No, you have to be in the right place and doin' all the right things or . . . it could bring a curse down on me head! I could never do that, I couldn't!" Robert sighed and poked at the ground with a stick. "But you don't believe in spells and such anyway, so—"

"Now, wait a minute!" Katy felt herself growing slightly curious. "Where *is* the right place to be when you . . . say the words an' all that?"

"Where?"

"Come on, Robert! Tell me!"

"Well, it's quite close by, you see. If you stand under that banana tree, I could show you meself." Robert pointed to a stand of trees a few feet away.

Katy looked at him warily. "All right, I'll do it. I'm not afraid of anything, you know!"

"Ooh! Aren't you the brave one!" Robert stood to his feet and reached for Katy's hand.

Pulling her to her feet, Robert tugged Katy along and the two youths ran silently to the banana trees and stood beneath them.

"Now what?" Katy looked up at the grinning boy, silhouetted in the ghostly glow of the far-off torches.

"Now you close your eyes and say these words—Moon, moon, give me good luck!"

"Is that it?" Katy was not impressed.

"That's it! Simple!" Robert placed his hands on his hips, the moonlight glinting on his auburn curls.

Closing her eyes, Katy repeated after him, "Moon, moon, give me good luck!" Waiting in the silence, she slowly opened her eyes and found Robert standing directly in front of her.

"I forgot to tell you somethin', I did, Lady Katherine."

"What now?"

"You have to kiss the moon."

"Kiss the moon? Robert, that's impossible! How could I kiss the blasted moon? It's too far away!"

"That's the enchanted part, you see. That's why this island is so magical an' all. If you stand on your tiptoes, close your eyes and pretend you're kissin' the moon . . . it'll kiss you back!"

Katy sighed with exasperation. "That's it! I'm goin' back to the ship!"

Robert gripped Katy's arm gently and pulled her near him. "I thought you weren't afraid of anything."

"I'm not afraid! This is just . . . foolish!"

Robert's face softened and Katy felt her heart quicken. She turned away, not wanting to read his thoughts. One part of her held tightly to the child within, while another seemed drawn to the early stirrings of womanhood.

"You'll never know if it works or not if you don't try."

Katy eyed the young man and tried to mask her suspicions. Suddenly her lips gave way to a bashful smile and she gazed into Robert's mischievous green eyes. She felt him release her arm and watched as he turned his back to her in disappointment.

Katy sighed. "Oh, all right! If it'll shut you up about all this kissin' the moon business!" She crossed her arms self-consciously at her waist, her lips still graced with a smile. With guarded abandon, she stood up on her toes. Closing her eyes, she chanted the words again, "Moon, moon, give me good luck!" Keeping her eyes tightly shut, Katy drew her lips into an adolescent pucker. A strange emotion, like fear mingled with awe, swept through her as she braced herself for the inevitable. Suddenly she felt a warm breath across her cheek as a set of soft boyish lips pressed against her own. Feeling long arms wrap around her waist, she opened her eyes to find young Robert embracing her. Jerking her face away from his, she felt her cheeks blush and her heart pound against her chest. "Stop! Don't!" She pushed away in embarrassment and shame. What would her mum think?

Robert, still holding the girl in his arms, laughed quietly. "Is this your first kiss?"

"Me first kiss?" Katy sputtered. "Why . . . I would've saved it fer me 'usband if you hadn't stolen it from me! You . . . you highwayman!"

"Stolen!" Robert's eyes glistened, not in a roguish way, but rather like a child who had found a treasure. "You the same as gave it to me. And now I'm a criminal, am I? But I can solve yer problem, I can at that, Lady Katherine."

"How?" Katy asked indignantly.

"Marry me, Lady Katherine! I'll whisk you away to me castle in the sea."

"Marry? You?"

"We'll have servants by the hundreds and twelve children!" Robert tried to whirl Katy around.

"Let me go!" Katy demanded.

Robert looked quietly down at the lovely girl. He hadn't meant to embarrass her so. "I'm sorry, Katy. You're just so . . . so beautiful." He pulled his arms away and Katy dropped back on her heels, still gazing shyly into his eyes. "Will you forgive me, Lady Katherine?"

"All right, Robert." She accepted his apology. "But you have to promise you'll never tell anyone about this . . . it's a secret."

"*Our* secret, Lady Katherine." Robert placed his stout fingers over his heart in oath.

"Now, will you walk me back to the ship? I *will* be in trouble if I don't get back soon."

"I would be honored!" Robert held out his elbow and Katy took it hesitatingly. Beneath the banana trees, the young boy and girl ran through the foliage, down the beach, and to the *Sirius*. The only sound was the ceaseless breaking of the surf as their feet padded up the gangway. Under the shadow of the crossbeam, they bid adieu and slipped quietly into their quarters. Katy glanced over her shoulder to watch her midnight friend disappear into the darkness.

18

SILENT
REPRIEVE

Tossing back its crimson comb, the rooster crowed from its usual perch on the barn just as the pale pink hues of dawn were penetrated by golden fingers of summer sun. But the rural alarm was disregarded by the servants of Stoney Manor, who had been awake for hours after being rudely summoned into the white ballroom by their distraught matron, Emily Breach.

"I'm innocent I tell ye, Mrs. Breach!" Watson stood before Emily Breach, held tightly on either side by two broad groomsmen who stood silent and somber.

Emily Breach let out a long, exasperated sigh and seated herself in a large tufted chair, her maids at either side. Cozette Frye stood with brow furrowed and plump arms crossed, still gripping a feather duster. Shaking her head at the accused thief, Watson, she turned her remarks back to Emily Breach.

"I caught 'im red-handed, I did, Mrs. Breach! I found 'im in me room early this mornin' tryin' to place some o' your silver in me bag, I did." Cozette scowled at Watson. "Tryin' to get *me* blamed for your thievin' ways, now, weren't you?"

Watson glared for a moment at Cozette, then jerked his face around to stare obstinately out the window.

"I'd venture to say, he's been the one gettin' the others arrested all along, Mrs. Breach!" Cozette shook her feather duster at the thief. "Those two maids o' Mrs. Breach's were 'anged fer it. And that poor Prentice woman, her with the little girl an' all, who knows what could've happened to her?"

Emily Breach bit her lip. How many servants had she fired for this man's offenses? "Is Cozette correct, Watson? Did you allow the others to take your punishment?"

Watson stared silently at the floor, refusing to answer the accusations.

"Want me to blow 'is head off, Mrs. Breach?" Jiggs stood with a loaded musket aimed at Watson's jaw.

"No, Jiggs. Let the authorities do their duty with the man. You men take him into town while Jiggs holds the gun to him." Emily turned back to Cozette. "You'd best go with them. You're the witness, Cozette."

The ladies' maid curtsied. "Yes, ma'am. I'll change right quick out o' me apron."

Emily raised herself from the chair and dismissed the servants before retiring quietly to her study. Watching through the great oak doorway until she was certain the servants had all gone about their business, Emily turned and closed the door. Seating herself at her late husband's desk, she fidgeted first with the cameo at her throat and then smoothed her emerald green skirt. Reaching slowly for the quill, she hesitated and let her hand rest on the desk top, making nervous circles with her index finger. It was all Watson's fault the Prentice woman had been transported. Emily Breach sighed loudly. "How I hate being a party to his contrivances!"

She picked up the quill pen with her thin, chalky fingers and pulled a sheaf of ivory paper from her desk drawer. Resting her forehead against her hands for a moment, she deliberated upon how she should word the letter to her nephew, Commander Arthur Phillip. Although a servant was not considered a high priority in Emily's caste system, she did feel the wording should justify her error in order to maintain a certain amount of family integrity. Suddenly the encouraging thought struck her that the embarrassing letter might never reach her nephew. Either way, her obligation would be fulfilled. "No," she muttered to herself, "the wrong must be righted." Placing the quill to the paper, the words began to spill from the pen's tip as she resigned herself to her duty. However long it took the letter to reach her nephew, if indeed it ever did reach him, the Prentice woman would have to be pardoned. Emily purposefully dipped the pen in the indigo ink again and addressed her letter to the commander of the Botany Bay Expedition.

◈

"Do we have the search party arranged, Lieutenant King?" Phillip looked up from his desk.

King leaned over Phillip's chair, his eyes weary. "Aye, aye, sir. We think the convict's been missing since last night, sir. He can't have gone far, though. No one around Tenerife wants to give aid to a criminal."

"What was his name again? Power?"

"Yes, John Power."

"Have officer Tench make a note of Power's escape, will you?"

"He's doing so now, I believe, Commander."

"Very well, then. You *will* keep me posted of any further news, I trust?"

Lieutenant King dismissed himself. "Yes, sir."

Phillip scribbled a brief note in his diary while at the same time on the *Charlotte*, Corporal Watkin Tench chronicled not only the escape of the prisoner, but highlights of the First Fleet's week in Tenerife as well. As he noted the supplies they had taken on and blotted the page, Brock Chaney entered the doorway, sucking the juicy pulp out of a bright green lime.

"Taking your daily dose of medicine?" Tench asked absently.

"Scurvy's not my favorite bedmate. Have the prisoners been given their antiscorbutics?" Chaney asked, hefting a large sack of citrus under his broad arm.

Watkin Tench shook his head. "Not today."

"I'll take these to them, then. I've been asked to keep an eye on the prisoners while the search party scours the port."

Heading for the convicts' hold, Chaney approached the guards. A lethargic guard on duty nodded to the officer. "Yes, Corporal, what kin I do fer ye?"

"Pass these out to the convicts, will you? I've come to relieve you for a bit. I'm certain you'd like to be freed from these females for a while."

"I would at that, Corporal!" The mariner laughed. "I've tried to live wif three of 'em in me lifetime and I kin tell ye they's all trouble!"

Chaney noticed the hatches were open. He could hear the females below complaining and fighting with one another. Sighing at the thought, Brock reached into the bag and stuffed some of the fruit into his pockets. "Better save a few of these for myself."

After taking the citrus from Chaney, the guard walked with it down to the last hatch and began doling out the fruit.

Rachel Langley sat cross-legged on the hard floor of her small cubicle tending to Faye Flannery, who had weakened during the voyage. "Don't fret, Faye. They're bringin' us somethin' good to eat. We'll be eatin' like kings soon."

Betsy lay curled up against the wall. Fatigue had overtaken her and she was sleeping soundly.

The sickly older woman moaned. "Just let me die. I feel like I'm in a bad dream an' I can't wake up, Rachel."

Fearing that Mrs. Flannery was growing gradually worse, she sighed. "Should we send word to your family?"

"I don't 'ave no other family. Me 'usband died a few months before me arrest. That's why I was stealin' to begin with."

"I'm sorry." Rachel struggled with words as she sought to speak comfort to the old woman. "Maybe Charles is in a better place now, Faye."

"Knowin' Charles . . . not likely." A tear coursed down her cheek. Grasping Rachel's hand she asked, "Where's your family, Rachel?"

Rachel sat silently, unsure of her answer. "I don't know. They're scattered to the wind, I vow. I'll probably never know."

Rachel grew still and seemed to reflect upon a matter. "What happens when there's no one left to mourn us?"

Faye gazed from lifeless eyes and spoke darkly. "We cease to exist."

Rachel dabbed her wet forehead. "I suppose that would make a lot o' sense, now wouldn't it? But still—"

"What? What hope is there, Rachel?"

"I don't know," Rachel shrugged. "What makes me keep goin', Faye? Why haven't I given up?"

"Somethin' *I* can't see, that's for certain."

Rachel contemplated the old woman's words intently, searching through her ramblings for a grain of truth in them. "Somethin' we can't see," she whispered.

A pounding sound startled their conversation as bright green limes rained down abruptly upon them, tumbling around their feet.

Rachel frowned up at the sailor who stood tossing the fruit down into the hold. "Careful now! We've a sick lady down 'ere!" she scolded.

"Shut up, wench! You think I want to spend me whole day playin' nursemaid to an old crow?"

Rachel felt anger rage through her. Her fists clenched as she rose to her feet.

"Don't say nothin' on account o' me, Rachel," Faye pleaded mutely, her lips parting to one side. "I'm dyin' anyhow. I ain't worth it."

Rachel gazed piteously down at the older woman before giving the sailor an angry look. "Worth! Who decides what any of us are worth?"

Faye lay still, her eyes closed in a futile effort to seek a peaceful rest. With a heavy sigh, she answered hoarsely, "Whoever 'olds us prisoner, Rachel." Her abject tone faded as she fell into restless slumber.

"She has a valid point." A different voice spoke from the hatchway.

Rachel looked up to find Brock Chaney had sent the sailor on his way.

"Whoever or *whatever* holds us prisoner, that is," he added with a sardonic smile.

Rachel straightened her prison frock as best she could. Seeing the corporal made her feel self-conscious of her homely apparel. "What would you know of bein' a prisoner, Corporal Chaney?" She swallowed nervously, for impertinence could bring a punishment of ten lashes.

"We're all slaves to something."

Rachel nodded warily. "Some places is worse than others, I vow. This'n's the worst one I know of."

"Oh, everyone has their own private hell with which to contend."

Rachel's brow furrowed upon hearing Chaney's cynical philosophies. "I don't think that's true of everyone, sir."

"No?"

"Some people has it easy."

"Or so they say."

"I wouldn't know about that as much. I only know what I sees."

Chaney chuckled. "You haven't learned yet to read the soul, Miss Langley."

Rachel shrugged. "I don't know. I've never given it much thought." She smiled and relaxed as the young corporal laughed. The corporal had such a nonthreatening tone that Rachel felt drawn to his words. She was lonely and hungered for normal conversation.

"I'll bet you think about a lot more than you realize, Rachel." Brock crossed his arms at his chest. He seemed to regard Rachel with a sympathetic gaze. "I need some of the healthier women to store away the food in the bosun's stores."

"I suppose that means me." Rachel sighed before bending down to freshen Faye's face towel with water from a bucket. "I'll be back to tend to you, Faye. Why not try layin' on your side? It'll 'elp you breathe better, I believe."

"Betsy, wake up." She nudged her slumbering friend.

Betsy awoke, startled by Rachel's prodding. It was common to be awakened by disgruntled sailors for head count and rations. Convicts who were too slow to respond often paid a high price. "What is it, Rachel?" she asked, rubbing her eyes.

"We 'as to load some citrus in the stores. Corporal Chaney

wants us to go up top quick like."

As the younger convict women climbed out of the holds, Rachel stepped onto the deck and stretched, gazing out toward the harbor. The beach had only a sprinkling of sailors, some hoisting large sticks bearing stalks of bananas, while others carried crates of flour and other staples. Most of the officers were either away at the Santa Cruz market stocking up on more food and wine, or enjoying the sudden break in monotony with the manhunt.

Brock led the females starboard where the citrus was being brought aboard. "All of you gather the containers and follow Corporal Tench to the stores."

Rachel followed the corporal's instructions. He wasn't as harsh as the others and was a natural leader, one who was easy to follow. Her thoughts became occupied with the handsome marine officer, and the notion of conversing with him again gladdened her heart.

"Aye, aye, Captain Aimsley!" Chaney saluted and stood to attention as the captain of the *Lady Penrhyn* strode by. Glancing at the corporal with admiration, Rachel then quickly cast her eyes down at the deck. "Rachel, why don't you take these bushels of citrus over here and carry them below?" Chaney asked politely.

"Yes, sir." Rachel found herself curtsying rather awkwardly.

"I'll help," Betsy answered. "Rachel, we can talk on the way."

As the two women grasped either side of the heavy bushel and began to carry it, Rachel couldn't help but notice Betsy's marked concern. "What's wrong, Betsy?"

"You were talking with that Corporal Chaney in the hold, weren't you, Rachel?"

"I thought you were asleep."

Betsy's eyes grew wide but were full of sincerity. "I was asleep. I promise you that, really. But with all the commotion, I couldn't help but be roused. You're fond of him, aren't you?"

"I told you before, an' nothin's changed with me . . . I won't be used by a man again. But I'm not tryin' to gain his affections if that's what you mean, Betsy."

"I didn't say you were, did I? I wouldn't be a friend if I didn't warn you to be careful. Even the nice-looking ones will use you, if you don't watch out."

"Corporal Chaney talks to me. If ever I could pick me friends, I'd pick one like him, Betsy. He's right intelligent, that one. Knows about a lot o' different things, he does. Why, he's the type that could sit down an' talk wif a cockney girl like me an' then turn around an' have a conversation with King George himself, if he had a mind to."

"Rachel, how could you know all those things about the man? You haven't known him for very long, and if you'll listen, you'll find he really says very little. I know . . . I grew up with men like him."

"There you go puttin' on your airs again, Betsy. I wish I could make one decision that you agreed with, I do." Rachel was growing disconcerted with Betsy, who always seemed to have an immediate opinion and a ready answer.

Betsy's brow furrowed as she cast off her defenses. "I'm sorry, Rachel. I didn't intend to sound judgmental. I know I'm no better than anyone else on this fleet. No one knows that fact better than I do. It's by God's grace that I grew up in such an educated family myself."

Setting down the heavy bushel basket, her arms akimbo, Rachel turned to stare at Betsy. "I suppose me own lot, then, was due to God's anger?"

"That isn't so, either. But as time goes on, perhaps I can help you understand. Pain is like an uninvited educator. It teaches us to choose our destinies more carefully. Not only do we suffer, but our children suffer as well."

Rachel lifted the basket again and they continued on toward the storeroom. Rachel contemplated Betsy's admonition, pondering the wisdom of her words. Of course Rachel knew her own life was the product of many generations making poor choices. But why had Betsy been thrown into this place of torment? "Why are you here, Betsy? Why can't you tell me?"

"Rachel, people have died trying to help me."

"I don't care. I've nothin' to lose. Tell me, Betsy . . ." Rachel's face softened. ". . . please?"

Betsy sighed heavily. She pulled Rachel into a dark corner where they wouldn't be seen, then set the basket down again. Slowly, she reached for the ragged scarf and began to untie it from around her neck. "But you have to promise me you'll never breathe a word."

"I swear it, Betsy. I'm your friend, ain't I?"

Pulling the worn scarf away from her throat, Betsy's face grew sorrowful. Her bared neck was marred by a reddened scar that completely encircled it.

"What's happened to you?" Rachel questioned with concern.

"I was a political offender. When my widowed mother died, I was taken in by her husband's family. My step-uncle was a ruthless magistrate who used his power to feed his own greed." Hearing someone approaching, the two women hurried on with the bushel of fruit. Rachel followed Betsy down the dark stairwell, fascinated by the intrigue of her story.

"He was involved with every political figure in London. Somehow, he even had connections with the contractor of this fleet. I slipped away one night and followed him on horseback to one of his midnight rendezvous, and that's where I saw all of them—merchants and politicians involved in a clandestine operation. They met in the back of a pub . . . there were lots of women about. When Uncle left, he disappeared into a brothel and I fled back to our home." Betsy guided the bushel into the dimly lit storage room, where Tench was making note of the inventory.

Rachel waited for Corporal Tench to disappear up the stairwell again. "Did you tell his wife?" She helped place the bushel of fruit next to the others and began meeting the convicts at the door to take the next load from each female.

"No. But I threatened to inform the authorities if he didn't change his ways. He promised to end his meetings with the merchants, but that was just his way of delaying it all until he devised a new plan."

"What plan?"

"A plan to involve me in a political plot to spy on the British government. I was accused of being a spy for France."

"That's insane, Betsy!"

"Yes, but my uncle had the power to do it. I knew too much about him and could implicate too many important people."

"What happened? Did you report him?"

"I tried, but every effort failed. As a last resort I tried to inform my aunt. She wouldn't . . . or couldn't believe me. She enjoyed her place in society too much to risk losing it. The next day I was arrested, and I never heard from my family again. I wasn't even allowed to say goodbye to my sisters."

"So they transported you?"

"Transportation wasn't part of Uncle's strategy. I was sentenced to hang. He wanted to be completely rid of me. But something went wrong."

Rachel studied the pinkish wound around Betsy's neck. "You lived?"

Betsy nodded, her eyes grave. "Now you know . . . the Lord spared me, Rachel. I know He did. He has something in store for me. God's plans are always greater than our own."

"I wish I could feel that way, Betsy."

"Let's hurry it up, ladies." Brock Chaney's familiar lilt was heard from the stairwell.

Noticing Rachel's anxious eyes, Betsy crossed her arms at her waist and looked sideways at her friend. "Give it some time, Rachel. Don't be anxious for anything. I want the best for you, but people can't satisfy our need for happiness. If you think that's so . . . I'm afraid you'll be disappointed."

As the women stepped back up onto the deck, Captain Aimsley approached Chaney and Tench. "If you'll return these prisoners to their cells and batten down the hatches, I'll need every man on deck to join us in the manhunt. Commander Phillip wants Power caught before nightfall."

Chaney saluted and walked abruptly forward, his face still turned toward the captain. Suddenly he felt his shoulder collide with another, and turning he apologized. "Oh, excuse me, Rachel." His eyes met with the convict girl's.

Rachel swallowed nervously. She wanted to prove Betsy wrong. She could avoid trouble, if need be, for she was strong-willed and determined. But the corporal drew her in with his eyes. They were merciless and beautiful.

"Won't you need some of us to watch the convicts, sir?"

Chaney asked of Captain Aimsley, his eyes still fixed on Rachel.

"I've already taken care of that situation, Chaney. Boswell and another sailor are standing guard while the navy searches for the escapee."

Chaney nodded. "Yes, sir."

"Shall we go, then?"

Chaney saluted absentmindedly, seemingly transfixed by the red-haired convict girl. "Aye, aye, sir," he all but whispered.

Rachel moved away, her cheeks on fire.

The corporals busied themselves assisting the females back into their cells. Rachel glanced sideways in Chaney's direction. His face had resumed the cool, professional demeanor of an officer. Then he turned to face her again, as though he remembered something.

"Rachel," he said quietly to her.

"Yes?" She turned to face the corporal again. A hopeful smiled graced her lips.

"I'm sorry to say, they notified us a moment ago that Mrs. Flannery has just passed on."

"Hurry it up, men! We don't have all day." Aimsley was growing impatient.

His duty plain, Chaney prodded the women with the handle of his whip. "Let's hurry, prisoners," he said flatly, his countenance assuming a melancholy stare. He assisted Rachel into her hold, his grip on her arm like that of a jailer.

Rachel climbed into the dark cubicle with rejection and despair descending upon her. The cold reality began to set in that nothing ever improved on a transport . . . it only grew worse. *Poor Faye.*

How foolish for me to dream of having Brock Chaney, she chided herself. She didn't mean anything to him. She was just one of many convicts.

Climbing slowly down, Rachel leaped from the last rung of the ladder and landed on the hard floor next to a sleepily yawning Betsy. Mrs. Flannery's body had already been removed. Nothing remained but the old scarf she had gripped in her hand. Rachel hadn't bothered to ask why, but there lay the scarf without a trace of history to its credit.

"Are you all right, Rachel?" Betsy's voice sounded weary.

"Why shouldn't I be?" Rachel answered evenly.

"It isn't just Faye, is it, Rachel? It's Corporal Chaney too."

"It's useless anyhow. Just like everythin' else."

"What's goin' on?" Cally called sleepily from her corner of the cell.

"Nothing, Cally. Go back to sleep," Betsy answered.

"Why don't you all quieten down then so's I can get some sleep?" Cally's tone was less than genteel.

Rachel and Betsy watched the hatchway close overhead, turning their day into another long night. Rachel had tried to catch a quick glimpse of Corporal Chaney, but the officer never bothered to look back, leaving her with nothing but the memory of a screeching gray albatross that had passed quickly overhead just before the sunlight was extinguished. "I suppose we've nothin' left to do *but* sleep, Betsy."

"We could talk, Rachel."

"I've nothin' to talk about. Could you leave me to me thoughts, Betsy?"

"Sure." Betsy squatted on the thin mattress and nudged Wanda so she would move over. Settling on the floor, she grew still.

Rachel listened for Betsy's breathing. *How can that girl be so perfectly content in this horrible place?* Rachel tossed and turned before finally falling into a restless sleep.

19
PRAY FOR DEATH

With the escaped convict captured and flogged, the Botany Bay Expedition left Tenerife behind them and pointed their bows toward the Cape Verde Islands. Loaded down with fresh meat and more liquor, the ships were boosted south-southwest under the relentless northeast trade winds.

"Thar's Port Praia on Sao Tiago off the port bow, Captain!" the lookout cried from the crow's nest, pointing to the peak of an island just appearing southeast of the fleet.

A surly jack-tar labored with the sails. "With this wind we can't make easting, sir!"

The mates strained at the capstan, their muscles stretched tautly as they battled against the adverse winds beyond the reefs of the Cape Verde Islands. "We're hove down to the hatches, sir!" a sailor shouted to Captain John Hunter.

Hunter glanced up at the canvas, the three sails, unfurled and fast under double gaskets, were threatening to blow loose as they pulled from the yards. "We're struggling to change to starboard tack, Commander Phillip. We can't bring 'er about, sir!"

Commander Phillip stood beside his second captain, vigilantly watching the striving efforts of his crew. Hunter's voice rang out the vain commands as the wind continued to slant the flotilla in the wrong direction. Phillip's eyes narrowed as he stood windward of the men struggling at the wheel. He could feel the entire ship being shaken to her timbers under the constant barrage of slab-sided waves.

Not wanting to take unnecessary risks, Commander Phillip made a quick mental assessment of their stores and shook his head at Hunter. "We'll not make easting today, Hunter. May as well head 'er on to Rio de Janeiro."

"Jibe about!" Hunter shouted while the yellow and black signal flag was raised to indicate their change of course.

As the Cape Verde Islands disappeared from their stern, the flagship led the expedition with three reefs in the foresail, and a goose-wing spanker sailing before the northeast wind like a kite.

"Aren't we goin' to Cape Verde, Commander?" Katy had positioned herself against the bulwark on the starboard side.

"No, I'm afraid the sea is an unfaithful wife. The winds aren't in our favor today, Little Kate."

Katy tried to pull her hair back into a ribbon as the wind whipped around her blond locks. She was somehow relieved they weren't making landfall again. When Commander Phillip was involved with loading up more supplies, he didn't have time to speak with her. She watched him stroll across the deck. "Commander Phillip?"

Phillip stopped and looked at the girl. "Yes? What is it?"

"I need to talk to you, sir. If you have a moment, that is?"

Phillip nodded. "Go on."

"It's about me papa, sir." Katy took a deep breath. She realized the commander's opinion of her was probably about to change. "He's not dead. I never told your aunt that he was, though. I swear it, Commander, I do."

"Not dead?" Phillip eyed Katy, his face perplexed. "But where is he? Why did you wait to tell me?"

"I was afraid to, sir. You see me father is . . . a convict, sir.

I needed the work and thought perhaps you wouldn't hire me if you knew."

"So your mother and father are both . . ."

"Convicts, sir. Please believe me, though, when I tell you . . . they ain't bad people. Me mum would never steal from your aunt. I even tried to catch the real thief, but he got away."

"I see. Well, my aunt believed she had evidence."

"I know, sir. With all due respect to Mrs. Breach, she was tricked, I believe."

"I'm sorry you feel that way, Katy. Were they hanged?"

"No, sir. At least not me papa. I believe he's aboard one o' these ships. I found his name on a roster, sir."

"My roster?"

Biting her lip, Katy nodded.

"Well, let's go look it up. Let's be certain!"

Katy beamed. "Thank you, sir!"

Scarcely able to contain her elation, Katy attempted to stand quietly beside the commander in the cabin. She couldn't believe that he hadn't gotten upset with her at all and that he actually was going to help her. "Thank you, God," Katy breathed.

Phillip perused several of the lists until he found the rosters with the male transports. "What is his name, Katy?"

"Mr. George Prentice." How Katy enjoyed speaking forth that name so openly. She had hidden from her past for so long that her papa's name all but sounded foreign to her.

"Look here." The commander pointed to a name on the *Scarborough* roster. "Could this be your father?"

Katy read the name George Prentice and smiled. "I just know he's me papa, sir!"

Phillip sighed. "When we reach Rio de Janeiro, I'll arrange for the two of you to meet."

Katy was mystified. It had been too easy. How much longer would she have had to wait if she hadn't trusted the commander? "I'll get to be with Papa?"

"You may visit with him for a bit. You can't actually stay with him. Remember, he's a prisoner. Besides, I feel you're much safer when you're with Gertie and Daphne. They keep careful watch of you."

"I keep careful watch o' Lady Katherine, too!" Robert appeared from around the cabin entrance.

Katy turned with a start to see the cabin boy had been listening. "Oh, Robert!" Her face was full of excitement. "You'll never guess! I'm goin' to find Papa!" she beamed joyously.

Robert smiled upon seeing the approval in Katy's eyes. He held out his arms to the girl, who hugged him warmly. "Good. Then I can ask fer your 'and in marriage, I can!"

"What's this?" Phillip's brow arched.

Katy shook her head at the commander. "Oh, nothin', sir. We're just friends. He's bein' foolish is all!"

"I don't mean we'll marry right away. First I has to make me fortune in this world. Then I'll be so rich, you'll be beggin' me to marry you."

Phillip laughed ruefully as Katy stood with her hands on her hips.

Rachel stood before Captain Aimsley, her head bowed and fists clenched. "I didn't take it, sir! I can promise you by God Almighty I didn't steal yer watch, sir."

Aimsley paced in front of the convict girl, his gaze stern. He was a sinewy man with sun-darkened skin and cropped gray hair. His brass medals displayed his service to the Crown and his knowledge of war. A gold pocket watch, presented to him years ago by an admiral, had been missing for several days. He had known for some time that the convict women often crawled between the bulkheads at night and prowled around the apartments of the sailors . . . usually looking for company. So it stood to reason, that the watch found on this girl's person had been stolen in the night as he slept. "Why would you defend yourself when the watch was clearly found in your pocket?" he queried harshly.

Rachel shook her head forlornly. "I can't explain it, I tell you. All's I know is that when I was busy with the swab this mornin', I found the watch in me pail. I put it in me pocket fer safe keepin'. I wouldn't have kept it, sir! That sailor, Mops Jernigan, saw me slip it in me pocket. But I ain't a thief!"

The mariners watching from behind Rachel chuckled to one another. The girl had been caught red-handed, and after the trouble she had caused their comrade, Jake Hessler, they were glad of it.

"Quit yer lyin', wench!" Mops hollered, stirring up the other sailors to mock and jeer the girl. Beside him, a sooty, barefoot cabin boy watched in silence.

Hessler stood on the other side of Mops, a scowl defining his face. He spat at the deck and rubbed the snuff from his chin. "Flog 'er, Captain! Teach 'er a lesson!"

The mariners volleyed their approval, shaking their fists and swearing.

"I'm afraid we've no choice, Langley." Captain Aimsley shook his head at Rachel. As much as he had grown to like the girl, he couldn't allow the prisoners to believe they could steal without punishment.

"No! It ain't fair, sir! Please don't flog me!" Rachel, not wanting to cry in front of Hessler, held back the tears, her eyes downcast.

Betsy and Cally, who had stood silently waiting for the verdict, suddenly became verbal. "Captain Aimsley!" Betsy shouted. "I know Rachel, sir. I don't believe she would steal." Betsy defended the girl while Cally nodded her approval.

Aimsley laughed sarcastically at the females. "Not a thief! Why do you think the wench is being transported? For selling oysters?"

The seamen laughed crudely.

"She's changed, sir. Which is more'n I kin say fer meself!" Cally crossed her arms defensively.

"Get these women out of here!" Aimsley ordered. Two brawny marines seized hold of Betsy and Cally.

"What's happened here?" Brock Chaney stopped abruptly, his eyes rapidly assessing the scene. He and Watkin had dashed from their cabins when the sound of angry voices reached them. He could see immediately the triumph in Jake Hessler's eyes.

"It ain't none o' yer concern, Chaney!" Jake barked as he stood surrounded by his cronies.

"She was caught with my pocket watch, Corporal," Aimsley explained. "You know the rules. She has to be flogged!"

Brock studied Rachel's face and shook his head. "I don't believe it. You didn't . . . did you, Rachel?"

"No, Corporal! I promise you I didn't take it!"

Jake mimicked Rachel, batting his lashes. " 'No, Corporal!' Blast it all, Captain! Don't you see what Chaney's up to?"

Rachel took a step toward the forecastle, and then, fear and panic overtaking her, she bolted and ran straight into the wind. The bloody lashings she and her cellmates had frequently witnessed were too gruesome and horrible for her to face. She would rather pray for death than take a flogging.

"Bring her aft!" the captain shouted, and the sailors took off after Rachel, stumbling over one another in eagerness for the new game of chase.

The first mate emerged from the forecastle and stopped dead in front of Rachel while the other men scrambled up behind her and laid hold of her.

Rachel said nothing, but turned her head slowly and stared at Brock with hopeless eyes while the sailors dragged her aft.

"I'll spread-eagle you, wench, fer all the trouble you've caused me!" Jake held Rachel tightly by the face, his coarse hands spread around her face and hair.

Rachel stood glaring back into the hard face of the man she hated so much. She closed her eyes tightly, refusing to acknowledge his depraved presence.

"Don't be all day, Hessler!" the captain barked. "Seize her up!"

Jake Hessler, with the help of the other mariners, shoved Rachel roughly against the shrouds, tying her wrists and feet up tightly to the cables that held the mast in place. Tightly gripping the whip in his hand, the captain took several paces back and swung around halfway so as to deliver the blow with twice the power. Throwing himself around forcefully, he delivered the first lash, followed by a brutal second.

Rachel collapsed in excruciating pain as the sharp leather stripped the fabric from her back.

Gripping the windlass with his shaking hands, Brock slumped forward, helpless. To protest would be mutinous.

Guilt marked his countenance as a third and fourth blow was delivered across the girl's frail back. Only one soft whimper was heard as unspeakable agony followed the racking pain.

"Wait, Captain, sir!" a quiet voice called near the gangway.

Aimsley turned to see the cabin boy standing at his side. "What is it, little John?" He sounded annoyed at the interruption.

"I fear to speak, sir. But I fear God worse to stay silent!"

Hessler stepped toward the lad, his eyes threatening.

"It's him, sir!" Little John pointed at the menacing mariner. "Jake Hessler put your pocket watch in the lady's pail. I saw 'im do it meself, I did, sir!"

"Why didn't you say so sooner, lad?"

"I feared fer me life, sir. Everyone on board the *Charlotte* knows you don't cross Hessler. He'll cut yer throat while's you sleeps, sir, he will!"

"Oh?" Captain Aimsley dropped his arm to his side, the whip still dangling in his sweating grip. "Is that so, Hessler?" he scowled.

"The boy's a liar! Everyone knows how he runs up an' down the ship spreadin' his tales." Hessler eyed the boy directly. "Ain't that right, boy?" he snarled menacingly.

Little John swallowed and shook his head, his eyes full of fear. "No, it ain't true, Jake Hessler! You put Cap'n's watch in the pail just so's you could take revenge on that convict girl . . . all because she shamed you in front o' the others."

"Unlash the convict girl!" Aimsley ordered while the sailors pulled Rachel, bleeding and unconscious, from the shroud. "It's you that'll take the lashes, Hessler!" the captain threatened as Brock Chaney stomped toward Hessler.

Seizing him by his collar, Chaney spun the tall mariner around to face him. "You won't live to take your lashes, Hessler. I'll kill you myself!"

Hessler drew back his fist from under his chest and leaned away from Brock, striking the corporal in the abdomen. The wind knocked from him, Brock recovered quickly and followed with a powerful right hook, launching Hessler across the deck and into the capstan.

The sailors circled eagerly around the battling men, as

though they were witnessing a cock fight. Their loyalties divided, they bantered one another about in a shoving match. Before Hessler could stand to his feet, Brock lunged into the man with his boots, sending the mariner's head reeling against the capstan for a second time.

With blood streaming down his ears and neck, Hessler flew in a fury back in Brock's face. With a swoop of his bloody hand, he pulled a sharp blade from his pocket. "You're dead, Chaney!"

Rachel was coming to and tried to raise herself up from the deck, but crumpled in burning pain. "No, Brock, don't," she whispered as Betsy, freed during the distractions, ran to tend to her wounded friend.

"I'll run fetch water." Betsy gently brushed Rachel's hair from her face, then leaped to her feet.

Rachel lifted her gaze to the sentry seated on a barrel next to her. He cheered first for one man and then the other, boyishly slapping his hand against the pistol that lay at his side.

"Put the knife away!" Captain Aimsley warned Hessler. "You'll hang for it!"

Hessler laughed as he pointed the shiny blade at Brock's throat. "I'll risk it! Just fer the pleasure o' watchin' you squirm!"

"Let it go, Hessler!" one of his buddies called out.

"Shut up, you coward! I'll slaughter the lot o' you." As Hessler drew back his right arm, a shot echoed from across the forecastle. It was a sound that would continue to ring for hours in the ears of all who tried to sleep that night. Like a cannon shot, the bullet tore through Hessler's shoulder, burning dead center into his heart. Hessler stood as rigid as the mainmast that overshadowed his shaven crown. Then his head fell back limply and he collapsed at Brock's feet, the dagger clattering across the wooden surface.

Brock's head snapped up in astonishment. The crew followed his gaze. The circle of bewildered men parted to reveal the one who held the smoldering gun—the final offal of proof.

Rachel held the weapon awkwardly in both slender hands, the tip black and hot from the explosion. Cally, standing beside Betsy, straightened herself and smiled with admiration at the cellmate turned gunslinger. "I didn't know she had it in 'er!" she whispered.

Aimsley, with a worried frown, marched toward Rachel and stood before her. "You've somethin' to say?"

Rachel handed the weapon back to the careless guard who had been so carried away with the brawl he hadn't noticed his pistol was missing. With a sorrowful face, she held up her wrists toward the ship's chief and surrendered. "Arrest me."

"Wait, sir!" Mops called out. "I didn't see anythin'"—he turned to another sailor—"did you?"

"Not me!" the man shook his head. "I didn't see who shot 'im!"

One after another, the mariners stepped forward to confess their ignorance of the whole affair as Rachel sat dauntlessly, her wrists extended before the captain.

Brock wiped his bleeding lip with a stout wrist. "Me neither, sir. I was too busy defending myself."

Captain Aimsley shrugged at the titian-haired girl who had suddenly won the popularity of all aboard the *Charlotte*. Turning toward the bleeding Corporal Chaney, he commented dryly, "I suppose we don't have any witnesses, then, Mr. Chaney. I'll make a note of it in my logbook. Jake Hessler was accidentally shot during a brawl of his own making. The gunman was never discovered." Aimsley turned to make his way back to his cabin. "You're all dismissed."

The crew cheered as Brock smiled down at Rachel. But Rachel couldn't smile, for her eyes were fastened on the body of Jake Hessler whom she had just murdered. A thousand nights would pass before she could forgive herself. Suddenly the last remaining ounce of her will to live was crushed within her as guilt and accusation flooded her thoughts. *My life for his*. The reasoning didn't add up, even when coupled with her hatred for the man. No satisfaction being gained, Rachel refused the aid offered for her wounds and quietly limped back alone to her hold.

20
TROPICAL MADNESS

Captain Woodrow Fox could smell a storm the way a doubtful mother can smell the lie of a wayward child. Before the nimbus clouds grew heavy and gray, and before the wind began to whistle through the canvas, the captain stood at the bow of the *Scarborough*, watching and pacing. His face was worn and hard, with leathery folds of sunparched skin resembling the hide of a walrus. Like searching sentinels, his faded blue eyes gazed into the telescope of his sextant as he studied the atmosphere.

Captain Fox rolled up his cotton sleeves with thick fingers, his nails coated in tar. Drumming his thumbs against the bulwark, he parted his lips and the words came quietly and simply —"Storm's comin'."

The first mate, a tall lanky sailor, stopped upon hearing the captain's words. He craned his long neck as his ears caught the phrase from the man who rarely was wrong about matters of the sea. Anyone who ever worked under Woodrow Fox knew of his irascible temperament when crossed. This attribute was his downfall, causing him to make many mistakes with people. As a result of his disposition, his own family was fractured and scattered from one side of England to the other. But when given a feisty storm with which to tangle, Woodrow Fox was boss.

"Say again, sir?" the sailor muttered meekly as he stepped cautiously toward Captain Fox.

Captain Fox inhaled a big draft of air, his chapped lips protruding from the prickly gray beard. His great frame heaved as he leaned back on his heels. Then settling himself down again with his eyes stationed on the horizon, he muttered the same phrase —"Storm's comin'."

The first mate whirled around and cupped his hands to his mouth. "Storm's comin'! Batten down the hatches! All hands on deck!"

As the mates issued from the companionway and forecastle, manning the wheel and gathering around the capstan, Lieutenant Wallace, the second lieutenant of the *Scarborough*, emerged from the officers' cabin. Approaching the captain, he pulled off his cap to scratch his receding hairline. "Are you certain, Captain Fox?"

Not bothering to reply, Fox pulled a meerschaum pipe from his pocket and lit the tobacco with a flame from the headlamp. Then turning to position himself on the platform, he stood with his feet planted firmly and said nothing. He merely rocked back and forth like an old bull elephant, a circle of smoke enclosing his head in a fog.

Wallace turned to see if any signals were flying above the *Sirius*, which was two knots starboard of the *Scarborough*. The *Sirius* bobbed through the choppy water, disappearing behind the swells like a toy boat.

"The wind has picked up, that's one thing for certain," Wallace commented, watching the northern horizon. Turning back to face Fox, Wallace pulled a few shillings from his pocket and held his hand out to the sea captain. "Look what one of the mates handed me, sir."

Fox gazed down at the coins and reached to pluck a shilling from the officer's hand. Jostling the coin back and forth

in his stout grip, he scowled as he expelled a big puff of tobacco smoke. "Counterfeit?"

"But quite good counterfeit, sir. If it hadn't been made with
such lightweight metal, I might not have detected it myself."
Wallace dropped all but one of the coins back into his pocket
and held the remaining one between the tips of his fingers.
Turning both hands downward, he bent the coin. He then held
up the warped coin for Fox to inspect. "Do you think we
picked them up in Tenerife?"

"Could be." Captain Fox appeared to speculate on the matter. "What did the crewman tell you about them?"

"Only that he bought a few things from the island market
and a few things from the bosun's stores."

"Are we still checkin' each prison hold every ten minutes?"

"Like clockwork, sir. It's downright impossible for the prisoners to set up a coinery. . . ." Wallace contemplated for a moment. "At least, I *believe* it's impossible, sir."

Fox studied Wallace with a skeptical gaze. "You believe?
Tell me, then, are there any prisoners who have earned privileges?"

"No, sir. That is, I don't recall any prisoners being given
privileges. They're all a pretty miserable lot, Captain Fox."

"Are any of them in charge of anything, Wallace?"

Wallace thought for a moment. "It seems we do have a few
men who keep the others busy swabbing and maintaining the
quicklime."

"And are *those* men watched carefully?"

Wallace sighed, tiring of Fox's pointed questions. "I suppose we could put a guard on them, sir."

"Who are they?"

"One is Thomas Barrett. The other two, I don't recall."

Fox stretched out his arm over the bulwark and tapped his
pipe tobacco into the sea. "Where are they now?"

Wallace looked toward the convicts who were busy swabbing the deck, and yelled toward one of them, "You there,
Prentice!"

George Prentice looked up from his work and gazed
guardedly at the officers. "Yes, Lieutenant Wallace, sir?"

"Where are Barrett and his two men?"

Setting his jaw firmly, Prentice seemed to contemplate the question intently. "I can't remember, sir."

The cabin boy standing behind him answered, "Sure you know, Prentice. Ol' Barrett done told you they was goin' below to bring up more swabs and buckets."

" 'Course, you're right," Prentice nodded woodenly. "I suppose I forgot."

"Take me to them, Prentice." Captain Fox strode toward Prentice, his great belly protruding like the bow of a hulk.

Prentice swallowed hard, wanting nothing to do with Barrett or his two cronies, Worley and Jenkins. "I'm really not sure where they are, sir. Per'aps you should ask the cabin boy to take ye."

Fox frowned. "I want *you* to take me, Prentice. Now!" the captain ordered.

Moving slowly, Prentice placed his mop in the pail and pushed it against a wall. His hands suddenly felt sweaty and he could feel his heart hammering against his chest. He had managed to steer clear of the forgery ring, always finding excuses for not being available to aid in their crooked endeavors. Staying within range of an officer had helped a great deal as well, although Prentice seemed to fall prey to Barrett's angry threats as the forger cursed him under his breath for not going along with him.

"Let's go, Prentice!" Wallace barked, regarding Prentice suspiciously.

As Prentice climbed down through the companionway, he struggled with his new faith. Should he inform on another convict? He shook his head. *No, they'd all label me a tipster*. He resigned himself to taking Captain Fox and Lieutenant Wallace on a wild goose chase through the between decks.

The decks below were full of the sound of clatter as the three men clambered down the stairs and tromped onto the wooden floor. Ambling through the narrow passageways, their shoulders swayed back and forth while they passed the oil lanterns swinging from their cords. Prentice walked toward the food stores where the dried meat was kept. Pulling open the hinged door in the floor he squatted and peered into the dark cellarlike room. "Hey, Barrett!" he yelled.

"Quiet!" Wallace sputtered. "We don't want them to know we're coming!"

Prentice looked at the two men and realized they were without a doubt trying to entrap the men. "I don't know where they are, sir. May I go topdeck again?"

"No, Prentice." Fox stood with his thumbs clasped. "I believe you *do* know where they are. You may as well take us now—get it over with—unless you're in cahoots with them."

Prentice knew how easy it would be to lie. But something within him desperately wanted to hold on to the truth. "I believe I do know, Captain Fox, sir. Truly, I'm not for certain."

"Take us there, Prentice," Wallace insisted.

Prentice dropped the hinged door and it closed with a thud, sending dust skittering around his feet. Walking slowly down another corridor, he crossed a passageway and hesitatingly made his way toward the storage room. He reached to pull on the door and felt the ship heave beneath his feet.

Wallace cocked his head. "Wind's pickin' up," he commented.

Fox smiled smugly, then pulling a thick monocle from his coat pocket, he held it to his right eye. Squeezing his cheek and brow to hold the glass in place, his pale blue eye was magnified and seemed to protrude fiercely as he scowled toward the storage door. "Open it up, Prentice," his gravelly voice whispered.

Prentice heaved a sigh upon hearing the sound of heavy metal clatter against the hard floor from inside the room.

"Do I detect a rat?" Fox whispered as Wallace nodded and drew his pistol.

His arms flexed, Prentice reached for the door and flung it open with a powerful force. His eyes stayed fixed, emotionless, as they met the surprised gazes of Tom Barrett and his two forgery friends.

Barrett's first response was one of fear as he beheld the two large officers, one with pistol drawn. Then turning to look at Prentice, he glared at the informer. "I should've strangled ye in your sleep long ago, Prentice!"

"You're as good as dead, y'are, Prentice!" Worley spat at the floor.

Jenkins dropped the homemade counterfeit plate to the floor and spilled the newly made coins from his hands.

"*You* won't be able to kill anyone, Worley! After the floggin' you'll get for this offense, you'll be lucky if you're still alive!" Fox remonstrated.

"You men come with me," Wallace demanded. "Prentice, you gather the evidence and put it in a bag."

Prentice stared down at the floor. He felt as low as the scum whose arrest he had just witnessed. *I thought doin' right would feel better'n this*.

While Wallace led the men past Prentice, Barrett gnashed his teeth at the man whom he'd vow to see dead. "I hope you got paid good fer this'n, Georgie! You'll need it fer your funeral!"

"Go on!" Wallace shoved the back of Barrett's head forcefully. "Move along, vermin!"

As the men trudged through the dank belly of the ship, a sudden light flooded the galley ahead, followed by a heavy wet spray of green from above. A crewman wearing an oilskin coat was making fast down the ladder, and the ocean seemed to be following him.

"It's that gale you spotted, Captain Fox! She's comin' in fast an' blowin' hard against the yards!"

"I'm on me way up!" Fox answered, pushing himself in front of the others like a mother hen running for her chicks. "Wallace, you lock these three convicts in a hold and bar the hatch! They'll wait, I vow, 'til this thing blows over!"

Captain Fox clambered up the ladder, followed quickly by the others. As he lifted the hatchway, his cap was torn from his head by the gale wind whipping through the spars with such force that it swept every loose object from the topdeck. Fox eagerly accepted the oilskin coat handed him by a mate and threw it around his frame. Taking a quick glance windward, he spotted the *Charlotte* on the gray shelf of the clouded horizon being lifted to the sky like a peace offering. "Hold your own, dear lady—hold your own!"

Fox turned and slid his way toward the wheel, where three men held on grimly, their faces tight-lipped and rigid as the ship began to heave to and fro like a wounded animal.

Watkin Tench pulled the rope around his waist as he lashed his rain-soaked body to the base of the mizzenmast. Losing some of her fight, the *Charlotte* had wearily nosed into the last green wall of salt water instead of riding it, and had flooded the upper deck from bow to stern, sweeping away everything that wasn't battened down. "Chaney!" he shouted to the corporal, who was blindly feeling his way along the bulwark, the sea bludgeoning his face.

"Tench! Where are you?" Chaney shouted into the wind, holding his stout arm over his saltwater-burned eyes.

"Here, man! Grab a rope!" Tench hurled the end of the rope at the sea-soaked officer.

As Chaney clutched the rope with his red and swollen fingers, Tench dragged the corporal toward him. Drawing him close to the mast, he yelled, "Better tie yourself on, Chaney, or you'll be washed overboard!"

"Give me a hand, Watkin! My hands are slipping." Chaney struggled with the rope as he fought to shove himself up against the other side of the mast.

Tench snugged a bowline against his waist and reached to hold on to Chaney while the sea smashed against the ship, shattering one of the cabin doors. Running to make a fast repair was the carpenter, who dashed endlessly from one end of the ship to the other, keeping the *Charlotte* nailed together.

Stationed grimly near the forecastle, the captain stood bellowing out his orders, while overhead the sails blew adrift and the fittings broke loose. Seamen streamed back and forth from the cabins, alternating in shifts as they ran through the waterfall that flowed over the forecastle like cataracts.

"I'm tied on, Watkin! Now if she won't drown me like a cat, I might live to tell!" Chaney coughed, then lay his head back against the mast to catch his breath.

"You must live, Chaney!" Watkin winked. "All the ladies aboard ship would go into mournin'. That's all we need is a bunch of blubberin' women!"

"I wonder how they're doing, Watkin . . . the women, I mean." Chaney was short of breath.

235

"They're safe, Brock. We're the poor fools left up here to drown!"

Brock looked toward the hatchways, which were barred down securely. In the roar of the wind, he couldn't hear the screams that emanated beneath their fasteners.

"Somebody help us!" Cally wailed as more water flowed into the hold, saturating her hair and skin, while below, the overflow swirled back and forth between her feet.

"God help us!" Wanda shouted, desperation in her voice. "Are they goin' to leave us down here to drown?"

"Surely this place won't fill up!" Betsy tried to reassure her.

Cally lunged for the ladder. "I'm breakin' out o' this crypt!" As she reached for the slippery rung, another wave of ocean swept across the topdeck sending a stinging spray through the hatchways and into Cally's face, bringing forth a curse. "Help us, you dogs!" She shook her fist toward the hatchway.

"Cally!" Betsy tried to warn. "We've got to keep our heads!"

Whirling around, Cally spewed, "Keep our heads? Let's see your God get us out o' this mess!"

Betsy remained silent as Cally slumped to the floor and held her head. "I wish I could just die, I do!" She moaned despairingly while the murky warm water soaked into her prison gown. "Nothin' makes sense anymore!"

Rachel leaned against Betsy and sighed, fighting back the terror.

"It's bloomin' hot, it is!" Another cellmate, Hilda, pulled at the neck of her dress, her hands clammy from the tropical heat. Nauseous, the old woman crouched down next to Betsy, her head being doused with more water from above.

Cally jumped to her feet, sending Hilda sprawling headlong into the ankle-deep water. "We *are* goin' to die, that's what!" Cally screamed while lunging for the ladder again. "We'll all drown like rats!"

"Out o' me way!" Wanda shrieked, fighting Cally for a place on the ladder.

Cally swung her fist around and hit Wanda in the cheek, sending her swerving into the cell wall. Hilda jumped to her feet to join in the brawl and grabbed for the tattered hem of Cally's dress.

"All o' you stop it!" Betsy shouted while Cally and the other two careened onto the watery floor, their arms and legs flailing and kicking.

"Maybe we are goin' to die, Betsy!" Rachel grabbed Betsy's shoulders. Perhaps tonight would bring to an end her misery and her self-hatred as well. "I want to die too. Hell can't be worse than this place!"

"Rachel!" Betsy pleaded. "Please keep your head! We can't all go mad!"

"Mad!" Cally laughed deliriously, untangling herself from the other two. "Who's mad? Are you mad, lady?"

Wanda gripped the sides of her head and screamed as Hilda grabbed her and shoved her face into the water to drown out the sound.

"Drown 'er, Hilda!" Cally shrieked hysterically, succumbing to insanity. "Then drown me next!"

Betsy and Rachel stood barely breathing, their backs flat against the wall, fearing for their lives. Rachel whispered so only Betsy could hear, "Maybe I should let them kill me too. No more pain. Livin' ain't worth the bother."

"No!" Betsy wailed as she lifted her face toward the hatchway. "Dear Lord!" she called. "Help us!"

"Time for Sister Betsy's preachin'!" Cally mocked, shaking her head like a wet dog.

Hilda jerked Wanda's head around and shoved it again into the turbid rainwater. Wanda fought back violently.

Betsy couldn't be silenced and continued to whisper her fervid prayer. "I trust . . . I trust." Hot tears coursed down her face.

Wanda reached over her shoulder, grabbed Hilda, and dug her grimy nails into the convict's shoulder, forcing Hilda to loosen her grasp. "Tryin' to drown me, are you?" Wanda lifted her face from the water, and gasping for air, she spun around and yanked Hilda's hair.

Hilda howled and wrenched her wet locks from Wanda's grasp. Far removed from reality, she blubbered, "Don't pull me hair, Auntie Luce! I'll be good . . . I promise!" Hilda was still shrieking insanely while Cally sat splashing in the water, giggling like a two-year-old.

"Send your calm, oh God! Calm the storm!" Betsy's persistent cry rang fervently above the crazed women while a mixture of rain and sea and tar continued to sweep past their feet.

Rachel placed her pale, trembling fingers into Betsy's hand. Betsy's confidence was beginning to have a calming effect on her. Betsy seemed assured her God would answer, even when surrounded by madness. As Cally launched into another screaming paroxysm, Rachel realized her misjudgment of Betsy. *I've been listening to the wrong voices.* Betsy had never pretended to be perfect. Rachel would have seen through that falsehood. But it was the peaceful demeanor pervading Betsy's life that nagged at Rachel's thoughts. *God, are you really the key to peace?* Or was Betsy staging a performance to draw Rachel in . . . to pull in another convert to her own brand of religion?

The *Charlotte* groaned, shifting starboard, and then eased steady to the center as the sea parted to cradle the bow. Rachel squinted, her eyes peering through the gloom toward Betsy, where a single pin dot of light glinted from a crack in the hatchway, falling onto Betsy's auburn hair. Rachel blinked at the light, at the same time realizing the water beneath her feet had ceased its churning. A tranquil smile crossed Rachel's face and she squeezed Betsy's hand. "He did it, Betsy. Listen!" Rachel drank in the peaceful silence. "God calmed the storm for you!"

A welcome breath escaped Betsy's lips as her forehead smoothed. "For us all, Rachel."

Rachel could feel Betsy's hand relax in her own and heard a relief-filled sigh, followed by a whispered, "Thank you, Lord."

Their mad tantrums arrested by the sudden calm, the women on the floor sat still for a moment, staring up at the light that sifted in from the hatchway. A distant rumble reminded them of the maelstrom that had just rocked their lives.

Cally moaned and pulled her hair away from her face. "Well, I *don't* believe in miracles! It was just a coincidence! That's not proof to me!"

A soft laugh spilled from Betsy's lips, not cruel or mocking of Cally's disbelief. But a sweet, joyful laugh that broke the silence like a stream breaking through the ice in the spring. "That's all right, Cally. You've nothing to worry about. He only speaks to those who listen."

Thunder rolled across the heavens once again as the storm departed, revealing glimpses through the cracks of the crisp blue Atlantic sky.

21
AMELIA'S BRIBE

While the land-hungry sailors milled around the Rio dock, Katy donned a dress she had dried in the sun, pulling its starchy folds around her waist so Daphne could fasten up the back. She had no sooner dressed herself, when Robert appeared at the door wearing a pair of long brown trousers and a dingy white shirt.

"Ready for your escort, ladies?" he asked as he rubbed the toe of his old shoe on the back of his trousers.

"Ready?" Daphne answered with mock desperation. "If I ever gets meself off this bloomin' ship, I'll never step foot on another!"

Tying the lavender cord of her bonnet, Katy asked, "What sort of dainties are we to buy for the commander on this round, Daphne?"

"We better buy ourselves some fabric, I vow. Our clothes are startin' to wear. Look at this sleeve!" Daphne ran her finger down the frayed edge of her sleeve.

Gertie appeared, having finished her list for Commander

Phillip. "I don't see how the convicts are survivin', I don't. What with wearin' but one garment, they're practically naked."

"If we still had the freezin' weather to contend with, they'd all be dead, I vow." Daphne shook her finger.

"Can they sew, Gertie?" Katy asked, her voice ardent.

"They can sew well enough . . . the females anyway. But we've got to find 'em some material that'll wear better'n what they 'ave now."

Looking beyond the rail toward Rio de Janiero, Katy sighed. The Rio harbor sat sparkling like a jewel in the Atlantic, its sandy beaches and bright blue water a welcome respite for the sea-weary aboard the First Fleet. The waters of England being a murky dull brown, the blue tropical brine was an exotic spectacle to the European eye.

"Let's go then, shall we?" Gertie was the first to head for the gangway.

Katy should have been excited about an excursion to the seaport's markets, but she was feeling anxious about the reunion Commander Phillip had promised her with the George Prentice listed on the roster of the *Scarborough*. *What if it's not Papa?* Playing a disappointing scene over in her mind, Katy had imagined walking into the prison hold and being introduced to the wrong George Prentice. She had even cried herself to sleep the night before as she convinced herself to expect the worst. *What if I never find Papa?* Katy swallowed the lump in her throat and turned to follow Robert and Daphne through the doorway.

While the flagship docked at port, the remaining ships in the fleet were anchored out in the harbor where the officers were preparing to go ashore. The *Charlotte* was undergoing some repairs, so the carpenter and his crew were ordered to remain aboard until she was made shipshape. The hatchways were all pried open, as was the routine after sunrise. The first women to emerge blinked from hollow eyes and stretched their aching muscles. While most launched into their various diminutive complaints, Rachel and Betsy walked quietly to the ship's railing and gazed peacefully toward the sea.

"We're not dead yet, Rachel," Betsy said gently. "We're almost halfway to New South Wales."

"You're right, me friend. I hadn't stopped to realize it's God that's keepin' us."

"It's your heart that speaks now, isn't it, Rachel? I've prayed long for you. Don't give up on what you've found." Betsy's voice bore an urgency.

Rachel turned her eyes toward the harbor. She reflected upon the night after the fitful storm. Rachel had prayed a simple prayer. She had cried softly as she confessed aloud the pain within her soul, asking forgiveness of God. But forgiving herself became the more difficult half of her restoration. Throughout the days, Rachel slaved under the watchful gaze of the mariners and had little time to think on her past. But at nightfall, the darkness seemed to envelop her thoughts like a cavern, echoing endless, guilt-ridden scenes across her mind. On most nights she would awaken and bolt upright, feeling eyes from the past upon her.

Betsy turned sideways so the wind would blow her hair away from her face. She found Brock watching them. She smiled at the corporal politely. After all, it was he who had come to Rachel's rescue twice already. "Good day, Corporal Chaney," she murmured as Rachel turned immediately upon hearing the name.

"Are you women ready for your morning rations?" Brock approached them. He smiled at Rachel in a resolute manner, his eyes sparkling as they reflected the sky's warmth.

Rachel cast her blue eyes up at the corporal and then at Betsy. Rachel found herself transfixed momentarily on her faithful friend. Betsy's brow was pinched with a hint of worry. Rachel then turned and stared down at the deck, damp from the last storm. "Let's go fetch our rations, Betsy. If you'll excuse us, Corporal Chaney. . . ."

"Miss Langley, I wish to speak to you in private." Brock smiled warmly.

Rachel rose slowly from the railing and, straightening her back, turned to face Chaney. His gaze remained fixed on her, anticipation lighting his expression. Vulnerability filled her countenance while the dark, comely eyes welcomed her. Rachel knew if she looked again toward Betsy, her face would betray her own anxiety. Determinedly, she fixed her eyes on Brock. "Yes, Corporal, sir . . . I'll speak with you." Only the sound of Betsy's weary sigh rose against the breaking of the distant surf.

Pulling the cloth away from the infant's arms, Amelia fanned her baby boy and blew softly against his face. Even in the heat, the baby had managed to fall asleep. As Caleb slumbered, his tiny dark lashes rested in soft wispy curls upon his ivory cheeks. He was considered by all the convict women aboard the *Lady Penrhyn* to be a "good baby." He seldom awoke at night and when he did, Amelia was right at his side on the mat where they slept on the floor. Fearing she would not produce enough milk, she had coaxed the guards into giving her extra rations. Her last possession, a single shilling, was still hidden in her shoe in the event she would need to bribe a guard for more food. "I love you, Caleb," she whispered gently.

"Want me to watch 'im fer you, Amelia?" Ollie asked, the light of sincerity marking her gaze. "Go up top now and get some fresh air while I take 'im. It'll do you some good, it will." She was wan in appearance with a frizz of gray hair protruding from under her scarf. A kind grin pinched her cheeks. She had rocked Caleb many nights when Amelia had come down with a fever.

"Thank you, Ollie. That's kind o' you." Amelia gently placed the small bundle in the old woman's arms. Bending to tenderly kiss the child's forehead, she turned and pulled herself up the ladder toward the open hatchway. "Where are we, again?"

Ollie swayed back and forth, instinctively rocking the baby. "Rio de Janeiro."

"Where's that?"

"Not in England."

Amelia looked out over the blue harbor. "You're right about that, Ollie. It looks like paradise."

Ollie's voice held a hopeless inflection. "For everyone but us, Amelia."

Glancing again down at Ollie and Caleb, Amelia climbed out of the hatchway and stepped onto the deck of the *Lady Penrhyn*. She spotted the captain, along with the other officers, heading for the lifeboat to go ashore. As she stepped toward them, a strong hand gripped her arm and jerked her around.

"Where do ye think you're goin'?" the broad sailor snapped.

"I just wanted to speak to Captain Meeks . . . that's all, sir . . . I swear it!" Amelia regarded the sailor with a soft gaze, trying to appear as nonthreatening as possible.

"No y'ain't. Cap'n's leavin' for the day and 'e don't want no convict botherin' 'im."

"I won't be a bother, really, sir. I just need to give him a message for Commander Phillip."

The sailor laughed coldly. "Why would Commander Phillip be gettin' a message from the likes o' you?"

Amelia sighed. "I'm trying to find me 'usband."

"No," he answered flatly. "Now be on your way."

She frowned, a thought suddenly striking her mind. Placing her hands on her hips, Amelia opted for further persuasion. "Might you be interested in a bit o' lolly?"

"Eh? Where'd you get such as that?"

Slipping her foot out of the old shoe, Amelia reached and pulled out the shilling. "It's all I have, sir. Would it interest you?"

Setting his jaw to the side, the sailor studied the coin, taking it in his hand, trying to bend it, flipping it in the air. "It's good. I'll take it. But don't stay more'n a minute or two." He spotted the officers climbing over the rail and into the boat. "You better be quick or you'll lose your chance. Not my fault, it ain't." He slipped the shilling into his large pocket.

"Captain Meeks!" Amelia called, running after the man. "Wait! I need to speak to you!" She waved her arms wildly above her head.

Meeks wore a scowl on his thin face. He glanced rather blandly toward Amelia, impatience evident in his gray eyes as

245

he crossed his arms at his chest. "What now?" he muttered.

Marching toward the boatful of officers, Amelia's demeanor was dauntless. "Please, sir! I'll only be a moment if you'll listen."

"No you don't!"

Amelia felt a blow across her back. Her knees buckled and she slumped awkwardly to the deck. Opening her eyes slowly, she beheld the dissolute mariner who stood with the whip drawn back to strike again.

"Sorry, sir," the sailor apologized to Meeks. "One o' the females must've slipped past the guard. I'll take care o' the matter."

"Hurry it up, then," Meeks chided.

Amelia held her trembling hands to her face. "I need to get a message to Commander Phillip. I . . ."

Meeks grew indignant. "What?" he interrupted before Amelia could finish. "Unheard of!"

Another lash cracked the air and the whip wrapped around Amelia like a stinging tentacle. "Quiet, convict!" the mariner shouted.

Amelia fell flat against the deck. Her nose smacked the wooden plank hard, and she felt the warmth of blood soak into the back of her garment. Turning her face toward the captain again, she spilled her words quickly. "It's important, sir." Her voice quivered.

"To whom?"

Amelia hung her head, feeling embarrassed at the accusing stares of the officers. She lay her face against the deck and wept softly. *It's no use. They'll not bother with me. No use.*

A corporal turned to the captain and quietly commented, "Couldn't we at least listen to the female, sir? She's the one with the infant an' all."

The captain blew out a hard breath. "Blast it all! I'm not a nanny!"

Sitting quietly looking at one another, the officers said nothing in reply. But each face reflected pity for the woman.

"Oh!" Meeks spat at the deck. "All right! If it'll ease your consciences . . ." He turned to Amelia. "You! Convict! On your feet and state your problem! But be quick about it!"

Amelia's eyes held a faint glimmer of hope as she pushed herself up. She closed her eyes a brief moment. *Thank you, Lord. Thank you for your mercy.* Studying the mariner guardedly, Amelia addressed the captain. "I . . . need to find me 'usband, Captain Meeks, sir," she explained weakly. "I feel George might be on one of the other ships." She stood before the officer, her arms wrapped around herself. "I would like to see if he's on a transport, sir . . . and sorry to be such a bother, I am at that." Amelia's shoulders stooped while she bit her lip. Pain from the whip seared her body . . . but not as strong as the pain she felt for the loss of her family.

"It most certainly *is* a bother!" Meeks shot back.

"*I* don't mind tellin' the commander, sir," the corporal intervened. Amelia smiled at the young officer. He didn't look much older than Katy.

"Then you do it, Corporal!" Meeks was stern. "I wash my hands of the matter."

"Yes, sir. Thank ye, sir." The corporal acknowledged Amelia with a faint smile. "What's your 'usband's name, ma'am?"

Feeling elated at the young man's kind heart, Amelia answered eagerly, "George Prentice is his name. He's a good man, really. Just fell on hard times."

"I'll try to remember. I've a cousin named George who's a blacksmith's apprentice. I can remember George Prentice."

"If you can, sir, when I'm able to find work later, I'll send you some pay if you like."

"No, Mrs. Prentice, pay won't be necessary." The corporal shook his head as the mates began lowering the boat into the sea. "I'll let God take the credit for this one."

"Glory be!" Amelia beamed. "You're a religious man?"

"Me mum is more religious than me . . . an' you remind me of her, you do."

"It's a sign, it is!" Amelia held her hands toward the sky. "Thank you, Lord Almighty, for noticin' a worm like me!" Turning her misty eyes toward the harbor, Amelia dabbed at them with the tattered cloth that hung loosely from her sleeves.

The corporal turned his face away, as though taken by the sight of the white clouds mirrored in the glassy bay. A beam of sunlight radiated through them, drenching the bay with a supernal warmth. Amelia stood for a moment, basking in the glow of the sunlight before the guard prodded her to move on. She would always remember the light of goodness that pierced through the darkest days of the exiles' voyage.

22
ANGEL FACE

George Prentice lifted the empty salt-pork barrel from the cook's table. "I'll haul it below if you're ready now," he remarked to the cook, sweat spilling from his brow.

"You can take it. I'll fill it up in a day or so with the goods we bring in from Rio de Janeiro." The cook removed the spoon from the bean pot and wiped it on his apron.

Good, George thought. He wanted to go below. He had devised a makeshift prayer room for himself in one of the stores. He tried to pray there every day if he could find an excuse to go below. Not that he thought the storeroom was a fit place of worship, but it gave him the solitude he sought. Under the lantern's oily glow, he continued his search for truth. His faith growing, Prentice found a new contentment rising from his dark life and hungered to read his Bible.

"I'll be back shortly," he told the cook. "Do you need me to bring up anythin' else?"

The portly cook thought for a moment, then shook his head. "Nothin' else I can think of, Prentice."

George heaved the barrel through the doorway and carried it to the companionway, where he hoisted it below. He landed firmly on the floor below deck, then rolled the barrel down the corridor. He felt tension rising in his chest. Tom Barrett had vowed to kill him since the day he and his two forgery friends had been flogged. The convicts had been chained in their holds for weeks, but George was warned that they would be allowed above deck within days. He peered cautiously around each turn, shoving the barrel up to the storeroom door. Turning the handle, he breathed a relief-filled sigh at finding no convicts on the prowl. After placing the barrel against the wall, he quietly closed the door and turned to kneel on a wooden box, propping his elbows on a barrel.

Growing still, he began to pray, his eyes open. "It's me—George." His words were barely audible. "I wanted to talk to you again today, Lord. Thank you for listenin'." The language of prayer did not come easily to Prentice, but knowing that God understood his halting words, George opened up his heart. Quietly waiting, the ex-pickpocket felt a subtle breaking deep within and the tears began to flow. It wasn't the first time he had cried while he prayed. But some days were lonelier than others. "Please keep me wife and daughter safe. Me heart's heavy for them today." Tears spilled from his eyes and his chest heaved convulsively. "If I ever see them again, I know it'll be a miracle," he sobbed. "I can't do anythin' proper, it seems. Forgive me of my sins which are many. . . ."

Prentice felt a lump rise in his throat, choking further attempts to speak. His head dropping, he lay sobbing against the barrel for a few moments before lifting his face to the darkness. Strangely enough, the silence enveloped Prentice in a wave of peace. He couldn't explain the sensation except to whisper, "I feel you, God."

Standing to his feet, Prentice bowed his head reverently and opened the tattered Bible once again. Biting his quivering lip, he read from the Psalms: "Why art thou cast down, O my soul? and why art thou disquieted within me? hope thou in God: for I shall yet praise him, who is the health of my countenance, and my God."

Prentice raised his face upward while the tears continued

to course down his cheeks. "Help *my* downcast soul, dear Lord. Teach *me* to hope only in you." Knowing the crew would come searching for him soon, Prentice closed the writ and secured it in the waistband of his trousers. "Give me strength to live through another day, and . . ." he concluded, "grant me one request, though I know it to be great—please let me see Amelia and Katy again." Breathing a swift "In the name of your Son, amen," Prentice stood to his feet and left the storeroom.

As George sauntered down the corridor, his heart was light. Whether he remained bound or was set free, this new liberation from his own past was worth its weight in gold. Admittedly, he struggled with the temptations that had mastered him for so many years, but he assured himself often he would never turn to pickpocketing again. The more he resisted the former desires, the stronger his courage grew and the more quickly the old desires began to fade. He frequently reminded himself that the Lord would provide somehow—*and if He don't, there's always heaven*. Nearing the ladder, he saw a bright shaft of light appear from above, indicating the companionhead had been lifted. He hesitated, fearing he was about to be flogged for lingering too long below deck. *Ahh, it was worth it, Lord*.

George stood motionless, gazing above while two small white-stockinged feet in white shoes stepped onto the ladder. A flutter of lace and white taffeta surrounding a golden-haired girl filled the grimy companionway with the scent of flowers. In her delicate grasp was a small nosegay. The sunshine glinted from her flower-adorned hair as she descended the ladder.

Staring at the back of the adolescent's head, George stood spellbound at the sight of the girl. "It's an angel!" he exclaimed fearfully.

"Papa?"

The word rang in George Prentice's ears. *Papa?* He hadn't heard it for so long, the name sounded foreign—and cruel. "Don't play tricks on me, Lord!" his voice quivered.

"It's me—Katy!" She turned to face her weary father.

"It can't be! Katy?" George moved toward her, his steps

timorous. Reaching out with his hand, he drew it back quickly, realizing its dirty appearance.

Katy smiled, the tears gliding down her cheeks. "I can't believe I've found you!" She leaped from the ladder and ran to him.

George rushed to embrace his daughter. "Look at you, child! You're practically grown!"

Unable to hold back her feelings any longer, Katy sobbed against her father's shoulder. As she threw her arms around him, she could feel his bony frame in her embrace. He was even thinner than the last time she had seen him at the jail-house. "I thought I'd lost you forever!" she cried.

"I'm alive as can be, Katy!" George grinned serenely. "How sweet your name sounds . . . me Katy!" Holding her out at arm's length, he asked anxiously, "Where's Mum?" Stepping toward the ladder, he looked eagerly up the companionway but only found the curious face of a gentleman dressed in a red tunic. "Hello, sir!" he called politely to the gentleman.

"I can't bear to tell you, Papa . . ." Katy shook her head sadly. "She's gone. She was falsely accused, she was, o' stealin'. And I never heard from 'er again."

George stood stunned. "My Amelia . . . gone? Dear God! Don't tell me . . ."

"I miss 'er too, Papa!" Katy wept, bitterness tinging her words. "It's not fair! Why would God allow a good woman like Mum to be . . ."

"Wait, Katy," George interjected. "Don't blame God for all our misery. It's me who's to blame, it is! Most of it's been brought on by me own stupid mistakes."

Katy stared at her father in bewilderment.

"It's been a 'ard lesson fer me to learn." His eyes stared with a haggard look as he reflected on his past. He had spent many long nights in the hold punishing himself with regret and guilt. "I'm trying to put it behind me, love." His eyes grew tense, pierced with grief. "But, oh, dearest Amelia! The thought of her . . . oh, it breaks me heart in two." Prentice gazed upward, his face wrought with anguish. He closed his eyes and breathed a prayer that seemed hopeless. His thoughts turning to Katy, Prentice composed himself. "But you've a good life ahead, Katy. You can find yourself some work. Forget about me, love. You'll be grown an' married by the time I've finished me sentence at Botany Bay."

"But I found meself a good job with Commander Phillip, and he brought me here to you—just like Mum thought he would." Katy's eyes were pleading. "I'll never leave you, Papa! I'll stay at New South Wales until you're free. We'll go back to England together. Commander Phillip will 'elp us . . . I just know 'e will!"

"So I've 'im to thank."

"Yes." Katy stared up the companionway and smiled. "He's a good man, Papa . . . like you."

"Don't tell me the man's standin' right 'ere!"

Katy nodded and blushed. "He escorted me, Papa."

George shouted up the ladder. "Thank you, Commander Phillip, sir! You're an instrument o' God, y'are!"

The commander nodded politely at the convict and turned to Gertie, who had accompanied him. "Stay with young Katy, Gertie, for about an hour. I'll have one of the men escort you back to the ship when she's finished with her visit."

"Are you leavin', sir?" Gertie asked, curious.

"I've one more convict to see. If I don't take care of the matter, she'll never give me a moment's peace."

"Troublemaker, sir?"

Phillip shook his head. "No, nothing of the sort. A convict's lost her husband and believes he's a prisoner on one of the ships."

"Poor wretch. Good luck, Commander Phillip."

A crewmate ran up, breathless, to Phillip. "You better come quick, sir! Thar's a fight on board the *Alexander* and a convict's stolen a weapon!"

"Thank you, sailor. I'm on my way. Can you man the lifeboat?"

"Aye, aye, Commander!"

Phillip glanced at Gertie one last time. "I suppose the convict woman will have to wait."

"It's probably for the best, sir." Gertie began sauntering toward the companionway to retrieve Katy.

Worley grated his chains across the floor as he stumbled away from the waste can in the corner of the hold. "Cursed sailors! You'd think they'd empty it out sometime!"

"We'll die down 'ere in our own refuse, that's what!" Jenkins rubbed his scraggly beard. He was slumped in a corner of the dank cell, chained to the wall.

"We've one man to thank for our situation—George Prentice!" Barrett spat on the floor, feeling another rodent scamper across his swollen leg. The flogging had initially rendered Barrett unconscious, and when he had awoken he was given only a little salve to nurse his wounds. The surgeon warned that he would likely lose his leg. "I'll kill Prentice, if it's me last act on this Godforsaken sea! I'll cut him up piece by piece and feed his bloody bones to the sharks, I vow!" Raising his bad leg in the air, he slammed it down savagely, crushing the rat across the back and killing it instantly. Barrett howled with pain and jerked his knee to his chest before kicking away the bloody remains of the rodent with his good foot.

The hatch overhead lifted and a ruddy old sailor scowled into the cell. "They're goin' to bring you out today, convicts. Surgeon'll be seein' you first, Barrett." The old salt's words drove through Barrett like a dagger.

"Not me leg!" he yelled up at the old man, his eyes threatening. "They'll have to kill me first! I'll not allow it!"

"You'll do as they say, Barrett . . ." he snapped. "Or you *will* die!"

Two sentries appeared and stood with their muskets aimed at the convicts while two more ambled down the ladder. Barrett pushed himself against the corner. "Keep away! Just leave me 'ere to die, I tell you!"

As a large guard bent to lift Barrett, the convict jerked his chained wrists and smashed his fists into the man's face. The guard stumbled backward while the armed sentries overhead threatened to blast the convicts at once.

"Stop, Barrett!" Jenkins' eyes were wide. "They'll kill us all down 'ere like rats in a cage!"

Worley shoved himself behind Jenkins, who in turn swung

around to strike the convict in the face. "Tryin' to save yerself, you devil?"

"Halt!" A shot blasted overhead as a guard fired into the air. Immediately, the two sentries were surrounded by additional armed sailors.

The hold grew quiet.

"Bring 'im up, men!" the lieutenant overhead barked as the guards lashed Barrett's back to a long, flat board and tightly secured his arms and legs.

"Heave to!" the order sounded, and the sailors began hoisting the subdued prisoner out of the hold.

George Prentice had observed it all while standing behind the mariner, with his swab dripping onto the deck. After having kissed his daughter goodbye, he had watched Katy and the commander's maid leave in the lifeboat that would carry them to the white sandy shore. Remembering he hadn't secured the latch on the storeroom, Prentice laid the swab aside and took a step toward the companionway. His errand was interrupted by the sound of a scuffle and gunfire. He edged over to the hold where Barrett was imprisoned. He could hear Barrett swearing and begging the surgeon to save his swollen leg.

Prentice shook his head upon realizing Barrett's plight. As the felon was lifted to the upper deck, Prentice thought he had better leave and turned once again to go down into the between decks.

After clambering up the ladder, Jenkins and Worley stood wearily while their shackles were opened.

"You try anythin' else an' you'll both be hanged!" a corporal threatened. "You're allowed out for a bit, but mind yourselves or you'll be back in the shackles." The officers and sailors left them and returned to their duties.

Jenkins breathed the salty air and squinted at the beach that lay ahead. The felon's face reflected the distress of being caged like a beast for weeks. His eyes connected to the shoreline in a calculating manner, measuring the distance from beach to ship. Hope for escape was never far from any exile's mind, and Jenkins was beyond the point of being threatened by punishment. Desperation and revenge now weighed heavily in his thoughts.

Turning his head, he caught sight of the companionhead being lowered. Narrowing his eyes, he scowled at what he was seeing. It looked as though George Prentice were sneaking below. Jenkins nudged Worley and leaned his head toward the companionway, directing Worley's gaze with his bloodshot eyes. "We've some business to attend to, Worley," he grinned viciously.

Worley rubbed his wrists. "Not me. I'm stayin' out o' this 'un. I'll not 'ang fer nobody. Not Barrett—not nobody!"

"You're a coward, 'at's what y'are!"

Worley turned his eyes from Jenkins' accusing stare and slumped away toward the stern.

Jenkins edged toward the head, but cringed at the sound of an animal-like scream. The sound diminished into a pain-filled wail and then to silence. "Ol' Barrett must be gettin' 'is leg sawed off, 'e is."

Jenkins searched the topdeck with his eyes. No one seemed to notice as he sauntered toward the companionhead. Stretching out his arms he yawned and then leaned indolently against the head on one grimy hand. Glancing around, he lifted the hatch and clambered below.

As he stepped quietly into the dark corridor, Jenkins caught faint sounds of someone murmuring. The sound was muddled, and it faded to silence when he stopped at each turn to listen for Prentice's voice. The murmur began again, and Jenkins slid his body along the wall, catching his coarse shirt on protruding rusty nails. Continuing, he banged his forehead against a blackened lantern. He bent to creep along the base of the wall, searching for the possession he had dropped and kicked away when he was arrested. His hands slid into every crevice, feeling the dark holes along the wall. "Where's me blade?" he mouthed with worried impatience.

The murmuring voice commenced again, and Jenkins jerked his hand from behind a barrel. As he did so, his knuckle bumped something long and smooth, sending the object spinning. The convict peered behind the barrel, and the glint of a dagger blade caught his searching eye. His mouth curving into a foul grimace, he squeezed his stout body between the wall and the barrel and grabbed hold of the knife. He chuckled as he pulled out the blade and held it in front of his face. "This'll cut open the fool like a cold meat pie."

Jenkins crouched low and began to move more quickly, drawing near to the voice which was distinctively that of George Prentice. Fearing Prentice was not alone, he slowed down, adapting his plan with the skill of an experienced assassin. Rounding the final corner, the convict saw the storeroom door was slightly open. The murmurs continued, but no other voice returned the conversation. Jenkins chuckled, deciding Prentice was mad. Peering inside the crack, he could see Prentice with his back to him and on his knees. Clutching the dagger, Jenkins stood cautiously upright and drew back his right arm. He would charge through the door, stab the traitor straight through the heart, and then cut his throat.

"An' please 'elp Mr. Thomas Barrett," Prentice prayed from inside the room. "Don't let 'im die, but touch 'is leg and heal it, Lord." His prayer was quiet but sincere.

Jenkins shrugged off the melancholy that swept through him.

"An' help Jenkins and Worley to know you, Lord, like I knows you."

Jenkins huffed as he crossed his arms at his chest, the dagger still held tightly in his grasp. "Fanatic," he whispered to himself.

"Help me to be more forgivin'. I forgive Barrett and Jenkins and Worley too, Lord."

"That's it!" Jenkins whispered. Drawing back his arm again, Jenkins whirled around but stopped dead at the sight of the large man who suddenly blocked his path. "Out o' me way," he snapped. The man was enormous and muscular. He stared down at Jenkins with penetrating blue eyes, his broad arms held out to block entry to the storeroom. Jenkins did not remember the man by name, although he looked vaguely familiar. With his long blond hair and rough brown attire, he could have been a Norwegian who joined the crew while they were docked at Tenerife. Many foreigners landed on the islands, only to leave with the next passing ship in search of better pay or a more reasonable sea captain.

The huge man looked into Jenkins' eyes. His expression was tranquil but left Jenkins uneasy. Jenkins drew back his weapon once again. "Out o' me way or I'll . . ."

Pulling a sword from a leather sheath, the Norwegian held its tip toward Jenkins. He said nothing in return, only continued to look deeply into the convict's eyes as though reading his soul.

Jenkins' hand began to tremble and the dagger clattered to the floor. A powerful fear seizing him, he backed away. "Wh-who are ye?" he asked shakily, pushing himself against the wall.

The man gave no answer, but his eyes seemed to smile.

Jenkins stepped to the side, then turned to race back down the corridor to the companionway.

Hearing the convict's shrieks, Prentice cautiously pulled open the door. He frowned as he saw Jenkins disappear around the corridor. His gaze falling back to the floor, Prentice saw the dagger thrown against the base of the wall. Bending to retrieve the weapon, he spun around thinking he saw another figure from the corner of his eye. A shadow crossed the corridor and disappeared. Prentice looked up and down the dim pass-through, but soon realized he was alone. He turned the knife over in his hand. "Thank you for protectin' me, Lord. You're a mysterious God, you are."

23
SEED OF TRUST

"Life has become purposeless, Watkin. What we need is a good war." Chaney gulped down another glass of gin as the door to their cabin opened slightly.

Tench mused, "War. It takes our minds off ourselves, don't it now?"

"And takes my mind off home. For a bit, anyway. But I do hate to lose. I still say the colonists'll come to their senses soon. They'll be begging Mother England for help." Brock looked up to see Rachel Langley had entered with a pail and a mop. Her hair hung in soft strands around her frail shoulders, the titian locks a severe contrast against the coarse prison gown. The corporal's eyes seemed to light up at the sight, though his expression was guarded.

"What makes 'em so cocky, anyway . . . the Americans, that is?" Tench closed the logbook he'd been scribbling in and stood to his feet to stretch. Tipping the shot glass, he guzzled the last drop of liquor.

"Ignorance," Brock replied. "But they'll tire of their starvation. You wait and see. They'll be begging for a ruler to meet their needs again. Independence does have its price."

"What's the difference, Chaney? They were starvin' anyway, weren't they?"

"They'll forget their roots. Everyone does eventually."

Tench nodded, his thoughts racing to the tasks of the day. Dutifully, he placed his glass on the table and secured his hat. "I'll be gone for a bit. Captain's needin' me to chronicle for 'im today, he is."

"Good day, Watkin," Chaney yawned sleepily, deciding to take full advantage of his time off. He nodded politely at Rachel who had begun the task of cleaning the wooden floor. "Captain sent you to clean, I trust?"

Rachel stopped for a moment and nodded. Casting her eyes to the floor, she wound a strand of hair nervously around her finger. The last time she had spoken with Brock, he had only needed her to assist with another mundane chore— much to Betsy's relief. But working next to the virile corporal had sent a spark through Rachel that unnerved her. Rachel had eventually confided her fears to Betsy—that she felt drawn to the handsome officer. There were nights she struggled, sometimes hopelessly, with unpractical thoughts that filled her mind.

Chaney swallowed the last drop of gin he and Tench had picked up in Rio de Janeiro. He eyed the convict girl, who was carefully swabbing the floor around his bunk. His eyes seemed to trace the soft sunlight that wrapped around her statuesque form.

Without glancing up, Rachel commented, her voice empty of emotion, "I know you're needin' your rest, Corporal. I'll be quickly about me chores."

"No need to hurry, really." Brock's tone held a soothing, gentle quality. "I truly appreciate the company. You're a pleasant girl to speak with."

"Thank you kindly, sir." Rachel curtsied, then swiftly turned to complete her work.

Feeling the drying effects of the sour gin on his tongue, Chaney puckered his lips and squinted at the convict. "You seem to have a sensitive spirit. Are you religious?"

"I have a deep faith, if that's what you mean, sir?" A faint smile crossed Rachel's lips. She was relieved at Brock's question. Never had anyone commented about her in such a way.

"My parents are good Anglicans. Never miss a day of church."

Rachel relaxed upon hearing a topic she hungered for. "You come from a Christian home?"

"Yes. Knew my catechism backward and forward."

Rachel bit her lip. Her past was not so pleasant to speak of. "I only wish that I . . ."

"It doesn't matter," Brock interjected, seeming to read Rachel's thoughts. "Yesterday is water under the bridge. Today and tomorrow are all that count."

A smile radiated across Rachel's face. "That's what I'm finding to be true, Corporal, I am."

"Do you have family back in England?"

"Yes. But I scarcely know what's happened to 'em all."

"Well, if you'll write a letter, I'll see what I can do to reach them for you when I'm sent back to England."

Rachel's brow furrowed as she bit her lip. "Why would you do that for me?"

Brock hesitated, contemplating his answer carefully. "I'm not sure I know myself. You appear as though you need something good to happen to you for a change. I'm sorry if I sounded forward." Brock drummed his thumbs upon his chest and sighed as a void settled upon the room.

Feeling awkward at the sudden silence, Rachel gazed apologetically at the corporal. "I didn't mean . . ."

"No need to apologize. I think you've every reason to be suspicious of everyone. I'm not so certain I'm the one who should help you anyway. To promise such a thing could be a grave error on my part. I'm sure you've had your fill of disappointments in life."

Rachel started to agree, then felt disillusionment sweep through her. Brock's tone was beginning to reflect finality, as though the conversation had ended. A thought struck Rachel's inquisitive mind—a question that drove her to speak. "I only meant that it wouldn't be right, would it, Corporal . . . a fine man like yourself wasting your time on a convict girl?" She felt her hands trembling. She knew she should leave, but the urge to remain was too strong.

Brock cast his eyes reflectively upon the girl and broke into a smile. "You're not a waste, Rachel. Never let anyone tell you that about yourself. You're as bright and beautiful as any fine English girl . . . perhaps better than most. Don't you agree?"

"I'd be a fool to answer that one, sir."

Brock chuckled warmly. "When you feel comfortable with the idea, please call me Brock." His deep voice resonated through the room, filling the quietness with an atmosphere of welcome.

Rachel's lips parted, but she was only able to answer in an awkward whisper—"Brock." Taking a few steps closer, she forced herself to look at the officer, who remained stretched out on the bunk, aloof and quiet. He had a fine, strong face. With hair uncharacteristically ruffled, it hung in soft, unkempt strands across his broad forehead. He appeared as guileless as a schoolboy. Deciding to further indulge her curiosity, Rachel studied the dark, mysterious eyes which had captured her memory. Though he was within inches of her, he kept his distance and made no advances toward her.

Brock returned the same studious gaze and smiled reassuringly. Suddenly his brow drew up pensively, and he slowly pulled himself up, bracing his strong hands against the thin coverlet. "You're trembling. I hope I haven't frightened you, Rachel."

Rachel shook her head, worried that her curious gaze betrayed her thoughts.

"I'm glad you came by today, Rachel. When I feel the need to talk again . . . would you mind?"

A broad smile crossed Rachel's face and exuberance washed through her. How desperately she needed to hear those words—someone to talk to. "That would be wonderful, Brock."

"I'm glad you feel that way. And I do admire your smile. You light up this whole dreary voyage."

"You speak such kind words." A seed of trust was sown within Rachel's injured heart, causing her to risk sharing her anxiety. Hesitating for only a moment, she allowed her thoughts to culminate into words. "Brock, I've been speaking to a girl named Betsy. She's taught me a lot. I want to live me life right, you know, like reading the Bible and all that."

"I understand." Brock's eyes remained steady on Rachel, as though her words were paramount.

"I'm finally straightening out me life . . . with God's help."

Brock weighed the girl's concern, his gaze assuming a paternal nature. "I'm sure you need something to lean on. But there are many answers out there. Don't get bound up with fanaticism. Such things deaden one's sensibilities," he added with an air of great consequence.

"Oh, no, I wouldn't do that," Rachel said quickly, trying to shroud her confusion. She didn't want Brock to think she was foolish. Suddenly, all the spiritual conversations between her and Betsy seemed secondary.

Touching Rachel's arm in a friendly manner, Brock assured her, "You'll make it well in life, Rachel. You seem to have great strength."

Rachel swallowed hard, feeling Brock's gentle touch against her arm. Gazing again into his eyes, she believed all he said was possible. The sensation of his touch sent a fire through her that further melted her resistance. At the same time, she couldn't help but heed the warnings that flashed through her mind, though the signals were weakening.

"There you go, looking worried again," he laughed softly. "I think you should go now. I can only trust myself for so long."

Rachel lifted her face and looked into his eyes again. They were as deep and beautiful and mysterious as ever. "Thank you for . . ."

But Rachel didn't need to finish the words. Brock gazed down at her and nodded knowingly.

She felt energized next to him. It was the most wonderful warmth she had ever felt from a man. Her father had never been around to offer the love she so desperately craved. "I need a friend, Brock."

Brock pulled her face under his chin and tenderly stroked the soft, fiery strands of Rachel's hair. "So do I."

A soft knock rapped against Phillip's door—so soft, in fact, that he almost chose to ignore it. "Who's there?" he called, laying his sextant on top of a chart.

"I'm the one you sent for, sir?" A strained and cautious voice broke the silence.

"*I* sent for you?" The captain's brow furrowed.

"You did at that, sir."

"Well, enter, please."

Amelia Prentice peered from around the oak door. In her arms, a blue-eyed baby stared out from the tattered fabric in which he was wrapped. "I'm Amelia, sir."

Prentice felt a wearisome sigh escape his lips. Departure time was imminent, and last-minute preparations were still pending. Then his gaze fell sympathetically upon the infant. "He's tiny. He must've been born on ship?"

"He was at that, sir. But a right healthy boy he is . . . an' good as gold."

"Now, let me think . . . you're the woman who's searching for . . ."

"Me 'usband. I'm beginning to think it's useless to try. We're so far from England an' all. He could be back in one o' the hulks . . . or worse."

Phillip studied the convict's auburn hair. Her skin was beginning to show the effects of the voyage, but she had a pleasing, almost familiar, face. *Perhaps I saw her during inspections.* "Have we met?" he asked succinctly.

Amelia hesitated, for she knew it would displease and perhaps anger Phillip to know of her crime against his aunt, and she also knew whom he would choose to believe. She kept her eyes to the floor hoping he wouldn't recognize her face.

His mind on the pending voyage, Phillip continued pragmatically. "Well, no matter. Let's pull out the rosters. We'll need to hurry, for we're departing shortly and heading for Cape Town."

"That's what I heard, sir."

"Your husband's name, please?"

"His name is Prentice, sir. George Prentice."

Phillip stared up at the woman in disbelief. "What did you say?"

Amelia stopped as gloom encompassed her. It was evident Phillip had recognized her name. Her words deliberate, she spoke again quietly. "His name is George Prentice, sir. There's no problem . . . is there, sir?"

A look of mild amusement lit the commander's eyes as he stuffed the rosters back into his drawer. "You're Amelia Prentice?"

"Yes, sir." Amelia's voice began to tremble.

"And you've been on the fleet all along?"

"I have at that, sir. Are you angry with me?"

The commander stood to his feet and placed his arms into his coat sleeves. His eyes now regarded Amelia in a quiet and familiar way.

Caleb fretted, his face turning red. Amelia responded quickly by placing the baby against her shoulder and rubbing his back. "Hush now . . . don't want to disturb Commander."

"Come with me, madam, and that's an order!" Pulling on his coat, Phillip marched out of his office and stepped out in front of the forecastle. A glimmer of amusement marked his face.

"Yes, sir! I—I'm coming, Commander Phillip, sir!" Amelia followed after the officer, her brow pinched with worry.

The commander rapped hard against the maid's door. Gertie appeared with her hair rolled in cloth rollers. "Dear me, sir! I do look a fright! What with us departin' an' all I decided to take a rest. . . ." she began to spill her explanation.

"Not to worry, Gertie. It isn't you I need. It's your little helper. Will you get the girl for me?"

"Yes, sir. I'll get 'er for you right quick." Gertie shut the door in haste.

Soon the door opened once again and Katy stepped out, dressed in a crisply starched blue dress, her hair pulled back in a ribbon. "Yes, sir. Did you need me, sir?"

"I've someone for you to meet, Katy."

"Who, sir?"

"Your mother."

The commander stepped away, and Katy and Amelia's eyes

met for the first time in eight months. Katy's eyes grew wide and seemed to fill first with anguish. Then, reality setting in, Katy's hands flew to her mouth. "Mum!"

"Dear Lord!" Amelia pulled Caleb next to her as she beheld her daughter. Katy was much taller now, but beyond noticing her increased stature, Amelia was impressed with the womanly refinement that had blossomed in the girl. "God in heaven, Katy! You're beautiful, child!" Becoming aware of Katy's piteous gaze, she stared down at her tattered gown. "I look a fright, I know . . ."

"You're alive!" Katy ran to embrace her mother. Throwing her arms around the frail Amelia, she gasped upon seeing the bundle. "A baby!"

"Your brother, Katy. He's a miracle, he is!"

Katy kissed her mother's cheek and reached to hold her tiny brother. "What's 'is name, Mum?"

"Caleb George Prentice."

"You're so 'andsome, Baby Caleb!" She pulled the cloth away from the infant's face. He lay softly snugged in his mother's arms like a pink cherub. Her eyes bright with wonder, Katy addressed Phillip. "I can't believe you found them, Commander Phillip. How did you do it?"

"It wasn't my doing. They found me."

Amelia grinned. "It was God that did it, Katy."

"That's what Papa said, Mum!"

"Papa?" Amelia seemed to choke on the words. "Don't tell me. . . ."

Katy glanced up at Phillip, finding his eyes alight with amusement.

"I haven't told her yet, Katy." The commander's gaze met Katy's knowingly. "I'll give you the honor."

Katy placed her hands on Amelia's shoulders, her eyes direct. "I've found Papa! He's on the *Scarborough*."

"My George . . . alive?" Amelia touched her trembling fingers against her lips. Her eyes seemed to dim at first as though the news were incomprehensible. Then her frail hand shot heavenward as emotions flooded her heart. "Dear God, you haven't forsaken me!" Amelia gazed into the sky that stretched like a blanket of blue. Tears of joy spilled from her eyes, tinging her cheeks with a rosy wash of color. In faltering tones, she acknowledged, "You heard my cries in the night, dear God. You saw my tears for George and Katy!"

Katy wrapped herself around her mother and baby brother. Mum felt so good next to her. "You prayed for Papa, Mum? I feared you didn't love him anymore." Katy wept as well, the new realization sweeping through her like a fresh ocean wave.

Amelia sobbed as she held her daughter and son possessively against her breast. "You must forgive your mother, love. I feared I had lost all feeling for your papa as well. But I was wrong, I was. I love George more than I love me own life. And I love you, Katy." Amelia stopped, drinking in the presence of her children. "Listen to those words, daughter! Let them ring in your ears!" Her face exuded the zeal of a poet who had just composed a masterwork. "I can never say it enough—I love you! I love you! My family is my wealth . . . more precious than gold."

The signal flag unfurled overhead, a bright flash of yellow against the blue firmament, alerting the First Fleet that departure was impending.

"I'm sorry, Mrs. Prentice, but I'm afraid your time's up. We're about to weigh anchor. I'll send a sailor to take you back in the jolly boat." Phillip answered abruptly, although his tone was apologetic. Turning quickly, he strode away to attend to matters of the departure.

"So soon?" Amelia's eyes were pleading.

"Oh, Mum! Kiss me again!"

Amelia held her daughter and baby boy in her arms as she kissed Katy's face and lips. *I feel alive again, Lord. I just know I can make it now!*

"When we arrive in Africa, perhaps Commander Phillip will allow us to see one another again . . . an' Papa as well." Katy sounded hopeful.

"Pray he does, Katy. Your father must be fretting something fierce by now."

"He is at that, Mum." Katy weighed her next statement carefully. "He thinks you're dead."

Laying her head against the hard wall of her cell, Rachel prayed silent, cluttered prayers, entreating God to honor her feelings for Brock. "He is a true gentleman and kind," she whispered. If only Brock could understand her faith! She reasoned within herself that faith could spring up in his heart with her help. *Brock can change. God, you can do that—I know you can.* Basking in the memories, Rachel's thoughts wandered from her prayers to linger over the warmth of Brock's gentle nature. Rachel felt a surge of triumph as she purposed in her mind to see him again. Concluding her swift but determined prayer, she lay her head on the hard floor. A faint smile was on her lips as she imagined herself once again in the presence of the handsome corporal. His friendship was important to her. She could be the instrument of his salvation.

The ship groaned and shifted beneath her as the fleet was put to sea.

24
ROBERT'S RANSOM

The cool spray of October sea misted against the *Scarborough*'s bow. The ocean was beginning to shift, rising and falling in huge swells, forcing the ship to nose up and dive down into the hollow of the sea. George Prentice had grown more introspective and had begun to regard each change in the wind and weather a spiritual dynamic. If the sea were calm as a mill pond, it reminded him of God's gentle mercy. If the wind began to whip through the spars, bringing the sailors up from their indolent postures, it was a sign of the Father's disciplining hand. To George, the ocean and the ship were his theological school and God Almighty his Schoolmaster.

Sitting with his back to the mizzenmast, he heard a grating sound coming from the stern. It was the sound of a cane scraping against the bulwark, and the man holding it limped along slowly toward George, running the walking stick along the rail. He wore a tattered coat that hung to the floor, hiding his limbs. Moving slowly, he seemed to use the bulwark as a support. Turning about-face, Thomas Barrett stared at

George long and hard. His eyes and skin were torpid and he looked much thinner than when George had last seen him— before the surgeon dragged him out. George looked up at the convict woodenly. He didn't know what to say to the man who blamed him for his own misfortunes. George had heard that Barrett was dying, so it surprised him to see the convict out walking the deck on this cloudy day.

"I'm not a ghost, Prentice!" Barrett snapped. "You needn't have wished me dead, for I lived to spite you."

"I didn't wish you dead, Barrett."

"No?"

"No," George answered flatly. "I prayed God would spare your miserable life."

"That He did, all right. So I could make things right, I vow."

"Have they made you a wooden leg?" George noticed the pair of worn leather boots protruding from under the coat.

"Wooden leg?"

"You lost your leg. Didn't they fit you up with a new one?"

Barrett laughed. "So you think I'm a cripple, do ye?" He opened his coat. "Take a look at this!" Holding out his leg, Barrett bent his limb at the knee showing George it was completely intact.

George stared in disbelief. "It's a miracle, that's wot!"

"Dr. Wilkes called it a miracle, as well. I begged 'im to leave it and let me die. He put up a fight, all right, but I won. Got to keep me leg, I did. Look at it . . . good as new, almost."

"You shouldn't take lightly what God's given back to you, Barrett."

"You sound as crazed as ol' Jenkins. That's what he kept babblin' about when I was put down in the hold to sleep. Said he saw an angel an' such."

George's brow furrowed, ruminating on Jenkins' comment.

"He would've killed your miserable soul, at that. But I don't want your blood on me hands. I suffered, I did, for weeks. Promised God if He'd let me live, I'd change."

"I tried to change for years, Barrett. I found I couldn't do it on me own."

"Well, Prentice, I've a strong will. I can change . . . if I put me mind to it."

"You'll fail if you don't put your trust in God, Barrett. I know . . . it's a bad road that way."

Barrett's gaze was hard. He was growing weary of this fool's advice. "You do it your way, Prentice . . . I'll do it mine!"

"Never fear, Lady Katherine! Lord Robert will save ye from the pirate kidnappers!" Robert leaped across the deck near the stern. The southeasterly wind rippled through his hair and blew his shirt behind him like a cape.

"Oh, save me, Lord Robert," Katy said rather indifferently. She stood to her feet and squinted to see the *Scarborough* on the horizon. She had grown weary of Robert's make-believe and was missing Papa and Mum. "Why can't I save *you* for once? I'm tired of bein' the damsel all the time."

"Because you're a woman and I'm the man . . . see me muscles?" Robert flexed his sinewy arm.

Smiling faintly, Katy nodded at the boy and turned again to watch the flotilla bobbing in the distance. The wind had picked up and another storm appeared imminent.

"Robert!" A corporal shouted from the bow. "Come stand at the capstan and help the mates with the rope!"

"Ah! It's a ransom they want, is it? Well, I'll go and fetch the treasure to save me precious Katy."

Katy laughed. "What am I worth to you, Lord Robert?"

"All the gold in England and Spain and New South Wales!"

"Will there be gold in New South Wales?"

"Yes!" Robert leaped toward Katy and pressed his face close against hers. "And fine jewels to 'ang round your neck." His gaze gentled as he rested his hands upon the soft ivory collar around Katy's shoulders.

Katy turned her face from his. "Don't you dare try to kiss me again, Robert! I'll tell me papa!"

"Robert!" This time it was Lieutenant King, sounding angry.

Pulling back his face, Robert smiled, tapped Katy upon the

nose with a bronze finger, and ran to meet the officers.

She peered from the corners of her eyes, watching the cabin boy run to obey orders. Katy had kept Robert at a safe distance since he had kissed her under the moon's glow of the Canary Islands. It wasn't because Gertie had called him common, or even that Katy feared him. Rather, it was because she wanted to earn the respect of this ruddy-faced boy. She liked him. He was hard to tame and fearless. He was like a lion cub tumbling in the thicket awaiting the day he could arise and claim his kingdom.

When Robert was far from earshot, Katy turned and looked into the horizon. "I'll let you kiss me again, Robert . . ." she whispered into the wind, ". . . someday."

Her eyes squinted at the antagonizing gust that whipped her hair around, loosening the ribbon from the back. Reaching to secure the blue ribbon, which was flapping like a kite's tail, she was distressed when it slipped through her fingers and blew up and around the shroud that held the jigger mast. Daphne had paid for the ribbon with her own money at the market in Rio de Janeiro and would surely think her irresponsible for losing it so quickly. Katy gripped the shroud with her hands and tried to shake its stiff riggings, but the rope was taut and scraped her palms. She looked up to find the silk tie was fast slipping from the shroud. *If I don't fetch it soon, it might blow overboard.* Lifting her foot, Katy positioned herself upon the rail of the stern and held to the rope with both hands. Stretching with her hands extended and her feet against the bulwark, she grasped the ribbon with the tips of her fingers and yanked it from the shroud.

"Blasted wind!" she yelled, the ribbon once again blown from her grasp. "Oh, no!" Her fingers flew to catch the silky hair-tie as it whirled over the stern and down into the foam. Drawing herself back from the shroud, Katy was suddenly swept off balance by a forceful gust of wind blasting against her. "Help!" she wailed, her foot slipping from the bulwark. The sky and sea mixed before her in violent shades of blue and green as her hands flew back and her body plunged into the churning sea.

Hearing her cry for help, the shipmates looked up from the

capstan. They briefly saw the flailing feet of the girl before they heard the sound of her body smack against the ocean's surface.

"Little Kate?" a crewman cried out.

"Body overboard!" The shouts erupted simultaneously from the throats of twenty or more men.

"No!" Robert shrieked. With wild eyes he tore toward the stern. "God, save 'er! Me Katy!"

"Someone grab him!" Commander Phillip was running from his cabin. "Grab the boy, blast it!" To the man at the wheel he barked, "Hard down your helm! Down! Hard down!"

The sailor at the wheel began to spin the spokes to grind down the wheel and stop the *Sirius*, whose bow was now fleeting headlong toward the east—toward Africa. "Wheel's hard down, Commander Phillip!" the man at the wheel shouted. The ship began to slow and came to a stop while the emergency flag was hoisted for the entire fleet to see.

Somebody threw a life buoy over the side, and at once the sailors gathered at the stern to watch for the face of little Kate.

"She's face down!" Robert cried, looking down at the unused life buoy tossing to and fro between the waves.

Katy's body floated lifelessly like a porcelain doll upon the brine, her ivory sleeves billowing at her sides and her skirt rippling around her slender legs. Her blond locks held a greenish cast as they waved soft and hempen about her crown.

God, don't take 'er! Robert's mind was racing. Looking around at the men who stared helplessly down at the girl's body, Robert lunged for the rail. Planting his bare feet upon the stern, he leaped from the bulwark and dove headlong into the cold, hard water.

The mates grappled for the lad but it was too late. One of them yowled, "Commander Phillip!"

"I see, I see!" Phillip sighed and looked anxiously after the boy. "He's bound and determined, that one!"

Robert grabbed the ring and began to swim frantically toward Katy. When he reached the girl, he plunged into the water and came up beneath her, pushing her head out of the water with all of his strength. Throwing the life buoy over her head, he lifted out her arms and secured her to the ring by wrapping rope around her chest and under her arms. "Pull 'er up . . . quickly now!"

"Grab hold!" Lieutenant King shouted. "We'll pull you both out!"

"No!" Robert demanded. "I'll weigh 'er down. Save the girl first . . . then me!"

The lieutenant shook his head and gave the order to hoist the girl from the sea. Turning to the second mate, he hollered, "Find the other life buoy!"

Robert positioned Katy vertically and then pulled himself toward her for only a moment to kiss her cheek tenderly. "I love you, Lady Katherine. Forever!" Then he blinked and his heart began to pound when he saw a fin break the surface. As the girl was lifted, Robert treaded slowly, his eyes guarding the surface suspiciously. Then allowing the waves to toss him around at will, he floated noiselessly—*Like a log*, he thought. *I'll look like an ol' log—tasteless an' dull.*

Robert looked up again and saw that Katy was suspended halfway, her body slowly inching toward the rail to safety. Her skin was pale, but she was still lovely, even with the kiss of death shading her once rosy cheeks. Something within him said she would live, and knowing he had saved her, he felt at peace with himself. Robert had always felt he had nothing to offer Katy, being the pauper he was. This was the reason he was forever making up tales with which to amuse her. "I've paid your ransom, Lady Katherine!" he shouted from the brine.

In a flash, a tall, blue dorsal fin broke the surface, knifing through the water with horrific speed. It was followed by an-other—then another. The great blue Mako sharks surrounded Robert, their dull eyes watching him fearlessly, for they were the swiftest predators in the sea.

"Sharks!" a voice shrieked from overhead.

A life buoy was hurled below within just a foot of Robert's frantic fingers. The lad reached out in desperation, causing just enough movement to send the sharks into a frenzy. His hand slapped at the water and the mate above hoisted the rope, finding no resistance in the line. Their tails thrashing through the waves, the Makos were masters at their craft, plowing into the lad with violent force. The boy's cries were heard on the deck, and the crewmen watched in terror, powerless to save their cabin boy.

Commander Phillip, watching with alarm, leaned over the stern as though he could will the life buoy to float within the boy's grasp. "Save yourself, boy!" Wrenching his eyes from the scene, he stood motionless in frozen horror.

The first life buoy was brought athwart the rail, and several mariners lifted Katy over the stern. She was placed gently upon the deck, her chin tilted up and her stomach down. Seaweed matted her hair and her dress hung limply at her shoulders. As the girl's face was turned sideways and her ashen cheek placed against the wood, salt water spilled from her washed-out lips, and a faint cough issued from the depths of her.

"She's alive, sir," the second mate turned to look up at Commander Phillip.

"Praise be! Our little Kate's alive!" Shouts went up from the men.

"Thanks be to God . . ." Phillip nodded, his soul dispirited, ". . . and young Robert . . ."

Phillip hurriedly took a blanket from one of the sailors and wrapped the girl in it. Lifting her limp body, the commander carried her to the sickroom. The doctor followed close behind, ready to attend the young patient.

The sailors standing at the stern removed their caps, bowed their heads, and closed their eyes. Sir Robert would cheer their days no more.

25

CAPE OF SORROW

The marketplace of Capetown, South Africa, offered the officers and the sailors no blithe welcome. The Dutch traders who bargained down to the sixpence were an annoyance, and according to the sailors, the locals spent most of their day "loaded to the gills on rum."

Phillip stood with his list trailing, the hot African sun blistering his skin and the red dust stinging his eyes. "We'll need more cattle and sheep for the last leg of this voyage. I'll want to strengthen the convicts for the landing." He turned to address the Dutchman standing between William King and John Hunter. "Sir?"

The man was a blue-eyed, hard-faced European of short stature. Wearing a wide-brimmed hat, he stood beneath a rough canopy. He spoke with a quick Dutch clip and never took his eyes from Phillip. "Is d'ere something else?"

"Have you any soft bread?"

"We've a good lot of it, Commander. Will you be needing vegetables?"

"Yes, and my list for seed and plants is extensive."

"Dhat's costly as well, sir." He took the list from Phillip. Studying it phlegmatically, he turned to three African men, scantily clad in bright swaths of cloth. Speaking to them rapidly in their native tongue, the Dutchman's eyes shot back and forth from the list to the men. The Africans nodded at one another and huddled together, muttering among themselves. Finally one stepped toward the trader, and with a long bony finger drew figures in his hand, indicating his price for the seed.

Phillip sighed as he spoke quietly to his two comrades whom he had joined in the shade. "We could be in South Africa for months at this rate."

"We may have no choice, Commander," King advised, "but to pay them what they ask."

"They're quite the bargainers, sir," Hunter added with resignation tinging his words. "I've dealt with these Dutch settlers before and they pride themselves on their stinginess."

Standing with his arms crossed and his eyes on the Afrikaner, Phillip muttered, "I suppose they do have us over a barrel."

"Their price is reasonable," the Dutchman snapped. Scribbling on a piece of parchment, he handed the numbers to Phillip, who gave no immediate reply. Adding rather matter-of-factly, the trader said, "I have some sheep of my own which truly I've already promised to a French trader. But for de right price I can sell dem to you, Commander Phillip . . . unless you want to search all over South Africa. But I can assure you dat my sheep are of de highest quality. . . ."

"That's quite all right, thank you." Phillip turned away to leave.

The Dutchman stood with arms crossed, his gaze unwavering as Phillip strode away.

After an unsuccessful attempt to deal with another settler, Phillip turned and came back to the original Afrikaner. "How many sheep do you have, sir?"

"Forty-four. High quality."

"I'll take them all."

John Hunter stared at Phillip, greatly surprised. "Where will we put them, sir?"

"Move the women off one of the ships and transfer them to another. They'll just have to be cramped for the remainder of the voyage. We'll have to take the livestock with us in order to live."

Hunter nodded deferentially. "Of course, sir."

Brock watched with mild interest two sailors engaged in arm wrestling. One was a husky street-fighter from St. Giles. The other was a Jewish sawyer from Whitechapel, north of the Thames, who had lost the sight of one eye. With his good eye, the sawyer glared at his opponent, who in turn snarled back at him.

"Think you can beat me, eh, Jew-boy?"

Brock shook his head and laughed. "A woman could beat you!"

The sailor from St. Giles pressed hard against the sinewy arm of the Jewish sawyer. His muscles bulged and the veins protruded as he gritted his teeth. "Who asked ya, Chaney?"

"He's right . . ." the sawyer studied the sailor's eyes, ". . . a woman could beatcha!" The sawyer slammed the sailor's forearm against the wooden stool. Standing up with a self-satisfied smirk, he picked up the bottle of whiskey at the sailor's feet and turned to leave with his payoff.

"How did you know the sawyer would win?" A voice spoke quietly from behind the corporal.

Brock turned quickly to find Rachel had been observing it all. "Hello, Rachel," he said warmly. "Simple. I've watched that big sailor loll around the decks when the captain's gone. When a storm breaks out, he's all wide-eyed and confused. He's big all right, but has no concentration."

"And the sawyer?"

"He's wound up tighter than a watch. I've seen him hard down the helms for hours on end without batting an eye. He's got what it takes to survive the rigors of the sea. He's a real man's man, that one."

Rachel smiled. "You seem to understand people so well, you do."

Brock sat silently for a moment studying her blue eyes. "I understand sailors. That's all."

"No," Rachel replied quietly. "You're one of the smartest men on this voyage."

"How do you know that?"

"You think about things before you speak. You don't rattle on about yourself . . . like all the rest of 'em do."

Brock regarded her comments thoughtfully. "Thank you, Rachel. You've been a faithful friend and a far cry from all the other convicts. It won't be long until this voyage ends. I'm glad to have known you."

"And me as well." Rachel stood shifting apprehensively. "You have to return to England, don't you?"

Brock nodded. "It's in my contract." His dark eyes glistened, seeming to ruminate on Rachel's beauty. "I need to take a walk back to the stern for a brief inspection. Why not accompany me, Rachel?"

"Surely." Rachel tried to mask her eagerness. "I can do some chores if you like."

The corporal shook his head. "No, not today. You need to rest sometime."

Rachel felt the care of his words envelop the harshness that had pervaded the voyage. The general treatment of her and all the other females had been demeaning and brutal. She was warmed by the corporal's kindness and followed him gratefully to the stern.

Brock stationed himself against the railing and peered toward the horizon. "Blasted dust is so thick it's difficult to see."

"What are you looking for, Brock?" Rachel's eyes narrowed as she strained toward the distance.

The corporal chuckled softly. "The future."

Rachel's brow furrowed and a humorous pout graced her lips. "What do you mean?"

"It seems as though I have none at times—a future, that is."

Melancholy washing through her thoughts, Rachel lamented, "Your future is bright compared to mine, Brock. After you return to England, I'll be at the mercy of . . . who knows what?"

"I know. I'm already beginning to worry about you. Some of the others, they deserve their lot. You're so . . . young, so intelligent and . . ."

"Thank you." Rachel felt her heart beating rapidly.

Turning gently toward her, Brock slid his hands down both slender arms and clasped her fingers. "You're so beautiful."

Rachel opened her lips to speak, but no words emerged.

Brock glanced down at the girl's delicate hands, which were clasped around his own. Her eyes were brimming with trust and she did not pull away. Drawing her toward him, he pressed his lips against her own and kissed her lightly, allowing his mouth to brush against her tenderly.

Rachel felt as though she were in a trance. Her mind was gliding on wishful seas, dreaming of spending her days locked in this man's embrace. She pressed her face toward him and felt her will melt as he wrapped his arms around her.

Brock closed his eyes and placed his hands on either side of the convict girl's face. Drawing her closer he kissed her again.

"I . . ." Rachel drew back slightly.

"You needn't speak. I won't take advantage of you. But I could bear it no longer. I had to feel you next to me." He turned the back of his hand toward her cheek and stroked it gingerly. "You feel more wonderful than I'd imagined."

"You'll never know how I've longed for this moment, Brock," Rachel finally admitted. But a distant fear seemed to rise from within her, eclipsing the joy in her face. She placed her palms against his chest and drew away slightly.

"I want to hold you forever, Rachel." Brock seemed to notice the desire drain from Rachel's face. A disquieting cloud settled in his eyes, but he refused to release his hold on her. "Tell me what's wrong, Rachel. I'll do whatever it takes to bring you comfort."

"You're so kind to me, Brock, and I'm so undeserving. But I'm frightened. I refuse to let go of the truths I've found over the last few months. I've found the answers to all my confusion, Brock. I've found Christ as my Savior."

Brock stirred uncomfortably. "That's good for you, Rachel. We don't have to believe the same way."

Rachel shook her head sadly. "That isn't true, Brock. I can't serve two masters."

"No one is asking you to serve me . . . or some god for that matter. Serve yourself, Rachel. Reach out and take happiness before it's gone . . . joy is a fleeting thing."

Disappointment marked Rachel's reply. "You'll never understand."

"I understand that I want to hold you. I want to hear your sweet laughter and feel your breath against my cheek." Brock flung his arm outward in a chivalrous gesture. "I want to make you forget about all this misery that surrounds you. To leave you with more than these cold bitter memories of your dark days of exile is my deepest wish."

Hands trembling, Rachel weakly held her distance as Brock attempted to hold her more closely. His poetic nature served effectively as an impetus to soften the determination that barred her mind.

"Don't you understand, Rachel? I feel your pain when you descend into that soulless pit! I want to steal you from your heartless keepers. I want to love you and you love me in return. When there's nothing left but hopelessness, why not settle for a morsel of bliss?"

Tears streaming from her eyes, Rachel felt torn between her feelings for a man and her love for Christ. "I'm not without hope, Brock. Don't you see?"

Gazing again into her eyes, Brock made no move toward her. He waited quietly, as he had in the past, for her to respond. "You need more time to think, Rachel. But before you drive me to insanity, allow me one final kiss. I cannot bear another moment without it."

Clutching his tunic in her grasp, Rachel felt his heartbeat against her hands. Tears continued to flood her fair cheeks while she battled the desires she had nurtured so long. Her feet firmly planted, she made her decision, and peace blanketed her mind.

Wiping the sweat from Katy's face, Amelia squeezed the wet cloth into a pail. "How do you feel today, love?"

"Terrible."

"You'll feel better tomorrow." Amelia reached beside the cot to pull the cloth away from Caleb's face and neck. He was sleeping restlessly in a frayed, handmade basket. His cheeks were pink from the heat, and sweat moistened the soft folds of his skin.

Amelia's face was taut and tears coursed down her cheeks. Stifling the sobs that rose up within her, she stroked her daughter's hair gently as though the girl would break at her touch.

Katy gripped the blanket tightly with her fists. She had been weeping for many days and her eyes were filled with grief. "I can't bear it, Mum. Robert's dead . . . I killed him!"

Amelia turned to pat the infant, whose tiny eyes fluttered at Katy's outburst. "It won't help matters to torture yourself, love. The boy was a brave soul. Leave it at that, Katy," she pleaded.

Wiping bitter tears from her eyes, Katy pushed her face into the frail pillow. Agony twisted her expression as she wrestled with the guilt demons in her mind. "*I* should've died. Not Robert!" She turned to peer through the open door and out beyond the stern. Beneath the waves, a boyish laugh seemed to emanate from the watery grave. A tender memory softened Katy's eyes for a brief moment. "Not sweet Robert!"

Amelia scooped a tin cup into a pan of water. "There, now, drink this down, a sip at a time. I want you well. Lots o' people asking about you, they are."

Turning her face stubbornly, Katy shook her head.

Placing the cup beside her, Amelia sighed and wished she could have come sooner to Katy. She felt like an outsider, being so little a part of her daughter's life. "Who told you, love . . . about Robert, I mean?"

"Commander Phillip told me himself. If he would've told me sooner, I wouldn't have fought so 'ard to live. It should've been me that was killed by the sharks . . . not Sir Robert."

"Don't say such things, Katy!" Amelia spoke in a whisper, her face filled with alarm. "I'm so grateful to the poor lad for saving you, I am. He must've been a special boy, that one."

"He was, Mum . . . the finest. He wanted to marry me . . ." Katy wept again, her voice marked with blame. "And I laughed at him! Laughed right in his face, I did!"

"How could you 'ave known the boy's fate?"

"God 'elp me . . . I should've been kinder!" She punished herself with her words while cradling the dingy blanket to her chest.

"Blaming yourself won't help now." Amelia placed her fingers on Katy's shoulder and began to massage gently. Even though she had never met the boy, a heaviness filled her heart to see her daughter so heartbroken. Watching Katy sobbing against the bolster, Amelia began to reflect upon what could be done to ease her daughter's pain. Standing slowly, she turned to close the door, worried that the draft would make Katy worse. "It grieves me to see you hurting so, love. Did you know . . . was there a funeral?"

"Funeral?"

"Did anyone say some words on Robert's behalf?"

"But he's gone, Mum. There's nothin' left of him to say over."

"Well, he had a soul, didn't he? It's the spirit of the lad we need to remember, not that he was killed by sharks."

Swallowing hard at the bitter taste in her mouth, Katy's brow relaxed. Her headache seemed to be subsiding. She struggled to imagine the boy's cheerful face as he had gone off to assist at the capstan. "You're right, Mum." Katy sat up and wiped her face on her gown. "Robert'd scold me if he saw me carrying on so. If you can help me with the proper words and such, I can make a wreath of flowers and float it out to sea."

Amelia pondered about the flowers. "All right, Katy. We'll have to talk to your Miss Gertie about getting us some flowers from Cape Town. You think she'll do that for us?"

"Gertie'll do it, Mum! She loved Robert too . . . just like I did."

"You loved him, Katy?"

"Dearly, Mum. He kissed me, they said, on the cheek before he paid me ransom."

"Ransom?"

"It was a game we played. He was always makin' up games for me. I suppose to keep me mind off you and Papa. He shouted before he died that he had paid me ransom."

"He must've loved you, too, Katy."

The cabin door to the sickroom vibrated against the oak frame. The knock was steady and firm, and it startled Amelia. She sighed. "I'll not be surprised if that's the guard. They reminded me that I could only stay a little while with you today, love."

"I hate to see you treated like a common thief, Mum."

The knock came again, only much louder.

"I'm coming, sir," Amelia dragged herself wearily to the doorway. Pulling the latch with downcast eyes, she seemed to look past the worn-out shoes on the feet standing outside the cabin.

"Amelia!" a voice exclaimed.

Amelia looked up in surprise and addressed the ragged-looking fellow. "Excuse me?"

"Amelia, don't you know me? Have I changed so much?"

Amelia studied the sallow cheeks and bloodshot eyes beneath the scraggly gray-brown hair. She felt frightened at first when the man drew near her. His eyes seemed wild, and he looked as though he were going to lunge for her. But in the space of only a second she studied the man's face again. This time she beheld not his clothes or his ragged appearance, but instead regarded the familiar tenderness that shone from his face. "God help me!" She reached out her hand gently and stroked his bearded chin with her fingers. "It's George!" she shouted. "Katy, look! It's your papa!" Her voice was jubilant and the tears began to stream from her eyes.

"You did it, Lord!" George cried, embracing Amelia. "You gave me back me family!" He swung her through the air as blithe as a young lad. "Amelia! Dearest, Amelia! You're the most beautiful sight me eyes have ever beheld!"

Katy tried desperately to pull herself from the bed. Her weakened state slowed her, and feeling helpless she yelled hoarsely, "Papa? Mum!" She watched entranced as Papa cradled Mum in his arms. Katy had lived for this wonderful moment and could scarcely believe her eyes.

"Don't get up, child. Stay where you are. Papa will come to you!" George set Amelia gently on the floor and she lovingly wrapped her arm around the thin waist of the husband she had lost a year ago.

Standing fondly over his daughter's cot, a devoted smile curved George Prentice's face. It was much like the weary half-smile worn by a war survivor. "You're as beautiful as your mum, Katy." He bent to kiss her brow and then turned to kiss Amelia warmly. Drawing his face away, he studied the gentle curve of Amelia's face and the soft contour of her mouth. "Your lips feel sweet as nectar against mine, Amelia. How I've longed to hold you again . . . without shackles."

From below them, a loud, demanding cry was heard. Caleb had kicked completely free from the strips of cloth and was working himself into a tantrum.

George stared down in amazement. He chuckled at the red-faced infant whose arms and legs were flailing wildly. "Who is this little fellow?"

Katy and Amelia smiled broadly at one another. Amelia reached to cradle the baby in her arms and comfort his cries. "His name is Caleb. Caleb George Prentice."

"Caleb? What a good-lookin' fellow you are . . . what's that you say?" George glanced up at Amelia and then quickly back at the child. "Did you say 'Prentice'?"

Amelia nodded as delight tinged her cheeks a rosy pink. "Greet your new son, George!"

"We have a son? This boy . . . he's mine?"

"What a question!" Amelia blushed. " 'Course he's yours, George Prentice. What do you take me for?"

Katy laughed upon hearing her mother fuss again at Papa. Then a tear slipped from her eye, glistening like a star upon her cheek. With joy she watched her father reach clumsily for the baby. "I've never seen you hold a baby before, Papa," she teased warmly. "Do you even know how?"

" 'Course I do!" George fumbled to hold the wobbling head in his grasp. "I held *you*, didn't I?" George steadied the boy and gazed into eyes that matched his own. "He's a handsome one, Amelia. You did good, you did!"

"I didn't do it alone, George Prentice! I haven't been away from you *that* long!" Amelia placed her arms akimbo in mock indignation. Lifting her chin, she cocked her head to one side and scowled at George, though her smile betrayed her pleasure.

"Oh!" Katy held her stomach. "Don't make me laugh again. Me sides are hurting."

"Here now . . . don't tire yourself, dear," Amelia fretted.

George held Caleb to his shoulder. "Whatever it takes, Amelia . . . Katy . . . I'll not see this boy grow up inside of a convict colony."

"I don't know what else to do, George," Amelia lamented. "My sentence is the same as yours—seven years."

Feeling the need to rectify her life, Katy offered, "I'll take Caleb, Mum. I'm thirteen now. I can take care of him and bring him to see you both."

"What a miserable life for a young girl," Amelia admonished, shaking her head. "It would be like stealing your childhood from you, love."

"I'm not a child anymore, Mum. Besides, I love Caleb. I'm sure Commander Phillip would allow it."

George awkwardly handed Caleb to Amelia. "A baby in the governor's house?"

Amelia looked up and saw the guards standing in the doorway holding the shackles in their hands. Sighing, she said, "We've got to pray for guidance, George. Caleb could die in one of those cells, he could."

"That's one thing I've learned to do, Amelia," George tenderly stroked the arms that held his son. "I've learned to pray."

26

CATTLE OR WOMEN

Weaving the last flower through the arrangement, Katy stretched out to the water's edge and floated the twig-gnarled wreath out to sea. Her eyes followed the coronal of red and white flowers to the place where the back door of the Atlantic met the threshold of the Indian Ocean. Crouching in the sand at the water's edge, Katy felt the coolness of the lapping waves against her fingertips. Wringing the wad of cotton skirt she held in her grasp, she stretched out the hem to dry it in the salty breeze.

Standing slowly, she gazed somberly when a distant glassy wave crashed upon the token of her memorial. Left bobbing above the surface was a lone white flower, struggling to stay afloat. Katy wiped her stinging eyes. The strain of her vigil had taken its toll. With the indelible memory of the white flower dancing upon a sparkling crest, Katy turned to walk back to the ship. It was a good final memory, for she could see Robert dancing along the deck battling imaginary foes. "I miss you, Prince Robert . . . lion-hearted Robert . . . my friend," was all that seemed appropriate to say. Katy slipped her sandy feet into the pair of worn-out slippers she had brought from England and ran to the ship.

Standing on the shoreline, Commander Phillip was defensive and growing weary of the complaints from the mariners. "I don't care if the men *are* cramped! They'll have better victuals this round and have more wine for their misery," he snapped at the surly seaman who stood beside Corporal Tench. "It's a fair swap for all."

"Whatever you say, Commander," Watkin Tench tried to be agreeable. "I finds the cattle to be better company than that miserable lot o' females, I do."

"If we don't take this load of livestock and seed with us, we could starve, sailor!" Phillip checked off the final cargo of seed being transported onto the *Friendship*.

"I just don't know, Commander, if we can load that many women on those two ships." The sailor shook his head.

Without looking up Phillip ordered, "Do the best you can! It's only for a few more months. England offered me no solutions, therefore I have none for you!"

"Aye, aye, sir," the officer grunted. Then saluting, he spun around to return to the *Lady Penrhyn*. Nearing the ramp where a group of shackled women stood swearing and jostling one another, he muttered under his breath, "Who knows what's ahead in that Godforsaken land? With or without the cattle, they're bound to starve anyway! Those convicts eat everythin' in sight!"

Amelia Prentice stood holding Caleb, trying to avoid the females who were prone to brawl. Since the *Lady Penrhyn* was overcrowded with the women transported from the *Friendship*, she had been selected as one of many who were to be moved to the *Charlotte*. Caleb was lying against her shoulder, clutching and unclutching her gown between his small fingers. He had not slept well the entire night and his brow felt too warm for Amelia's satisfaction. "Ollie?" she called to the convict who had delivered Caleb. "Feel his face. Does he feel hot to you?"

Ollie Feldman slid her bare feet toward Amelia and

reached carefully to examine the infant. She placed her long fingers over Caleb's brow and stood quietly for a moment to assess. "This baby's got a fever, he does, Amelia." She placed her hands on either side of his temples and studied the baby's pupils.

"I knew it!" Worry spread across Amelia's face. "What'll I do, Ollie?"

"Try a bit o' wine on a cloth. Let the child suck it into his mouth. It'll ease the pain and 'elp 'im sleep."

"Will it break his fever, though, Ollie?"

"Only God knows that, Amelia."

"I'll do it . . . and pray." Amelia turned and faced the forecastle, trying to comfort the wailing baby.

"Sir?" She flagged down an officer rushing past.

"Eh?" he muttered, his mind distracted by the list in his hand. "Don't bother me now. I'm busy."

"Please, sir. I need a bit o' wine for the baby. The child's sick with a fever."

"Fever, did you say? Keep 'im away from me! That's all I need is to finish up this voyage with sickness."

"What about the wine, sir? Just a bit on a cloth'll do the trick, I'm sure."

"Look, convict, we're tryin' to get you women moved so we can set sail today. I don't have time to do no nursemaidin'!" The young man turned on his heels and walked to the front of the line of women. "Let's go!" He began pushing the convicts down the gangplank toward the *Charlotte*. "Havin' a choice between cattle or women to contend with—I'll take the beasts any day!"

Suddenly the path in front of them was a flurry of dust and horns as eight men fought to herd two Afrikander bulls toward the gangplank of the *Friendship*. They were black beasts with a large hump on their backs and had long-reaching horns that spread from their heads like crescent moons. The breed was a surly animal that lowered its head to charge when threatened. The Afrikanders walked nose to flank, tossing their large heads at anyone who approached. Behind the bulls ambled three cows, some weary horses, and the herds of sheep and pigs bought by the officers. Several natives strode along, calling out to strays and balancing crates of squawking, bright poultry on their heads. The creatures were pushed, poked, and prodded until each had been secured in a makeshift pen aboard the *Friendship*.

Amelia pulled the cloth over Caleb's face to protect him from the fine dust particles. "I'll be so glad to leave here, I will. We eat dirt morning, noon, and night in this place."

With the other convicts, Amelia stepped cautiously down the gangplank, trying to prevent the shackles from chafing her. She wanted to prevent her legs from swelling with a new infection if she could. Once secured in her hold, she felt the "good" prisoners like herself would be loosed from their irons again. Amelia pressed her cheek against Caleb's inflamed face. "Poor innocent. What have I done to us?"

Katy watched the transports from the bow of the *Sirius*. She was hoping for a glimpse of Mum and Caleb. All she could see was red dust and bleating, clucking livestock. Daphne and Gertie stood with crossed arms beside her.

"I wouldn't want to be in with that lot, I wouldn't," Gertie commented rather dryly. "An' we think *we're* miserable!"

Katy squinted when she thought she saw a convict woman holding a baby. Sighing, she bent to rest her chin on her arms at the rail. "It's not them. Must've been a lot o' babies born on this voyage."

"Seems like a lot, don't it?" Daphne shook her head sadly. "A lot've died. Most likely the rest'll perish in that prison colony, I vow!"

"Don't say such things!" Katy shot back at the maid.

"I'm sorry, Katy." Daphne blushed. "I keep forgettin' about your new brother an' all. He's a healthy one, he is. No need to worry."

"Do you think Commander Phillip would let me keep him with us?"

Gertie frowned. "He's the governor now, Katy. The man 'as no children. Likely he'll not want a cryin' infant takin' up all our time. It's best fer the child to be with his Mum anyway."

"But Daphne just admitted most of the babies will die in the colony. I can't let that happen to me little brother!"

"We can't take 'im, Katy." Gertie's tone was insistent and her gaze direct.

Katy watched with a dismal glare as the convicts disappeared into the *Charlotte*'s holds. Her words had fallen on the wrong ears. She must speak to Commander Phillip directly, before Gertie warned him of her request. She watched as one young woman stood holding onto the rail of the *Charlotte* while a sailor pushed her back into line with the others. The red-haired girl looked familiar.

"Captain's sent fer you women." A breathless cabin boy approached the servant women. "He's moving to the *Supply*. It's a faster vessel an' 'e wants you to collect your things an' join 'im."

Gertie sighed. "All right . . .'ere we go again!"

"We better do as 'e asks, ladies." Daphne placed her arms around the two women and they began to make their way to the cabin.

Katy glanced back over the rail to look for the red-haired young woman again. But the girl had disappeared along with the other convicts who had been whisked back into their cells.

The cells, recently swabbed, seemed odorless and mostly dry to Amelia. She was happy to move Caleb out of the hot sunshine into the dark cell. "At least it's cooler in here," she muttered to herself.

"Why'd they 'ave to put a sick baby in *our* holds? We barely 'ad room to breathe as it was," a voice said beside her. "We could suffocate in this rat trap."

Amelia shifted uncomfortably. Her presence was obviously unwelcome by these females. She wanted to leave as badly as they wanted her to. "They need to get me to a sickroom with me baby. He's got a fever, he does." Amelia could see the profile of the young woman in the light filtering in from the hatchway. Even in the shadows, she noticed the girl had an attractive face and long lashes. She sounded young, but not as young as Katy.

"Bloomin' fools! I can't believe they brought a sick baby in here. The fever'll spread like wildfire!"

"May I hold 'im?" Another girl spoke from a corner of the cell. "I'm not afraid."

"Let me 'old 'im too, Rachel," another voiced chimed in.

"All right, Betsy. We can both help."

A faint smile gracing her dried lips, Amelia's expression was now one of curiosity. The voice of the first young woman held a familiar warmth like that of a long-lost relative. "Thank you, miss. Your name is. . . ?"

"I'm Rachel and this is me friend, Betsy. We've taken care of a few sick babies on this voyage. We do the best we can do fer the poor things."

"Well, Caleb's been a healthy boy. His fever didn't start until today."

"I want to be moved!" Cally demanded.

"Hush yourself, now," Rachel answered in a quiet tone.

Cally struggled to climb the ladder to the hatch. Her shackles rattled against the iron rails. "I'll get meself out o' 'ere, I will!" Pushing her hands against the unsecured hatch, she shouted to the sentry, "I want you to move me to another hold. There's a baby in 'ere with the fever!"

Light flooded the hold and Amelia squinted to make out the faces of the women. Her eyes fell upon the red-haired girl slumped against the wall with her arms crossed. *Rachel Langley?* Although she was much thinner and her skin colorless, the blue eyes were unmistakable.

The sentry grumbled to Cally, "Get back in there, wench!"

"Let me out! I want to be moved, I tell you!"

Heaving a heavy sigh, the guard marched to the hatchway to stare down into the hold. "I'll flog you with this"—he held up a whip—"if you don't stop your caterwaulin'!"

"What's going on?" Another man stood within inches of the guard.

"It's the dark-haired wench, Corporal Chaney. She's stirrin' up things again."

Brock chuckled and glanced casually down, his eyes directly avoiding Rachel. "So, Cally, up to your old tricks again?"

"It's not a trick, Brock." Cally's eyes were wide, feigning

sincerity. "I'm just tryin' to stay alive. Is that a crime? They've put me down 'ere with a sick baby! It has the fever, it does."

Brock groaned and looked with pity upon Amelia and Caleb. "We need to get this woman and her child moved to a sickroom, Mr. Thigpen."

"Yes, sir." Thigpen shook his head and walked away muttering under his breath, "Bloomin' convicts 'ave all the rights. We mariners are the dogs on this fleet. . . ." His voice faded as he disappeared around the forecastle to locate an empty sickbed.

Sighing, the corporal grumbled mostly to himself, "In the meanwhile, let's move this whining woman to the next cell." He reached for the opening, grasping the top of the ladder. "Move down the ladder. I'll need to unchain your feet. May as well get all the irons unlatched while I'm down here," he muttered brusquely.

Cally calmed instantly, elated at Brock's compliance.

After freeing Cally, Brock went at once to Amelia and freed her ankles from the iron fetters. Amelia rubbed her feet, which had already begun to swell. Turning to Betsy, Brock did the same for the young convict girl. After ridding the two older women of their bonds, Brock stood to reach for the ladder.

"Excuse me, Corporal?" Amelia spoke politely.

"Yes?"

Pointing to Rachel, Amelia asked, "Did you forget about this girl?"

"Hm?" Brock's brow furrowed. "Oh, that one, I suppose I did forget." His words were intended to be stinging and direct. Rachel sat quietly. She felt a new sense of freedom with or without England's shackles . . . with or without Brock's affection. Brock grasped her ankle mechanically and freed her legs.

If he noticed her newfound confidence, he didn't acknowledge it. Turning with a cold air, he hastened up the ladder, followed by the capricious Cally. The hatch fell shut with a loud ring.

"Rachel?" Amelia was cautious.

"Yes?" Rachel directed her eyes to the new convict woman with the baby.

"You're Rachel Langley, aren't you?"

Quiet filled the cubicle for a few seconds.

"How do you know me?"

"Because . . . I'm Amelia Prentice."

Rachel searched the recesses of her mind. "Amelia? Not the woman at . . ."

"Miss Marcella's place. Yes. I'm the same one. You rescued me and me daughter from the wretched plans o' those evil people."

"I thought it was you who saved me, Amelia."

"God saved us all."

"And where's Katy?"

"She's in good hands working for Commander Phillip."

"At least that's a relief."

"What brought you here, Rachel?" Amelia reached to place her hand tenderly on the girl's lap.

"Not what you think, that's for certain."

"I . . . I wasn't meanin' . . ."

"It's all right, Amelia. I deserve me reputation. I earned it, I suppose, forever. But I was hungry an' I stole some things. Not a lot, really. But it doesn't take much, does it, to have the finger o' the law pointed at you? Only to be poor an' looked down on by all."

Amelia was full of pity for the girl, but felt she should account for her own presence. "I was accused o' somethin' I didn't do, Rachel."

"I wouldn't have asked, you know."

"I feel I must explain. I'm trying to live fer God now. I've become a different person."

"You were a good person then, Amelia. Always."

"Good and godly are two different matters, I've found."

A soft sigh came from Betsy's corner. "Praise be!" she whispered.

Rachel grew introspective. "I'm learning what you've learned, Amelia. But I seem to fail God an awful lot, I do. I don't have much to offer."

"Let God be the judge o' that, Rachel. He sees things that

we can't see. He'll use you . . . for the good."

Rachel shrugged and answered flatly, "In this place? Impossible!"

"Just wait and see if I'm not right."

"But what if nothing ever gets better, Amelia? What if everything keeps growing worse all along?"

"Count it all joy to fall into trials. With hardship comes steadfastness which increases our patience."

"Patience I don't have."

Amelia sighed. "Nor do I, Rachel." Her thoughts quickened at Rachel's words. "Apostle Paul said that there were times when he was in need and times when he had plenty. But he learned to be content in every situation. That's what I'm learning, Rachel—to be content."

"I want those things too, Amelia." Rachel closed her eyes. "God give me strength."

"You can have it, Rachel." Amelia gripped the convict's hand. "That's the kind of prayer God answers. Pray with me."

The hatchway overhead flew open. "I need the woman with the sick baby to step out please. We're movin' you to the sickroom." The guard stood frowning overhead.

"Dear Lord," Amelia quickly entreated, "let Rachel know you as I've known you. You created her for a special purpose. . . ."

"Let's move!" the guard demanded harshly.

"You're worthwhile, Rachel." Cradling Caleb, Amelia stood quickly. The infant was sleeping soundly but his breathing was raspy. "I'll keep praying for you, Rachel—praying for God to give you joy."

"Please do, Amelia. I feel such a peacefulness. . . ."

"Now!" Flicking his whip into the hold, the guard snarled.

When Amelia and Caleb had disappeared and the hatch closed again, Rachel reflected in the silence. She was relieved at Cally's departure. *She's got a rough road ahead, that one,* she decided. She bowed her head and prayed aloud. She no longer cared what the others thought. "Dear Lord, please help Amelia with her infant. Please don't let the baby die, God. Let him live and let him live for you like I'm going to do from now on . . ." Rachel slid her foot along her ankle. "With or without shackles . . . bound or free."

27

WALK THROUGH THE FURY

Cold, dark waves vaulted into the sails, drenching the sailors and sending some hying below for dry oilskins. The winter storm had rocked the First Fleet through the perilous night with an unceasing cadence of battering wind and driving rain.

The convicts had been locked in their holds with the usual blind impetuosity dealt them by the begrudging mariners. Without the light of the African sun eking through the cracks in the hatches, the cells became fierce, inky confines, battering the prisoners around and hurling them against the walls and against one other. The storms of the Atlantic had been mild compared to the violent sieges dealt out by the Indian Ocean. With waves that reached beyond the ships' crosstrees, each ship appeared to be alone and surrounded by impenetrable walls of malachite glass.

The *Charlotte* seemed to topple, nose down and stern up, flinging open the forecastle doors as the sea roiled beneath the wintry sky.

"Every blasted thing's bein' washed overboard!" Tench shouted as he and the crew tumbled onto the dark deck, trying frantically to hold on to anything that was solid. Some held to the stanchions while others grappled for personal items. The cook, his eyes wild, tumbled toward the railing with a tin plate in his hand. Blankets and coats washed freely over the sides, undulating like manta rays. In shock, a cabin boy grabbed hold of a broken railing, just short of being washed overboard.

"Furl the fore and mizzen topsails!" the orders were yelled over the blustering wind.

Their bodies continuously battered by the unrelenting gale, the seamen crawled aloft to salvage the canvas. Straining against the tempestuous blast, the crew secured the sails and slid to the deck, bruised and exhausted.

Suddenly a scream whipped through the wind. The men looked with horror upon the wall of green and black ocean, towering high above their heads and rushing toward them. The huge swell lifted the vessel like a great winged sea creature, then dropped her like a toy.

Panic reigned in the holds. The females screamed and pled with the gods for their lives.

"By the saints, spare me!" wailed a woman next to Rachel.

"God help me!" another shrieked.

Rachel pressed herself against the wall. "You're all praying now!"

"I'd pray to the devil himself if I thought he'd listen!" another woman shot back as they were heaved onto the floor.

"Dear God, help us!" Rachel cried above the tumult.

"Pray, Rachel! Pray like you've never prayed!" a thief named Beulah beseeched pitifully.

"What do you think? That I wait for something bad to happen and then talk to Him like all o' you? I been prayin' to God all along, I have!" Rachel refused to show panic.

"Help us, Rachel. Show us how to pray!" An older woman fell against Rachel, her hands gripping her drenched sleeves.

"Rachel, it's me, Hilda. I want God like you 'ave."

Rachel wiped away the wetness, part sea and part tears, from her chapped face. "Just talk to God like you talk to me,

Hilda. Tell Him you're sorry for the bad you've done. Ask Christ to live in you."

The cries of the women went up through the hold as they pled for their lives and for their souls. When the waves grew more violent, their prayers grew more fervent.

"I'll never leave you again, Lord! I'll pay me tithe to the vicar an' not spend it on rum," Hilda swore.

"Forgive me of me wicked thoughts an' the way I behaves with men. I'll not let meself fall into sin again, Lord," Beulah blubbered.

Rachel prayed silently but made no requests. Instead she praised God for His mercy and His love. *Thank you, God, for allowing me to know you. If this is me final hour on this desolate ship, then I praise you for allowing me another day o' knowing you and your peace.* Lifting her face, Rachel perceived a lightheartedness entering her soul. It surged through her like a cleansing spray. Her mouth curved upward as the exultation swept through her. "Joy!" she exclaimed. "It's here, Lord!" Rachel pointed toward her heart. "You've answered Amelia's prayer. You've given me joy . . . in the midst of trials."

"Are you mad?" Beulah called out. The ship was swept up and tossed about again, sending her to the floor praying and cursing.

"No, Beulah, I'm free!" Rachel wept. "Don't you see? I've been afraid o' dying this whole voyage. And worse than death, I've feared loneliness. But I'm not afraid anymore. If I live or die, I'm not alone. And I'm not afraid."

In a cabin in the forecastle, cold water swept back and forth across the floor, moving seaweed and broken glass with it. Amelia crouched in the corner upon her cot with Caleb. They were the only occupants remaining in the sickroom. Two women had been taken back to the holds yesterday. Another woman had buried her baby at sea two days ago. Amelia had wept with the convict mother when the child had breathed its final breath.

Holding her son to her breast, Amelia felt drained. She had no tears left to cry. The baby's fever was high and had remained so throughout the night. With the wine bottles smashed on the floor, there were no painkillers left to administer. Amelia stroked his tender scalp and tried to encourage him to nurse. Caleb had suckled so little that her milk was beginning to dry up. "Eat, child, while there's somethin' left to eat." Her tone was vapid.

A sudden clash of the bow tearing into another wave thrust Amelia into the wall. Her shoulders struck the hard wood without constraint, but she continued to cradle Caleb protectively. Caleb no longer cried. His eyes remained shut and his mouth parted slightly, emitting a hoarse whimper. "He's dying, Lord." Amelia kissed his forehead, ignoring the pain from her bleeding shoulder. "Just don't allow him to suffer anymore, God. I don't want me son to be in any more pain. Caleb's suffered for months now. I place him in your hands entirely, Lord."

Amelia thrust her feet across the bed to brace herself. Suddenly her foot struck a hard object. Curious, she reached to pull back the damp blanket. Underneath was the last remaining wine bottle. She lifted the green bottle and held it up to swirl the contents. "Looks like a sip left fer you an' one fer me, my dearest." Amelia placed her fingertips on the cork to loosen it.

Abruptly the door to the cabin flew open. In crawled a man, drenched from head to foot. He sprawled across the floor, his breathing labored. "Can you help me?" His voice cracked, enervated by his vigil on deck.

Amelia hesitated. Unable to help Caleb, how could she be of any use to this stranger? "How, sir? How can I help you?" Hopelessness weighed heavily in her voice.

The man dragged his brine-soaked body onto one of the empty cots. Rolling over onto his back, he grimaced and clamped his eyes shut. "I'm in pain. Took a blow from a flying jib. Must have . . . torn off in the wind." His chest heaved as he tried to catch his breath.

Amelia stared down at the nearly empty bottle. "I was going to give this to me baby. Me boy is dying, sir."

"I understand, I do, ma'am." Noticing his bleeding arm, the man weakly ripped off the bottom of his shirt, and with trembling fingers folded it to use as a bandage.

Sighing, Amelia pulled the cork from the wine bottle and tossed it into the watery debris. As she tipped the bottle to dribble the contents into Caleb's lips, an urging within caused Amelia to stop. Regarding the man with pity, she asked, "Sir?"

"Yes." He coughed and opened his blue eyes slightly.

"I've some wine fer your pain. It ain't much, but perhaps it will help ease the pain." Amelia placed Caleb against her chest and slipped her feet with their weathered shoes into the cold sludge. Sloshing through the seaweed, she worked her way around the broken bottles and finally stood over the man. She held out her meager offering.

"But that's all you have, ma'am. What about your child?"

"Caleb's goin' to be fine, sir . . ." Her voice broke. "He's in God's hands now."

"The Lord bless you for your generosity, Miss . . ."

"Mrs. Prentice. Lord's blessed me for certain." Amelia remembered how beautiful Katy looked standing on the deck of the *Sirius*. She remembered the musky texture of George's bristly beard as he kissed her before being hauled away in fetters. Now with the look of death on Caleb's face, she would remember the scent of soft baby's breath against her cheek. Memories had become a solace to her.

Swigging the wine in hard swallows, the man gripped the bottle tightly, his fingers white. "I have to go back out there, Mrs. Prentice. Captain needs me. Fiercest gale I've seen in all me life."

"Go back? In your condition?"

The man pushed himself out of the cot and planted his boots against the floor. "Aye! We'll make it through all right, though. The storm'll be over in an hour, I vow."

"Will it, now?" Amelia stared at the man curiously as he braced himself to run out the door.

"The Lord bless you, Mrs. Prentice." Handing her the empty wine bottle, the man pushed himself through the doorway, against the gale that came rushing into the room and howled in his face.

It wasn't until later that Amelia remembered she had backed away and leaped for her cot to shield her son from the fierce wind. She recalled cradling Caleb for several minutes before recognizing the familiar feeling of let-down as milk returned to her bosom. She nursed Caleb, who was first lethargic, then opened his eyes as the first drop of mother's milk dampened his lips. The storm ended within the hour. And baby Caleb did get better. He was now as strong and healthy as any baby she had known. Amelia was stronger too. Her faith could now move mountains . . . which loomed ahead, far from Europe's shores . . . in Botany Bay.

28

LAND HO!

Serving as watch for most of the night, the crewman scowled at the loud albatross gliding over his head and screeching its gray-tongued morning song. "Blasted bird! Go away, you!" Then he stopped and blinked. Not because of the albatross, but because of the dusky rise of land he could see ascending on the horizon. The sailor pulled himself upright and scrambled to rise amidst the tangle of blanket and rope that twisted around his ankles in the crow's nest. "Land!" the strident cry rang from his throat. "Land ho!"

Commander Phillip stepped in the midst of the men scurrying over one another, each trying to be the next to set eyes on the harbor of Botany Bay. Phillip pulled on his coat and adjusted his cap before pulling out his glass. Peering through the scope, he observed the white beach rising before them, with trees tall, thin, and widely spaced. After the ship completed its exploration by circling a shallow inlet, Phillip ordered, "Anchor north of the bay and keep a watch for the other ships." Pacing briskly, he turned to Lieutenant King, who stood at his side.

"The dinghies are being made ready, Commander." Lieutenant King made fast work of putting away the charts.

"Let's go take a look at this Botany Bay, shall we, King?" Phillip put away his glass. "We'll see just how accurate old Cook was about the harbor." As the *Supply's* landing party drew closer, evidence soon revealed that the hasty scribblings of Captain Cook's previous observations were not as accurate as his records of other harbors.

King and the others paddled cautiously to shore while Phillip's boat rounded the harbor in search of deeper waters.

Behind a stand of trees, lying flat on the ground and tightly gripping their spears, fearful observers watched the white-skinned, strangely clad men approaching their territory. The onyx faces of the natives gleamed from the heat of the Australian sun. *Warra! Warra!* their chant began slowly and quietly. "Go away! Go away!"

Phillip observed with dismay the long pole protruding from the water's surface. The sailor held the pole solidly in his grasp, revealing the depth of the harbor. The commander shook his head. They had explored the entire cove and their findings were disappointing. "There isn't a suitable anchorage in the entire harbor!"

"Right y'are, Commander," a corporal commented. "Not just the shallowness of the harbor that's a problem, but the bloomin' bay's wide open. What if the Dutch decide to attack? We'd be an easy target."

Phillip sighed. "We may have to explore farther down the harbor. Take me to King's landing party on the shore. Let's search the area for fresh water." Phillip looked toward the beach and the landing party. Suddenly his jaw dropped and he sat forward on the seat, alarmed at the disturbing scene he beheld. With one brow arched, he stared at a group of dark-skinned men rising to their feet. He assessed they had probably been crouched behind the gray and pink eucalyptus for some time, observing King and his men. One tribesman drew back a long spear and screamed fiercely. Phillip's heart sank.

Brock Chaney shouted overhead to the man at watch. "See anything, Mops?"

"No, Corporal. Nothin' yet, sir. But we can't be far from land. Whit Fulmer spotted a twig on the water's surface this mornin', he did. Said it was like no tree twig he'd ever seen b'fore."

"Good work, men. I'm ready to see land, New South Wales or otherwise." Brock studied the convict women sitting cross-legged under the mizzenmast mending their ragged frocks.

Tench sat under a crosstree and chronicled the last few days of the voyage. He was careful to report that the behavior of some of the mariners and some of the female convicts was disgraceful. He purposefully left out the names of the officers in question. He sighed upon seeing Brock standing over a group of weary-faced convict women. To his journal Tench merely added, *They just can't leave one another alone.*

"Rachel, may I have a word with you, please?" Brock spoke, sounding astute and controlled.

Amelia, sitting next to Rachel and Betsy, shot a warning glance Rachel's way.

"Not to worry," Rachel patted Amelia's shoulder and stood to her feet. Cradling Amelia's Bible under one arm, she studied the corporal warily. "What do you want, Corporal Chaney?"

Brock led Rachel to the stern of the *Charlotte*. He said nothing until he was away from Tench's accusing glare. "I want to say I'm sorry for the misfortunes that have kept us apart."

"It's all for the better—" Rachel tried to speak.

"Tut, tut, Rachel," Brock interrupted. "Please allow me to finish. I'll be forced to remain behind with the other crewmen for longer than anticipated. Captain Aimsley just informed all of us." Brock reached to clasp Rachel's delicate hands in his own. Grasping them firmly, he smiled. "As officers, we'll be allowed one servant each in our dwelling. I want you to live with me, Rachel. I can't bear the loneliness and I want you near me."

Rachel hesitated for only a moment, staring into the corporal's dark, fathomless eyes. Her eyes wandered over his firm jaw and the strong features of his face.

Brock bent down with his lips near hers. "Just say yes."

Suddenly, as strength seemed to well up from within, Rachel's gaze became direct and resolute. "You're a handsome man, Brock, and intelligent. But I've given me promise to another."

Brock's chin lifted as his brow furrowed. "Whom?"

"Christ Jesus. I can't have you now, Brock. Not in the manner you want me, anyway. I'll wait . . . forever if I have to until the right one comes me way. Perhaps I'll never marry. It isn't the worst thing that could happen to me, is it now?"

"It's a lonely world ahead, Rachel." Brock studied the distance beyond the bow. "And a vicious one for a pretty female. Can your God protect you from those vile convicts you'll be thrown in with?"

"Whatever happens, Brock, I'll never be without Him, I'll not!"

"When will you realize you've been abandoned?" The corporal released his firm grip from Rachel's arm. His dignity shaken, he walked away without another word.

Rachel, dismissing the wounding words from her mind, lifted her face to the crystal blue sky. Her eyes fired with purpose, she opened the pages of Amelia's Bible. With a gentle peace soothing her spirit she read: "Who shall separate us from the love of Christ? Shall tribulation, or distress, or persecution, or famine, or nakedness, or peril, or sword? As it is written, for thy sake we are killed all the day long; we are accounted as sheep for the slaughter. Nay, in all these things we are more than conquerors through him that loved us. For I am persuaded, that neither death, nor life, nor angels, nor principalities, nor powers, nor things present, nor things to come, nor height, nor depth, nor any other creature, shall be able to separate us from the love of God, which is in Christ Jesus our Lord." Rachel wiped her tear-streaked face and squinted curiously toward the distant gray landmass slowly appearing through the mist.

The sailor from the watch shouted wildly, and the female

prisoners were shoved harshly back down into their holds.

Lieutenant King jerked around when he heard Phillip's warning shout from the dinghy. Hurled forty feet, a spear stuck fast and quivered in the ground near them. "Steady men," he ordered as they faced the tribesmen. "Jones, fire your weapon—blanks first."

The sailor complied and fired the musket over the heads of the slowly advancing party. The aborigines crouched low, trembling and muttering, but did not retreat.

"They're confounded naked, Lieutenant!" Jones remarked.

"Not a stitch o' nothin'!" observed another bewildered jack-tar.

John Hunter, second captain, asked cautiously, "What's that one saying, sir?"

King studied the aborigine man who had stepped forward.

The native's skin was blacker than any islanders they had encountered. He had a sagging stomach and a creased face. He seemed to be making a friendly gesture with his hand. Two others of the tribal party grabbed the man who had thrown the spear. They dragged the offender before the white men, slapping his head and kicking him vehemently in a show of their displeasure with his actions.

"I think they want to apologize for this man's behavior. At least, that's what it appears to be." The lieutenant waved his hand at the aborigine and shook his head when the tribesmen seemed to be threatening to spear the transgressor.

"I believe you're right, Lieutenant," Hunter agreed. "Let's offer them a gift." He pulled some cheap baubles from a bag. Shaking the beads so they sparkled in the Australian sun, Hunter held the gift out to the aborigine who appeared to be their chieftain. The chieftain walked eagerly to Hunter and accepted his gift. Soon the landing party was surrounded by all the tribesmen, waving their hands and standing with anxious smiles as they awaited a gift from the white strangers. The spear-thrower was the fastest on his feet and the quickest to stretch out his hand.

Hunter, Jones, and the others distributed beads and ribbon, which the tribesmen received eagerly. After being joined by Phillip and his landing party, Lieutenant King pulled a bottle of wine from under his scarlet tunic. First he popped free the cork, then swigged its contents to demonstrate how one drank from a bottle. Passing the wine to the chieftain, Hunter grinned when the man guzzled the brew greedily. The chieftain scowled at the cloying aftertaste. Spewing the drink from his mouth, he shook his head and returned the bottle to Hunter.

"Maybe he has a taste for tea instead," Phillip's expression reflected mild amusement.

After spending five days exploring the area behind the beach, it was quickly surmised by all that Botany Bay had a less than desirable harbor and would provide a wretched refuge for a prison colony.

"Hunter, come with me," Phillip requested. "We'll all be dead if a better harbor isn't found soon."

Loaded down with an exploration team and temporary supplies, Commander Phillip and John Hunter set out to explore Port Jackson, four hours north of Botany Bay.

Upon returning to the encampment a few days later, they found the officers, along with Surgeon White, entertaining the aborigines with a target practice using a paperbark scrub for a target.

"Nothing like wasted ammunition, eh, Dr. White?"

White's face flushed upon seeing Phillip had returned. "Sorry, Commander," he apologized. "They're so interested in everything we do."

"Find anything better in Port Jackson?" Lieutenant Bradley asked wearily.

"It's the finest harbor in the world, Bradley. We'll have all we need to settle there—fresh water to drink, safe harbor, deep water." Phillip was jubilant. "I'm naming the harbor Sydney Cove."

"Lord Sydney will be most appreciative, sir," Bradley answered blandly.

"Once we've colonized this wilderness, England will possess an impenetrable harbor against France, or any foe for

that matter. But first we need to address the problem of victuals. If our present food supply will hold out, perhaps we can
turn these miserable convicts into farmers."

Bradley shook his head. "It'll be a bloomin' miracle, sir."

Thunder and lightning streaked across the pink sky of
Sydney Cove. The wind had picked up and the tents erected
for the male convicts began flapping against the iron stakes.
The mariners ran past them, herding the females from the
ship to their newly erected encampment. Chaney and Tench
shouted to the mariners to hold back the convict men who
were whooping and calling out licentious oaths to the women
passing by.

"They're restless, Chaney. Look at 'em all, will you? Actin'
like a bunch o' wild animals let out of a cage." Tench eyed the
convicts apprehensively, pushing the women along at a rapid
pace.

Holding Caleb protectively in her arms, Amelia, along
with Rachel and Betsy, fled toward the tents, ignoring the
shouts from the men. Two women trailing behind them
turned and blew kisses at the convicts, waving flirtatiously as
the wind blew their hair wildly about their faces. The convict
men responded in turn, pressing against their jailers and bid-
ding the women to come near. Then the mariners took up the
diversion, offering themselves in front of the convict women
while tossing their maledictions back at the men.

"Quiet!" Brock shouted to the females. "Or you'll get more
than you bargained for, I vow!"

Suddenly, two of the convict males fell forward between
the guards. Leaping over them, several caught the sentries by
surprise, eluding their attempts to restrain them. "Let's get
'em whiles we can!" one shrieked, his eyes wide with excitement.

Rachel turned at the commotion. "Amelia, Betsy! Look!"
she cried fearfully. She pointed to the army of half-crazed
men swarming toward them. "Run! Follow me!" she shouted.

Streaking into a mound of gray-green shrubbery, the

women clamored over jagged rocks and ran through prickly bushes, frantically fleeing the screaming sounds reverberating from the mud-covered encampment. Overhead, another bolt split the Australian firmament, releasing a deluge of rain and continuous rolls of thunder. Caleb wailed in fright as Amelia pulled anxiously at his ragged cloths that were snagged on the shrubbery.

"Leave it, Amelia!" Betsy pleaded.

"Yes, Amelia!" Rachel was insistent. "They're too wet to do any good anyway."

Rachel reached for the baby and yanked him free from the drenched fabric. Peering distraughtly through the bush, Rachel could see the men, both convicts and mariners, grabbing the women, tossing them over their shoulders, and running off with them. *Lord, keep your hand on us!* Rachel shuddered and turned away from the sight of a woman beating a mariner across the head as he grappled with her. "Poor Cally," she muttered and then took off again deeper into the outback. She would not soon forget the look of terror that filled Cally's face or the hopelessness in her eyes.

"Those beasts!" Betsy cried, running behind Rachel. "They're nothing but a bunch of demons!"

Amelia plodded through the mud, draping up her coarse dress and wrapping it around Caleb. Holding up his head strong and firm, the infant gazed ahead in bewilderment. The rain collected on his long, dark lashes and upon the ringlets cascading down the nape of his neck. When a cloud overhead released another bolt of lightning, it glinted in his eyes like blinding silver. Jerking his head down, he burrowed into Amelia's chest and whimpered.

"It'll be all right, son." Amelia quickly glanced behind them one last time. "Where in the world is George?" she fretted despairingly.

George stared with shocked disbelief at the exhibition of debauchery that surrounded him. He scrutinized the faces of the women, searching for Amelia. Some were fleeing, while others appeared to be enjoying the riot. A group near him fought brutally over a pannikin of rum, jerking it back and forth while the contents sloshed freely onto the rain-soaked ground. A woman ran past with a screaming infant in her grasp. George jumped in front of her and grabbed her shoulders.

"Oh, no, please!" She looked up at George with pleading eyes. "I 'ave a baby! She's ill, sir! Please leave me be!"

George released the woman immediately, realizing she wasn't Amelia. "I'm sorry, ma'am. I'm looking for me wife— Amelia Prentice."

"I saw Amelia," the woman answered anxiously. She pointed toward the tents, which were blowing free from their stakes. "I saw 'er runnin' that way with two others, I did, an' a baby."

"Caleb," George muttered as the young girl fled away with her baby daughter.

George bolted for the tent site, his eyes searching nervously. Running behind the tents, he caught sight of a few females running into the thicket. Amelia was not among them, but perhaps she had fled in the same direction. "Amelia!" he called, tramping beneath the gnarled vines and eucalyptus.

"Oh, no you don't!" a voice snarled from behind.

George felt an excruciating pain across the back of his head and blackness engulfed him.

The guard who delivered the harsh blow turned to chase another escaping prisoner. "That's one that'll not get away," he muttered in satisfaction.

From the *Supply*, Commander Phillip glared furiously upon the chaos. "Even the sailors have lost their minds!" he raged.

Katy and Daphne stood beneath the covering of the forecastle. Gertie had hastened inside to the protection of the cabin. Katy begged Daphne to remain with her until she could locate her mother. She watched forlornly, her eyes gazing beyond the railing to the shoreline where the clamor and screaming was now mixed with singing and savage laughter. "Is this Armageddon?" Katy asked woefully.

"More like Sodom and Gomorrah, I'd say," Daphne answered with an air of distaste in her tone. "I wouldn't walk into that mess for all the riches in London, I wouldn't!"

"I'll go alone, then." Katy took a step out and the rain soaked the crown of her head.

"Oh, no you won't!" Daphne grabbed Katy's shoulder in a motherly fashion. "We'll just have to pray for God to protect your mum. There's nothin' we can do now."

"But Daphne!"

"Commander Phillip!" Daphne called in a threatening tone.

Gloom encompassing her, Katy dropped her head and pressed her chin to her chest. Tears streaked down her face and she clenched her fists at her sides. *If I were God . . .*

With dark coverings over their heads, the women stood behind the veil of rain watching the dismal shoreline. Motionless and dumfounded, the women had the appearance of mourners at a funeral. With sorrow they witnessed the birth pains of the infant nation as it reeled in the hands of its new parents—the outcasts of England.

29

SYDNEY COVE

Colored flags were hoisted just beyond the beach, lining the strung ropes with bright triangles of red, yellow, blue, and green. Flanked by an aromatic landscape of green, gray, and pink foliage, the wattle trees juggled their bright blooms while the song of the lyrebird drifted through the assemblage. Mariners placed horns and fifes to their lips while the drummers beat out their princely cadence just beyond the shore.

The dignitaries of New South Wales walked stiffly to the table holding the official documents for the commissioning of Captain Phillip as Governor. A safe distance away, the aborigines had gathered to watch the white man's bizarre ritual. Beyond them in the scrub of paperbark, a lone dingo stared out at the alien procession, then turned to serpentine into the bush, his red coat flashing as he disappeared.

Reading the edicts was the official judge-advocate, David Collins. During the ceremony, the convicts, both male and female, were made to kneel on the ground with their eyes cast down in punishment for the previous night's riot. The shrubbery behind the ceremony quivered slightly. Pulling herself up through the brush, Amelia moved slowly through the eucalyptus leaves so as not to awaken Caleb who had fallen asleep from exhaustion. Following close behind were Rachel and Betsy, who had survived the night with Amelia by hiding in a cave. Some aborigines had abandoned the area, leaving behind a kangaroo bone over a cold bed of cinders. The women had picked it clean.

"Everything looks normal enough," Amelia noted cautiously. "Let's go join the others while no one's looking."

"I hope they don't flog us for this," Betsy added disdainfully. "It wasn't our fault we had to run from the men."

Holding her fingers to her lips, Rachel whispered, "Let's go kneel behind that sentry over there. He'll think we've been here all along."

Governor Phillip accepted his commission without fanfare and then turned to address the convicts. He was unaware that his dear friend, Madam Bennington, had passed on back in England. "I want to be certain each of you realize the punishment that will be dealt to you if there is ever a repeat of last night's . . . spree. If any of you men are caught in the women's tents, you will be shot immediately. If anyone is caught pilfering from the stores or stealing any of our breeding stock or cattle or chickens, you will be hanged without question."

The convicts looked up somberly, most with hung-over expressions clouding their faces.

"I hope this is clearly understood," Phillip added with a stern note of finality.

"I hope so too." Rachel regarded her two friends worriedly.

Katy stood a respectable distance from the ceremony. She suddenly spotted the weary-looking faces of her mother and baby brother to the far left of the convict population. Relief flooded her mind.

To the far right was her father, George. His head was heavily bandaged and he seemed to be having trouble with his balance. He acknowledged his daughter with a faint, weary smile. Following Katy's eyes, which directed his across the crowd, he spied Amelia and Caleb. *Somehow, Lord, you brought us all here, although we're still apart. Somehow—you can bring us together again. But only you know how. In this land of exiles, how will we survive except through your guiding hand?*

Katy turned to gaze again upon the ocean that had carried her family far from England's shores and in whose depths lay the memory of a cherished friend. Perhaps she would return to England someday, but for now her hope lay in rescuing her family from a brutal system.

Her face filled with anxiety, Katy glanced toward the surreal landscape that stretched before her, full of strange hopping animals and odd foliage. This was Sydney Cove, and it would be her home until the longed-for day that she would be reunited with Papa, Mum, and Caleb. *Poor baby boy.* Her heart ached at the thought of Caleb growing up inside the cruel confines of prison. Her eyes fell on Rachel Langley. She had studied the girl's face for some time now, and she was certain of her identity. Her clothes were all but rotting off of her frail frame. She thought it curious the way the girl leaned against Mum as though she were her own mother. Finally catching Rachel's attention, Katy managed a faint smile.

Rachel returned Katy's smile, noting that the Prentice girl looked so unsoiled and so lovely compared to the convict women. But Rachel felt no pangs of jealousy for the girl; rather, she felt relief. For she was hopeful that someday she would be as free as Katy. Unaware of the days of starvation, cruelty, and sickness that would soon viciously crush them all, Rachel pondered her hopes, which were without plans. She had come to realize that nothing could be accomplished through her own contrivances. She would have to trust the One who had kept her safe thus far . . . the only One who could lead her far beyond the voyage of the exiles.

PATRICIA HICKMAN is a full-time writer and the wife of a pastor. She is the author of three books. She lives with her husband, Randy, and their three children, Joshua, Jessica, and Jared, in Louisiana.

ACKNOWLEDGMENTS

The most difficult part of the voyage is deciding whom to thank first.

My writer's group, the "Nubbing Chits," deserves more thanks than can be written. Professionals to the core, but never taking yourselves too seriously, your love and wit always gave me the strength to forge ahead.

Gilbert and Johnnie Morris opened their lives to a complete stranger. You taught me how to write. Your patience must have worn thin at times. I love you both forever. Your discipling of Christian writers *will* be duplicated—I'll do my best. Bobby Funderburk is the idea man. You were right, Bobby—the scarecrow needed a brain. Kate Blackwell, you encouraged me to write like a woman, to bring out the heart and soul of people, and to nurture a story with love. Thank you Lynn Morris for your assuring nature and for sharing your parents with the "chits."

A special thank you goes to Chuck and Sally Roach for your nautical knowledge. Your expertise with sailing added "salt" to the story. But thank you most of all for being my friends.

I especially appreciate Sharon Asmus, my editor, and the Bethany House family. You always steered me in the right direction.

Those dedicated ones who've lived every phase of the journey with me are my loving family: My husband, Randy; my children, Joshua, Jessica, and Jared—your patience with burned meals, the mountains of laundry, and my late-night jaunts to the computer deserves an award.

But my highest thank you goes to my Lord and Savior, Jesus Christ. You did it all, sweet Prince of Peace. I pray you bless this work to bring freedom to the prisoner bound by the darkness of this world.

Patricia Hickman